HEIRS OF FATE

THE GODS' FATE NOVELLAS

AMARA LUCIANO

Art by

GABRIELLE LUCIANO

WONDERHEART BOOKS

For information contact :

Wonder Heart Books, LLC

P.O. Box 44,

Carlstadt, NJ 07072

hi@wonderheartbooks.com

https://www.wonderheartbooks.com

Cover art by Gabrielle Luciano

Cover design by Eight Little Pages

ISBN: 978-1-7335031-3-6

First Edition: April 2019

❀ Created with Vellum

This one is for you, dear reader,
because you constantly remind me that I'm not just a mere purveyor
of stories, but am also an interminable believer in the magic they
imbue in a life.

And for my mom,
the first and most formidable reader and artist I know, whose
criticism and enthusiasm brightened
our dawning horizons.

AUTHOR'S NOTE

Back in June 2018, I published Bride of Dreams, the first of the Gods' Fate prequel novellas, under our then barely 4-month-old company. Gabi and I had worked tirelessly during that time to plot out what we wanted to publish first. There was a laundry list—in fact, there still is. But I remember thinking that novellas would be an easy way to test our mettle.

Ha ha ha. Ha ha.

All those trunked manuscripts I'd collected over the course of seven years? Those experiments were nothing like what it took to bring novellas to life. Telling an isolated story in less than 40,000 words was harsh training, but I needed it. We needed it.

Gabi and I are better for the stories inside this omnibus.

We now have a whole world to play with.

I hope this entrance into the Gods' Fate world creates within you the same joy and excitement it has for Gabi and myself as we strove to bring it to life through our art.

This is only the beginning. Read until the end to find out what else you can expect from Wonder Heart Books in 2019.

In the meantime, hold onto your wonder, dear reader.

BRIDE OF DREAMS

E very night Diya and her mother ferried desperate souls to the temple of the priestesses—a colossal structure cut into grass and gray rocks, which strad-dled a gritty chamber hiding the true length of the River of Souls.

Wanting more than this work was unpredictable. Unsafe, if the gods were watching. Yet Diya's heart thumped a tantalizing beat at the thought of fleeing it all.

It didn't help that their passengers were rarely interesting. They always boarded with prayers for honeyed horoscopes and a taste of tomorrow before end of night. They ignored the lumi-nous edifice in the distance. They relegated Diya's favorite mythical rumors to the playthings of children, forgetting the temple's images of strange, crystalline creatures wedging up from the river like pond weeds. And they always, always stared.

One glance at Diya and their fascination fell to smooth brown skin and dark, gleaming hair. Another glance for her mother and the whispers arose.

She had once heard her mother's hair compared to the

supple, midnight sleeve of river-water marred by their boat. How her eyes had gleamed a truer silver than the moon.

But the truth was Eta's hair was simply black and her eyes a pale gray, like most women in Novasi. Time after the war had not been kind to her.

She watched her mother quietly count heads and collect payment. A small child passed Eta with rounded eyes and Diya nearly hissed at the girl to finish entering the boat. The little girl's mother must have glimpsed Diya's impatience and rushed them both inside.

People had no idea how poorly they hid the cruelty in their faces. Diya could practically hear the thoughts aloud: *Old. Homely. Disappointing.* They would turn to each other and exchange surprised whispers. *This was the willful child who had started the war?*

And while it was true that Eta had lived her life assuming those who surrounded her were supposed to please her, she had paid for it. The past had diminished her.

This was the fate of unchecked beauty. This was a fate that Diya could never—would never accept.

And yet her mother seemed determined to make it impossible for her to refuse.

As Diya wound up the anchor embedded below the surface of the river, Eta stood beside her and spoke. "You've tried on your shoes, yes?"

"Not even in my dreams."

"You dream too much," Eta hissed. "I ask you for very little, Diya."

You ask for what I cannot give you. She nodded toward the impatient scowl of their first boarded passenger. The gongs had been struck eight times when they had started, and now nine clangs were underway. "You have work, *Ahma*."

Eta's face clouded like a storm. The little girl distracted Diya's mother from responding. She tugged on the waist of Eta's dress, rubbing the worn lily lace between two fingers as though mesmerized by the odd feel. "Will it be a long ride?" she said, blinking innocently. Her slim features were common, but a nameless Gildeshan ancestor might have caused her thick lashes and slashing brows. Diya wondered idly if that was why the girl's mother appeared so guarded. "I don't like when it takes so long."

When Eta smiled, it was the only time anyone found her beautiful still. Some of the gossiping whispers settled.

"Perhaps you'd like a tale," Eta offered.

Diya rowed the boat in earnest when the little girl nodded. Eta used to bend around the task at the start of their ferrying, though it had rattled her back. But Diya didn't mind taking over, especially on days like today. Her mother had a weakness for *other* children with imagination, and the need to please them indirectly pleased Diya.

She saw how Eta could have started a war and not known she had.

Eta didn't dare bring the child into her lap, but her back held a straight, elegant line before the passengers. Their dark heads leaned forward, their prayers forgotten. The boat went utterly silent.

This was Diya's favorite moment.

Eta savored the suspicion and curiosity of her audience before beginning. "Once there was a girl who would marry a prince among men. Her curls silvered like the wind. Her eyes rivaled the gold of her dowry. Her intended's love for her could not be measured in it's weight."

Faint recognition tightened Diya's shoulders. This was not the story she had hoped for.

"But the girl had never seen this prince. She'd heard of his loyalty. His courage. But these things covered her heart like a splash of rain on the window. She wiped it away, hoping to see clearly.

"Her youth gave her pause. Doubts pelted her once-bright thoughts. When the sky gave way to a storm, the girl left the shelter of home and ran for the heart of it.

"It was her wild chase of the thunder that snared the attention of a god."

"The god of dreams," guessed the little girl.

Eta only smiled, deliberately keeping her attention off Diya.

All the same, Diya felt the press of the story on her thinning resolve to stand quiet throughout.

"The god's sly tendrils of hair made the girl instantly want to reach out and grasp the feel of it. She imagined the god's red eyes clouding like rubies at the first touch of their lips. Her instant and startling desire was not unmatched.

"The god's hand swept up to her cheekbone. 'What do you run from?'

"'A dream. The longer my steps, the more it fades, but this dream haunts me.'"

"'Come with me,' said the god, 'and I will show you a new one.'"

The little girl released a delighted little clap. The other passengers traded looks, tossing out guesses for how the story would end. Despite her fervent rowing, Diya was riveted on the possibilities. It didn't matter that her mother was using the story to sway her. It was too late to block Eta from exploiting her weakness.

In more ways than one.

"Avoiding her parents' suspicious glances, the girl promised she would return before she was expected. She hunted the storm once more, despite their warning calls.

"But the god arrived with gemstone eyes dimmed. 'What is it?' trembled from the girl's lips. 'What's changed?'

"'You asked for a new dream,' said the god coldly. 'Here, take it.'

"Another pull she couldn't resist. The girl looked up into the storm as it changed. She saw the way the world had been—a cauldron of promise and excitement. Then the vision shifted, whirling into a nightmare.

"She saw her intended learn he could never have her love. He left her rejected before society, the weight of her wealth pinning her to her shame. No one in her family could escape from beneath it.

"It felt all too real. Despair split her heart.

"'You offered me a dream,' the girl whispered brokenly beneath the dying storm. Her accusation was hoarse, fragile.

"With a fanged grin, the god said, 'There are no dreams without nightmares.'

"The girl could not see the god wanted her broken. That this god who came to visit her was wrong-faced, wearing a mask. This was not the god who had offered her more than what she was destined for.

"Her skin had a grey cast by the time she was found in the soft, green distance from her home. The sky mourned viciously when the god the girl had meant to meet finally arrived.

"Immortal tears were rare and violent. They stained the earth black.

"When her family left to search for the girl, her body was gone. The storm had disappeared."

Tears fell from the little girl Eta had hoped to entertain. "That's a horrible story."

Eta blinked, frowning. "It's honest," she insisted. "This is a story to tell us we must guard against the dangers of our hearts."

Diya blinked away tears of her own. Oh, it was more than that. She saw now, too, how Eta could have started a war and not cared until it was too late. "Which was which?"

"What?" Relief was plain on her mother's face. Diya had given Eta a direction clear of a furious mother's glaring. Still, the little girl's sobbing caused a wince. "What did you say?"

"Which god was which?"

By the way the other passengers raised their long faces and furrowed their brows, they also wanted an answer. It was well known that the sibling gods enjoyed changing their forms, but the god of dreams had a natural inclination for it. At one time male, the next female. An immortal pillar for new beginnings as well as true love, while their infamous sister represented the heart of fear.

"It's up to you," Eta answered.

Diya flinched. She'd have given anything to hear her mother say those exact words several months earlier, when she had protested the need for a match of her own. But, try as she might, she couldn't break the promise of her impending marriage to a Gildeshan she had known as a child.

His name was Arien.

His family made up the backbone of Gildesh, while Diya had become the hand that fed her mother's penance from Novasi. Her village was currently teeming with relations until the seventh cousin for this disaster of a wedding—and all because her mother had been a capricious young girl with a foolish father, burning down the bridge of friendship between the two villages before Diya's grandmother could stop them.

"Don't be too hard on her," her grandmother had told her once. *"Loving your father despite what Gildesh wanted brought you into the world. Your mother sometimes forgets."*

Although those flames had died almost two decades ago, Diya was still haunted by their smoke, suffocating from mistakes that did not belong to her. Someone better than her— Arien, in fact—might have managed without hard feelings, but not Diya.

When the doors of the temple finally emerged, great gilded curves rising up from the river mist, her mother's old warnings rose up in her mind.

"There are always histories of beautiful girls who plagued both

gods and men so much they paid a terrible price. Do you understand?"

"Yes, Ahma."

"Would you like to pay your price now?" Her mother had lifted a kitchen knife between them. Moonlight caught the sharp gleam of it. *"It will be painful at first, but this way is less steep."*

Diya rubbed her cheek as she leapt from their narrow boat, the sparse beading of her work dress chafing the proud bone. The simple habit would have been painful had there been raw wounds from her mother's knife. But there was a part of Diya that regretted having said no.

She set about anchoring them without meeting Eta's eyes.

The gongs rang ten times as each passenger escaped the sudden nightmare of a ride, respectfully rushing into the waiting arms of the priestesses.

While Eta spilled the passengers' coin into their hands, Diya's gaze settled on an earthly tunnel hewn from black rock. It led from the mouth of the river to the true form of the River of Souls. She knew no name for it.

Sometimes there was a voice billowing from it. Sometimes there were many voices. The god of souls perhaps, or the murmuring of dead spirits. Diya imagined their frantic tugs on the god's shimmering sleeve incited pity or fury depending upon the day.

Looking at the cave, there was no room for Arien, his family, Diya's family, Gildesh, or Novasi. All of them fell off pedestals of expectation, landing in the water to swim after her. She continued into the darkness without a parting wave, giddy at the thought of what lay on the other side.

If she could get there, it would be like nothing she'd ever known.

It would be like... peace.

She didn't allow herself time to think or second guess. She ignored her lack of food or coin. The only thing she allowed in her mind was the thought of consigning herself to that wedding.

She was poised over the anchor when the hushed footfalls of Eta's sandals broke through her reverie. The rope slipped soundlessly through her fingers.

"Going somewhere?"

Diya slowly straightened. Her heart adopted a nervous rhythm. A long moment passed before she spoke. "I was readying the boat for us."

Eta came down a small decline of stairs. "Good."

Blinking several times before entering the boat did not make the world seem any less damp and blurred. Her mother's shadow fell over her head.

"You dropped this." Eta handed Diya the rope, but didn't quite let go until Diya looked up. "Let's go home, yes?"

She stung at the word. Home struck her as a rejection. Alcohol pouring on an open wound. Home was the place where eyes reached for her and mouths swallowed her name. Neighbors were already speculating what she would do. She knuckled her drying eyes before casting off. If she had found her anger sooner, she would have stopped herself from going back to such a place.

But guilt had gotten the better of her.

Her mother's gaze had conquered the rest.

"Yes, *Ahma*."

IT DIDN'T TAKE LONG. Her anger returned as soon as they arrived home. The fact that she had missed an easy opportunity riled her more.

"I hate him," she reminded her mother for the thousandth time, wincing as her grandmother's beloved hairbrush snagged in the black silk of her hair. She was thankful her cousins had gone to fetch her wedding dress, or they'd have teased her for it. She reached for an excuse her mother had not heard. "His hands are smelly."

There were a few days known as the confirmation period, in which she, Arien, and their parents gathered to ensure the two families still consented to the match. Diya had spent the entire two hours concocting ways to steal the bride-price from Eta's hiding place, her thoughts cycling sweetly around the shocked faces of her parents and the scandalous whispers that would come of hers and Arien's broken marriage promise. For a little while, she had allowed herself to pretend that escaping their families wouldn't snap the jagged truce between their villages. The lie brightened her mood.

Then, Arien, seated next to her, had tentatively brushed the back of her hand. His touch had actually jolted her back to reality, and left her scowling at him. Later, while inspecting her hand for evidence as to *why* his touch could interrupt a thought, she scented the vaguest impression of that too-sweet smell.

Eta's response was firm. "You'll get used to it."

Too firm for Diya's liking. But she couldn't defy her mother without making the hairbrush snag even more.

"Do they smell like jasmine?" guessed her older sister, Karula, with a sweet sigh while Diya thought up as many horrible names in the Old Script for her mother as she could. "Jasmine is just wonderful."

"How should I know?" Diya muttered. Jasmine was not *that* wonderful. The heat seeping through the windows stirred her anger, no less cooled by the moon than the slow, warm breeze dancing for the stars. Stars that Arien used to watch with her when they were too young to know what devious things their mothers' had cooked up for them. "And they're too soft." He used to be able to climb little mountains of stone with her to get as close to the night sky as they could reach, steadying her if

11

she ever lost her balance. Even then, his little hands had been rough-sure when they gripped her arm. Now, Diya felt more uncertain about their future than ever before. "They didn't used to be like that," she protested when her mother gave her *a look*.

"Hold on," said her younger sister, Lilia, without bothering to stop playing with Diya's wedding adornments, "why were you smelling his hands?"

"I *wasn't*."

"That's not what you *just* said." Lilia lifted what could only be termed a nest of rubies off her head. "You should wear this one. He'll be stunned."

The comment pleased Diya. Now she knew exactly which of the head pieces to avoid.

"If you're worried he's grown lazy, you'll teach him better," their mother said, calm in the wake of Diya's simmering irritation.

"I'm meant to be more than *his* teacher," she spat. As if a man who found time enough in his day to dunk his hands in perfume or flower beds or whatever he did to make them sour her nose was worthy of being *taught* by her.

"You'll be his student as well," snickered Lilia.

Eta smacked Lilia's temple before she could say something unbefitting of an unmarried girl. Never mind that Lilia's knowledge of innuendos ran conspicuously deep for an innocent maiden. There was metal beading wrapped around the hairbrush Eta had used, the back of it carved from moonglass, so the small blow was not a little thing. Diya felt a twinge of pity when Lilia's yelp turned into a pained hiss. Their sister's distress made Karula jump, and Diya wondered how either of them would fare if war broke like a yolk between Novasi and Gildesh.

They won't survive. Diya's heart sped at the thought. Eta was swift and smart, but was that enough to maintain their family's survival? If Diya ran from Arien now, would her family ever forgive her for putting them all in danger?

Diya put a hand to her temple. The thin skin felt hot against her fingertips. "*Ahma*, are you so eager to get rid of me you'll leave me in the hands of *Gildeshans*?"

Karula squeaked as though the word were a curse and Diya wanted to shout, *See? Doesn't anyone see?*

Before the battle between she and Arien's villages, Gildesh and Novasi were all but forgotten points on any map. Simple, if pretty stepping stones to the famed temple cut into the River of Souls, where magic and matches were made. Their wedding was the first time the two villages had reason to *behave* as though their feud hadn't happened. And yet, this culmination of nearly two decades of relative peace could not stop the fumbles as pink-faced chrysanthemums were wreathed along the buildings for the wedding. Could not soothe the startles at any shadow Diya's neighbors did not recognize. One more wayward war story and someone might very well light up the entire town instead of just a few dozen oil lamps.

Then again, if Diya shook off her mother's brushstrokes and ran as fast her bare feet could handle, she might very well be the blaze to burn them all. Her heart lurched even as her mind screamed at her to *go*.

"In the hands of a beautiful Gildeshan man whose family is honorable and well situated?" Eta lifted a brow in the mirror. On any other day, Diya would've tried to replicate the move in private. Would it have made her look as unforgiving? She wondered how long it would be before they shared the same crinkled lines in between the brows and around the mouth. "Yes, I suppose I am that eager," finished Eta.

Sweat prickled Diya's skin as her mother made a final rough pass through her hair. The strands were a black gleam in the moonglass, polished until they no longer looked snarled. Another exercise in Eta's patience. Another quest for penance.

Perfect the unruly daughter and the world would finally forgive.

"They won't let me pray to the moon and the night," Diya said with no less desperation than when she first understood what was expected of her. This was her future. She had to find some give in this woman who had borne her. "They won't like my hair styles or my eye color. The village will speak badly of me. They'll make me do what he does." Never mind that Diya didn't care much for prayer at all, and her hair was most often loose, obscuring her face as much as possible without scaring children.

"That's why he's going to live with you here."

Diya's mouth fell open. "*Here?*"

"Your father has already paid for a home with a portion of the bride-price. It was Arien's suggestion."

This time, Karula let out another gentle sigh. Even Lilia looked dreamy-eyed.

"How," Diya choked out, "is this possible? He's from *Gildesh*," she said again, wondering if both Arien and her parents were somehow confused.

"He was born at twilight, if you remember. He has the favor of both the moon *and* the sun. He can make the choice." Eta set down the hairbrush, meeting Diya's eyes for the first time since they entered their home. "And he was once your friend."

Diya's heart raced too fast for her chest to contain. It wasn't as if she needed any reminders as to exactly what Arien was to her or how much he had meant to her. A boy who soberly doctored her knee after a chase gone awry and kissed her cheek when there were troubles was hard to forget. He'd always been so *close* for someone so serious and timid. But putting aside his memory had been *necessary*. Thinking about him while they'd been separated was almost as exhausting as befriending him. Perfect, beautiful Arien always thought too much of others whereas Diya barely spared a thought. Competing with his goodness had stopped appealing to her the moment her parents informed her they expected her to do it for the rest of her life.

"You're *lucky*," said Karula, the only current gentle enough to sweep between such tight-knit animosity. She came over to Diya and planted a windowsill-flower behind Diya's ear, along with a kiss to the head. Both were bright weights, especially because the gesture made Diya think of her intended.

"You're so beautiful and he's so handsome," Karula continued, oblivious to Diya's wince. "It's like our bedtime tales. Or like a *dream*." Her special emphasis was not lost on anyone in the room. This was also the first time in near-to twenty years that the god of dreams had blessed a union. "It's just so perfect."

"A nightmare is not perfect."

"Sister," Karula gasped, paling. "Do not mock the Dream. The god of nightmares may be listening."

Diya snorted, often because, like mussing her hair, it made her less attractive. She'd seen it herself in a plain mirror she'd found, which she often used to practice morphing her face into something people wouldn't expect. "The Dream of Lovers is *one* star in the evening sea. It doesn't really prove anything. Besides, the gods have better things to do than curse me."

"Is this the next step in your plan to ruin this day for all of us?" snapped Eta, meeting Diya's eyes once more in the moonglass mirror reflecting them both. The light from the windows helped lend them both an ethereal glow to rival the images of the very gods Diya discounted. "Provoke the gods, call them down to the ceremony with ill talk? I taught you better than this, Diya. The gods know Arien doesn't deserve this. Neither do I or your father. Having a husband will offer you protection from the wrath of whoever might be listening, but understand me: if you continue talking this way, you won't be welcome back into this house. I won't have you spoiling your sisters' fates because of your selfishness."

No one in the room spoke.

Diya's cousins had returned with her dress only to stand with sick expressions on their faces. One of her mother's sisters came up behind Eta to offer a gentle pat, but Eta did not soften.

When has she ever? thought Diya, a bitter smile tugging at her lips.

"You're determined to take everything away from me, aren't you?" Diya whispered, her belly twisting as her mother's face darkened still. "You're determined to leave me with nothing. As if that would make what you did better somehow."

Eta's right hand clenched into a fist and Diya understood she'd barely escaped a fine slap. But, why mark her cheek *now*, when it might deter the husband her mother was so determined she have?

"*This* wasn't my doing," said her mother, that fist still trembling from what appeared to be a monumental effort. "I did not determine yours and Arien's stars cross over the Dream of Lovers. I did not ask the god of dreams to visit me with news of Arien's birth. I did not even presume your fate. I asked the priestesses for clarity and they saw in your horoscope what I already knew. And I did not make you so impossible and greedy."

The words were more punishing than any slap.

Diya's fists mirrored Eta's, but the fury in their trembling wasn't what was expected of her. She was meant to bend her head, scramble for her mother's forgiveness, and pretend away the disgusted look her mother was too angry to hide. Pretty Diya had a gift and she was squandering it with rude behavior and ungrateful talk, but she was also born in her mother's shadow and that was a curse of its own. *Quiet down. Sit still.* Eta's chiding had often followed Diya even in sleep, bleeding out the peace she sought. *Do as I say. But not as I did.* If she turned to the mirror now, would her beauty have spilled away? Would the girl in the mirror look as shrunken and shriveled as her pained heart?

Diya's aunt stepped between them now, coaxing Eta to relax, to apologize, to rethink staining this day with a memory like this one. But Diya's mother kept her lips pressed tight, so Diya did not bother with pretending away the moment as everyone else seemed to need.

She turned over her mother's words as the night sky slowly filled itself up with stars. If any of the women of her family thought to comfort her, they never stepped up to the sill. She was left alone with that tight fist in her chest as daylight slowly relinquished the length of itself to the night.

Her nails formed stark grooves in her palms. She was so tired of being loved and *hated* for all the wrong reasons. Why did it always feel like she had to surrender something vital in order for things to change?

Today was just one more bit of proof that beauty was a curse.

She kept hold of her enraged silence as her sisters and cousins slid and draped her wedding dress over her. She ignored the pleasure of the silken bodice, the soft marigold lace. Even the gleam of the beading couldn't blind her temper.

Her cousins crooned over her, the star-vines painted up their arms like miniature constellations still damp and strong-smelling. Lilia fixed her hair in the moonglass mirror, enjoying the effects before another aunt came and slapped her away. Karula clapped her own painted hands, bouncing in place. The entire scene should've landed on Diya like a petal across her cheek. A sweet surprise frozen in time, an unforgettable light in her memory.

Instead, she stuffed her feet into delicate beaded sandals that pinched. A cage for her feet and her mother's scowl the key turning the lock.

Because, now, all she could think of was the anchor she hadn't lifted fast enough from her little boat that morning. She'd allowed it to sink back to the bottom of the river, weighted down by the terrible sameness of things.

How Arien could stand the pressure and not drown these past years was something Diya would never understand.

Nor, if she was honest, forgive.

His wordless acquiescence had cut deep, and that single touch during their marriage confirmation had rustled up a small, intrusive desire. She would not sacrifice exploring what awaited beyond Novasi for the sake of exploring that foreign warmth he'd incited in the palm of her hand.

In the mirror, Diya's dark waves were looped around strings of rubies and freesias. Her gown was long and fragile, and each curve of the fabric clung to a curve of hers. A light sheen of almond oil seduced the moonlight to her skin.

She was the perfect quintessential bride, but for the panicked beat of her heart. *This isn't me.*

She swallowed her fear. *I won't let it be.*

What were a sprinkle of ceremonial words anyway? Their weight was determined by how much she decided to bear. Taking Arien for her husband would appease the villages and protect her family's honor. She could swallow her pride and play the part.

But the second she and Arien were alone after the ceremony, she'd demand he let her go. She'd threaten to injure herself if he tried to sway her to the marriage bed. She wouldn't allow her life to be eclipsed by his.

This was the only vow she intended to honor after today.

～

"YOU LOOK BEAUTIFUL," said Diya's father, interrupting her glaring contest with Arien's older brother. Unlike Diya's father,

Gabriel knew the redness along her shimmering cheekbones for what it was, and he sneered at her rage.

It had always been like this between them. She assumed he was jealous of her. When they were all younger, she'd steal Arien for another private adventure, exploring the forests and fields that hugged their borders while Gabriel called after them, warning Arien from danger and cursing Diya for the stubborn chase she gave.

Resentment set him apart from the crowd gathering at the end of a short, petal-strewn path leading into the village center. He seemed on guard in a way she didn't recognize. He'd always been wary of meeting new people, but this was different. His eyes had already been cold and alert before he spotted her coming toward them. As if he'd been spending his time assessing the crowd, sifting through the tension and excitement... for danger? Could he sense how the distress between their villages sat like a drop at the tip of a blade?

She hadn't even seen him during the confirmation visit. It was the one time she'd actually felt grateful to him. Then again, she wondered if a fight between them would have been enough to sever the match. Surely if she got along so terribly with his brother, Arien would have begged his parents to let her go...

As if he understood her thoughts, Gabriel's scowl deepened.

"Diya?" her father said.

A brute and an idiot. She muttered about missed opportunities. How Arien could share blood with the likes of Gabriel was just reaffirmation that the gods had whims rather than plans.

"Lovely," said Diya's father as he escorted her toward the priestess and her altar. They passed a small fountain, draped in more marigold than could possibly be found on Diya's dress. She missed it at first, her gaze focused on that altar, where offerings to the gods and sacred wreaths loomed. "Look at what they've done."

She blinked when her father gestured with his free hand.

He was right. Her village *had* outdone itself. Despite the skewed chrysanthemums, the buildings were brightened by gossamer turquoise fabric. Jasmine bloomed along the sides. Petals strung together to form a long hall of archways, leading to a garden outside the meeting house, where encouraging smiles littered the rest of Diya's view.

It took all her might to cling to her anger as lotus oil lamps were lit against evil and silver oaks peeled back to reveal a doting moon. It was a horrible thing, to feel so torn inside when all she wanted was the chance to run. To see what lay beyond the midnight beauty and dangerous legacies of her homeland.

"Diya, no young man could look at you and not feel blessed," her father tried again, clearing his throat.

Diya finally looked at him, studying his stiff posture and brimming discomfort. Their awkwardness might have been born when she was. She had distinct memories of climbing over his knees to sit with him and being replaced in another part of the house. "And do *you* feel blessed, *Ahba*?"

He shuffled his feet. The way he did on those rare occasions when Eta stepped between their bent heads, interrupting whatever fascinating story he hadn't had the chance to purge before seeing Diya. "My beautiful daughter is about to be married to a good man," he said carefully, as though he suspected a trick. He leaned in as if he were going to kiss her temple, but stopped short when she stepped back. "The gods have indeed blessed our family."

She wanted to snap at him. His sense of blessings was rigid and traditional. He was well-married and had fathered daughters to help him join families and villages together. A closed-mouth man from humble beginnings who gave up no protests when Eta had made distance a requirement of his and Diya's relationship. Why fan the flame of Eta's fears, when prosperity rooted in the *fact* of Diya's being rather than the state? Why risk a bond between father and daughter that might capsize their humble little world again?

Diya looked out at the open fields to her far left than at the place where a man only a few steps above a stranger walked beside her. "What does it matter to you anyway?" she said fiercely. "Besides the pile of coin and the new foot stool awaiting you?"

"Enough," her father hissed, staring at the crowd. No doubt heads had turned as her voice had spiked. "Come," he said. He tried to grab her arm, continue as if she hadn't spoken. His trademark method for dealing with her wildness.

She shook him off. Despite her father's hard looks, she wished he, rather than her mother, had been the one to oppose her choices from the beginning. Perhaps this was why Eta stood like a stone between Diya and her wants. "You listen to me," she hissed back. For once in his life, she needed him to *listen*. To understand that being beholden to Arien might dig out the core of her. "He is *not* my Dream. I want to... I want..." Her voice weakened when his expression only grew more bewildered. Frustrated beyond words, she forced herself to say, "Do you want to know what I want, *Ahba*?"

I want a history that belongs to me and not my ancestors. I want a life bright with new horizons. I want to know the place where the river's tail ends and the gods rise from the shadows they cast over this land. I want to live my life as I choose.

His mouth was shaped by disappointment and confusion. "No."

Blunt, quiet. These were her father's most renowned qualities, and still the truth crackled in her ears, distorting the murmurs rising behind her the longer she waited to walk toward her predestined future. Speaking with him was just as useless as convincing Eta. Neither of her parents ever saw beyond the form with which the gods adorned her soul.

"Will I not be welcomed back home, *Ahba*?"

21

He stared at her, his mouth a grim line. For the first time, Diya thought he might actually understand what she was saying: that if she managed to separate from Arien, could she count on something as simple as her father's loyalty?

He reached for her arm again. Squeezed.

Answer enough.

The lamps seemed to dim with Diya's hope, a wisp of a coming storm curling around the ritual flames like a snare. When she finally arrived next to the priestess, her father's arm fell away from hers. She was met with another look of deep resentment from Arien's brother, before he disappeared in the opposite direction. Arien likely awaited with the rest of the grooms' column somewhere among the trees.

Her mind grew frantic, flooding her with confusing images of a pair of children holding hands as they traced around the star that meant they would always be part of each other's lives... Gabriel pulling Arien from the thin line of the river that separated their villages when Diya had playfully goaded him... reaching for her mother's hand and finding Eta had already grabbed for Karula's and Lilia's... poking her father's side while he napped after a grueling night to demand attention...

Gabriel, swathed in a red as deep as his scowl, began the long column of men down the petal-scattered path toward Diya. With his eyes riveted on her, she remembered her fleeting thought to run before Eta had finished grooming her. If she ran to Arien now and explained herself... Her eyes darted to the shadows of the trees surrounding the gathering. She held herself back with a deep breath. *Patience.* She didn't want to risk an outburst between the villages. Frigid politeness was not impossible to crack.

As the procession continued to mimic the stages of the sun the Gildeshans so zealously worshipped, Diya had a vivid memory of Gabriel standing on the rooftop of his family home, haloed in crimson light like the sun god himself, demanding

Arien come away from Diya and return inside. Divine punishment could come at the top of the dawn they taunted by being
out so late.

"They're a danger together," Diya once heard him say to his
mother.

She'd been dangling from the roof with Arien's help. Her
frustration had made it difficult for Arien to hold his grip, but it
hadn't made sense how a discussion *about* them hadn't *included*
them. "He lets her think for him and she walks him straight
into disaster."

What Gabriel never understood was how rarely she forced
Arien to do anything on her behalf. She made suggestions and
Arien just seemed relieved that he didn't have to come up with
his own ideas. He *chose* to run wild with Diya.

Being reminded of that made her confident she could
convince him to let her go.

Diya's cousins followed after Gabriel and Arien's own array
of family and friends, holding some of the lotus lamps along
the path. When Arien took his first step, they would ensure the
light followed him.

But he stopped as soon as he saw Diya.

Thoughts of escape burned away from her mind.

Like paper lifting at the touch of a flame, she saw Arien's
golden-brown skin and straight, burnished hair through the
smoking remnants of her distaste. His gaze made a careful
study of her face, as if dreams and memories and a quick visit
hadn't allowed him, and when he smiled, gently, so gently, a
wish for that touch she'd felt months ago scrambled from her
heart. The full scope of him prized the resistance right out
of her.

How could someone so careful of his effect on others have
so worrying an effect on her? The innocent charms of the boy
she used to play with had always gone right over her head. But
the boy before her now was mercenary in his thorough regard

of her. She had no defense against his slow, steady perusal. Her thoughts bumped into each other.

Was it the finery he was wrapped in? His wedding clothes were a deep gold, complimentary but not overshadowing hers. His mother was a seamstress, but she used to confide in Diya when Diya was small that there were savings for garments beyond her skill when it was time for them to marry.

Arien's cheeks burned the longer they stared at each other.

Panic turned her palms icy. *I don't want this.*

The last time they were together before their imposed separation, they spent what should have been a normal night of chase and adventure crying in each other's arms. Their mothers informed them that it was time. Their bodies were changing, they said. If something untoward should happen, they would bring dishonor on both families. Like with everything else, their mothers were united in this.

I don't want you.

The pain of losing him for a time had eclipsed *everything.* Her taste for thrills disappeared into his shoulder, where her tears stained his shirt. They were both only thirteen. They still had little idea of the 'untoward' things their mothers feared. They hadn't even known what their separation entailed, only that it might kill the ease of their friendship.

She should have been used to her own mother's unyielding stance—but it hurt, as it hurt to be forced from the boy who *smiled* at her scraped knees and bruised chin and wild hair. She had been given someone who had accepted her completely, only to be forced away from him. No one in her family seemed to understand just how agonizing it was to separate yourself from all that heartache, then be asked to forget everything you'd done to fortify yourself against that kind of pain, to keep yourself whole and strong.

She could feel herself choking on that same sorrow as

Arien started to take a step in her direction. Her heart galloped to keep up with her spreading panic.

"You are not my Dream," she whispered the words like some ancient mantra, sweat beading her brow. "You are not my Dream."

And Arien *froze*.

There was a flash of something, a shiver in the air, like the river when rain hits its surface. Her fear should have barred her from noticing the faint sensation of being watched. And yet her spine still straightened and her thoughts began to turn.

Then Arien reeled back as though he'd been dealt a blow.

Shouts instantly broke out among his family members. Diya's eyes widened when he bent over his stomach, groaning like a knife had split his skin.

And there it was again! Another flash of... horns. Just the tips, shadowed silver in the moonlight.

Diya nearly ran toward that one brief glimpse, before everyone moved at once toward her groom, blocking her path.

The last thing she saw was Arien collapsing, seizing on the ground.

"Oh my gods," one of his sisters cried. They were twins, Diya suddenly remembered, who had liked to torment them as much as laugh with them. Now their tears fell in torrents.

Gabriel had already abandoned the groom's column, cutting a path for himself through the frightened medley of family surrounding his brother. He held his mother back and ordered his droves of cousins to give Arien space.

"Aren't you going to see what's wrong?" Diya demanded, breath shaking, at the priestess too shocked to move. "*Well?*"

"Yes. Right," said the woman, rushing forward with too youthful a face to relieve Diya of her fears.

Her father kept their family back from intruding. One wrong move or thing said and who knew how the Gildeshans might react? When one of his family members demanded,

"Was he poisoned?" Diya twisted her dress with white-knuckled hands. She caught her mother's gaze, shame burning her cheeks at the suspicion there.

Please don't be dead.

"Looks like you got your wish," Lilia said, as blunt as their father and just as grim-faced as they all helplessly looked on.

Karula's gentle hand fell on Diya's lace-clad shoulder. "Let's pray for him while the moon oversees. Maybe she can help."

Except Diya didn't know how. It wasn't like she paid much attention to the rituals of prayer. She loved listening to the stories the priestesses told in the temple, but that was the extent of her connection to the divine. Her knowledge was useless here.

Her father itched to be part of the solution, but that too-quiet part of him kept him from interfering. "Go," she told him.

Whatever tether seemed to hold him back fell away. Her father rushed to help Gabriel and some of his relatives lift Arien from the ground. "Bring him into our home," her father insisted. "Quickly."

Arien's parents followed, along with Eta and Arien's sisters. Diya's home wasn't large enough to fit the entirety of both families, so the excess lingered in silence.

Slowly all eyes roamed until they landed on Diya and stuck there. Her face grew hotter, that queasy feeling returning in the pit of her stomach.

She almost lost her balance when Karula tugged on her sleeve and whispered, "Go inside?"

Diya bobbed her head, making the world spin for a moment. A wriggling suspicion demanded her scrutiny, but she was too scared to really give it much thought. This couldn't be *her* fault.

With her head held high, Lilia took charge of her older sisters, pulling on both sets of hands until the three of them barreled through the crowd and into the chaos unfolding inside their home.

The second Gabriel caught sight of Diya, the shouting began.

~

"*You*," Gabriel spat, charging right for her. His father tried to block his path. "*You* did this. My fool brother loved you, and the thanks he gets is your black curse."

The priestess' head rose up from Arien's chest, suddenly intent on his brother. Diya wanted to ask after the strength of Arien's heartbeat, but her lips remained pinched, clapped together in case she ruined something else. That unnamed suspicion rushed up from the bed of her mind like a weed. Still, she said, "What are you talking about, Gabriel?"

"*I saw you*," he shouted, unraveling the paler Arien became. "You held his eyes and muttered something over and over. What spells did you learn so that you might cast him off? *What did you do to my brother?*"

"Gabriel." His father struggled to keep him back, but he was no more than a molehill between them. "Please."

"Gabriel," his mother tried to soothe, but he shook off her placating hand.

Diya tried steadying her breathing with little success. "I did nothing. *Nothing*," she said with a desperate wave of her hand. She couldn't afford for the opposite to be true. As much as Gabriel liked to be heard, this was no game he sought to win. The gleam in his eyes was terrifying. She would wind up dead if he could make it so. "I swear."

Gabriel spun to the priestess. "And I swear her mouth moved. She even began to sweat. I know she did something to him."

His cruel certainty sent Diya's heart galloping faster. Could he really think to declare her some kind of witch before a priestess? Did he really hate her that much?

What *had* she done? The oil lamps had cast shadows where there hadn't been any over her parents' faces, over Arien's parents. A dizzying heat had stolen her breath. Arien had watched her too steadily for comfort. And then she had said— but why should the words matter? A flash of those horns entered her mind and she did her best to keep standing, despite the ill feeling crowding her stomach.

"These are serious accusations, Gabriel of Gildesh," said the priestess, the wisdom finally outshining her apparent youth, "and you're not in your right mind. Let us take time to assess the situation. I'm sure Diya of Novasi can provide us with an explanation."

Once again, the entire focus of the room shifted to her. She swallowed nervously as her mother's arms folded. Every time she started to speak, her protests failed her. Her defenses had dried up the moment Arien had fallen.

"I'm sure it was just nerves," Karula said hurriedly. "Diya's been nervous all day. Right, *Ahma*?"

Without taking her eyes off Diya's guilty expression, Eta slowly said, "Right."

Karula elbowed Lilia, but Lilia said nothing. She was unaccustomed to lying. If she spoke then, no one would believe Diya was innocent of the crime.

Which meant Lilia suspected, too.

Sometime between Arien appearing and Diya's panic, Diya had felt out of touch with herself. She couldn't even remember exactly what she had said. Tears burned her eyes.

"They're her family," Gabriel exploded with no shortage of disgust. "Of course they'll defend her." He drew himself up to his full height, towering over the priestess. "My family will not stand for this. When word goes back to Gildesh, I promise you there will be a reckoning."

With wide eyes, Diya blurted the truth. "I didn't mean anything by it, Gabriel. Please stop."

Deliberately slow, he faced her again. "Didn't mean anything by *what*?"

Diya stepped forward, fists curled. "I don't know any spells. Let's get that clear," she said hotly, glancing at everyone in the room. "It wasn't magic. I don't even know what I said. I was only trying to calm myself."

"Then how do you know what you said wasn't harmful?"

Now, Lilia did speak up. "She said, 'You're not my Dream,' over and over." She stood beside Diya and stared Gabriel down. "That's *all* she said, all right? It's not good, but I don't think it's any spell. Could you step back from my sister?"

Gabriel leaned in, barring his teeth. "Sounds like a spell to me."

"Diya," the priestess interrupted. "Please explain exactly what you think happened. Tell us what you did."

Without much choice, Diya did. She ran through her feelings, no matter how embarrassing they were to reveal. "Then when he collapsed, I saw..."

"What?" the priestess demanded, leaving Arien's side. "What did you see?"

"A face," Diya rushed out. "It was there so quickly I could barely make out the features. I thought I saw red eyes. And... and horns. Just the tips before they disappeared. It looked sort of familiar, but I don't know how."

The priestess did nothing to alter the silence that fell upon the room.

"What is it?" ventured Arien's mother. "What's wrong with my son?"

A wintry breeze was no less grim than the priestess' heavy sigh. "I believe Arien of Gildesh *has* been cursed. But not by Diya of Novasi. Though I do not believe the bride was very helpful in preventing it."

"Explain," Gabriel demanded.

When she said, "I remember these children," no one was more stunned than Diya. The woman looked to be about her age, and yet she claimed to remember hers and Arien's births. "Their stars cross over the Dream of Lovers, yes?"

"Yes." This from Eta.

"It has been a long time since we've seen that star appear on a pair of horoscopes." The priestess faced Diya's mother more fully. "You received clemency for your past actions the moment we discovered it. But it seems your legacy continues."

Stunned, Eta's mouth sealed shut. Diya understood enough of her mother to interpret the color rising in her cheeks as insult.

Before Diya could fully appreciate the sight, the priestess turned to her. "The god of nightmares is always painted with horns pushing from her scalp in the far recesses of the temple," she said, and Diya shuddered at the thought of being so near to one such as they. "If our history is to be believed, this blatant rejection of the Dream of Lovers would have invoked the wrath of the sibling gods. The rare divinity of the god of dreams creates an unparalleled love between life-partners. A gift you dismissed, Diya of Novasi. Now it seems they have taken it back."

Just then Arien winced from some unseen blow, his eyelids flickering relentlessly, his mouth in the shape of a shout. A line from her mother's story haunted her:*"You asked for a new dream," said the god coldly. "Here, take it."* Diya's heart chilled as Arien struggled against her dining table, and his father was forced to hold him down.

"How do we fix it?" Gabriel stood before the priestess with that same indomitable glare. "There must be something. A tonic or some ritual." He gave Diya a meaningful glance, to which she narrowed her eyes. "Sacrifice perhaps? Or—"

Before Diya could punch him as she'd longed to since she'd

first seen him again, the priestess stopped him. "I'm afraid you have only two choices. You can give him over to my keeping and I will take him back to the temple. We will care for him until his body gives out." She stroked a finger down Arien's cheek, a shadow passing over her expression. The kind that made Diya wonder if the priestess had ever had a son before consigning herself to life at the temple. "Such a beautiful boy. Such a shame. It must be torture. There now, hush."

"And the other option?" whispered Arien's mother, reaching for Eta's hand as Arien's discomfort seemed to ease just a little under the priestess' gentleness.

Tears stained the priestess' venerable gaze when Diya looked up. "You may end his suffering, with my full pardon to do so. Those are your choices."

As Arien's mother cracked open from the force of her sorrow, Diya moved away, reaching blindly for the windowsill. She gripped the latch and shoved at the glass pane until she could breathe air stripped of guilt and heartache. This was Arien, was all she could think. Arien of the stone mountains, hunter of stars, navigator of her windstorm impulses. Suddenly, it didn't matter if he fancied himself too much, had grown lazy and arrogant and all the other things she feared had changed about him because of a pair of soft, scented hands.

This was Arien.

And he was dying.

Misery stained her conscience. When Arien had collapsed, there'd been no way of knowing that initial worm of doubt would grow into a wriggling pit inside her mind. It wasn't easy for her to be honest, not with a mother or a destiny like hers. But she could have found another way to end hers and Arien's match. At the very least, she could have *stuck to the plan.* Disgust left her feeling more exposed than any scathing glare from Gabriel or reprimand from Eta. She could have waited until they were alone to convince him of what she was really meant for. Instead, she had cowered before he'd even finished walking toward her. If she couldn't do the hard things, the things that required a bit of bravery, how was she supposed to have a life beyond Novasi?

A quiet rage built in her bones and the weight of it surprised her. She'd carried burdens before, but this had a punishing quality to it. Was it because she begrudged her family, Arien, his horrible brother, or was it because she begrudged herself? She had no idea what was right, but life-lessness did not suit Arien.

"I will save him."

At first, between Arien's mother's sobs and Arien himself, fighting against an invisible menace, no one heard her. She repeated the words with more force.

Gabriel's head lifted from watching Arien's helplessness. "What did you say?"

Diya regarded Gabriel warily, angling her chin high. "I will save him."

He scrubbed a hand over his face. His righteousness had faded into weariness. "How?"

She only had a vague idea. The priestess' temple was built on old lore, stacked high by ancient hands. Borderland history was sharp-edged and brilliant, more like a diamond than a pearl. She knew some of those stories. She knew the River of Souls harbored strange creatures and capricious gods, cunning eddies and a singular path to the rare miracles of their world. Maintaining herself on that path would be difficult, probably impossible.

But, with the burden of guilt weighing down on her heart, she had no other choice.

Careful not to glance at her mother, Diya declared, "By going to the land of the gods."

~

WHAT HAVE I DONE?

After the outrage and shock and disavowing had dissipated between hers and Arien's families, Diya was left alone to pack for her journey along the River of Souls. Her room was an ongoing conversation with her ideals of that river, crowded with sketches of fierce, supple-skinned creatures and gods like those embedded in the temple walls—heart-stopping, rippling with power. Somehow no one thought she might need comfort or reassurance for what she was about to do.

Even her sisters had abandoned her to care for Arien while Arien's mother went with his father to discuss the news with their extended relatives. But for the proud squeeze Lilia gave her and the soft hug Karula had laced around her, Diya had nothing else to hold onto.

She'd just *said* the words. And like a spell all of its own, no one had stopped her. A host of her own relatives and all of them had abandoned her to see to Arien and his family. She ruthlessly shoved travel dresses into her pack, then paused, wondering if she had enough to spare for the length of the river. *Will I be old and grey when I finally reach them? What will I say?* She couldn't imagine strutting into the realm of the gods, piping off demands.

Thinking about how Arien had once again resumed the central focus of her foreseeable future—even *without* marrying him—helped with her shaking hands. Undergarments were next, receiving a thrashing for the injustice of what was becoming her life. What would she do once she got him back? What would she tell her shamed family if she failed? She rolled her drawing papers into scrolls, though something told her there might not be much room for doodling on her course. As she took up an extra pair of sandals, she came to one certainty. It sharpened her mind, settled some of her doubts. When all this was over, she'd tell Arien the truth and get on with her life... even if that meant leaving Novasi behind for good.

She rummaged through wooden drawers and swept under her bed for loose things of supposed importance. Her hand wrapped around something small and smooth, and she pulled it out from some dusty corner.

At first glance, it was only an opal. But the longer she held the multi-sheened stone, the quicker she remembered how it had become forgotten.

Arien had given it to her just before they were separated. He'd found it at the root of the river, floating in the midst of leaves and moss. "It's okay if you forget me, because you'll have this," he'd said. He tried for a smile, but, like her, his eyes had been red-rimmed and damp. "Can't forget a rock when you're holding it."

"Unless I lose it," she'd pointed out, clutching it in a weary fist.

"You won't."

A couple years later and she'd found a new dream, one that didn't include Arien anymore. If her father hadn't worn indifference like a shield around her, she might have gone to him with questions about his travels. But she had planned, alone, a life that would take her past the sweet, unfettered heat of Novasi and into the dry prairies and biting winds of other regions. She could help the traders with their supplies or provide passage for weary travelers by ferrying them. She could apprentice. It didn't really matter so long as it dulled this restlessness beneath her skin. Stopped her life from descending into the dark and lonely monotony her parents had given her. She couldn't count on Arien for that any longer.

When her mother finally sat her down to explain about the marriage promise, Diya had lobbed the stone in a fit of rage and didn't look back to see where it had fallen. He'd had no right to confuse her, to intrude on what had already been set. She had once more put him far out of her mind.

Sixth months later and here she was, the stone gripped

tightly once more. "I'm never going to be rid of you, am I?" she whispered, an uncertain warmth blowing through her. She didn't dare trust it.

A shadow fell over her pack as she tightened the straps, the opal finding a home in one of the interior pockets. Eta sighed when Diya continued to give her back.

"You've been a difficult daughter."

"Something you know all about, I imagine."

Eta sighed again, tucking a greying strand of hair behind her ear. "Is this how it will always be between us?"

Shocked, Diya spun around. "*You* chose this for us, *Ahma*."

"And what about what you chose?" her mother snapped. "You're finally getting your wish. I hope it satisfies you."

"How would you know what I wish?" She almost laughed, but her voice tightened instead. "If your shallow observations are over with, you can leave the same way you came in."

"Shallow? You've always been an ironic child. Here," her mother growled, shoving a packet into Diya's chest. "You remember your lessons with a knife, I trust. This one will serve you well. Have a safe trip."

Diya opened the package as her mother walked away without a hint of worry or affection. Inside the paper wrapping was a knife unlike any she'd ever seen. It shimmered silver and blue and pink in the moonlight filtering through her window. The blade itself seemed too delicate, too thin to ever do anyone much damage without crumbling. Diya's lip curled. "What enemies will this vanquish?"

Eta didn't bother with turning back, ignoring the sarcasm dripping from Diya's voice, "The immortal kind."

"Really? By blinding them?"

"That weapon is an ancient one," said Eta, refusing to be baited, though she hovered in Diya's doorway. "It's been passed down by the women of our line since the priestesses first banned it out of existence. It's made from comet dust." When

Diya remained silent, there was a smile in Eta's voice. "You would do well to hide it. Priestess Ashani will react quite differently to that knife than she has to your witchy antics."

Was that a... joke? From her mother? Eta might as well have bopped Diya with her grandmother's hairbrush again. The sudden shift in attitude burned at the edges of a perpetual hollowness beneath Diya's heart. It made her arms itch to reach for Eta. It made her head boil with resentment. That her mother could still draw out the need to be held bespoke of a power Diya no longer wanted her to have.

And, thinking of how her mother thrived on holding that power, Diya said, "Why are you trusting me with this?"

For if the knife was imbued with comet dust, according to legend, Diya's new weapon was the undoing of all stars, all birthplaces of the gods. Some were loosely tied and others intricately knotted to the stars that birthed them. Comets were a symbol of rebirth and death, and could unravel a god from their star. Temple murals had stopped depicting this act centuries ago. Out of all of Eta's sins, harboring a comet-knife might very well trump starting a small-scale war.

"Because I see no other option," Eta answered, and Diya thought, *Of course,* but then her mother continued with, "My daughter's safety is not guaranteed to me otherwise."

A truly open expression sat on her mother's face when she turned back. Diya wanted to turn away from it, but the hollowness inside her whispered something almost welcoming. Forgiving. "Safety is not what I want, Ahma."

A shadow filled the crack in her mother's pride. Still, Eta seemed to balance her words on the scale hovering between them. "You've never kept secrets from me, Diya," she finally said. "Your sisters exist in their own little worlds from time to time and I let them have that freedom. Do you know why?"

"No."

"Because they understand there's a greater world at play.

Greater good, greater costs than one woman's fancies and fantasies. I've never given you that same level of freedom because you don't hold with the lessons I learned long ago. You think our world is yours to mold, but there are consequences to living your life as though it's entirely your own."

Eta held up a hand when Diya started to respond. "My feelings will not change," she said, casting one last look of mild worry on Diya before turning to the door again. "Stay safe."

Diya could only stand there as her mother disappeared from the doorway, choking on the arguments she might have made and the pain for which she held her mother accountable.

When Gabriel appeared just outside her doorway, she shut the door behind her and crossed the hallway with a hoarse voice. "What are you doing here?"

His family had already left her home. They'd carted Arien with them. Gabriel should have followed. She didn't need to contend with his judgement on top of everything else. Her mother's words still stung her eyes.

"What do you want?" she repeated, not daring to give him her back. He was a wall of danger blocking her most reliable exit as far as she was concerned.

He took his time answering, gazing about the slim hallway connecting her room with the dining area, where Arien had fought for his life. There were little silver statues of the gods of fortune, wilderness, and souls on a long, simple wooden table, their edges turning a dark, worn gray. She pushed the god of souls back in alignment with the others, dragging dust. When Gabriel finally spoke, his eyes landed on a painting Diya had always admired of the priestess' temple protruding from the cusp of the river like a large, lone star teetering into the night. "You say you're going to save my brother."

"And?"

"And you realize the kinds of creatures that lurk there? Rejects of some of the other gods. Demons."

"Demons?" While she didn't pay much attention to prayer in the meeting hall or give much weight to pilgrimages to the temple, her visits there as a child felt much like opening a precious box. Her feet were tentative and quiet as she wandered closer to the fables written into the walls. The domed glass above her head had gods arching around and between the stars. She'd watch the lamps cast bronze shadows on the painted creatures of the river and hold her palms aloft, waiting for the magic of immortal heroes and villains to fall into her hands. "Trust you to distrust what you don't understand."

His perpetual sneer was back. "Have you ever seen them?"

"Are you saying you have?" Had anyone else told her they'd ventured beyond the temple, her eyes would've bugged and she would've blathered all over the lucky person. It was a peculiar thing to be both afraid of someone and envious of them, like being hot and cold at the same time. "Getting drunk on the border and imagining things doesn't count, *Gabe*."

"It's been some time since we've seen each other, *beauty*, so you might not have heard. I'm a guard for the border now. I've also patrolled the cavern that sits next to the temple." Her eyes must have widened, because that almost-smile reappeared. "You know the one, I take it? It's the entrance to the true River of Souls, not the harmless puddle you drink and bathe from every day. You have no idea what awaits beyond that cave. So, again, I ask how you intend to face those creatures?"

She almost showed him her mother's knife, just to see that superior smirk slip off his face. But beneath his bullying, he really did detest her. Worse, he showed no sign of respecting her. She couldn't count on him not to blow smoke into the priestess' ear before they left Novasi.

And, yes, it would be *they*.

If he was a guard, then chances were he knew a thing or two about fighting. Diya only knew a little of self-defense backed by a knife, and she was trying to be responsible.

But if he thought she'd go begging for his help... She sidled up to him with a broad grin. "*I* don't intend to do anything about them," she said, patting his thick shoulder. When he shrugged her hand away, her grin widened. She wondered if he thought she could curse him too. "That's what *you'll* be there for, Gabe. Thank you for volunteering. I already appreciate all the manual labor you'll be doing on my behalf."

"I—What?"

"Isn't that what you were hoping I'd say?" Her wicked smile dropped. She didn't know what kind of guard he was, whether he fought with a sword or combatted his enemies with strategy. But there was a part of herself, the part everyone but Arien shied away from, that liked to question. To gamble. An inner wildness that she found herself shrouding with her hair and a bent head to appease her onlooking mother. That was the part that faced Gabriel now. "Was I supposed to crack and break apart, weep for good measure, begging you to help me? My apologies, Gabe, but I'm not that sort of girl."

He took her measure anew. "You've always been clever," he said after a moment. "But that won't be enough to save you when there are sharp-toothed jaws hovering over you in the water." He thumbed his chest, a scowl morphing his face into something impatient and unapologetic. "*I'm* going to save my brother. I won't stop until I've dragged back his spirit myself. And I'm not going to waste time stopping you from joining me. But we'll see just how long you last, pretty Diya."

"Is it worship of the sun that makes you so horribly domineering, Gabe?"

"No." His smile held no humor. "If anything I get it from my mother. I'll be sure to pass on your opinion of both of us."

Diya shut her eyes. *Their mother.* How that woman had wept. Diya had confused the wind's soft howls for her groom's mother a few times while she packed. "Maybe you could be kind and merciful enough to pass on my apology."

Gabriel paused, his features less harsh outside the shadows of her doorway. "Arien's curse is not on *my* conscience. Tell her yourself."

She intended to use the silence against him. If she said nothing, she could blame him and keep her dignity. But, as her thoughts crowded with his mother's keening and Arien's shouts, she winced. The truth of her silence came to her like a blow.

Gabriel had shoved aside his pride in coming to her. And her fear of judgement had her curling inward rather than reaching out to his mother. Her hands fisted uselessly at her sides.

Righteousness curved his lips in a ghost of a smile.

"I'm leaving on the next sunset. Don't be late." He started to leave, then stopped. "I don't know if we're coming back. Now is not the time to leave anything unsaid. My mother and father will leave before we do."

She landed on her bed as soon as he left, jolting her pack high. The opal Arien had given her clinked against the comet-knife until it found somewhere new to settle. Through the relief was yet another doubt she could actually save the husband she had succeeded in wishing away.

And if Gabriel couldn't guarantee their safe return...

"Arien," she murmured up at the moon framed by her window. "I hate your brother. I hate him more because he's right about making amends." She waited a moment, half-hoping Arien's spirit might appear outside her window, ready to be dragged back inside the house no matter how unlikely. It would mean she could speak with him, let him go. Not to eternal torment, but back to his simple life. And she could go on living her own life as she chose. When nothing happened, she said, "I hate you less, but I can't marry you. You'd under-stand why if... I just hope I'm not too late to tell you why. And to save you."

She meant every word. But she couldn't help but wonder what wonderful sights lay ahead. What magic might fall into the little boat she planned to repurpose for their adventure.

Her heart betrayed her. It had no interest in even the slightest tenor of excitement. When she hitched her pack over her shoulder, her shame dragged on the load. A useless, punishing weight that not even the deepest of breaths could shake loose.

~

BENEATH A NARROW SEA of banyan trees banked by their region's matchmaking temple, Diya and Gabriel accepted offerings of advice and supplies from their families.

His mother handed him corn-flour bread with bits of onion and roasted potatoes with garlic-covered skins wrapped in small towels. Their sisters had the same idea: both pairs had sent along hand-woven blankets against the chill of the river at night. Their fathers pulled them each aside, but Diya could still make out a small, humble sun god statue passed to Gabriel. She herself received a plain leather sheath for her knife.

Surprised, she looked to Eta, who only had a small nod left to give.

Priestess Ashani, along with two of her temple sisters, cut Diya's thanks to her father short when they stepped forward. She wasn't actually sure what constituted a full-fledged priestess, but the other two women led her to believe their only mission was to listen carefully to Priestess Ashani's wishes. They kept their heads bent low and carried identical moon-glass trays of burning incense, the ash sparkling like stardust.

The priestess reached for Diya's hands first, then Gabriel's, slowly lifting them as a chanting prayer rose up from her throat. Plumeria smoke weaved closer, latching onto their clothes. Diya coughed, stepping away, but Gabriel kept his hold. His mother prayed with them, clasping hands with his father.

Despite what he had believed, his parents hadn't left when it came time to journey to the temple, instead sending their daughters back to Gildesh ahead of them. They accompanied Diya and Gabriel, along with her parents. Her own sisters remained home. Karula had promised them both they wouldn't leave Arien's side. Gabriel had stiffened and blushed when Lilia pointed out their bladders might beckon them otherwise.

"I didn't realize you were so... prudish," Diya had taunted. "And if you say something awful about my sister, I'm going to hit you."

"You're always spoiling for a fight, but we both know you can barely handle that knife in your bag, let alone throw a solid punch. Otherwise, you wouldn't need me. So." He had thrown his own pack over his shoulder, and it tangled with the thin orange shawl tied in a knot over his long tunic. "I'll say and do whatever I please, beauty."

Because she couldn't have risked him knowing about the comet-knife, she'd fumed in silence.

But, oh, it wouldn't take much to wipe that smug smile off his face. A quick adjustment of her body weight and he'd teeter right out of her little boat. If there were demons, they'd be his problem. They just needed to get onto the water.

This close to the River of Souls, Diya felt a familiar hum seep into her bones, in that way the earth had, sending small shocks up one's body to let them know something lived beneath. She understood why people sometimes scooped some of the river into skeins and called themselves healed or invigorated.

The tawny branches of the trees netted her well-wishers' voices, the leaves nicking her green wonder. A cold breath wound around her, gusting from the cave Gabriel seemed to know better than she did. It had always stood as a teasing taste of something more, a banquet that told her she was hungry for more of the world before she knew.

But, now, staring into the darkness, Diya almost expected teeth to shoot down and a growl to pool in the back of its black-bouldered throat. She shivered.

"Let's go," Gabriel said shortly.

Before she could follow him, his mother wrapped her arms around her. She smelled of rising dough and fire-lit nights. "Thank you," she murmured in Diya's ear.

Diya fumbled with returning the embrace. Her ears felt too hot and her stomach lurched. She could have blamed the sensation on close quarters with a Gildeshan, but this was Arien's mother—the same woman who used to braid Diya's hair and make silly faces with her in her pocket mirror. She was being thanked for fixing something she had broken in the first place. Her stomach didn't turn now for fear and disgust. Instead, shame made her as awkward as her father.

"But please hurry," Arien's mother whispered. "Gildesh and Novasi haven't forgotten their worst memories of each other. It won't take much for them to relive the past."

The request held the same flavor as her mother's expectations. *Marry quickly and save us from each other.* Diya bit her tongue to keep from protesting. A few short words from her the night she'd declared herself capable of saving Arien, and Novasi had turned tail, leaving her alone to once again bridge the gap between their enemies, spewing a fountain of gossip as she went. She knew they called her selfish, but what were the villages in all this?

At least Gabriel cared enough to go after his brother while her own family had stepped back. They had always planned to lose her anyway. They had always had *plans.*

Eta stepped up to her when Arien's mother let her go. "You have the knife?" she said in a low voice. Diya nodded. "Good. The river is dangerous. Be cautious."

Diya nearly said, "Fire take your caution," unwilling to accept a scrap of sentiment after years of waiting for caring and praise. But, looking back at the cave was enough to quell the rebuff. A bit of caution might do her some good, no matter where it came from.

Priestess Ashani stepped forward next, after Diya's father offered a stiff hug that Diya did her best to return. "You are the first common woman to travel past the temple in a long time, Diya of Novasi," said the priestess, watching her with dark, solemn eyes. "As our acolyte, your mother knows a little of what lies beyond the river, but you may not detail your journey to anyone in these lands. Even her. Do you understand?"

Diya thought of rich brushstrokes bringing bull-headed fish and serpentine women to glorious life in the corners of the temple where lamp-light could not reach. Heat had risen to her cheeks the first time she had seen them, but not because many of the creatures were beautiful in the dark. Her mother's fear of her lived inside the temple walls too. The knowledge had scraped her heart afresh. The people she knew risked too little and protected too much in the name of their quiet terror. "It shouldn't be kept secret."

"The creatures there will try to deceive you, seduce you." Pity tangled with firmness in the lines of the priestess' face. "They will prey on any thought for the ones you love. They will kill you if they have the chance. Do you understand now, Diya of Novasi?"

"How do you know all of this?" Diya demanded. It was one thing to sit atop a hill and look down at the way of things, passing judgement on surface qualities without really knowing the truth. Actual *experience* was something else altogether.

"Every priestess must undergo a journey down the River of Souls." Diya's hope deflated as the priestess revealed jagged scars beneath her sleeves. "We let the gods decide our fates, and those who return with the scars to prove they endured may join the temple. I have seen all that you deny. You must be vigilant, or you will not succeed."

"Thank you," Diya managed, blindly turning to the boat where Gabriel waited, his impatience filling the interior. They said their goodbyes one last time and she entered the boat on the opposite side of him.

"Give me your pack," he ordered as soon as her attention fell on him.

She only clutched it more tightly to her chest. "Why?"

He held out his hand with an exasperated sigh. "We can't have any kind of token or reminder of those we love. Trust me when I say we will die if you don't listen to me."

"I didn't bring anything like that," she lied smoothly. The opal Arien had given her would remain tucked in her bag. She wouldn't even think about it, just like she wouldn't think about parting from it. Not now, when Arien's fate was in her hands. "Maybe I should search *your* bag."

"Fine," he snarled, settling into the boat as she pushed away from the shore. "Don't listen. But the second some beast comes for us, I'm feeding you to it, understand? You will not get in the way of me finding my brother."

A part of her wanted to laugh. This was typical Gabriel. She couldn't count the number of times she and Arien had laughed off his henning. His expression had been too adult for a child's face. She wondered now if he'd ever had any fun playing the hen while his brother pretended to be a hero in one of her grand reenactments of old epics in the woods.

"You're just jealous," she said, paddling *without* his help. She kept her pack between her legs as she worked. "Saving Arien is the only way you're going to have your chance in the sun without burning for it." Paddling with their supplies weighing down the boat strained her muscles. She jutted her chin to the other oar, expecting him to help. But he didn't.

He didn't move at all.

She eyed him, another jab ready on her tongue, but he stared into the water. His tight jaw sent guilt clunking down to the pit of her stomach. For the first time in all the years she'd known and loathed him, he couldn't conceal how her words had struck him. And, in a cruel flick of Fate's wrist, causing a wound like that was like wounding herself.

"I'm sorry," she relented. "I'm just... I'm just angry." She fully expected him to ignore her apology and strike with a blow of his own.

Instead, he cut his gaze to hers and said in low, precise tones, "Did you ever write back to him?"

Her thoughts stuttered. "What are you talking about?"

"So it wasn't enough to curse him." If his fury had started to crumple, her confusion spread it out again. "You're the one who will burn for your sins."

"How many times do I have to say *I didn't curse him*?"

"If you really believed that you wouldn't be here," he said. "You would've found a way to make it somebody else's problem, just like you used to. Then again, here I am cleaning up after the two of you, same as always." He rummaged around in his bag while she reeled. He had fine aim after all, right down to the disgust in his voice. "My mother wrote to you, didn't she?"

"I received all her letters." Impossible to guess if another blow was coming, but she decided to meet the possibility now, while she was prepared. "Every day until the wedding." She'd barely been able to tolerate the words as her mother read the messages aloud. *Oh, Arien's hair has grown an inch. Oh, he's such a fine, tall man now, wait until Diya sees him. Oh, he's learned her name in the Old Script and has set the words in ink. Where? Over his heart of course!* "I'm surprised her wrist never crippled."

"Arien wrote to you too." When he had what he wanted from his pack, he hesitated. She studied his struggle, not sure why the thing in his hand mattered so much. She thought of her opal, but doubted he carried anything belonging to his brother. Then his gaze settled on the cave looming before them, impatient for them to begin. He handed her a wrinkled piece of paper. "This is the last one he meant to send. I was supposed to deliver it." He didn't need to explain why he hadn't, but Diya wondered if it was guilt or duty that prompted him in this moment. "You're going to want to read that now."

She scanned the letter.

Diya,

Immediately, Arien's face entered her mind. Her eyes screwed shut automatically before she blinked them open again and continued reading.

Do you remember when we tried to build a bridge over the mouth of the river? We started with ropes. Carted planks. We worked on it every night for weeks. It fell apart the first time we tried using it, but for one moment, before we fell through, I was happy that we had tried. That we had spent so much time together trying, laughing, despite the uncertainty of the future. That's what I hope our marriage will be like.

I know we haven't been friends for some time, and maybe that's part of why I've gone along with our mothers' plans. We built that bridge between our villages to be closer together. And I miss being close to you.

My father used to tell me a light like mine no god could resist. Even now I don't know what he meant by it, but today it made me think of you. You've always been a light I could not resist. Without it, without you, I feel lost.

I'm happy to marry you. I think it must be too much to hope you're happy to marry me, but I cannot leave hope unspoken. I'll stop there, before I embarrass you.

But let me finish by saying I miss you very much, Diya of Novasi.

I'll see you at the priestess' altar.

Yours,

Arien

Her head tightened, her mind wrapping itself wholly around each word. She blinked, and was surprised by the tears that fell. Longing and guilt and agitation all tangled together, leaving her undefended against Gabriel.

He moved too swiftly for her to stop him, snatching the letter from her weakened grasp. Again, there was that brief battle behind his eyes. A flicker of pain as he clutched the letter in his fist. Then, without warning, he ripped it to pieces.

Fragments of Arien's words fell into the water streaking behind them.

Diya's arm rose before she could stop it.

Gabriel inclined his jaw to take the hit.

But, through the haze of her anger, she saw he was pale, his lips pinched tight. He looked to be bracing himself for her fury... as if he knew he deserved it, but had seen no other option. He'd sacrificed his brother's token for the chance to save him.

Her fist fell before it could connect. And she could regret. She was no longer in any mood to make his life miserable. Her plans to knock him into the river evaporated.

"Keep away from me." She dipped her chin, letting her dark hair curtain her face. She didn't care if the silence ate away at her resolve. Anything would be better than staring her mistake in the face. "Just... keep away. I don't want to hear you anymore."

He listened, sidling closer to the opposite end of the small boat.

They continued their strokes across the water in silence. Soon, the cave engulfed them, shared pain and history and all. Neither of them noticed how the water formed tight rings around the boat, pieces of Arien's hope falling into waiting, hungry mouths.

SHE HADN'T WANTED TO, but the terse silence between she and

Gabriel under the immensity of the stars, over the endless span of the river, made Diya dream of her grandmother, Kiaana.

From dark spills of the night sky, her grandmother emerged like a figure flowing from predawn fog. Her light brown eyes were her wealth in beauty, two copper coins under sooty lashes, as the rest of her sagged toward the earth. An ache bloomed in Diya's heart as she walked through soft grass blades and pressed Diya close.

"You made a mistake," she told her grandmother. "I am not beautiful because I am interesting or special or brave. I am dangerous because of my beauty."

"You make less mistakes when you shake off your youth," said Kiaana. "And we didn't call you wild one for nothing."

"I'm like her," Diya whispered. "If I don't bring Arien back, his brother has already promised there will be a price. One that none of us can pay. The villages still haven't fully recovered."

Kiaana sighed. "You could have just married the boy."

"Not you too, *Ahnan*."

"You *are* like your mother, Diya. But it's still not too late to make a better choice. Eta would have too, if she'd been given the chance. You have that chance."

"Do you remember Arien, *Ahnan*?"

Kiaana's laugh tickled the top of Diya's head. "Of course I do. Beautiful boy," she said as her granddaughter sighed. "Bright. Thoughtful. He always had a smile for you. You never failed to tease it out of him. Your mother did well there."

Like Diya, her grandmother never put much store by the priestesses and their magical matchmaking reputation. Kiaana had met Diya's grandfather by working in the fields with him long ago, when harvesting was as rough on skin and bone as the scarce winter seasons. No one had approved of the match and yet they'd made each other better. In a matter of years after they married, they had owned enough land to stir envy in even Novasi's most innocent living souls. Kiaana had always believed

Diya's mother's dreams were telling and special, simply without any divinity attached to them.

"I miss you, *Ahnan*," said Diya. "Only you have ever cared about what I wanted."

"But have you been honest about what you want? Have you told anyone what it is *you* find beautiful?"

"You think I'm to blame."

"I think you expect to be judged before you've acted." Kiaana continued stroking her hair. The motion sent the wrist bangles she'd been buried with chiming. "You have growing to do. Don't worry so much about Arien, little one. No god can part you."

Diya pulled out of her grandmother's arms. She wished Gabriel hadn't shown her that letter. Now she was mesmerized by the possibility of Arien having written to her. A part of her desperately wanted to know how long the letters had been coming, how many she would have found if she knew where they were. Now there was not just one but two secrets between them: The reason she wished to let him go. And why she wished that she could stay.

"See?" Kiaana said, smiling over Diya's head. "Your bond was set long ago."

Diya spun around.

A hand caught her forearm when she lost her balance. Soft against her skin. Her heart warmed before she could stop it. "Arien?"

Twilight lit his dark copper hair aglow and he swallowed his own confusion. "Diya?"

"*Ahnan*, how is this possible?" she called back to her grandmother without taking her eyes off her intended. "You're in the realm of the gods," she told him. "You can't be here. Oh gods, am I too late? *Ahnan*?"

Kiaana melted back into the cool night when Diya tried to find her.

"Take the Dream," her grandmother urged from somewhere deep in the fog. But Diya didn't want a dream where Arien lived at the center. She hoped Kiaana hadn't just made her preference clear or she was doomed to wear a stain of disappointment into her next life. "Tell your mother to stop using my hairbrush as a weapon," her grandmother scolded faintly. "Tell her, her father is proud of her."

Then she was gone, leaving Diya with an overflowing heart and damp eyes.

Alone with Arien.

Gods, what did she say to him?

Going with her first instinct, she alleviated her burning curiosity by reaching over and pinching his arm. "Did that hurt?" she had to ask, because he never shouted when it did. Countless accidents and mishaps thanks to their mischief-making had taught her that.

He rubbed the sore spot and nodded, gaze delicate on her face.

"So then you're here. I don't understand it. Where were you before you got here?"

"I don't think I should tell you."

"Why not?"

"You'll make yourself sick with worry," he said.

Diya seized his shoulders. "Are you being hurt?"

Arien kept his silence. Stubbornly. Everyone had always thought he was slow-witted when he did things like that, as though he were too pretty to be seriously pigheaded.

Diya gave him more credit than that. "I'm so sorry for what's happened." She dropped her hands, fisting them at her sides, longing for a way to make an apology *mean* something the way he did. No one could question his sincerity when he had looked so earnestly into your eyes and asked for your forgiveness. "Tell me how to find you. Where are you?"

"You can't save me." His mind must have been turning over

her next steps. He was the opposite of slow, especially when he was concerned about those he cared about. "Take my brother and turn around. Stay away from the river."

"Not happening."

Terror made his eyes wide and pleading. "Diya, *please.*"

"Arien, it's my fault," she blurted. Then shut her eyes. "It's my fault you were cursed. I rejected you. I rejected the Dream for us. I was overheard. You... you must have seen my lips moving."

The weary tilt to his shoulders told her he already knew. "You looked sick," he said, as gently as she'd come to expect. "I was worried."

Never mind that he had been the one to keel over and nearly die. He could be dead now for all she knew. She felt desperate in a way she couldn't explain. The feeling pushed her to speak although she was considering how to wake.

"I will tell you something," she said, pricked by vulnerability and regret before she could escape them, "if you promise not to press your advantage."

Her hand somehow fell into his. Their fingers threaded together. "Tell me," he said. No recriminations. No questions about the letters he sent that went unanswered.

Like saving him, there was only one choice. She ignored the fear pulsing beneath her skin. "I could marry you," she said on a deep breath. "And a part of me would be wholly content." She met his eyes then, watched pleasure leave a shine that hadn't been there before. "But there's another part that wouldn't be satisfied as your dutiful wife living in Novasi. I'm going to save you," she said, trying to be clear and quick. "But that's all I'm going to do when you are returned. I just thought you should know."

His gaze dimmed, but he didn't let go of her. He blew out a breath. "What if I could give you more?"

She shook her head. "That's the problem. I don't want you to be the only one who gives."

"And what about what *I* want?"

"You want to marry me," she said uncertainly. A flush rose up in her cheeks the longer he stared at her. His thumb dipped past the knuckle of her index finger, brushing a warm path back and forth.

"I want you to trust me," he said.

She tried to shake her hand free, but he kept hold of her. "I don't know what you mean." Her voice sounded thready and panicked even to her own ears. She forced herself still and made herself calm. "This isn't up for debate."

"I won't leave you alone again. I'll go with you."

"Stop it," she whispered, because her first instinct had been to shout the words. "You have nothing to prove to me."

"Don't I?" Arien said lowly, letting go of her hand to cup her cheek. "Why am I here, Diya?"

Why did he stare at her as if she had his answer?

"I'll go with you," he promised. He'd lowered his head to look directly into her eyes. "Anywhere." His certainty, his gentle determination was too much. Some wall she'd spent years manning against him collapsed.

Gabriel had accused her of casting spells, but why was it Diya who had to frantically clear her head? Why was it *her* feeling enchanted and safe and not at all sure of this blooming warmth as Arien reached up to delve his hands into her hair?

This close, she could feel him trembling. She could see he wanted to draw her nearer. She wanted to leap from his touch, the way she had during the confirmation of their match.

But she lingered, also locked onto the *why* of his sudden power over her. *Why* a part of her still dreamed of staying with him.

She couldn't resist him this way—sure-eyed and serious

and strangely soft-handed, the strands of her hair clinging to his skin. The both of them roped in and coming undone.

"Consider that," he said. His breath was hot and sweet. "Consider that the choice is finally ours. Our mothers... the gods... they can have our charts and our prayers, but they can't have our destiny anymore."

One of his hands dropped down to reach for one of hers. She sucked in a breath. He kissed her palm. A picture was building in her mind, stirring heat beneath her skin. Her emotions hovered at the tip of her tongue and she wanted to share the taste of them with him. Ask him if he understood what she didn't dare put wholly into words.

But she was shoved awake.

As the dream dissipated, she saw Arien's deep flinch. Naked fear blanketed his expression as he slowly vanished from her mind. The last thing she felt was the brush of his warm hand.

"No!"

She screamed this into Gabriel's pinched face. "Diya," he growled. "What have you done?"

She struggled for air, whipping her head as she searched for Arien, for her grandmother, anyone other than this hateful boy. The dream had been a tangle of hope and fear, but by the end of it, Arien had given her exactly what he'd intended— more. And Gabriel had ruined it before she had time to understand the clue she'd been given. The future she wanted lost its shape, waiting for a choice she thought she had made.

"What is this?" he snapped, tugging open her clinched palm.

The opal clinked against the wooden bottom of the boat, the last of the moon's light catching on its surface. Diya had no idea how it had gotten into her hand.

Before she could tell him, a shadow with gleaming teeth rose over them, yanking a shout from Gabriel's lips.

DIYA WRENCHED AWAY from a deadly comb of teeth. She felt them skim her shoulder, but her blood did not fall. The creature darted over the lip of their boat, hitting with a hard splash. "Did you see—"

"You need to get rid of it," Gabriel shouted as more long, muscular fish arched out of the water, making violent jumps toward them. Diya screamed and Gabriel unsheathed the sword he'd kept hidden behind his orange shawl. "Move!"

She lost her balance. For a moment, she was cheek to wood and reaching for the opal caught in a crevice of the boat. Beady eyes and powerful, snapping jaws changed her course, sending her scrambling back. She dug around for her knife as several of the ones Gabriel had missed wriggled toward her.

"Get it out," Gabriel snapped.

"I'm a little busy at the moment."

"I *warned* you."

Her fingers wrapped around the handle of her knife. "Oh, get a grip, Gabe." Something landed in her lap and she stabbed without thought, loosing a scream. "I didn't put the stone in my hand."

"Do you think the river is without tricks?" They slashed and stabbed at any sudden motion. "*Hurry up,*" he ordered.

She let go of her knife long enough to dig her fingers into the damp planks. She tried to pry the opal loose but it wouldn't budge. Gabriel suffered a bite as she struggled.

"I don't see," he gasped, "how you're worth any of his efforts these last years." An angry wound spilled red onto his shirt-sleeve.

"Penning letters isn't much of an effort." She panted from her own efforts. Her fingers twisted to reach the damn stone, but she couldn't get so much as a nail under it. Damage to her knife might not keep her safe for very long, but... She used it to dig beneath the opal. "And you're worse than demon droppings."

"You never really did manage to grow up, did you?" He swung his blade at an oncoming sea of predators. She was grateful not to see where all the blood ended up as his sword sliced through a few of the bodies. "He worried over touching you with shepherd hands. For the past two months, he'd bring a pot over from the kitchen after all his work and soak his hands in hot water, scrubbing until they were smooth again. He became fixated on the task. You don't deserve that kind of effort."

"Don't worry," she choked out. Fear had her by the throat as more creatures leaped for her side of the boat. There was no room for the guilt lurking beneath. "I'll remove myself from your family soon enough."

Gabriel's sword blocked her from harm with a vicious swipe. The violence of the feat dislodged her hard enough to send the opal skidding out of its hiding place.

He spared her a glance. "See that you do, beauty," he warned in a soft voice. "Or I will end things for you."

She picked up the stone as more ripples arrowed toward them. Screeching trailed the disturbances of the water. Gabriel tensed. "You know what," she said, diving for her knife as a creature double their size slid out of the river with a roar pouring from its throat. "It's not really you I'm worried about."

There was no time for him to argue against that.

Her last conscious thought was, *Live. I hope I live.*

THE SUN FELL behind the trees. They fought demon after demon, their breaths loud and labored, their sweat pouring. Vines dripped down from the trees like shadows of disparate souls watching from the banks as they parried green-tailed creatures with female torsos and white, wrinkled snouts hiding rows and rows of teeth.

"Gabriel," Diya rasped. Beside her, his weariness was a palpable thing. "I don't think I can take anymore."

"We can't die here."

"I don't want to," she said wearily, quivering each time the river gurgled around the boat. "But I can barely hold this knife." Anticipation of the next attack had saved her through the dawn, but she struggled to raise the shield of her fear. She pushed sweaty tendrils of hair out of her face. "If it comes down to it, don't stop if I fall. You have to save him."

Arien's brother took his eyes off the river. "That's what I said I'd do."

Her smile was thin. "How many times did you yank me out of the way last night?"

He scowled, then winced. The answer was, *countless*. A rogue slash striped his jaw from when one of the demons had tried to gouge and pull him. He'd helped himself before Diya had been able to reach him. The wound still bled.

"I think... it's safe," was all he said.

"Gods." She dropped her knife. Sat down hard. "Thank the gods."

"You shouldn't say that if you don't mean it."

"Gabe, no offense, but shut up."

He muttered something obscurely unkind. The tone shifted and she realized he was praying. In earnest.

"What the hells are you doing?" Was he trying to conjure the very beings who'd started this mess? The irony of Gabriel calling *her* the witch was not lost on her. Recanting a small piece of her horoscope had been enough to pique a god's wandering interest, ending in a curse on his brother. And here was Gabriel, inviting the divine into his uncharted life with a deferential head tilt and a few mumbled words. "We just barely escaped our deaths."

"It's unholy to be out where the sun walks without his blessing," he said testily. "I disobeyed him this morning."

Diya reached for the thought that such rigid customs from Gildesh had never seemed reasonable. While her people rarely walked about during the day, it was only because they basked rather than feared the moon and the stars. That at least was more welcoming than the worry spread out over Gabriel's harsh features. "You'll notice that the god of sun didn't care enough to step in while we were fighting for our lives. Yet here you stand."

"Mercy does not mean forgiveness," he snapped.

She shook her head and reached for her pack. She had the sense they had a long, wet road ahead. Reversed images of the trees stood up from the river, hiding any places where darkness coiled to spring once more. But she'd collected so many new truths about these waters, she wanted to tell the god of souls not to bother with hiding anymore of its ugliness. What she knew would forever change her thoughts of this place. And if this was what she could expect beneath water that had appeared harmless all her life, what was it truly like outside of Novasi? She no longer knew if she was prepared to find out, Arien or no.

Gabriel interrupted her darkening thoughts. "You did well today."

"Wow." Diya paused. "That actually sounds like a compliment."

"I judge someone by their actions."

She snorted. "Keep telling yourself that, Gabe."

"You want to know my first clear memory of you?" He sloshed the boat a bit when he stood, fists clenched, as if she'd challenged him in some way. The abrupt change in mood did more than teeter the boat. Her sanity might be threatened for the rest of this trip. "You're laughing, leading us on a chase through the trees. My brother is behind you. I'm behind him.

You climb up a boulder, then another. My brother doesn't hesitate until I pull him back. I tell him what mother said about climbing so high before you're ready. I warn him that one of us could fall. You're beaming down at both of us, but he only has eyes for you. He shoves my hand off his shoulder and climbs up. He makes it to the top and I'm still on the ground. Then you laugh at something he says until you lose your balance. To keep you from falling he ends up with a broken arm and a split temple. My mother wept when my father and I brought him home. Can you honestly tell me that there are no similarities between then and now?"

"No, I can't." But Gabriel was wrong about something. From his perspective, he was always in hers and Arien's shadow. Yet his loneliness had not been overlooked for long. Arien had always gone back for his brother. It was part of the joke that day he broke his arm.

Let's not leave him sulking, Arien had said to her with a grin.

"Why do you think I didn't want to marry him in the first place? There's been enough pain behind us and not enough of anything new."

"You've had *years* to live your life like it was new. Yet here the three of us are, trapped in the sameness of things." The outburst forced him to sit, swallowing down the past with a pained scowl. "You know, I thought becoming a guard and serving on the border would help me focus on my own path. But now I'm beginning to think I will never stop worrying over my flighty, foolish brother."

She finally saw something in him that rationalized his fear and hatred of her. The harsh feelings she had toward him. It was no longer a wonder they couldn't stand the sight of each other. How else might two mirrors react when you set them in front of each other and asked them to speak?

"It's funny," she said. "My mother told me this story of the gods of dreams and nightmares before the wedding." She retold it to him. She let the worry pass that she wasn't doing the tale enough justice. The point was for him to see himself inside the tale. Telling him taught her that stories shaped themselves around the person listening.

"Am I the god of dreams or the god of nightmares?" he said at last.

She shrugged, as tentative with him as she was with her mother. "I think it depends on what you believe." When he met her eyes, she continued. "Whether you choose to hope or to exploit the weaknesses of others. But no one is perfect."

"So, I should hope that my brother wakes up to his own mind."

"No. I'm saying that what you perceive as weakness he perceives as strength. And you should hope you'll learn from each other. Otherwise, you'll just end up a scowly old man, brother to no one."

His weary reluctance faded into a small smile. For the first time in too many years to count, she smiled back at him.

Impish laughter echoed down from the canopies above them. A flash of horns appeared out of the corner of her eye and banyan vines lowered to the edges of their boat. They looped around Gabriel's chest like iron bands and swooped him up into the air. "*Gabriel*," Diya screamed, as the vines dragged him into the forest.

"Go!" he shouted, his voice struggling, his veins bulging in his neck.

Arien's words echoed in her mind. *Let's not leave him.*

Diya leapt from the boat, comet-knife in hand, and swam to the hedgeline wrapped around the River of Souls. She glanced back once and saw her boat disappear with Arien's opal—and the rest of her pack. Then, she pushed herself up to chase after Arien's disappearing brother.

〜

"Gabriel," she called out. The trees were too quiet. Her fears showed him being swallowed whole.

Her legs were unsteady yet. Worse still, she rarely had cause to exert them like this. Her job was to ferry a few people daily to the temple of the matchmaking priestesses, which built up the muscles in her arms and not her legs. It seemed this entire situation was designed to prey upon her weaknesses instead of her strengths.

"Gabriel," she tried again, hurdling deeper into the darkness. Her eyesight was sharp, but the terrain so unfamiliar. She knew no name for this area near the river and so did not know how to battle it's thickets and coils. She found herself running into trees in her haste, flying over low-hanging bark, and crashing into underbrush. She coughed up leaves and tasted blood. Her mind wobbled before the enormity of the dark, but she pumped her scraped legs faster.

Must you always pick a fight, Gabriel would have asked her.

And the answer stopped her, forced her to set aside her impatience. She held herself as still as possible, heeding the sounds playing havoc on her urgency instead of hunting them. Her father had taught her a little of the forest whenever she'd happened upon him. He'd sometimes find her in the middle of playfully hiding from a seeking Arien, after returning from the northern and western villages with new crops and new methods of harvesting and distributing the old ones. In his rare moments of speaking, he taught her that if ever she wanted to avoid danger inside any forest, she only need listen for the birds. Were they flying away or had they nestled down nearby? If they flew, then she and Arien should run. If they settled, then they were still safe.

Diya heard them then, the nightbirds shrieking and flapping. Peering up through the intricate lattice of the boughs, she found her course.

When at last she found Gabriel, the forest had tired of him.

The vines had strung him up by his wrists, leaving him to carry all his weight from the weakest part of his limbs.

He was already unconscious.

Diya barely skimmed his ankle. "Come on, you rat-bastard." She tried nudging his feet. "You've led me on a lively chase. Don't die on me now."

"Worst..." His voice was weak, distant. "... comrade... ever."

Taking out her knife, she tried indulging him with a light laugh, light talk, hoping to keep him awake as she pieced together some kind of plan to get him down. But the trees were so high up and she'd never been much of a climber. She likely had the strength, but not the dexterity. And he was as far away from a reasonable perch as one could get after being dragged away by an inexplicable net of forestry. "Can you get loose at all?"

He wiggled in the vines' grip, then scowled down at her.

"I can't do this without you. You said it from the beginning." She couldn't imagine anything more painful than being stuck fast, rendered still. Not to mention the physical agony and exhaustion. But worry and guilt were doing her no favors, so she forced herself to shift away from his predicament. To be as brave as he. She'd risk her neck to get him down. "You have to help me here."

"Keep going. Can't get me down."

"You can't stay like this. You'll die."

"Have some time," he said, almost gently. "Kill you. Leave."

"Save the threats. Even if I wanted to go on without you, I lost the boat. And *you can't hang there indefinitely.* Maybe try swinging a little this way?"

"Weak. Numb. Stings."

"Gods, Gabriel you can't ask me to—"

"Haunt you forever," he wheezed out. Straining to hold his body weight made him sag. "Promise."

She squeezed her eyes shut, the comet-knife as light and

useless as a feather in her hand. "Just... try not to pass out while I think of something."

He barely managed a nod.

She couldn't help but panic as she always did when she couldn't break free of something out of her control. Never mind that she wasn't the one left hanging in the air. Gabriel had been taken and she could only run after him, pitifully helpless. Her confusing muddle of feelings for Arien burned in the back of her heart in much the same way, at once comforting and caging.

Her eyes landed on fallen logs as her thoughts circled. She wondered if this tumultuous tide was what Gabriel felt when it came to his own family—free to keep them safe but unable to truly protect them. Unable to be completely true to himself.

A single solution bubbled up through her agitation. It wouldn't spare Arien's brother from the forest... but it could get her to Arien. And while it certainly wouldn't be her best work, she had done this twice before when the river flooded and swallowed her only means of transporting the priestesses' patrons. Her mother wouldn't be there to lend a hand, but...

Diya set to work.

She found a heavy, yet manageable branch to use as her hammer. Embedded her knife in the logs she'd found, using her new hammer to create a small split. There were wedges and more hammering, until halves and holes made up the state of things.

It took hours to lock everything into place.

But she managed to build a raft in the relative dark.

"Gabriel," she said, her heart pounding and her body lined with sweat. "I did it."

The answering silence prompted her to look up, no matter how much she dreaded doing so. She knew before she saw his shut eyelids that he had done the opposite of what she'd asked.

He'd fainted.

"Come on, Gabe," she said, though it was useless to pretend she could do anything for him. "Your mother named you for a warrior, didn't she? Some foreign ally in the battle between our villages. I remember her saying so. You need to fight as she would have."

"Diya?" He sluggishly blinked through sweat and exhaustion.

"Good. You're awake."

"Do... *not*... fail... me..." When he lost the fight against his weariness and faded again, she nearly cried.

For Arien's brother, of all people.

But she'd known from the beginning that she could only go so far alone. She hadn't needed much convincing to bring Gabriel along because she hadn't wanted full responsibility for the safety of Arien's soul.

Wanting things was not enough. Her mother was living proof of that. And yet Diya's desire for others to regard her with admiration for her *accomplishments* was costing her two lives outside of her own.

Stories had been her only comfort amongst the gossip and speculative looks, shimmering at the border of her imagination, waiting to become real. She had only wanted a chance to live inside a story she could take ownership of, despite a past and a face stitched into her being before she was born.

And, instead, *this* was what her story had become, resewn by her callousness into something she would rather forget. A beast too untamed for her to contain, her wildness more curse than blessing.

They can't have our destiny anymore. Arien had been so certain of his place in her story. He'd been willing to gamble on whatever shape it might take, so long as he got the chance explore it with her.

So why hadn't she been willing? When had she become so gutless?

It's still not too late to make a better choice.

She didn't know if she could do what they all asked of her and still be true to herself. But she *had* made a promise to Gabriel and to herself that she would save Arien from the gods.

Steadying herself, she spent some time marking as many of the trees as she could find with whatever stones could burrow deep enough into the bark. She did not stop until she found her way back to the river, then back to Gabriel, sure of the trail she'd created.

With a last glance at him, looking bloodless and helpless, Diya whispered, "Keep an eye on him for me, *Ahnan.* I'd really hate for Arien to lose his foul brother."

Hard shell, she silently warned her grandmother's spirit. *Good heart. Impossible boy.*

With great huffs, she carted her makeshift raft back to the eddies of the river and hung on with all her might, hoping beyond all doubt, just as Arien had taught her to long ago.

HER GNAWING belly pressed down on the raft, making unhappy, frustrated sounds.

The river had become mercifully quiet. Whatever mask had slipped off had fallen back into place, the creatures beneath no more than filmy wisps. If she pushed her face into the water, she was sure she would see their savage faces peering up at her, waiting for her memories of loved ones to summon them again.

But her mind was too cluttered for love. All her thoughts centered on her body, at how frail she felt. Myriad leaves and coy shadows were not going to sustain her. She couldn't afford to leave her raft behind to hunt for food she wasn't sure existed. Hadn't the priestess said she was the first common woman to come here in a while? Why would the river and the forest provide for creatures like her, whom they had neither invited nor permitted to linger?

 She could do nothing but wait for her stomach to grow angrier, make her retch. *Feed me,* the emptiness inside her demanded.

Night turned into day, the cycle resuming again and again, while hunger stuffed Diya's mind full of cotton. The winding flow of the river seemed endless. She didn't know how the priestesses had borne the journey. They had clung to their packs and a stone-cold resolve was Diya's bitter guess.

Some part of her begged her not to dream, to avoid remembering things that would end up killing her. She had no chance of fighting off those who waited to dine on her.

But her eyes grew spotty. The tree line blurred. Her body was too warm, too shivery. She couldn't settle herself down. Not even giving in and drinking from the river helped. Her hope that the gods' silhouettes would appear in the distance was fleeting. Eventually, she lay her head down and shut her eyes.

Sleep seemed to take pity on her. She was swept off the raft before she could stop herself.

Soon, there was no wind. No water. No hunger.

Soon, there was nothing but *Ahnan*'s lap, made up of velvet-soft fabric and warm legs. One elderly hand cradled Diya's cheek, while the other smoothed her curls. She wrapped herself around her grandmother's calf like she used to when she was small enough not to really burden Kiaana's gait. "You can't leave me again."

"I will not anger the god of death for you."

"Is he real then?"

"They all are, wild one."

"I wish they wouldn't bother with us anymore," Diya said, too comfortable to hate how childish she sounded. Whether dead or alive, her grandmother still smelled like sandalwood and cinnamon, similar to that of the temple, where she had spent countless hours daydreaming of how she would astonish everyone, including herself. It was the only time she ever felt truly free. "No matter what they do, I won't store my faith by them. I don't regret breaking the match."

"It doesn't matter," said Kiaana. "That is not why you are here."

"Don't go, *Ahnan*."

"But you need to see, wild one. You need to see what it is you regret."

Her grandmother disappeared. Disappointment rested on Diya's tongue and she was so used to the taste, she barely noticed how it made her heart sink. Her head felt heavy, hard to keep straight. But when she looked up, her parents loomed over her, wearing expressions that stole her breath.

Do you think the river is not without tricks?

"I used to wish you simple instead of cunning," her mother spat. "Look what you've done."

"Do you think me a coward?" her father said in his quiet way, but for his gaze. His eyes were filled with hate. "What does that make you then, Diya?"

"Look what you've done," her mother repeated, and the world changed. It moved so swiftly Diya's concentration lagged. Her stomach heaved while her deepest fears tumbled forward.

"Stop!" she shouted.

But no one listened. The world kept spinning too fast for her to pin down.

"No one can hear you." Gabriel unfolded from the new landscape, taller than before because she'd ended up on her knees. "For once you can't say something you'll regret."

Everything had been blank as a fresh sheet of paper. Now, the scenery shaped itself around Novasi, modeling it's familiar heat and purple-flowered fields and the sway of cypress and silver oaks. At first, that cadence of calm was the only thing

Diya could hear. She wondered how long it had been since she found her cage so appealing.

A whisper of tension broke through, like a knife meeting flesh in the dark.

She saw Gildeshans and Novasi crashing into each other on those fields, two great waves turning into an all-consuming flood. She saw innocent hands reaching out for help, scrambling for purchase against the clash. She saw her sisters trampled, her mother's throat cut, her father dying in battle.

She saw Arien's family dead, Gabriel hanging lifelessly in front of their door, robbed of the chance to save them. With white lips and sightless eyes, he mouthed, "I warned you."

"Where's Arien?" she sobbed, searching frantically for him. "Where's Arien?"

She hadn't wanted to claim responsibility for this. She hadn't meant to bash the walls of her cage so completely that she caused its entire destruction. She hated the thought of its beauty being ripped out at the roots, drowned in bloodshed, and then ultimately forgotten. She hated that a dream had forced her to confront that thought. Nothing was as simple as it had seemed.

She regretted her dishonesty.

She regretted telling herself her beauty was the problem when it only existed as a convenient way to hide her flaws. To nurture her carelessness with others.

Her sobs grew wilder. "Where's Arien?"

The world laid itself bare ahead of her, a dark void waiting for her next step. She could walk—hells, run—to it as she'd always intended, diving for the deep unknown. It was what she wanted.

A light spilled onto the map of her despair, the red-stained deaths of those she loved clotted by that golden-ink gleam. Arien's hair appeared first, then his smile. Despite the spreading glow, looking at him made her think of the plain mirror she trusted to tell her the truth about herself.

It wasn't that she was incapable of taking the risk. She was persistent and passionate enough to wade through the unknown, no matter what awaited her. It wasn't even a question of whether she should. Diya breathed slowly. This was her home. She couldn't separate her heart from it. And whenever she returned to it, she shouldn't feel ashamed.

Wherever she planted her feet next, home should be a tale worth remembering.

She fell into Arien's waiting arms and said, "I don't want to be a being of regret." His mouth pressed against her temple and she said, "I don't really want to leave you."

He stroked her hair. This time she let him.

"You're close," he told her. "You'll find me where the night ends. I believe in you."

She nodded against his chest. And woke.

REMORSE DID NOT MAKE a desperate situation less so. Hunger rose up inside her even as demons rose from the water. She quickly dragged her legs up from the river and knelt in the center of her defenseless raft.

She could barely feel her fingers wrapped around the comet-knife. "Go away," she pleaded, hoping there was something of remorse inside the creatures watching her. Gabriel's sword would have already swept across their hides, no matter how human some of the faces. Tightening her hold, she lifted her small blade the closer the demons circled.

"We love you as you love them," said one of the half-serpents, green tail flicking up drops of river-water. There was a musical quality to its voice and Diya's mind lulled. Keen eyes watched her struggle against some invisible pull. "Come into my arms, pretty human, and I will show you my love."

Diya arced the knife over her head, hoping to hit an eye or a cheek when the creature lunged. But light and angle did something unexpected. The demon fell back, a thin, piercing scream smothering the desperate, starving growls in the air.

Shrieking, it slid away from the boat, scraping its claws down the center of its mesmerizing face. "Hideous," it hissed. "*Hideous*." It thrashed in the water, crying tears of blood and crazed sorrow.

Diya stared down at her knife with wide eyes. Angling it sent the other demons in a frenzy and she noticed the moonlight had hit some of them in their milky eyes and others' newt-like skin unwound like a fruit-peel.

When another demon leapt for her, she made sure the light bounced off her knife.

That creature burst into dust.

She nearly missed her chance to duck the next attack. Teeth still scraped her shoulder. When the river took a sudden dive, Diya's raft plunged with it and she nearly toppled. She held onto the planks as best she could, her wounded shoulder singing, but a violent current sent her rushing into a wall of rocks.

She crashed. Or close to it. The loud crack of her raft hitting stone scraped her skin raw.

Caught between two boulders, she couldn't adjust the raft no matter how she shoved. Shifts of the water made her flinch. Hissing followed her movements. With a sobbing breath, she *pushed*.

The raft did not budge.

She was going to die here.

Eta's stern face swam up to the surface of her mind.

A child who'd been taught the moon was painted solely for her, then watched as her world peeled away could only grow into a survivor. Eta hadn't minded her daughter's safety for nothing. But she'd go on.

She'd see to it that Diya's sisters had matches that were just as perfect as the one Diya had rejected. Somehow, she'd see to it that their family had their best chance in any conflict between Gildesh and Novasi, for Eta's atonement lay in her shifting tendons as she learned how to hold a grieving Gildeshan mother's hand. She had made friends even without Diya's help.

Diya's head fell into her drenched hands. She didn't want to be a forgotten name in their household, a stain her village sought to remove because of shame. In her new life, she wanted no regrets. She couldn't leave Novasi without carving a place for herself in the bedrock of her family, her village.

The demons wove through the water toward her. Diya ordered herself to think.

If she couldn't fight them off, she needed to get around them.

Or above them.

She kicked off her sodden, broken sandals.

The boulder at her right was just coarse enough for her hand to dig in. She wasn't a climber of trees, but all her jaunts with Arien came back to her as she hoisted herself up, bare feet scrambling for rivets in the stone. She used her knife to steady her. Despite the blade's delicate feel, it balanced her body weight. It helped her gain momentum.

When she arrived at the top, she sank down to her knees, breathing heavily. Ignoring the screams below her, she used the comet-knife as a traveling lantern, illuminating the distant dark for any secrets that might prove useful.

A light winked back at her, so tiny it was no more than a flicker. She didn't know if it was possible for her possessions to have survived. But she hoped despite all doubt.

Taking another deep breath, she leaped for the banks,

catching herself against moist soil and clamoring for grass roots. She pulled herself up through gritted teeth, giving into the burn in her chest and arms, the welts and bruising on her shoulders, for motivation.

When the creatures' ravenous screams fell away, she sobbed out a breath.

It didn't take her long to find the glint. It seemed tied to the shine emanating from her knife. When she reached that tiny beacon, her reward tasted sweet as fig fruit.

She fell onto her little boat, intact but for a few scratches, clambering for her pack as hunger pains bellowed in her empty stomach.

But the first thing she touched was the very thing that had led her there.

Arien's opal winked up at her from the crook of her palm.

She clutched it tightly. And smiled.

~

DIYA WOKE with ash in her mouth. At least, the dream had made her think so.

War and death had snuck into her mind while she slept properly for a change. She half-expected a quicksilver flash of horns while the brutal reminder not to fail still crowded her eyes.

She wiped her damp cheeks and packed everything back into the little boat. The wind was strong enough she didn't need her oars. She gave them a rough toss. But, hearing wood slap against wood failed to smother the dark tenor of her dream.

Rain hit her head, slapping down hard. Inky-grey clouds hung like a ravenous smile. A provoking wind slipped through holes she didn't have time to repair in the main-sail. Her temper spiked. Her slick hands slipped from tacking the lines and it reminded her too much of a bloody grip letting go.

She exploded.

"You think I don't feel you near," she shouted into the brewing storm. Her legs took her to the muddy edges of grass meeting water. "There's nothing between us now." Diya tucked the comet-knife against her wrist. It warmed as she spoke. "Will you hide from me?"

A thunder strike seared the air, drumming the stillness of the river.

Diya covered burning eyes as a bright light flashed.

A woman's shape divested itself from the crackling, walking across the water with two horns crowning hair thick as smoke. Her skin was like the bronze of sunlit valleys. If Diya touched her, the face would be smooth as the opal she clutched tightly in her other hand.

Laughter hit the air like a spark.

Diya dropped her hand and squared her shoulders.

"Have you enjoyed my gifts, Diya of Novasi?" said the god, walking as if the river was no beast to buck her. Her eyes might have been rubies winking in the moonlight.

"I wouldn't call desperation and survival gifts," Diya spat.

"No?" Needle-like teeth emerged in an almost friendly imitation of a grin. "I take back the love you did not want, the companion you have long hated, and I don't yet have your thanks?"

Diya thought of her mother's story and how a girl had died for wanting a god. "Do you thank the god of dreams every time they steal from you?"

The god's grin faltered. "Careful, mortal." Thunder painted vibrant threats above.

"I'm sick of your games, god," Diya hissed. The knife seared her flesh, demanding to be set free. "Where is Arien?"

"Why would I keep him?"

The gods had always proved themselves to be careless, but not with this. Not with him. The question wasn't really why but where. "Because you're a thief too. You steal back from the god of dreams."

The god cut a finger in Diya's direction. A sapphire light shocked Diya back a step. "You were warned." The god balled more power in her hands while Diya's breaths escaped like sharp whistles.

Fighting for breath wouldn't stop her. "For isn't that what happens when innocence comes before you? Is love not a dream you hope to twist?" Another shockwave slammed into her. The god's head cocked. It was only then that Diya understood she was meant to be dead, and wasn't. Following instinct, she made sure the god took no notice of the growing gleam beneath the sleeve of her dress. "How many have died coming too close to your storms?"

The god of nightmares growled. Fury made her fanged smile deadly sharp.

Diya braced.

She saw an explosion of black mist, and then the god was a breath away, lunging for her.

The clash of Diya's knife and the god's ferocious nails emanated a thunderclap of sound. A laugh split the god's lips while Diya groaned from the effort of holding her back. "Mortals. You never cease to amaze me."

Diya stole an opening. She mimicked something she'd seen Gabriel do against a demon with lethal claws. Her knife went up, breaking their hold, and then she ducked her arm.

The thin, little blade slashed the immortal's chest. White light gleamed across the motion.

And a jagged scream stirred the storm anew.

Even that was not enough. "*Where is Arien?*"

The god brought a shaking hand to her smudged chest. Her fingers came back stained.

"Where is he?" Diya cried, ready to leap with her knife again.

Lightning flashed, boiling the river. The god of nightmares stared at Diya with hatred sharpening her face. The look promised a world of retribution. She stepped into the storm and vanished before Diya could stop her.

The forest went so quiet it hurt Diya's ringing ears.

Almost instantly, the river felt different. Quiet in a way that did not hide a threat. She hung onto Arien's opal, but no demons arose to challenge her thoughts of him.

You'll find me where the night ends.

She poured her weary body back onto the river in the echo of stunned silence.

You're close.

And prepared for night to finally end.

WHAT THE GOD of nightmares hadn't said turned uneasily in Diya's stomach. And while her small victory jeweled her study of the night sky, she knew the sweet sting of her body's efforts would soon give way to numbing fatigue.

Suspicion replaced anxiety. She couldn't shake the feeling that Arien's curse, and everything following after, had landed far outside the margin of the gods' usual spite.

Comet-dust wasn't merely a legend. The god of nightmares had been repelled by Diya's knife. But she didn't know where the line between fact and fable began and ended.

What made lovers a dream? Why were she and Arien chosen before birth, only to have their separation exploited?

A ripple in the water distracted her. She reached for her knife.

But there was no time to react when the river rose, flooding uncontrollably.

The boat flipped over and she sunk.

She fought to swim, the water sliding over her head. A flash of a demon's face stole her breath. Her arms pinwheeled. Her legs kicked hard. But she couldn't seem to break the surface for more than a few seconds.

She sucked in a huge breath. Sunk again. Her hand fumbled for her pack when the water tried to steal it from her. Her hair snagged on a branch, yanking her further downriver.

Can't die. Beat gods. Arien.

Sputtering and thrashing, her fury at her own inabilities grew.

Stop fighting. The words came in Gabriel's low voice. He sounded angry with her.

She was slowing. Losing air. Her world was faded blue.

Then, like a pin in her panic, she remembered the river had swelled from nowhere. The surprise of that slid under her alarm.

Stop fighting.

What if the flood was not real?

Calm spread out from her mind. Diya arrowed up, gasping as the water parted.

Air was sweet. Her mouth ate more of it. She stood, strong and straight.

She walked through the roiling current as if she couldn't be drowned.

The longer she moved through the water, the more her skin dried and the river leveled. Grass smushed between her toes. She focused on what lay ahead.

And, for a moment, she couldn't bring herself to blink.

Diya drank in her first glimpse of night ending above her as water drained from her calves.

Worry for Gabriel couldn't touch the glittering arch of coral-skinned trees topped with diamond fruit. Fear for Arien couldn't cool milk-white hills looking soft as sand.

The sky was a vespertine sieve holding back the fires of all worlds, the ashes and rebirths of all stars. And beyond that an endless horizon tattered the edges of night, flowing out in a melon-bright sweep that pained her eyes.

The familiar burn of her knife brought Diya back to herself. Where was Arien?

She cleared her head with a light shake, then bent her neck. An infinite wheel of stars turned above her, but it didn't take long for Diya to find the Dream of Lovers.

It looked different here. The true scope of that single star glistened with the same two-sided sheen as the river. Maybe the sibling gods were like that too—inspiring one thing but meaning another.

The star was brilliantly blue, more like fire than water. Her breath caught.

And she wondered if her answer waited for her in the flame.

Turning her back on the familiar unfamiliar, Diya tilted her comet-knife, angling it so that the night sky waved in the reflection like a dark, fraying flag. She circled slowly, her eyes focused on that reflection.

Then she let the knife drop.

Stars scattered like pearls at her feet.

DIYA WALKED the stars in silence. Then the air thrummed to let her know she wasn't alone.

At this distance, she could see an impossibly tall man. She blinked, and questioned whether he was not small and hobbled? As she walked, the god's image changed again. No longer was there a man, but a woman with rich amber skin and a long, golden shimmer of hair languishing against an elaborate seat made from moon-shards and sun-seeds.

Queen was a word barren of meaning in Diya's time, yet she thought it of the god in their female form. The royalty of old had never had anything so elaborate or ethereal, not even before the priestesses had spread their divine tarp and covered the lands with their power. But she knew that the long-ago kings and queens of Novasi and Gildesh would have envied the self-possessed way the god loitered in splendor.

Perhaps that was why Diya didn't feel green.

After all, she had no use for a stationary chair in the heavens.

The god's head lifted. "Ah, at last. Won't you join me, Diya of Novasi?"

"Where has your sister taken Arien?" she said.

"Sit." Their voice smoothed over the air like a caress. Diya felt her hackles rise.

She avoided the plain seat that emerged between them. "Where is he?"

The god's smile was a gleaming cache of secrets, revealing nothing before they were ready. "Here." With a wave of their hand, a cage made of iron-colored prisms appeared. "Will this ease your mind enough to speak with me?"

Shock blew through her like an errant wind. The god of nightmares didn't have her intended.

"Diya," Arien breathed.

Somehow the injustice of seeing him trapped was worse than seeing him near to his deathbed. He had fought as he lay dying. He couldn't fight a cage and win.

"Let him go," she demanded.

The god of dreams rose from their seat. "Do you know how much time I spent carving your path to this boy? Do you know how long it's been since I've given my blessing?" Their footsteps were lush whispers against the softness of the stars as they circled her. "Why would I reward your ingratitude, mortal?"

"Let him go and punish me."

The god drew closer. "Not sufficient. I offer you one chance to spare yourself more pain."

Impatience bit at the hand holding her knife. It was that hand to which the god pointed.

"Let the river take your ancestors' knife where it cannot be found and Arien will not be harmed."

Which wasn't the same as Arien having his freedom back. Diya opened her mouth as smoke entered the room, tasting of a winter storm.

"Keep the boy," said the god of nightmares in a tone full of menace. "But the girl is mine."

"I've heard that before." A small smile was akin to a wicked wink from the god of dreams. It was then Diya noticed how one eye was slightly angled and silver while the other was yellow-bright and straight. The reason for this didn't have to be important. But she also noticed that his eyebrows and his cheekbones didn't quite match each other either. "I'm afraid I have need of her yet," said the god to their sister.

"I'm *tired*." The declaration sounded strange—and deadly—coming from a god with horns gleaming in the soft light of the stars. "Look what she's done to me."

"Sweet sister, why do you think I bargain with the girl?"

An idea dawned on Diya. "We haven't reached an accord," she said. "I want a new deal."

"You think to negotiate with one such as me?"

"Think of it like an exchange of gifts if you must." The god narrowed their eyes, but her voice rang clear. "Give Arien back and you live."

The boy in question watched with growing horror. He was silently pleading with her to fall back.

"You would *dare*?" the god of nightmares seethed.

Her sibling studied Diya with a face full of bitter arrogance. "I am not the god of death," they said. "I can pleasure the body with dreams beyond imagining. House the mortal mind in a gorgeous prison until that body leaves in the wind. No more than memory, no less than dust. Will you risk your beloved suffering a fate far worse than death?"

"I don't have to. You need us."

"You are replaceable," the god snapped. "I could have any mortal of my choosing."

"But can you wait for the gods of fate and fortune to take pity on you?" She saw that she was right to implicate their pride. Pity was the last thing the god wanted. "You're weak."

If this realm were a room, the darkness of it would have squashed her like a bug. The hot beam of her knife might have been the only thing that kept her from flying back into the river a carcass and not a girl. A crack sprang in the god of dreams' throne. Their finger lifted to tap against it.

"War has made you weak. That is why *we* were born to your star. The infamous Eta's daughter and a son of Gildesh born at twilight. Tell me something," she said, walking and smiling without guile though her heart pumped frantically. She planted her feet in the god's star. "Are all the legends true?"

Lifting her arm back like a snake poised to strike, she plunged the comet-knife into the heart of that star.

The night sky splintered when the god of dreams screamed.

Diya pulled back the blade before it could finish its work and sever the star in half. The color was changing from silver-blue to onyx, and the veins of the god glowed like shattering glass.

An electric shock streamed for her chest. Arien shook the bars of his cage, shouting her name.

She kept her ground despite the blazing pain. The knife had deflected the worst of it.

"Would you risk my power, mortal?" said the god of nightmares, murderous lines pinching her satin features. "Would you risk a world without dreams?"

Diya's breath labored. She hoped the sound concealed her

lack of skill with a bluff. "I don't care what happens to any of it if Arien does not come back with me."

"You can't fool me, mortal. I took him from you because he meant so little to you."

Diya found Arien's bent head inside the cage. "You took him because you could," she said. "And he means far more to me than just a little."

Arien's mouth tightened. He was barely concentrating on her, but she knew he heard, just as she knew he was formulating a plan to free himself. She couldn't allow him to interfere.

"Do you think I will spare your friends? Your family?" More of the god's energy collected in her palms.

"Do *you*?" Diya asked, and the god's thunder wavered like a flame. She turned her face in the direction of the crumbled god of dreams. "War is a nightmare you barely survived once. Can you survive it twice? If I don't return with Arien, what do you think will happen?"

It was a gamble, but Diya was familiar with great risks. She took them in coming here, playing the gods like she had all the advantage. But she had to believe this was the reason the god of dreams had kept Arien from returning. Even now, their face undulated like static, unable to hold forms with the simple ease temple stories had taught Diya to expect.

"I will not give up anything," she said into the silence. "But you have only to give up what doesn't belong to you."

For a long moment, the silence stretched. The god of nightmares festered beneath the tether Diya had placed on her. The god of dreams lifted a hand.

Arien's cage swung open. He ran to Diya. She warned him with a look not to sweep her up into his arms as she could see he wanted.

He settled for kneeling beside her across the star that had set their destiny in a mold. When their thighs touched, he seemed to relax a fraction. With her free hand, she reached for his, as much to anchor herself as to hold him back should everything go wrong.

"If you think," said the god of dreams with no shortage of effort, "you will survive the outcome of this bargain, you're mistaken."

Diya's hand went cool against Arien's. "But I have a new bargain for you. Love is a powerful dream in our villages," she said. "Swear you will never bother with us again and I will help you."

"How?" demanded the god of dreams, face a deadly mosaic of fissures.

Diya took a deep breath. She pressed her advantage. "I have a story to tell the world." When she had sensed the god of nightmares by the quality and depth of her merciless sleep, an understanding of the balance between gods and mortals had shaped itself in Diya's mind. "When I marry Arien people will only be more inclined to believe that story." His surprise bumped against her steady voice, but she was ruthless in pretending she hadn't felt it. "They will see his hail return as a sign of your goodness. Your blessing. They will flock to your altar in the temple and leave their wishes at the feet of your statue. They will think of you should war ever fall upon on them again. They will beg you for hope. The farther I go, the more this will be so."

She read desire in the god's expression and could have crumpled to the ground had she been standing. "That is, of course, if your sister will have it." She arched a brow at the lethal weight of the god of nightmares' power.

Even weak, the god of dreams conquered. Diya saw Eta and Gabriel in the look the god of dreams settled on the god of nightmares.

She saw more of herself than Arien when the god of nightmares lowered her hand. Pity stirred for the immortal. Perhaps this was why the god's brother-sister could harm an innocent who had worshipped her in a story and still remain defended in reality.

However, the god of nightmares did not fully back away. "This bargain appeases one god, not two," she said. "A grudge can grow and leap for you when you forget to look, Diya of Novasi."

Pity evaporated. "What do you want?"

She had an image of fangs, dripping with the blood of Arien, her family, spreading in a smile while she slept. She released Arien's palm.

"Your agony," said the nightmare god. "Are you willing to pay such a price?"

Arien curled his abandoned hand around Diya's over the comet-knife. "No," he stated clearly.

Would you like to pay your price now?

"Arien..."

This way is less steep.

"No, Diya."

"Look at me." When he did, she said, "Trust me." She lifted the comet-knife between them. "Yes?"

There are always histories of beautiful girls who plagued gods... they paid a terrible price...

He gave her more than she probably deserved. "Yes."

"Stay with me?" No matter what, she thought. No matter where I go.

"Yes."

She turned the knife up to her face. She locked eyes with the god of nightmares. "Watch me."

Do you understand?

She did. She made her choice.

Appeasing the gods was no small thing.

White-hot pain flared bright and powerful, bringing out her

scream. Her consciousness dimmed. Blood flowed hot over the handle of the knife. Her eyes remained open.

But her body plucked like a string and spilled back. She was caught against Arien's chest.

She could hear his wedding tunic tearing. "You have your tithe," he spat at the gods, pressing torn strips of cloth to the barbed wound Diya created. "Now set us free."

A thundering gust swirled around them.

Diya kept her fist tight around her knife, the bright red eyes of the god of nightmares cutting through the icy spots in her vision. "Don't bother... us again," she said. *I am quite the restless spirit. Death will not stop me.* She couldn't say the words without feeling her pain rip the seams of her torn face.

But the god of nightmares smiled as though she'd heard what hadn't been said. "Die soon, Diya." The god kept her honor, if such things even mattered to immortals. "I look forward to meeting you in your next life."

That was the last thing Diya heard as she arrowed out of the gods' realm, locked in Arien's arms. The explosive shriek of their fall eradicated all else as they barreled endlessly toward the earth.

Diya lifted her head to smile at Arien as the final words of the tale fell into a quiet circle of pale-skinned young men and women. Her audience swallowed the ending down as Diya's scarring caught the sunlight.

Fear and awe had rearranged their solemn stares.

"That's..." A woman with a white cotton apron cleared her throat. "That's a tale if I ever heard one."

Soft murmurs agreed with her. Diya was pleased that she understood many of them. Her recent travels had uncovered her gift for learning languages.

"Where is this River of Souls?" said one man, still riveted on Diya though her words had faded.

Snow painted down the mountains outside the window of the *tavern*, and the sun streamed ribbons through golden and straw-colored hair common in this region. A shiver tickled beneath the wool frock protecting Diya's warm skin. "A good distance from here," she responded, thinking of the blistering heat of the borderlands. "But if you can find it, anyone from Novasi or Gildesh will welcome your stay."

"If they're still recovering from war," the man said skeptically, "why would they welcome strangers?"

Arien came over with a strange concoction of alcohol. He was forever pushing her to sample each new food and drink he ran across. "For coin," he answered the man, bending to kiss Diya's largest scar. The word was one of the few he had mastered. "And for marrying."

Everyone heard him. Laughter erupted.

"Will you go home soon then?" another girl asked. Pink spots dotted her cheeks when Arien had joined the circle.

Diya smiled. "Yes."

"Why should you have to?" a boy muttered, frowning at the bright white of his homeland framed in the window.

She wanted to say that it was because she couldn't remold the world into a shape that best fit her. That there were other people who had to live in that world with her. But she said simply, "It's my choice. It can be a choice."

Her voice still held the echoes of her story.

The boy nodded at her, perhaps understanding.

"We will miss these tales of yours," said the woman with the apron. "And your wares."

Diya clasped Arien's hand lightly in hers. "We'll come 'round this way again."

Later, when night removed the pale blue veil of the sky, and they had settled in their straw bed, Diya turned into

Arien's chest. Her mind was restless. "I never thanked you for this."

His finger trail through her hair halted. "I don't want to be thanked."

She smiled against his skin.

"Don't you?" she said when he stirred beneath her.

"Never mind. You were right to thank me."

It felt so good to laugh, though it strained the right side of her face. They hadn't waited long to marry, but it had taken a little time for them to settle into new roles as traders. She had spent months learning everything she could from her father before they left.

Her impatience with him, with waiting, sometimes got the better of her. But Arien had withstood her. And by the time Novasi had become a green gleam in the distance, she and her father had shared less awkward, tense silences. Eta had learned to put less conditions on her trust, while Diya had worked to do the same. These things were helped by the marriage they had asked of her.

But the choice had been hers entirely.

"Somehow Gabriel got a letter to us. He's on his way back from patrolling the southern border," Arien whispered in her ear. His breath sent wisps of her hair shivering. "He wants to stay with us when we return."

The home they came back to from time to time straddled land sitting like a narrow island between the temple and the cavern leading out of the River of Souls. Despite all that had happened on the other side of that cave, it was the only place Diya had felt she belonged.

She sighed. "That news is no way to thank *me*."

Arien kissed her softly. "Please."

Weakening—because she could be weakened by him—she said, "I suppose it's all right."

Miraculously, Gabriel had been found breathing and relatively intact despite the distress to his wrists. It was almost as if time had slowed down the effects of his capture while they searched for him. When they managed to cut him down, he was hardly untouched by pain.

But he lived.

"He says he misses you."

"Like the god of death misses his victims."

Arien's laugh burst out. He was so beautiful. She could admit that to herself now. His face and form were just the start of it. "They're not victims," he said. "Death isn't an ending."

"You're right." Talking of the gods made her uneasy now, so she spoke lightly. "What would the god of souls do if it was?"

A memory of their first attempt at marrying floated in her mind. She remembered feeling everything she had made herself into would shuffle off, like forcibly shedding skin she still wanted. She remembered being afraid of who she might become without being so hard on a world which had blamed her more than it had warmed her.

But now she believed any part of herself that perished would be reborn in other ways. And these new phases of Diya, like the one cocooned in Arien's arms under a different sky each night, felt unburdened.

Whole.

It was like peace.

HUNTRESS AND THE NIGHTINGALE

*S*he should have stayed inside.

By Zahria's count, there were seven women with rosebud mouths from the pleasurehouse, two unattended pints of honey-ale, and a queen carved from finery sitting alone on a vine-wreathed dais. All while Zahria stood alone in the tempting swath of Red Saint's Day.

Red cloaks and dyed flower petals oppressed the bright ivory gleam of the city. Blood grails lay open to drunken revelers, protected by the queen's most watchful bloodguard. Citizens of Luren held out their wrists to perform the Exchange with sleepy delight on their faces. The guards kissed those wrists with their knives. Blood bloomed and dripped past the bronze lip of the closest grail.

Zahria watched the queen's mouth fall open, cheeks flushing, breath deepening. The narrow cracks in her youth filled, leaving Zahria to reach for a forgotten pint. Ale dripped down her collar. Her eyes shut to close out the queen and her magic.

She should have stayed inside. The palace would have been solemn and quiet and without temptation.

With a swipe across her mouth, she looped an arm around

the first available female lingering at the edges of the crowd. The girl didn't squeak or squeal. Some distant part of Zahria's mind registered surprise. "Dance with me," she whispered into the girl's neck as fiddles and mandolins plucked the festivities to a higher note. Her heart pounded with the rise of drums as the girl wriggled. "Is that a no?"

Her breath must have tickled the hairs at the back of the girl's neck, for she shivered. Golden clouds of hair had blocked the girl's face, but when a face did reveal itself, Zahria was met with shrewd seafoam eyes.

"Let go of me."

It was then Zahria noticed that the girl's neckline remained buttoned and she did not have crossed-over rose stems tattooed over her collarbone. Instead, the girl stood draped in burgundy velvet, with black beading trimming her collar—and the waist Zahria still clung to. "Do you accompany the queen?" she asked, drawing her hands away from an area where the dress didn't appear to be properly cinched. The girl's hips were lost in a sea of fabric.

"Of course." There was a stubborn tilt to her chin. Those jeweled eyes crystallized into sharp points of annoyance. Impatience.

"And your name?"

The impatience deepened, but the girl said, "Elina, my lady."

Zahria arced a brow. "A pleasure." Was the girl mocking her or did she truly not know? Impossible *not* to know who Zahria was while in service to the queen, but both possibilities thrummed her heart faster. The girl was stunning... and suspicious. It had been too long since Zahria stopped at the verge of collecting something that wanted to stay hidden. When the Old Zahria had desired, nothing had halted her pursuit. Nothing could have kept her from the truth.

"Might I escort you back to Her Majesty?" The invitation

left Zahria's mouth imbalanced. She reached for the girl's arm and missed her target, landing near the girl's drowned hip. "My deepest apologies," she said, tacking on a small giggle.

Elina of the summer-sea eyes frowned. "Who are you?"

"You don't know me?" Another giggle. "I am Zahria."

"No," said the girl with quiet ferocity. She tugged Zahria's arm off her shoulders and gripped a free wrist. "*Who* are you?"

"Easy," said Zahria with an uproarious laugh. Heads turned in their direction. She was loaded with long stares, though her drunken behavior had little to do with it. Her dark skin set her apart in this kingdom. "Too easy. I'm huntress. I mean, I'm the huntress. Royal Huntress."

There. Awareness flashed behind the jewels, before flitting away. The girl's hand lifted off Zahria so quickly, Zahria lost her balance and swung around in a near-perfect circle. "It's Red Saint's Day," she said on another laugh, reaching for the girl again. "Let's have a dance, Elina."

"I'm afraid my mistress awaits," Elina said hastily. So hastily her prim accent slipped. She hadn't sounded like a Lurenite at the tail-end of her sentence.

Zahria barely had time to blink before the girl dove for the crowd, ducking under limbs and chasing the outline of the palace. Her balance caught and she straightened, eyes narrowing. She wondered just what Elina of the bright medallion hair was running from.

Or running to.

She thought about pursuing. Her curiosity was big enough. But, as she tipped back more of her ale, the queen's gaze collided with hers.

And decided her.

She chose the opposite direction, the heady rush in her chest slowing, growing cold. *I should have stayed inside*, she thought again. Beneath the welcome chaos of lust and intrigue caused by Elina, the queen rendered Zahria empty and tired with no more than a glance.

She was so tired.

A handful of drunken ministers with piss-smelling robes sat beneath a painting set in the wall behind them. "Spare a coin for a verse?" one roused himself enough to whisper as Zahria walked past.

She hesitated before patting down her pockets. She wordlessly handed over a few stray coins.

"Saints be," he whispered, before dropping into sleep again, his left fist slacking around a wineskin.

Moonlight rippled across the golden face in the painting and Zahria toasted the Red Saint herself. Saint Lura, the city's wealth in pride. She stared out at Zahria with bold eyes and black hair, guarding—some believed—the red sun at her back. Her robes flowed from her body like blood, and Zahria wondered, as she always did when confronted with any one of Osolda's backward saints, how anyone could mistake this woman for a saint of mercy.

Saint Lura's true mirror was the god of fire. Those cupped palms in the image looked like they were ready to bathe in the crimson heat of the sun, taking greedy handfuls of its burning rays.

Zahria's older sister, Jenya, had been training to become a priestess before Zahria had left home, and would have scorned the Osoldans' tendency of worshipping gods for the wrong reasons.

Her sister's face flashed in the moonlit dark, stirring an ache in her heart.

This was why Zahria could spare no pity for the people of this godsforsaken kingdom. Even when they painted the truth, they still found false meaning.

She found herself on a white stone bench, pretending she was happy to sit, looking, watching. Awaiting nothing.

Pretending she didn't feel the weight of her own heart more heavily, that being still didn't feel like surrendering.

She could still see over the precipice of what was one of the lowest mountain-made towers of the city. Her gaze stopped on the Unforeseen Forest. She remembered her first time riding through it, unable to believe the enormity of the trees. The banyans of her homeland were always dragging their hair, whereas the green pines and firs of Osolda arrowed gracefully toward the sky. Or they had. Now the forest was no more than a gray net of ancient trees losing verve.

Music and laughter swelled at her back, but none of it comforted her. The wind raked icy, brusque fingers through her hair despite the mild warmth of the night. Her eyes strained and she realized she was willing the warning fire of Greyhold to light. The flames of the garrison city would call her to track beasts loose from the forest again. Mighty ones with thick, gnarled hides and crushing jaws. She no longer cared if she was faced with the trees in the distance. She could ignore their fervent whispers to finally have some sport.

But there was only the cold and quiet. And the bitter lie frozen inside her whispering she was far from content to sit back while her gifts remained tucked inside her, collecting dust. The tiny silver statues dangling from her belt turned icy in the wind's breath.

Perhaps this was her punishment. Perhaps she felt the sharp cut of the wind and the pointed silence of the city in the distance because the gods were angry with her.

Saint Sumora. Saint Becan. Saint Holt. These were the Osoldan names for the ones who had blessed her. The saints of new life and power, of messengers, and of the hunt. But their true names were ripe with real magic.

"God of sun," Zahria said in the borderland dialect of her country's language. Her fingers flitted over the faces of the statues at her waist. "God of wind. God of forest. Give me the strength to break free."

She was no longer alone.

"What are you doing here?" she said, staring at the grey husks splintering the horizon. She wanted nothing more than to reel her words back. Hold onto the spoken relics of her home in private.

"You should give them real names." Somehow that long, dark hair remained a bold shadow in the dark, haloed only by the milky light of the moon. The length of it swayed below the waistline and brushed Zahria's fisted hand.

"Who?"

"Your gods," answered the queen, straightening her skirts as though she had endless time at her disposal.

"It's not my place to give such things."

The queen wore white tonight. Like the ministers of Luren once did. It was a way of standing apart from suspicion that Red Saint's Day was of the queen's own making. That while Saint Lura herself was not fabricated, the need for bloodletting was. But anyone who took the time to observe her throughout the celebration would have known the truth.

But Osolda was blind.

Questions perched behind Zahria's teeth. Questions like how dull skin could glow in the span of an evening because of a gathering of blood. Why guards were abandoned to take up the seat next to hers. Where the softness between a queen and the shadow of her huntress had gone. But she didn't flood the silence with all her accusations. Instead, these questions curled like a vise around her heart, not because she didn't know the answers, but because she'd lain with them in her bed on the long nights of the last half-century, squeezing them so tightly the pain had etched itself somewhere far down inside her. They were not the answers she wanted, even now. Hearing them out loud would only cause meaningless anger. And, despite everything, the last thing Zahria wanted between them was something of too little meaning.

"You roam the city like a caged animal. The guards are frightened of you."

Zahria sucked in a breath. "Are you frightened of me?"

"Should I be?"

"You had me kill a man," Zahria said after a long moment of that painful, empty silence. The wind howled like a weeping woman as she spoke. "You used me to ease something inside you without care of the cost." She looked over at the queen. "This is the cost, Liana."

"I am *above* cost."

"You've always thought so." Zahria looked out again, following the long tangle of the Unforeseen Forest. Her heart tripped at the thought of being lost inside those seeking, labyrinthine limbs, but could she take much more of this city, this kingdom? Its queen? "Let me go, Liana. Please."

Skirts rustled. The bench hissed. Zahria felt the punch of emptiness beside her. "I will not abide this useless wretch you've become." Black eyes set into Zahria's bent head, demanding she rise, but she refused to be baited. "Get up. Find work, if you must. Roam the forests and hunt up the creatures that live there. But I will not abide *this*."

Zahria's hands fisted. The gap between them was widening, swallowing the questions, the desires, even whatever was left of kindness. "*You* will not abide it? You don't command me, Your Majesty. " She'd always thought the cold, set face above her beautiful, but even that was lost in the chasm of their turmoil. "After all we've been to each other, I ask that you find me a way home before the worst happens."

"What," Liana said coldly, "do you suspect that to be?" Her willowy length stood illuminated by starlight and fury, every muscle braced and every hint of pale skin heightened in color. Her eyes looked wild, brimming with righteous rage.

"We'll kill each other," Zahria murmured.

The wind died. The only sound came from Liana's harsh breathing.

"Before much longer, hatred will be all we have left. In hate, we'll do unspeakable things," Zahria whispered. "We've already begun. We will both go mad."

"There is no way out," Liana said with finality. "The southwestern border is blocked by the Feydlans. The Unforeseen Forest and its creatures to the east. The mountains at our backs. You are not the first to ask me for what I cannot give. This city —no, this kingdom—would empty if I allowed it. And I will not allow it. Not even for you," she finished quietly.

Now Zahria stood. Her voice was soft. "Then you doom us both."

Cawing like Zahria had never heard before thwarted whatever Liana might have said next.

"What is it?" shouted Zahria as bloodguard poured out of the shadows, soundlessly taking up defensive positions around the queen. A few remaining guards broke before joining the formation, hands tightening on their pommels as they ran toward the district center.

Zahria chased after them.

Something exploded.

Glass.

Shards of it rained down on the Belle District in the upper tiers of the city.

Screams soared above the merriment as palace windows shattered in a symphony as sharp as the cry of a hummingbird.

Birds burst from the destruction and spilled into the night.

They wove through stars, shivering from their freedom, their feathers flapping like falling, rippling gems.

Sea eagles with snow-dust shoulders, dipping herons, sparrows with dark underwings, lilting kestrels, doves with jade necks, larks darting in bold streaks...

Zahria watched the wild-hearted windstorm of birds in sheer awe.

"The bird clans," someone shouted, pushing against the throng of people looking on in horror.

A storm of wings sliced through the air, diving lightning-quick for the Angel District.

"An attack," another cried. Sobbing and shouting erupted. *"What do they want?"*

The song of a nightingale pierced the question. A lone bird arced out of the chaos, winding down toward the pointed tip of Saint Lura's Church.

A girl flipped out of the bird's body, one form emerging as the other vanished.

Medallion hair. Summer-sea eyes. Sweat gleamed on sun-fed skin.

Zahria's breath fled. *Elina.*

That was the name this girl had given, in clothing Zahria now understood hadn't belonged to her but another of the queen's ladies-in-waiting.

She towered above the people of Luren.

"Osolda has defected," Elina shouted down, her voice echoing off white stone. "Your queen has corrupted the lifeblood of this kingdom. She has betrayed the Skies."

Zahria could see the queen give the order to shoot the clanswoman down, but when the arrows finally did come free, Elina had shifted effortlessly between bird and girl to deflect them all.

Steel clinked like hail against stone.

"We will no longer be burdened by the curse upon this land. But I warn you," said Elina, her voice and color high, "We may forgive, but the forest will come for you. The forest is *starved* for you. Beasts will dine on your families until bones are all that line the soil.

Osolda will not forgive. The land curses you."

An arrow nearly clipped her shoulder, but Elina twisted away from the tower, free-falling before her enraptured audience. She took flight just before landing in front of the queen, her eyes a crackling green against the black fire of the queen's gaze as she arose a nightingale once more.

The nightingale cut a glance to Zahria, the beat of her wings circling near. She resumed her climb for the sky above Zahria's head.

Wings extended into the night. Legions of birds swam for the moon beckoning in the horizon.

Sobs ended in the Angel District.

Gasps exploded.

Then silence reigned.

A feather had landed at Zahria's feet, but she waited until birdsong faded before plucking it from the nose of her boot.

And meeting the violent gaze of the queen.

WHEN ZAHRIA ENTERED the Hall of Kings, the queen's screams tore through white rock walls and lofty, crystal beams like gossamer. "How does one girl set my palace to ruin alone? Is there no loyalty in this room?"

"Your Majesty, we've searched for signs—"

Liana's control slipped. Her palms were especially thin-skinned and littered with scars. It was easy for her to make herself bleed. She called upon her magic and made the Exchange.

The guard's gaze fell. His struggle for breath echoed in the vaulted room. Soon, pride and training vanished. His hands scrambled for the grooves in his throat.

"My queen," said Alistair, a nobleman from the south of Osolda. Like the others of his ilk, he wore crimson robes and a ring inlaid with garnets. When he addressed Liana, Zahria's mind pricked. His words rang hollow in the Hall. "This was a plan set in motion long ago."

Liana spun to him. "And yet, my Master of Spies knew nothing of it. Had she had a sword, might she have cut out my heart in my sleep?" The guard's choking breath dissolved and he collapsed at her back. "Shall I lay the blame at your feet next, Alistair?"

"You summoned me?" said Zahria, flicking a wet strand of her smooth curls. She sounded impatient and unassuming even to her own ears.

"You took your time." Liana's gaze chilled to black ice. "You bathed."

"A pity the maids were too frightened to send word."

Several moments passed as Liana took cleansing breaths. "Is it not your task to prevent the desertion of those in my keeping?"

Zahria didn't sting at the attempt to score her pride. She let the silence hum for a moment. "I am not aware of all that is in your keeping, Majesty." It took all her control not to wince as she said the words. The inexplicable screams deep within the palace had kept her from sleeping these last months.

Liana's smile could have seduced the god of death as Zahria's meaning seeped in. "I am not required to apprise you of such things."

"Then I cannot be held accountable for your actions."

"It would be easier for you to think so."

They shared hold of the silence then, a weapon refusing to fall into either set of hands. Anger flitted between them, murmuring embittered things.

You swore to love me.

You swore to honor me.

You would leave me alone.

You sacrificed what was yours alone.

Never forgive you.

Never forgive you.

Zahria could hear the furious tenor of her own heart. The nervous breaths of ladies-in-waiting and manservants. Nobles flexing their fingers behind their backs. Her senses had always been heightened, but sound—and its lack—expanded the breadth of even the smallest moments.

Everything was gold and marble. Everything was set alight by a pale, luminous woman wreathed in scarlet before the throne. And yet the beat of Zahria's heart thickened, as though fighting through ice. She wondered why she and Liana were still so proud they couldn't voice the accusations screaming from the chasm between them.

Especially, Zahria thought, meeting Alistair's speculative gaze, *when everyone else strained to hear the unspoken.*

"There is a thief at large, Huntress," Liana said finally. "You know what must be done."

"Her people were already in her possession, my queen."

"Were they people?" Liana turned to Alistair. Zahria wondered if the queen could see the muscles flexing in his smooth jaw. "Unless my eyes deceive me, it was only a flock of birds that escaped. My collection, in fact."

"The crowds saw the girl change," Zahria said.

"The crowds in the *Angel* District," returned Liana. "They see shapes in their smoke and chase rats for their supper. We fed them well and the rest of the celebrations only gorged on their reputation. They know nothing."

"They knew enough to identify the girl as sky clan," Zahria said, thumbing the feather hidden behind her belt. "They know enough of the Unforeseen Forest to understand that these beasts that tear at their family's lands are no accident of nature."

The souls dwelling in Luren know you're the reason.

Liana's eyes blazed. "The sky clans have no rights here. Find her for me."

"Then set me free."

Liana swept toward her golden seat. Zahria had seen her do this before. Liana liked to deal with disobedience by staring down into the face of it. "Is this how you ask me to invest in your service?"

Zahria smiled. "The gods know I haven't taken payment of *any* kind in many years."

All murmurs ceased in the Hall.

Liana cocked her head. "Your gods know nothing." And yet Zahria could almost hear her say, *Well played.* "But what exactly does your freedom win me? You are a valuable asset to Osolda. The beasts of the Unforeseen Forest will return as soon as their conqueror abandons us. No," said Liana, finger ticking against the polished metal of her throne. "Subduing the sky clans will not be enough."

"Might you rid the forest of all the beasts, Huntress," one brave noblewoman stepped forward. "Surely that is within your great powers."

Zahria barely spared her a glance. "Name your price. Majesty."

"We both have a problem that requires the same solution," Liana said, her tone full of quiet menace. Could anyone see how her nails curled? How her eyes became bottomless? This was no longer a queen, but a demon. How long before everyone else noticed? It had taken Zahria far too much time to see the signs. "Rid us of the forest altogether, and we shall both have our freedom. You to leave. Me to rule beyond our borders. Osolda has been isolated long enough."

Zahria said nothing. Her heart kicked faster. She nearly crossed her arms over her chest before she remembered how that would show weakness. The defense would immediately signify the accuracy of a blow.

She remembered how freedom had once felt. The way she had roamed the earth with a berry-sweet taste on her tongue and the damp smell of wet bark around her. She remembered being accompanied by the thought that if she could roam the earth and scent the god of forest near, she need never be afraid of how far she travelled.

Now the inside of her mouth tasted sour. The air smelled of ash. How long had it been since she'd been among a forest clean of the queen's poison?

"I cannot," Zahria murmured, but it was as if she heard herself from two directions, like a split reflection. There was a part of her that did not recoil at the loss of the Unforeseen Forest. This part of her had tracked this same conclusion in the muddle of Zahria's darkening thoughts and had simply waited. It was not within her to pounce on a whim. But it was Liana pointing out the logic and opportunity. Tearing down forests was an evil damned by the gods, but did that matter anymore after everything Zahria had done?

"I wonder how else you expect me to release you from service when there is nowhere left to go." Liana smiled from her seat, her crown a cold gleam in the evening candlelight. "Magic? My power has no effect on the forest. Men? The Feydlans would skewer them for sport and then I would have no one to defend what matters most in this kingdom. Of course," she said, "you're welcome to seek refuge in the mountains. Live out your days in some hovel until the wind steals your warmth. I won't stop you."

A guard burst through the tension, his words like the warning gleam of a blade. "The garrison city has lit their beacons," he panted out. "Greyhold calls for aid, Your Majesty."

"What impeccable timing these beasts have," said Liana, eyes locked on Zahria's. "It seems your duty remains here in Osolda, Huntress. Will you refuse it?"

Zahria's fists curled. Refusing would be reason enough for Liana to take action against her. No one would stop the queen from imprisoning a foreigner with strange magic, no matter how reluctant those in the room to lose their champion against the beasts of the forest. A rigid belief in the absolute right of the monarchy superseded even the deterrent that was the queen's dangerous reign.

"The soldiers there won't last long, Huntress," murmured Alistair, drawing Zahria's gaze. She remembered then that much of Greyhold's responsibilities fell to him. "Please."

Her breath caught in her chest. She turned to the queen. "I will empty the forest of its beasts." The taste of her freedom didn't return, but, in that moment, the idea of leaving this wretched kingdom far outweighed the wrath of her gods. With a heart that felt deadened, she said, "And then I will empty these lands of the forest."

The queen rose, her mouth parting. With flushed cheeks, she held out her hand to Zahria.

Zahria's eyes travelled down to the obsidian ring nestled against Liana's third knuckle. She herself had slid it into place almost a century ago. She had knelt as she did now, swearing her fealty. The woman standing above her had been sitting in the middle of twisted sheets. But when Zahria's lips met the ring in front of an audience in the Hall of Kings, the gesture was a far cry from loving. Her knees touching the cold tile told her something vital had been taken from her—the loss of which could never be forgiven.

She rose. The queen's hand fell to her side. Zahria leaned in close enough to cause stirs among the onlooking nobility. "May you rot behind these walls," she whispered. "I will never again give you a moment's thought." She pulled away, bitterness changing the shape of her smile. She could the taste the lie in her words, but hadn't been able to resist delivering them.

Liana's hand did not rise to detain her. Her soft laugh quieted the whispers in the room. "Go ahead. Free yourself of this place, Huntress," she said, leaning forward this time. Her voice was low enough none could hear but Zahria. "But I wonder what you will have left to comfort you after a century. Or should I say... whom."

Zahria's thoughts went to ice. The sudden burn of it made her flinch.

Liana smiled. "Run along then." She returned to her throne, languishing in a right she had stolen long ago. "You are dismissed."

～

THE RAINWATER LOOK of her window made Zahria think of blood.

She'd seen it flow in reflective pools along the white stone paths twining around the palace. The Belle District had suffered when the palace had ruptured and the birds had flown free. Men and women who had begun to think themselves safe in the queen's inner circle would forever bear scars from what might have been an innocent stroll. Not even their fine dress could hide their brush with the god of death.

Zahria took her hand away from the cracks in the glass and finished her packing. She hesitated over her wineskin. Then she slowly lifted her hand, leaving it in the shadows made by the bedpost.

There was no one within the palace worth giving farewells, so she cut through the quiet of the halls at night and left.

The passage between the Belle and Angel Districts was low and winding. Zahria's footsteps paused. A fallen statue of the last king, Henul, lay on its side. In the lamplight, his eyes were wide and shadowed. The edges of his face were roped in vines. His hands were missing, but if the stone-king could speak, his words would have pinned her. Death was supposed to be a rite of peace, and yet he looked tormented.

Zahria hadn't killed him.

But that wasn't why he might have blamed her, this golden-eyed son of gray-bearded kings. The paintings Zahria had seen in the palace burnished the man who had decreed Luren a symbol of wealth, prosperity, and innovation for all of Osolda. Liana had daggered herself to his side long before Zahria had found her already crowned. She'd ushered bloodcraft from the shadows and into the brilliance of court. Henul had soon stripped a word from the base of this statue. He'd replaced innovation with blood because the two had become the same. Zahria tried to turn the blame onto his ambition for what this kingdom had become.

And yet Zahria and the stone-king were both centered in the darkness tonight. The moonlight wanted nothing of either of them and the silver-softened silence was deafening.

She turned away from the gray shadow of Osolda's fallen king.

It was Liana who had convinced Henul to entertain the idea of a bloodguard and the Exchange. It was Liana who had fitted them to his regime. And it was Liana who had used these men and women to claim the throne for herself. Henul may have given her room, but Liana had never needed much of a foothold to take what she most wanted.

Zahria used to dote when Liana spoke of how she had ensnared a king and killed him, how she had besotted the people into believing immortality was her divine right. Zahria had always believed it was the right of the predator to enjoy the catching of prey.

She laughed in the darkness.

Maybe that had changed when she had stopped aging. When their bed had grown cold while the nights stretched on. When the screams in the far reaches of the palace lost their distance and had become unmistakable. Zahria had killed an innocent man. So much had changed. Everything that had come before vanished like a dream.

She'd met with the trap that had taken Henul. She still

wriggled in its jaws. But for Liana's greed—or softness—Zahria still wasn't sure which—she remained alive inside that trap, bleeding soundlessly over the ivory stones of this city, waiting for a dawn she could bear.

Jenya might have said Zahria and the queen were destined. Zahria's sudden immortality in this realm—in the queen's presence—would have been proof of that destiny in their homeland. And yet if they were meant to love each other, why was it that neither still knew how?

This was why they brought such misery to each other. Who had the greater right between predators of equal match?

"You could be so much more."

A dagger slid into Zahria's palm, and then up into the neck of Liana's Master of Spies.

His body slammed against the wall. His breath exploded.

Zahria stopped herself just before piercing flesh. "You're a fool to follow me alone, Alistair." She hadn't heard his footsteps, but she would've spotted his waifish spies. Their desperation made their steps heavy and their waiting brief. "Could your little pests not catch me?"

The fool in question stood rigid, staring down at her with something like contempt. "Shall I ask you for mercy then, Huntress?"

Zahria smirked. "What better place." They stood at the dilapidated edge of the Angel District. There was no place in greater need of mercy. Liana, of course, had made a mockery of that need by holding Red Saint's Day in the bowels of this city, offering spectacle rather than real sustenance. Zahria brought up her other arm, pinning Alistair with her elbow as she returned her dagger to its sheath. "What do you want?"

He considered her for a moment. "The alarm in Greyhold is false."

She said nothing at first, searching for openings in his closed expression. "Why tell me this?"

His gaze stayed steady on hers. "Because you have finally relieved yourself of the queen."

"And you're so certain I will not return to the palace and tell her her Master of Spies betrays her."

"No, I am not certain," he said, without hesitation. "But the risk of trusting your ended allegiance outweighs the possibility of you returning to her side."

"This still does not explain what you're after, Alistair."

"To offer you your freedom."

Zahria scoffed. "That is beyond your reach, my *lord*." She didn't doubt he was anything less than a complicated man, but if his power didn't concern the queen, it certainly didn't concern her.

"I cannot offer you surety without revealing the source of my confidence."

"In other words, you're asking me to trust you when there is none closer than you by the queen's side."

Alistair smiled. Zahria did not like its shine. "Your jealousy is misplaced," he said, and she nearly brought out her dagger again. "And, yes, I ask that you trust me. I ask that you consider I am not the only one displeased with our queen's... methods of diplomacy."

"Oh?"

"There is a council."

"Secret, no doubt."

"Yes."

She sneered. "You plot your queen's destruction with the curtains drawn and you expect me to trust you'll see to my freedom?" From the first day he'd arrived at court, already carefully dressed in the queen's favored attire, Zahria paid special attention to how he wooed others at court, all the while omitting much of his own origins and accomplishments. In some respects, he'd appeared in the Hall of Kings much like a ghost. Some cunning spirit of Osolda, for Zahria had seen the gleam of his eyes when the queen spoke. She knew what admiration looked like, and Alistair had never borne a trace. "Will you stand in my way should I give the queen what she wants, Lord Alistair?"

"You are not the only soul in Osolda in dire need of liberation. The difference between the queen and myself is that I ask you to heal the forest rather than strip it from these lands."

She let him go. His boots created a small echo when they touched the ground. "Then you've wasted your time. It cannot be done."

"Do you know what is said about you, Huntress?" he said, smoothing out the crinkled lines of his black collar. "They say the queen was seduced by a spirit of the wild. A forest sprite. They say this is why you do not age at her side. If the queen lives so long and so imperviously because of her magic, they say you also live because of your own. I've watched you," he continued, taking a step away from the wall. Zahria was forced to move back. "I've partied to your hunts in the Unforeseen Forest. Your methods of tracking and scenting. The way you move. What is this, if not magic? It is the first I've seen that does not require more of the lifeblood of this kingdom. Yours is a magic that can heal Osolda's wounds."

"Not magic. I was blessed by my gods," muttered Zahria, and her gods felt more distant than ever before. Saving a kingdom held even less appeal than somehow begging their forgiveness. "Leave it to an Osoldan not to know the difference."

"The queen believes you can rid us of the forest. Why?"

"Go back to your clandestine meetings, Alistair."

"Why?"

When next she freed her dagger, it flew for Alistair's neck. The blade wedged his collar to stone. Moonlight fretted over him, illuminating his finery.

Zahria enjoyed seeing him powerless. "Good night, my lord."

"You asked if I would stop you," he said quietly as she turned her back. "I will."

Zahria allowed him a glimpse of her smile. "This wretched kingdom will collapse long before you do."

"I don't understand, Huntress," he called as she left him. "I have what you seek."

"No," said Zahria, hands itching for a wineskin, "you only thought you did."

Freedom wasn't all that would save her soul. She was starting to wonder if such a thing were even possible any longer. But Zahria knew she'd never again take anything from an outstretched hand when there were strings attached.

THE GOD of storms was giving her a deserved beating. It took a moment for Zahria to realize that dawn was fast-approaching. She wouldn't have even been out in this tearing wind if she had simply waited for morning to pass.

Her head churned as thunder spiked. She'd given in and stopped at a tavern before she had set out. The wineskin she'd purchased was all but empty at her side.

Her horse bucked beneath her. It took all of her muddled concentration to cling to its sides as the sky snapped its temper. "Steady," she ordered her stolen mount. The soldiers responsible for its safekeeping had been throwing dice down for bets, which meant she'd been able to sidle into the lower stables despite her drunkenness. "If you live," she said, "I promise to name you." When the horse whinnied a protest, she said, "No? Not interested in my friendship? Well, then."

Her dismount was clumsy, reckless. She crumpled into a pile of sodden clothes and tangled hair, mud splattering her face. Her arms trembled as she rose up, but she told herself it was because she needed to train her muscles to do things like saving her from her impulses again. "On with you," she shouted at the horse. "You needn't suffer this anymore."

The horse snorted, stamping its foot. Mud hit one of her little silver idols. When she looked down, the god of forests' blank eyes peered at her through the mud. "I think I'll call you Heathen," she told the horse. She dragged at its reins, but it refused to move. Its stubbornness would have made her laugh if they weren't both caught by the hooks of a summer storm. Dusk was turning the world into toasted ash. She didn't want to anger the sun god on top of everything else.

But where could she go?

Even in her bedraggled state, she'd chosen to veer away from Greyhold altogether. She had seen its valiant spark in the distance, but couldn't bring herself to follow it. Should beasts actually make an appearance, the garrison city's needs could be met without calling on the men and women behind its stone walls. Men and women she had cost something dear. She had cut west, straight for the forest, in the hopes she would never have to see their lost expressions. The trees were still a good distance ahead, but even that was more of a comfort than it should have been. She could at least find refuge from the storm in the forest, though shelter was a different matter.

She tugged on the horse hard enough to send herself sprawling again. Her bow creaked when she landed. When she lifted her head, she thought she saw sandaled feet. She rolled onto her back and rainwater made an image of her sister. Jenya looked down at her with fierce contempt, her priestess markings sliding down her face like tears. It was the kind of bracing look she gave when Zahria was in need of motivation. It was made up of guilt and demand and Zahria had never been able to hold herself back from either when they came from Jenya.

"But you're not real," she murmured, her hand wobbling as it rose to touch her sister's hem.

And the truth sliced her heart. Because, indeed, the vision of her sister was nothing more than a rush of water slipping between her fingers.

She would just lie here then. Perhaps the storm would drown her and that would finally put an end to things.

Heathen let out something like a squeal. Squelching sounds were approaching, horseshoes meeting mud under the whip of the wind. Zahria didn't bother lifting her head.

"Well, well, well."

Pressed against the earth the way Zahria was, she could sense eight horses, all with masters astride them. She wondered how they had spotted her in the smoke of the wind and the blaze of the sky. "You knew I was coming," she said after a moment.

"We were warned you might come this way. We watched for you." Booted feet landed beside Zahria's head. When she looked up, Ardith knelt beside her, a girl made up of hard falls behind a smooth face. She teetered over the edge more than a soldier should, but Zahria had always liked her unpredictability—even now, with Ardith twirling a knife between her fingers, her eyes sheened black by the storm. "Avoiding something, Zahria?"

Zahria understood. *Alistair*. She had to admire a nobleman who kept his promises. But how had he gotten word to Greyhold so quickly?

She rolled over to her side and spotted Dell in Ardith's party. She quickly recognized many of the faces there. She'd exchanged a word with some, gambled with others. But she wasn't surprised to see they had run out of welcome and cheer.

She grinned at Ardith and picked up a strand of the girl's hair, letting it spill like black paint across her palm. "Did you miss me, beautiful?"

A backhand cracked across her cheek. The flare of pain woke up her senses, but she laid back, laughter pouring out. "My sweet demon, are you still angry with me?" This time it was a kick to her hip. She hissed. "Kicking someone while they're down, Ardith? Now *that* isn't like you. Are you going to disappoint me?"

"You will say nothing," Ardith spat, her voice hitching. "*Nothing.* I owe you nothing. You do not deserve honor."

"Funny thing about honor," Zahria said softly, "It's personal. You only hurt your own, Ardith."

Ardith slid her knife back into the sheath strapped to her thigh. "Get her on a horse. We ride for Greyhold." She knelt down again. "If you struggle, I will save Lord Alistair the trouble of killing you."

"That's what you want? Go on then," said Zahria. "I don't want to go to Greyhold."

"You will face your sins, the witch-queen's favorite or no."

"Haven't you heard? The queen and I have parted ways." Zahria turned her face up. "Do you not know me after all, Ardith?" Zahria allowed her faint smile to collect the rain. "I will not face anything."

"Get up."

"I know very well what I did. The young general is dead," Zahria said to the violence turning over the sky. "I killed him. Your mentor. Your friend." She heard Dell dismount. Heard his sword come free. "Where is *his* honor, I wonder?"

When he swung for her, Ardith blocked his blade. Their swords locked in the rain, harsh breaths filling the silence.

Zahria pushed to her feet. She met Dell's light eyes over Ardith's dark head. He had grown from boy to man and his movements just then had been graceful. He'd finally learned how to meld with his sword. She remembered how he used to wrestle with his arms and walk like there was cotton stuffed in his boots. Dell had come to Greyhold like wet wood. There were still many outer layers for his superiors to cut through before they might have found kindling. Now, he stood with the rain melting off his skin, his gaze like smoke.

"I told you," Zahria said to them both, "honor is personal. You don't have the right to kill me. But... I'll allow it, just this once."

"I'd like nothing more," Ardith growled, "but we're under orders."

"Then you should understand," Zahria said quietly. "I was ordered to kill him."

"You had more than that." The words dropped from Dell's mouth like leaves catching the wind. They cut as they blew past. "Now you have nothing. You're not one of us. You never were."

Hurt rippled like a confused substance with nowhere to go. There was plenty of space inside her, but what right did she have to claim the ache? She'd heard the whispers these last years since she'd murdered the general. He had been an idealist and he hadn't been quiet about it. Word had spread quickly that he'd been rallying support not just in Greyhold, but in the farming villages under constant threat of attack by the beasts of the Unforeseen Forest. Farmers and millers and smiths who stubbornly clung to their village livelihoods instead of the lustrous promises of the city had pitched forward like water. They had been dammed so long, it hadn't taken much to fill up a cause that seemed to hold true.

The subversion hadn't lasted. The tide had barely impacted the ivory towers of Luren. By the time Zahria had cut General Tristan's throat, resistance against the queen was no more than a slow, meek trail from a blocked valve. By the time she had realized what she had done, and who she had become, clarity came like a curse. Zahria never expected it to take root and darken her view of the world.

She blamed the queen for the order. Liana had made

Zahria believe her life was threatened, and, in most ways, that was true. But, in the end, defending Liana's life hadn't rung of justice. Instead, all Zahria was left with were the dim echoes of Tristan clinging to his draining life.

She instinctively reached for her wineskin, then remembered it was all but empty. "You can blame me," she told Dell. "I spend so much time blaming the queen, I have no time to take responsibility."

Ardith opened her mouth to speak, but then *they* lunged from the darkness of the forest just as the sky began to lighten.

And Zahria hadn't sensed *them*.

A horse roared. Its panic sparked wild abandon in the others.

Just as one man was shoved from his seat, a wooly mouth leaped to tear out his throat.

"Swords!" Ardith shouted. "Swords, now!"

Zahria's movements were fluid as she drew her bow from her back. She notched twin arrowheads and watched them fly into the skull of a charging beast.

WERE HER POWERS FADING? Had the gods finally abandoned her?

Zahria should have *sensed* them. Thoughts with the same frantic beat pounded her head as her arrows cut a swath in the direction of the beasts tearing the ground.

Asarak. Her people would have called them demons.

Gods, was that her hand trembling on the grip? She couldn't already be tiring.

"Dell!" Ardith shouted. Her dark hair flew like a banner as she thrust herself between beast and comrade. Her sword came up, reflecting the vicious snarl of the beast before her. "Get behind me, Dell."

"I'm not green anymore, Ardith."

Together they plunged forward.

"Zahria," Ardith called back, grunting as her sword drew blood. "How is this possible?"

She didn't know. The beasts weren't supposed to rise at dawn. Her arms weren't supposed to strain from exertion. "Didn't I tell you its bad form to talk in battle?"

When she didn't hear an answer, she turned back to see Ardith's breath explode as teeth sank into her arm. Dell had his own demons to face, but panic spread across his face. "Ardith!"

Zahria moved before the next beast could engage her. She flipped over the back of one, stomped the head of another. She shot up in the air. Her arrows flew at the peak of her jump. There was a wet snap as steel entered flesh and Ardith's attacker collapsed.

Zahria's landing sent pain shooting up her legs and she fell forward. She fisted her hands in grass wet with blood instead of dew. "What's happening?" she muttered.

These were reactions she had never experienced. She was graceful in battle and even more so in the thick of a hunt. For the first time in her life, Zahria felt sweat running down her cheeks. She reeked of fear. Her vision was gray.

It took her too long to distinguish the gray came from the cloaks around her and not a fainting spell. The thought wasn't much reassurance. She remembered asking Tristan why he and his comrades represented themselves so plain.

"Is it only to stand apart from the queen's guard?"

"So curious about our ways." His eyes had twinkled. He always seemed to be on the verge of smiling despite the dark cast over his habitual dealings. "Are you a spy?"

"I revel in your humor."

He winked at her. "It's to ward off death."

Zahria cocked her head. When she thought about it, the Osol-dans had no death saint. Perhaps that was why they lost all color when death left a body behind. They did not know the soul was often led to where it was meant to return. Time and place did not alter that. "But how does this help you?"

"Well death is attracted to life, is it not?" *he said, another smile tipping over the first.* "And is life not full of color?"

Red joined the gray. Bodies were falling around her. Ardith had come with eight and now only four remained, she and Dell among the count. Zahria did not know if the god of death was indeed attracted to color, but she aimed to stop him before he lured those who had once been friends away from the battlefield.

"Pull back!" Zahria shouted over the din of desperate snarls and tiring defense. "Pull back!"

Ardith's head sprang up from stabbing down on her prey. "We will not leave you here."

"You're outnumbered." Zahria shot a beast just as it lunged for her. White eyes rolled back.

"We have *orders*."

Zahria turned away from shooting another creature and aimed her arrow at Ardith. "*Go,*" she snapped. "Or I will kill you myself."

Ardith's disgust formed a word in the silence. *Murderer.* Zahria refused to allow it to sink in and make a mockery of whatever remained of her soul. "Do I have to count?" she shouted.

Dell yanked on Ardith's bleeding shoulder. One of the other soldiers carried the last, whose blood fell from her side.

The beasts tried to give chase, but Zahria barred them. Muttering silent prayers to her gods, she let each arrow fly in a succession that tore at her screaming muscles.

Ardith whistled for the horses when they were a good distance. To Zahria's surprise, Heathen remained, forcing her to protect him.

The first dawn she had allowed herself in over a century

kissed her neck, rising over her head in increments that caused her prayers to shoot faster from her lips. Her arrows could not keep up with the words. She only hoped the sun god would protect her despite her sin.

Asarak. She could almost hear her gods urging her movements, blessing her with precision despite the numbness in her arms. *Defeat the demons of the poisoned dark.*

When there were only breathless carcasses at her feet, she sank to the ground. Her knees drowned in mud and ichor. She breathed in death after hours without food or water and forced herself not to gag.

She picked up her wineskin and shook out the last drops into her mouth. Her stomach roiled, begging her for something more soothing.

A wren landed on the dead body of one of Osolda's beasts. The strangeness of seeing it there, in austere whites and violets, had her focusing. "You're no ordinary bird," she told it, still panting from her efforts. She had yet to regain feeling in her hands.

The wren said nothing. She liked to think its silence was for self-preservation, but she could barely take a step in its direction.

Once, she had come to this country layered in the furs of all her game, coins from every known port clinking along her waist. There was no company, no opportunity or entertainment her skill could not afford.

And, over the course of a century, Liana had stripped Zahria of all those proud layers, leaving her with only... *this.* This woman who felt broken after her first taste of death since she'd killed a man who had considered her a friend. She'd allowed Liana's elegant hands to go unspoiled while dried blood mottled her own. While she cringed at the thought of the woman she used to be—a version of herself who would ultimately lead her here.

Her eyes felt bruised. Her body spent. She forced herself to stand despite the exhaustion whittling her down to nothing but cold, weary bones.

She didn't know if she'd crumble to dust the moment she destroyed the forest and ran for the clearing beyond. But she was so tired. She was past caring if it was death that would finally set her free from this excuse for a country.

She rose up on unsteady feet. The weight of past sins made it more difficult.

Her gods were abandoning her. If she was to be abandoned, that meant she had nothing inside her worth redeeming. There was relief in that. All that was left was that elusive taste of freedom, waiting for her in the outstretched arms of the trees.

She turned to Heathen. "Wait here," she said softly. If she lived through this last hunt, she'd take him with her. "If you're so inclined."

The horse said nothing, but she could feel its eyes on her back as she entered the Unforeseen Forest.

STRANDS of summer heat filtered through the cold bogging down the forest. Zahria wished its icy nature made it less luminous, that the gray stalks of the trees looked sickly rather than polished. The forest would haunt her with its defiant beauty.

You're here.

Finally.

Come closer.

We must tell you...

Zahria rooted inside her for breath. She grew impatient waiting to be soothed by the sounds of her body and drew a knife, twin to the one that had hopefully kept Alistair pinned until he was found and questioned.

Perhaps the queen had killed him. Zahria shook away the

thought. It evoked too much of Liana in a place where Zahria was supposed to feel safe, most like herself.

It seems your duty remains here in Osolda, Huntress.

That was the last thing Zahria believed, and yet, she was combing through a dying forest to vanquish beasts on Liana's order. This had to be the last time she bowed. This was her only freedom from the very kingdom she couldn't seem to escape.

Twigs snapped. Her boots kicked small rocks. She cast a suspicious glance at every shuffle that did not belong to her.

Gods, this wasn't her. Here she was, a huntress of her caliber, quivering every time the forest's skirts lifted in the wind, scattering lichen. She was supposed to expand on a mission and become something greater than herself. Excitement was supposed to seep into her, fueling instinct. She had always been the sum of something that had little to do with fear.

But she was afraid now.

The air was fertile with pleading whispers. They floated through Zahria's mind like spiraling leaves.

We have so much to tell you...

"Enough," she snarled at the trees, wincing at the amber stems of light poking through the spaces between the boughs. The sun god was weaving a curse for her wine-soaked brain, pricking her eyesight and knotting a headache. Those insistent whispers clawed, snagging on that knot. She didn't have time for ill will from the divine. She didn't have time for a forest she didn't want to understand. "I'm not going to rid the world of you yet."

First, she had beasts to track.

The pack that had attacked Ardith's hunting party had likely been scouting an area to den. The scent of human prey had lured them away from settling down at dawn. How they were capable of *leaving* the forest when daylight had begun to smear the sky was still a mystery, but Zahria hoped their patterns had remained otherwise the same.

Asarak traveled in small groups. They were rarely encumbered with young. And their sleep was just deep enough at this hour for Zahria to make several easy kills.

She just needed to find them.

When she'd defended Ardith and Dell, the beasts had howled. Not long sounds, but deep and brief. And yet no other packs had come to their aid.

She had some distance to go, then, before she'd find the first den.

Cocking her head, Zahria listened for water. She could never miss the way a rivulet smothered a twig cracking or a day bird flitting. Nuances of forest sounds stuck in her like spurs. Ever since she could remember, Zahria had known the difference between the rain god's crying and the gently drowning tongue of a stream. As soon as she dismissed the pleas of the trees, she could hear the faint blue gurgle of a river or lake.

A lost echo always had a source. She followed its trail.

Rain darkened the sky, forcing her vision to adjust. A wet pine smell fretted beneath her nose.

She didn't often mind the dark, but today there seemed to be a plot against her. Some cosmic decree that kept her from feeling truly sure of her footsteps. Nature had never been so compelled to hinder her before. Ancient stretches of wilderness had never made her feel like a frightened guest. And yet her footsteps were hesitant, as if she were a poorly hidden thorn hedging the seams between the trees. She could be wrenched free at any moment, made to stand bare and vulnerable to judgement.

You do not deserve honor.

Ardith had meant those words. They had carved something cruel into her beauty. She had been living with that painful sentiment until she had seen Zahria again. That was how

Ardith dealt with anguish. She made sure she passed it onto others. She'd likely given Dell a taste these last few years. Perhaps that was why he had stared at Zahria like an open wound. Seeing her for the first time since she had killed Tristan had been a slow-motion punch through mottled scar tissue.

"Curse you, Liana," Zahria murmured, her feet carrying her over a fallen stump. She had not become all that she was without understanding the mechanics of surrender. She had laid herself out for conquest and lost her pride. Friends. Honor. Anger began filling that vast empty space inside her. It pumped hideous images through her. Ways she could make Liana pay, which she might not have considered before. And yet suffering and death were not always exclusively mutual. Who better than she knew that? "You should hope I die before I come to you."

She was careful not to rely on the trees for balance. Their whispers were muddled, but they fuzzed the edges of her mind. It wouldn't take much to give into their pull.

Her distraction cost her a moment of warning.

But she heard it. A footstep out of time with her own. Her knife slowly returned to its sheath.

Then she whirled, her bow sliding down into her hands as though it had been waiting for her summons.

Elina waited on the other end of Zahria's arrow. She peered at Zahria from the mid-branches, bold eyes gleaming with satisfaction. The tension in her body told Zahria she believed she had found a fight she could win.

"It seems," Zahria said, a slight smile warming her lips, "I'm surrounded by fools today."

"I pity the company you keep."

"No need. I excel at teaching the foolish to be less so."

"And yet you come to this place," Elina said in tones befitting a death lament. Her voice held a thrush of winter at odds with the way her sea-storm eyes crackled. "And think yourself better than a fool."

"The queen would see you dead," Zahria said, dropping her smile. "Don't force me to give her what she wants."

"Do you think I'd be here if I thought you could give the witch-queen what she wanted?"

An arrow slid free.

Leaves spun into the air.

Elina hadn't had time to move. If Zahria had made her a target, the shot would have taken an eye.

"That was a warning," said Zahria, notching the next arrow. Her fingers had regained some of their strength after the morning, but just looking at Elina made her tired. The girl was so young. Beneath the natural command in her words and the pulse of ice in her voice, she was earnest. She wanted something from Zahria. And while helping a traitor might have once appealed, Zahria did not give easily anymore. "Fly away, little bird. I have more important things to do."

Elina shifted forms. Zahria quickly lost sight of her.

She returned her bow to the company of her quiver and kept walking.

The ground stirred beneath her feet, stealing her balance.

She caught herself before landing on the ground, but the sound of the earth coming undone heightened. The forest coughed an angry rumble.

And Elina appeared before her.

Zahria paused in her next step. She carefully removed her knife from her belt, turning it over in her palm. "Do you really want to challenge me, little bird?"

Elina cocked her head.

And released a twinned pair of knives of her own into her palms.

Zahria stared. Incredulity tugged a small laugh out of her. "Are you any good with those?"

Elina spun the handles with little effort. She tossed one at Zahria, catching her off guard.

Zahria watched tiny, tawny strands of her hair flutter to the soil.

Elina waited for Zahria to meet her gaze. "You need to listen to me."

This time Zahria sent *her* knife flying. She'd been waiting for Elina to speak. Marring Zahria's hair was a personal offense. Her patience had snapped. The knife sliced a cut across Elina's cheek. "You're—" Blood bloomed a narrow path across Elina's skin. "—in—" Elina blocked Zahria, swinging with her remaining knife. "—my—" Zahria dodged the knife and hooked a forearm around her prey's neck from behind. "—way."

Elina's color rose. Her frantic inhales turned to coughs.

Zahria didn't intend to kill her. She pressed down on Elina's head with her other arm. She only needed a few moments to get the girl unconscious.

But before Elina's eyes rolled back, the ground erupted.

Tree roots spiked up toward Zahria's legs, wrapping around her torso.

The next thing she knew, she was dangling in the air.

"THERE'S NO POINT IN STRUGGLING."

Zahria glared down at Elina. If the girl's bout of coughing had gone on longer, Zahria might have been mollified. But as things were, her hair was dipping into mud. She curled her fists at her own helplessness. She tried for calm. "Well," she drawled, careful not to touch the spokes of her trap. "You certainly have my attention. What message have you for me, little bird?"

The girl couldn't help herself. She liked the idea of Zahria being helpless. Having the upper hand had caused her to grin, though it didn't make the shape of her mouth more or less pleasant. She walked to Zahria's prone body and lifted her silver statues to eye level. "Your gods?" she said.

"I wouldn't," warned Zahria. "But I *would* start praying if I were you."

"Why's that?"

"Because the god of souls is about to receive another visitor."

Elina laughed a little. "You were testing me, weren't you?" she said, stroking the face of the forest god. She stepped back and the trees oriented Zahria upright. Zahria's head swooned. "During Luren's celebrations, when you pulled me away from the crowds. You weren't really drunk."

"Little bird, I am a hopeless drunk." It was Elina's turn to glare. "But I will say those in the queen's service fear almost anything without being told. You were too angry to be afraid and that made you suspicious." Zahria smiled. "If it helps, I found you terribly attractive."

"It doesn't," Elina said flatly.

"*Shame*," said Zahria. It was no trouble to rake her gaze from top to bottom. It gave her the satisfaction of Elina's bright blush. "We never did have that dance."

"Is this how you take back your advantage? Flirting with your captors?"

"Seems to me the trees are my captor. You're just a *very* attractive mouth-piece. Are you going to have your way with me now, little bird?"

Elina caught herself before she sputtered.

Zahria admired that small sign of the girl's control. She dropped her teasing and asked what was truly on her mind. "Who are *you*?"

Those seaglass eyes sharpened. "I am Elina of the Nightingales."

"No," said Zahria, echoing their time at Red Saint's Day. "*Who* are you?" She understood that the question had been

126

acknowledging more than the obvious signs of Zahria's otherness. Elina had sensed something of Zahria's place in her world and had been confused by her presence. Zahria found that she was intrigued by the same questions. "You're more than just Sky Clan, aren't you?"

"*Clans* of the *skies*." The emphasis held a bit of temper, though it did little to hide the bitterness in the statement. Listening to the words, Zahria recalled the feeling of broken weeping and wanted to turn away from even the hint of another's sorrow. Her throat suddenly slaked with thirst. She wished her wineskin full. "Though I doubt that would make much difference to you," said Elina. "My people are leaving Osolda. Some have decided to take their chances in the mountains, though many of them will likely die from the transition. Others are beginning to scatter."

"They let a little thing like you face me alone? Or perhaps you thought you could handle me all by yourself?"

"I wasn't wrong, was I?" Elina gave a pointed glance to Zahria's entanglement.

"Why track me down at all?" This piece of them all did not fit into the puzzle of Elina.

"Because the forest asked me to. It cries out your name."

Zahria's breath caught. She didn't realize she was holding it until the lack of air stung her chest.

"You're right about one thing," said Elina, staring up at the trees. "I'm not the one doing this. They need your help."

"Not my problem," Zahria finally choked out.

"You keep telling yourself that," said Elina gravely. "But do you really believe your own words? You see, I've learned many things about you, Huntress. We have eyes and ears inside that palace. Your queen thinks herself untouchable, but you know how wrong she is. You've seen the way enemies have begun flocking to her like hawks. They're already calculating their first true strike."

This time, Zahria's laugh was almost hysterical. "If you think you're going to threaten me by threatening the queen's life, then you know much less than you think you do."

Elina waited for Zahria to quiet. "I know you still care." Silence bore down on them both with enough weight to make their breaths deepen. "But if I could kill the queen, I would have already done so. I know you still care," Elina repeated. "You see, those eyes and ears tell me how you share wine with the thirsty and spare coin for the beggars. Simple kindnesses, really. These things don't have to mean what they seem. But I also know how kindness costs you when rage follows your shadow. I know how badly you want to see this kingdom fall, if only so you could escape. Have your freedom. And yet, while you might have taken coin and drink for your skills in the forests of the world, you're sworn to your gods. You can't help but find compassion for every tangled thicket and soft cry that comes from the darkness between these trees."

"I came," Zahria said, her head light, her breath unsteady, her voice sharper than an arrowhead, "to *destroy* this place."

The wind stirred the voices fighting for intrusion. Zahria's eyes pressed shut.

"You only thought you did," said Elina. The words chilled the sweat on Zahria's skin. She wondered if this was Alistair's feeling behind his mask of indifference the day she had left. "I'm going to show you how much you still care. I'm going to show you what your queen was accomplishing while you hid in your wineskins. I'm going to *make* you feel my pain."

"Do you think you can?" Zahria choked out. She hadn't considered the girl might have a stomach for torture. It took an intimacy with a kind of pain that no bandage could muffle to dole it out in kind.

And here Zahria was, shriveling from her fear again. This was what Elina had hoped for. Somehow, she had known Zahria's weakness was like a second skin. Fleshy, pink, new. It wouldn't take much to draw out what lay beneath. Zahria twisted inside the spindly arms of the tree's roots. She stretched her body downward and reached for the knife in her left boot. She had had enough of this.

"I wouldn't do that if I were you," Elina said softly. "They're coming."

The slow rise of the moon did not comfort Zahria. "What in the *hells* are you talking about?"

"You must have heard the screams over the years." Elina's face was set, hard. "You should have asked your queen then."

THEY ROSE UP like an endless fleet of chestnut sails.

They cut through the smoke of the night—a razor-tipped blockade of the moon and stars, sweeping through the uppermost tiers of the trees. Their yellow gazes swelled with malice in the darkness, their beaks viciously curved and bright.

The trees had formed a lattice of boughs over Zahria. When Elina followed, a kind of entrance had shut behind her. Zahria's panic burst thin trails of sweat down her back. She couldn't see a way out, except for seeds of moonlight dotting the lacing of the wood above her.

"You wanted me to see owls," Zahria spoke with a deadly softness.

"Look closer," said Elina.

The small dots allowing her to see into the night expanded to spots. Owl bodies sailed over the spaces for Zahria's sight, graceful as silent arrows. She saw what Elina wanted her to see.

There were remnants of human skin burrowed into their feathers. Their shadows were actually a part of their width— they were larger than any owls Zahria had ever seen. They were bloated with Liana's magic. When they did not find what they were looking for, the cries they made sounded human... yet wrong. These creatures were not like Elina.

"If I were to kill one of them now," Elina murmured, "there would be a human shape for a few moments. And then the beasts of this forest would fight over the crumbs of blood and bone left behind."

"They cannot switch their forms," said Zahria.

"No," Elina said, a mournful note in her voice, "they cannot. The queen has petrified them somewhere between the two. Easier to control them like this."

"I give my sympathy," said Zahria, with no shortage of reluctance. "But this doesn't change my mission. I'm sorry you thought it would, little bird."

The fibrous hold on her limbs suddenly dispersed, sinking back into the earth. Zahria stared down at the ground for a moment, then up at Elina. Perhaps that roiling gaze had scared the god of forest herself.

Elina snatched Zahria's collar. "You *have* to do something," she spat. "You have the power to help us. Help this entire wretched kingdom."

Zahria shoved her away. "You think you know something about me?" An amulet sea drifted above them, prisms of moonlight changing the hue of the leaves and filtering the colors into the underbelly of this insular world. Frustration was ripe in the air and not all of it came from Elina. But Zahria just didn't care. She wouldn't stop herself now. "You're so clever, are you? Do you think I would waste my birthright on this *godsforsaken* land? I don't care for your clans or your wars. I don't care about the people fooled or afeared by the queen's power."

Elina struck out. Zahria barely had time to block. Feeling was slowly returning to her limbs.

"Then what *do* you care about?" Elina hissed. "Shall I steal coin for you? Kill men for you? What will it take?" She swept past Zahria's defenses. "Name your price."

Zahria's hand wrapped around Elina's neck. She lifted her off her toes. Elina struggled for breath, twisting to kick Zahria in her side.

Zahria deflected. She wanted to snap the girl's neck. Her gods-blessed strength hadn't completely drained away. It would be easy. Elina used her nails to pry her way free but Zahria clung tighter, until Elina's veins strained. Her death would be so easy.

But that had been her mistake before. Thinking that because her life had extended so long, one death wouldn't poison the current of it. She remembered Tristan as Elina's eyes bulged, and the way his skin had gone ashen. The way his gaze lost light. The way his mouth, forever curved in some kind of smile, slackened. Even when she had taken the lives of her quarry, the choice had never been made lightly. She hadn't wasted a soul. The sport wasn't in the killing, but the skill it took to see it done for reasons that meant a village had meat or a shivering child had a coat. She had never been meant to deal out death and judgement this way. She was never meant to take a *human* life.

She still hadn't forgiven herself the offense.

Her head bent. Her hand shook above Elina's collarbone. The weight of her own betrayal made her drop it altogether.

But Elina gathered her breath back. Her fury had not been doused by a lack of air.

Before Zahria could defend against the blow, Elina had punched her hard enough to fall back into the base of the tree protecting them. Her hands slapped bark and she tasted blood.

Then her gods-given gift erupted.

At first, the sensations were as gentle as sleep kissing her brow. The world was but a whisper of a hand stroking her hair.

Then that world jerked her into awareness. She entered a waking dream of lush nightfalls, swept cool with midnight rain. Hot stars and laughter and wisps of long hair clinging to silk pillows. Weathered faces ringed in welcoming smiles. Secret sips of a ginger sun in the window.

She remembered her home. A place where banyans clustered around a secret living behind a temple. A place where magic lived a simple life, and yet burned like a lightning pulse if you got too near.

She saw her mother's tired face, stretched thin by time and work that curved her back. She saw herself as a young girl, dewy-eyed and near-frantic to live inside the stories her great uncle had told of a world so vast, its people took on all manner of shapes and colors. She saw Jenya taking the steps of the match-making temple two at a time, eager to pluck the gods from the walls like golden fruit.

Sometimes, in their homeland, you could catch a glimpse of them. They speckled themselves with moonlight and rain, but if you looked closely, night turned supple and vigilant. If you looked closely, flecks of strange light turned into eyes staring back at you.

She *missed* that.

Zahria wanted to tear herself open and let her screams loose. She wanted to burden the trees for holding the relics of her history and sharing them as though they had a right. Elina had asked her to redeem the land, but redemption wasn't available upon request. This forest hadn't earned the right. This forest was poisoned and beyond help. Just look at its cruelty.

Zahria was tired of living in the excess of cruelty. She was tired of being a victim of the gods, this land, her own ill-conceived ideas and impulses. What she had become had been nurtured inside the queen's selfish embrace. If the forest could be cruel, so could she.

Her eyes sprang open. A white film changed Elina's face.

She was a wraith haunting Zahria in the present. A curse from the gods made flesh to remind her of her many sins.

"Get me out." The strain behind the words drained her body of strength.

Help us.

We have something to tell you...

"No," she moaned. This wasn't her responsibility. The faults of this kingdom were not for her to mend. She just wanted to be free of demands that kept her so far from home. "No. Destroy you."

She hissed out a panicked breath, her body a bow snapped taut.

And then she was free. Falling. The taste of soil hit her tongue. Gentle hands turned her body over.

"Zahria," Elina shouted. "Zahria. You're all right. *Zahria.*"

She sucked in a harsh breath, her body bolting up from the ground.

Elina's head dipped as Zahria taught herself to breathe again.

"I didn't know that would happen," said Elina.

"What, pray tell," Zahria said, still panting, "did you think would happen?"

Elina evaded the question. "What did you see?"

"Nothing that's any business of yours." Zahria's temper had never needed much kindling. Helplessness was the quickest way to set it alight. She let it blaze. "I *will* kill you."

She noticed then that Elina's hands were bloodied. Had she dug Zahria out of the tree's clutches? Her temper towered higher. Heat crept into her thoughts, emblazoning all the ways she had lost scraps of her pride over the span of an unwanted century. There had been almost nothing left when the tree had reached for her, but Elina had stripped her of even the ghost of dignity.

She rose. Unsteadily, but she managed it.

"I'm sorry," Elina murmured.

There was no guile in the words. No expectation of Zahria caving to forgiveness. Once again there was that sense of acknowledgment. Elina left nothing to the shadows in their shared silence. Whatever she thought, she revealed. Even if it cowed her.

Zahria didn't like seeing Elina repentant. Not when she blazed this hot. She wanted someone to combat her, to give her purpose for this fury that had suddenly awakened. A part of her was relieved to feel the burn of it. It meant that something within her still cared enough to breathe fire.

"Zahria, I'm sorry."

She couldn't handle the flush of guilt on top of everything else. She didn't know if Elina was wrong to apologize to her. She only knew she couldn't bear this sudden, inexplicable gentling in the clanswoman.

Her hands reached for Elina's face.

She heard a sharp intake of breath, like leaves rustling before settling again.

"I don't want you to be sorry," Zahria snapped, the world still tinged in feverish scarlet.

Her mouth found Elina's. Not soft. Not tentative. Tongues of heat laved her skin, coaxing the fire in her to a more indulgent place. She demanded a clash from Elina's lips. She savored the taste of her own desire, using it as an excuse to have what hadn't been offered.

Elina snapped them apart. Zahria looked down at the hand digging a bruise into her chest. Her breath was still laced with want. Her heart still pounded with need. She wondered what Elina felt with her hand pressed against its beat.

Recovery was quicker for Elina than for her. "I might have done the same sooner or later," she sneered. "To scratch an itch."

Zahria's brow lifted. "I make you itchy. Interesting."

"We're all itchy," Elina deadpanned. "But I'm usually choosier about my scratching partner."

"You angered me."

"And there, you got your revenge." The clanswoman crossed her arms over her chest. Zahria thought that she suddenly looked very young. Guilt flared brighter. "Satisfied?"

"Not nearly, little bird," Zahria crooned. Damned if she would apologize. "But I have too many beasts to dispatch. Sadly, I don't have time to play with you."

"You'll still set about the queen's task." The statement was flat, devoid of emotion. But Elina couldn't help a gleam of disgust in those seaglass eyes. "I don't understand you."

"And why should you? You can't imagine what I've done in her name. How the choices I made took something from me." Zahria sighed. It burned her chest. "I'll tell you something else, Elina of the Nightingales." She brushed away bits of growing things stuck to her clothing. "The way to catch prey is hidden in their desires. If you don't know what they want, then you can't coax them. You can't anticipate what they'll do next."

Walking over to the tree that had burdened her with visions she'd have rather not seen, she rested her palm against its rugged surface. The bark sang beneath her hand, plucking a rumble from the earth.

A cavity reluctantly opened in the net of its limbs. The dark hollow on the other side was spotted with starlight and empty of owls.

She turned to Elina, whose eyes were wider than moonbeams in an open valley. "When you think you've won," she said, turning back to her escape, "the beast will show you otherwise."

Leaves prickled her skin as she passed through the opening. Damp, wet earth conjured a sharper smell than before. The wind lingered in her hair. Moonlight rendered a milky path in the soil.

Zahria rubbed her still-tingling palm. It had been so long since she'd embraced the power inside her. She didn't turn around. Instead, she followed the sound of the water's song. It was no longer frail and faint in her ears. The flow of it reached inside her, dancing over something just beginning to bloom after a long sleep.

∼

"REALLY?" said Zahria to undulating shadows clouding the canopies above her. "You're going to follow me?"

Something expanded in those shadows. A small implosion. Zahria realized Elina had shifted forms to do her stalking.

"We have no need of drunken, useless cowards in my world," Elina called down. "Go back to yours, or give me the satisfaction of chasing you out. Your choice."

"You want to threaten someone, look them in the eye until they believe they have a reason to fear," Zahria said. "So much to learn, little bird. Then again, it wouldn't make much of a difference. We'd likely end up right back where we were. And I have a feeling that's not where you want to go."

She couldn't see Elina blush. But she imagined her cheeks ripened to peaches. It gave her a reason to smile a little.

They were close. The beasts. She could all but feel them stirring in their dens now that the moon hung high.

The sensations of the forest belted through her senses, awakening feelings that had wilted with time behind a city made of mountain-stone. Her bones felt strong and fresh, like new spring growth. If she could eat this feeling and keep it inside her forever, she would. She didn't want to go back to being emptiness writhing inside living skin. For the first time since she'd set out on her journey, she felt hope rouse at the thought of her own future.

"You can't go back to the way things were," Elina called

down, closer than before. "The past haunts you, but it can never take shape and sit beside you. Not even returning to your homeland will change that. If it even exists."

Zahria's fists squeezed hard. "Last warning, Elina. Go away."

Careful. Take care.

Gnarled whispers spoke from the knowing depths of the forest. She couldn't ignore their tenor of alarm.

Careful.

Leaves exploded. She heard Elina's gasp hit the air.

A piercing screech echoed in the darkness.

Claws raked through Zahria's hair before passing over her. She spun around.

Owls circled Elina, tightening a band around her frantic movements. Lashing at her body. Clipping their beaks until blood fell.

She fell out of the trees.

And didn't transform.

There was a sickening thud as her body cracked against the ground, her face in bloody ribbons.

Zahria had her bow in hand before she'd realized. She was ice in gauging her shot. Water in letting one arrow flow after another. Grounded like the earth as her body moved, her arms moving quicker with each pull and loose.

Bodies slumped and fell through the quiet. Owl screeches spread like flame. Some went airborne. Sleep turned to dust for the true residents of the forest. Howls crested and blended together in the distance.

The beasts would come.

She had to get Elina aboveground.

Rushing forward, she pulled the clanswoman's arm around her neck. She braced, then hefted her weight as gently as she was able. The queen's creatures had nearly removed an arm. And the blood had already made them targets.

Had the owls been tracking Elina or Zahria? Which did the

queen favor more, Zahria's progress or tracking down the traitor who had made a spectacle of Osolda's thrall?

Zahria huffed a breath. It didn't take her long to decide which outcome meant more to Liana.

Snarls erupted at her back. The sensation of being watched shivered against the back of her neck. She couldn't remember ever feeling this vulnerable. Not even in Liana's keeping had Zahria ever felt like prey. That had always been the role of the nobility.

She grasped at bark, imbuing her touch with desperation.

The tree beneath her hand responded. There was a long groan, like abruptly being risen from sleep. She actually felt a twinge of sympathy for the caving bark. This tree was old, older than her.

"Help us," she murmured. Then swallowed. "Please."

Help us.

We have something to tell you...

Will you listen?

Zahria sighed deeply. "I will try," she said. "Now take us up." She might have tried to burrow down in the tree's base like when she was held captive, but she was afraid of what the beasts might do should they snag on the scent of two women lost in a place they each considered a kind of home. The beasts might tear open the trees. Not only would that spell their doom in their weakened state, but Zahria didn't relish the thought of seeing something helpless, though ancient, take the brunt of suffering meant for her. That wasn't who she was anymore. She didn't allow others to pay the price of her sins.

Branches unfurled. They reached for Zahria, careful not to jostle Elina in her arms.

Once aboveground, Zahria settled Elina against the sallow rind of the tree. The beasts were picking up speed down below. If Zahria climbed higher, she could have confirmed their path. Instead, she quickly fashioned a tourniquet from the ends of her tunic for Elina's tattered arm. There was barely a stir from her charge as she worked. Blood seeped outward.

Zahria's hands came away crimson by the time she sat back. She didn't have an ease with healing the way Jenya had. She'd never needed much in the way of remedies or poultices.

If Elina died, Zahria would know blame.

It hadn't been her fault. It hadn't started with her. None of this had. Like with Henul. But, maybe, in the twisted brackets of time, responsibility *did* belong to her. Her choices had been too hard, too arrogant. She'd seen Liana as a prize at first, something dazzling and not unlike her. She'd treated Liana as a mirror and perhaps that was why her reflection had become so distorted she had stopped recognizing herself. Their relationship had been inlaid with a repeating pattern and Zahria's reluctance to see it change cost her principles she had once honored.

She finally felt separate from Liana. A force of her own making.

"Thank you," she said aloud, though she wasn't sure where her gratitude belonged. The gods? Elina? The forest? "Thank you," she repeated, hoping that whatever convergence of deities saw fit to restore her felt her sincerity.

She started to try waking Elina—her lack of consciousness worried Zahria—when a scream cracked open somewhere below.

A thready female sound.

Who would enter this place?

WHORLS OF TREE limbs made Zahria's desire to help seem foolish. They hindered her. Branches tried to fell her. But the scream she had heard had sounded lost and desperate. It had thrummed inside her, resonating with what she had felt in coming here despite all her training and instincts. Whatever the trees had awakened in her—call it compassion or foolishness— prevented Zahria from leaving someone in the mire of their own need.

"Enough," she hissed at the forest as wooden ropes slithered for her feet. She was grateful she'd left Elina behind, instead of risking her further injury. She hated that she felt like an echo, especially when what she needed was silence. *Asarak* hunted the quiver of her breath and the steady softness of her steps. They knew she was a creature made of meat and sinews. They would not rest until their jaws closed over her belly, inhaling her panic and bleeding her body of tension.

Longing for a filled wineskin still nicked her, but she didn't *crave* it. She could withstand the edge, the need to reach for something to balance her.

She kept her posture low. She made herself a ghost. Her boots flattened rain-slick soil in silence. Sage and umber fists coiled from the ground, but Zahria had regained too much of herself to fall prey to gnarled underbrush.

She hoped the wind changed direction and that her scent would follow. The far-off sounds of the beasts' hunger cooled her mind, kept her nimble and careful.

And still she nearly tipped into a bowl of pale blue water. The trees loomed protectively over the lake's restless murmurs. This was the source of water she'd been hunting. Zahria imagined it used to be wide enough to sate the throats of an entire village. Now, only children would find entertainment in its depths.

She could see where the beasts had burrowed for sleep. They had been rough in exiting their den, carving the soil with claws like axes.

A pillar of moonlight shone like quartz over the scarred expanse before her. Her gaze roved until it pinned on the source of the scream.

If the beauty of the forest was made of defiance, the beauty before her was like the night. Stained, bruised, and silvered by the stars. Complicated and unflinching. Zahria's heart hammered.

Liana turned slowly, her hair rippling like a bolt of silk. She wore no crown. Only a bodice of pearls and a skirt of plump white feathers. The amber-tailed bugs pooling above the lake flecked a fragmented glow across her ivory skin. She was a spark of warm ice against the indigo gloam.

"Don't tell me you were the one crying for help." Zahria heard how hoarse the words made her voice, but couldn't find a way to smooth it down. "We both know that isn't like you." Seeing Liana walking toward her, unguarded, Zahria forgot her resolve for one stunned moment. It was enough to give Liana an opening.

"My love," Liana murmured, reaching for Zahria's hands, "I'm sorry."

The world teetered.

But pain kept Zahria standing.

Despite the questions racing through her mind, her hatred didn't dissolve. And yet she could feel a weakening. Like spindles splintering apart, making space for something familiar to enter. But Zahria did not have wine pumping through her blood nor sins burdening her thoughts. It was still impossible to see clearly with beauty this blinding, softness this tempting, but the last half-century had ground out the truth of what Liana was to her.

Poison. A concoction of pain laced with absolution to trick the tongue. Lie to the mind.

Her shoulders shook. Her first question should have been whose scream she had heard. "Why," was all she managed. Her heart felt stiff, strained past the point of breaking. "Why won't you let me go?"

"Do you remember how we first met?" Liana stroked

141

Zahria's palms, sensitizing the skin until it yearned. "Do you remember how your smile fell? How your eyes stayed on mine as you drew near?"

Desire was reflexive. Zahria wanted to lean into the heat unfurling between them. She wanted to forget the decades of hopelessness, appleseed bitter and as unforgiving as spilled blood. She had been destroyed by those years. Too alone with her thoughts. Too angry to share her fears. Desire had bridged many of their gaps. Now it seemed a pale light in a cavernous hollow. The gleam was too weak when you considered the darkness.

"I remember empty nights," Zahria said, clutching Liana's fingers. "I remember cold rooms and secrets behind closed doors. I remember thinking I loved you enough to leave you to your spells and to sacrifice myself for your ambition. But I can't."

Those early nights between them had sutured something palpable in its lightness. Almost innocent. The sensation had been in the curve of Liana's body as she wept for a long-dead friend, killed by the brutality the rare magic-user had once faced in this kingdom. In the resurgence of nightmares that would rip her into waking, splitting her mouth with what life had been like before she had tricked the king into thinking he could control the spectacle she had made of her magic. Zahria hadn't wanted to abandon a woman so constantly invaded by the past. She had loved feeling needed by someone both strong and weak.

"I want you to consider," Liana said, her own grip on Zahria's hands just as tight, "what it would mean to truly turn against me."

"Would you kill me, Liana?"

The wind stilled.

The silence was deceiving. It lay like velvet over them both, but there was no comfort for Zahria in its settling.

"With the forest gone, you could leave. And come back."

"Is that what you think will happen? That I will return to you someday?" Zahria's smile wasn't designed to ease the regret plain on Liana's face. But seeing it softened Zahria. They had been estranged so long, she had only seen a heart of polished onyx. She had assumed loneliness and anguish were things that rebounded from its surface.

"I hold your heart," Liana whispered. There was a note of desperation inside the words.

"No," said Zahria. She let go of Liana's hands, apology in their final grasp. "I didn't lose my heart to you."

Saying the words aloud was both burden and relief. It made sense of the fire and ice, the desert and windstorms within her. She was still in possession of her heart. She hadn't lost it. A century imprisoned in Osolda hadn't stolen it. There hadn't been enough of herself to give. Not from the moment Liana began ruling Osolda without honor.

"Let me go," Zahria repeated, hoping Liana might finally hear her plea as it was intended. She wanted to disappear from Liana's grip. She wanted to be free to redeem herself. She had many wrongs to right.

Liana's gaze darkened. The whites of her eyes drained, leaving the pupils room to expand.

Zahria's breath shuddered out. "Don't do this."

Blood flowed from palms Zahria knew to be callused as well as blemished with past Exchanges. Liana's nails elongated, until crimson rivers spilled onto the ground. Zahria was reminded starkly that the beauty before her had been paid for with the blood of others. It wasn't real. That was Liana's price for stealing a century's worth of a life.

"Liana."

"I know the truth. My spies keep nothing from me. You've consorted with traitors," Liana hissed. Her voice grew coarse, bottomless. Her gaze became too opaque. "You've resisted my

143

commands. I told you I would allow *none* to abandon my rule."

"Your people rot behind your walls. Let us go, Liana."

"*I will not.*"

"Your magic won't harm me."

Liana relearned her smile. It was edged with cruelty. "I don't spill my blood and the blood of others for *you.*"

Zahria heard them then.

The owls.

They stormed over the forest in endless droves, washing out form and shadow.

Leaving Zahria blind.

"I will rid my kingdom of the sky clans' dissension." Liana's disembodied voice rose above the din of frantic screeching. "And then I will wield a fire so great, this forest will die." Zahria didn't have to witness her disappearance to know Liana's presence faded with the light. "May you burn with it."

HOWLING AND SCREECHING CHORUSED TOGETHER. The Unforeseen Forest was alight with commotion—and yet without light. While Zahria's sight was sharper than most, even in her former homeland, she couldn't prize the contours of the world out of nothingness.

The owls, however, would have no problem doing just that. Zahria had seen proof of that in Liana's black gaze.

She leaned in to her other senses. Like smell. *Pine musk... withering wildflowers... blood.* She followed the sharp, rusted scent, letting sound and touch and taste guide her through the darkness.

Only once did she stumble, her chest kissing damp bark hard enough to expel her breath. She tasted blood in the corner of her mouth and knew it wouldn't be long before the beasts turned frenzied.

Zahria swore in such a way her mother's face would have turned plum. Zahria had always done so anyway, enduring her mother's lashes. She had always done what felt good and bore the consequences. But in all that time with her indomitable lover, she had never really learned how to handle Liana. This was why they were forever clashing.

And now Elina and the entire forest were caught in the middle, about to suffer consequences of Zahria's own making.

Despair would make a feast of her body if she let it, nor would the feeling need much coaxing since she would soon be prone to the maws of demon-hounds. Despair could have her corpse then.

Help us...

And we will help you...

What do you want from me, she thought wildly. *Why do you haunt my steps?*

Growls sundered the answering cries of the forest. Zahria pushed herself harder, faster. Every step was soundless, steady. But the ruthless dark was effective. Every mistake cost more than it should have, all while Elina lay injured and possibly frightened. The owls would not stop until they finished the job of killing her.

Zahria dropped to her knees and dug her hands into the soil. She toyed with the crumbling mounds between her fingers, drawing history and turmoil into her body. Juniper anguish writhing in the bed of an old, silvering wood. Empty silences brimming with untreated poison. Weeds weeping in memory of heavy blossoms that rustled in the crisp wind. Wishes for someone to remember that the long gray fringes of Osolda's woodlands had once been bursting with devotion for its people.

Tears blurred Zahria's vision. Owl screeches dropped from

the black belly of this new sky. "For what you have lost," she said, "I give some of myself over to your will."

Zahria's fists tightened in the earth, and the trees trembled with something like delight. To be awake. To be needed. Twisting their shoulders and blinking their dark eyes. Their arms speared up.

"May it be enough," Zahria whispered.

She had no need of her arrows. The queen's owls had no time to scream.

There was only a wide berth of silence. Like the kind Zahria would prop for a creature more menacing than she, whose arrival was unexpected.

Dying owls fell like shards.

Soon, the night was once more an open window inviting twilight.

ZAHRIA'S BOW locked into her hands the moment she reached the canopy of Elina's hiding place.

Elina was not alone.

A dusky white-and-violet shadow perched over her prone form. Recognition tickled Zahria's senses enough to keep her arrow from sliding free.

"Who are you?"

The shadow turned. A wren became a man.

Zahria dropped her bow.

"You surprise me, Huntress," said Alistair.

"You haven't," Zahria managed, "up until now."

Alistair's gaze was dark and troubled. "She won't survive much longer. She needs a healer."

"I forgot one on the way up."

"I'm going to signal the greyguard. Meet me at the southern edges of the forest. She'll be taken care of."

Zahria reached down for Elina. "You have some explaining to do."

"Are you sure you want to hear the answers?"

Zahria paused, her mouth a firm line. "I think I've kept my head buried long enough," she said finally. "Wouldn't you agree?"

∾

"You people," Zahria muttered.

She tightened her hold on Elina, who lay still in her arms. The soldiers of Greyhold had ridden to meet Zahria where Alistair had asked to her wait. Their expressions hadn't changed since she'd last seen them. There wasn't even a thread of gratitude unraveling among the party for the way she'd saved them. Dell held out his arms, all hard lines and angles besides. Ardith watched Zahria's reluctance curiously and it suddenly became a struggle not to shift her feet.

"Her blood will draw the creatures."

"We can protect her," said Dell in his quiet way.

Elina slipped into Dell's arms without a murmur, staining his armored tunic with her injuries. Her tan skin had drained of all color. Her arm had turned the stomach of an ashen young guard, sent to replace one of the fallen Zahria hadn't been able to save from the beasts. Alistair dismounted, walking over to Elina and stroking a strand of hair back from her face.

Zahria cleared her throat. "Who are you really, my lord?"

"A son of Osolda," he said after a moment. He turned away from Elina, but his stance was protective, wary. "A subject of my queen."

Zahria snorted. "Don't play games with me, Alistair."

"Your queen and mine are not the same."

Zahria's stomach dropped. She stared down at the seams of Elina's eyelids, willing them to open so that she might see the truth crystallize. "Some servant you are," she said, keeping her tone light. "Letting your queen enter the Unforeseen Forest while I hunted. I might've mistaken her for an enemy."

Alistair cocked his head. The gesture reminded Zahria of Elina. "Didn't you?" He turned his head up to Dell. "Take her back to Greyhold. See that she's given immediate care."

Dell's horse hastened away.

The remaining silence pressed against Zahria like spikes, insisting she reveal something she'd rather keep tucked within. She withstood the small torture of maintaining Alistair's gaze once it returned to her, but resentment for the mysterious lord swelled.

Don't expect anything from me, she thought, her lips tightening. Instinct and emotion were two very different things. Zahria was far from ready to trust the latter. She wound a hand into her knotted curls so that her fingers wouldn't make restless movements against her holstered knives.

"So you're Sky Clan," she said flatly.

"I am of the clans of the skies, yes," he returned, still watching her with speculation. "A part of you is unsurprised. You watched me closely at court. I was flattered."

"I didn't do it to flatter you," she bit out. She hated this uncertainty that bounded inside her. This confusion of loyalties. It wasn't as though Liana would have been hurt by Alistair's true allegiance. The queen had confidence in nothing and no one. Hadn't Zahria seen that only hours ago in the forest? For a moment, she had been willing to believe that Liana's sudden appearance was a belated show of trust. Instead, it had only been some sort of spelled mirage. Zahria owed her nothing. And yet... "How long have you been watching *me*?"

Alistair smiled, and it forced Zahria to wonder why she hadn't guessed his origins sooner. The clans were a proud yet secretive people. Alistair had been the only one at court adept in shielding what he most wanted to keep hidden.

"Even before my queen commanded it," he said. "I told you your magic intrigued me. I made it a personal mission of mine to seek out your history. Compare fact from fiction. I had my suspicions that you were... essential to my endeavors."

"I don't understand why you would risk your position at court," said Zahria. "Inquiries about me would have made their way back to the queen. She would not have been pleased. What could my past tell you about Osolda's future?"

"Simple." He folded his hands at his waist. "I learned that only you could answer my questions. For instance, what happens to an animal that refuses to adapt to new surroundings?"

Zahria didn't have to think. "They face extinction."

"And when there's a divergence of species?"

Zahria thought of wolves and bears and their many hues. Even the demons of the forest. "They no longer mate with one another."

Alistair nodded. "And so we have stopped breeding harmony in Osolda. Each of the communities here—those with magic, those without, and us clansmen—have tried to exist independently of the others, but this country was not meant to be so. Now we have beasts and dying fields. Isolation." His blue gaze turned unyielding as ice. "Your queen has fostered and wielded all this hostility. She believes she's tamed this kingdom. And yet both the land and the people starve. They linger under constant attack. And so, my final question, Huntress, if you please."

Zahria did not move to invite him.

He continued perhaps because of her silence.

"How does one stop a predator like the queen from consuming our world?"

Zahria remembered sitting next to a bored Jenya, brimming with youth and expectancy as their father explained the ways of hunting. *Your prey will try to disappear into its surroundings. It will try to make itself small. But when a creature becomes unrecognizable, it also becomes dangerous. Turn away from its secrets, or the god of death will teach them to you. And you will go to your ancestors at the end of your lesson.* She'd spent years learning this from her father until she was able to repeat the lesson back to him. Only then had he set her loose in the woodlands of their home.

Despite her natural talent, and her inability to be anything than less than a predator in her own right, Zahria had never forgotten this truth.

Prey must become predator if it hoped to survive.

This was at the tip of Zahria's tongue.

If the world couldn't shrink, startle, or warn the queen away, then it had to disrupt. Osolda had to become the greater threat. The better monster.

The queen would not expect this.

Zahria had neglected her gift so long, she'd shrunken to far less than what she was. Liana had only a faint recollection of what it was Zahria could do in a forest. But even then, she had not been trying to lay siege on foreign soil. In some ways, she had succeeded in hiding her utmost strengths and weaknesses from the one person she had believed understood those very qualities within her.

If she laid down a direct challenge, Liana had already lost. Liana would not recognize the stranger stirring inside Zahria. The advantage was hers. *Theirs*, she thought, looking between Alistair and Ardith, for she wanted nothing of this kingdom once it was out of Liana's grasp. She just had to make the choice.

"What would you do if the queen were gone?" she said finally.

The guards turned wary glances on Alistair. When their mounts nosed the ground, they were too distracted to stop them.

Alistair didn't fall into any of their warning gazes, nor waver as he stepped forward. He didn't question Zahria's question. He didn't condemn her fulfillment of the former general's death warrant. Zahria wondered distantly what this man saw when he studied her like this—a liar, a murderer, a drunk, or something altogether new?

"A council will rule Osolda," he said at last.

"And then?"

"And then we will redeem ourselves."

Zahria nodded. Her heart clutched in her chest, but she stepped forward. Offered her hand.

He took it into his own.

"I'm going to need to borrow your guards," she said.

"Take them," he said. "They're yours to command."

Ardith hissed at this and was ignored.

"What will you do?"

Zahria turned back to the Unforeseen Forest. "I will show the queen a better monster."

The horses whined as howls crescendoed at the first stirrings of dawn.

"Would you kill her? The queen?"

She had no answer for this. She wasn't sure she ever would, despite all that Liana had done. She let Alistair's question hang between them.

Without waiting to see if she was followed, Zahria led the greyguard into the depths of the forest.

TEETH SNAPPED at Zahria's collar, stinking of death.

"Why won't they sleep?" demanded Ardith, her breath short. Her sword was damp with blood. "It's dawn."

Zahria absently muttered a quick prayer to the sun god. She pointed out that she was thankful she had placed her hair in a knot atop her head, lest the beast steal a taste and ruin its glory.

"I'm wearing Elina's blood," she commented calmly as her knife stuck in the jugular of her own beast. "I'm sorry. I thought—" her breath punched out as yet another beast leapt for her "—we would have more time."

Ardith was quiet, but this time Zahria didn't turn. She could hear Ardith's shallow breaths. "What?" she snapped.

A keen cry was cut short. "You apologized to me," said Ardith.

"Is *that* what you really want, then?" said Zahria, shoving another beast back, before plunging her other knife in its spine. She reached for a fallen soldier's bow to save time when another beast came barreling toward her. "An apology?"

"I don't know," said Ardith. Her sword whistled in the air, blending with the twang of Zahria's arrows. "But it's a start."

Zahria smiled. "I always forget how sentimental you are." She turned just as blood splattered into Ardith's eyes.

Several clearing blinks later and Ardith's answering smile was small. A weak light. Something that would take time to stoke and brighten. But Zahria felt something loosen inside her, some pain that had raveled tight in the center of her chest after Tristan's death. The idea that redemption might not be as elusive as she had once believed wrenched her heart. Fueled her shots among the sunlit kindling the forest had become. The world was aglow with her hope, even as beast-blood watered the soil.

A ravenous growl made her head turn.

She loosed an arrow in its direction.

And lost time in stopping the beast lunging for Ardith from behind, its mouth wet with the blood of a fallen comrade.

Ardith toppled under the beast's weight.

She struggled against its wild, snarling mouth.

Zahria sent two arrows plunging into its hide. There was a squeal and a huff. Ardith shoved at its weight, but she didn't have the right leverage.

Zahria ran.

Another beast interceded.

She slew it before it could leap.

But when she turned back to Ardith's prone form, her hands slackened around her borrowed bow. Only instinct held it in place. Its limbs were cold inside her palms.

Ardith's gaze was blank. Her body still.

Her throat was mangled flesh.

Zahria's scream was dangerous. Her anguish pulled guards away from their own battles. When they spotted Ardith, their fighting stances weakened.

The less seasoned suffered.

Death littered Zahria's feet.

She moved like the god of death were whispering strategy in her ear. Her innate skill became a vehicle for his will. She pulled her own bow free and tossed aside the one which had failed her. Her hands and feet were a blur. Her arrows an extension of her being. Beasts fell. Their choked squeals raked the forest's ragged silence.

But, still, it wasn't enough.

More poured out from cracks in the daylight.

Their hunger eclipsed Zahria's.

She didn't know that keen sense of desperation. She only knew agony. Regret. Exhaustion. The beasts' need was strong and her gift was weak.

She was pinned in the span of a blink.

Her back hit the ground. Her arms came up to defend her face. Her breathing only incited the beast.

No.

The word echoed from dirt and seeds and stone. The beast reeled. It didn't lunge for the opportunity Zahria's confusion afforded it.

The earth *remembered* her. Was angry for her. Would protect her.

No.

No.

No.

Roots rose up from the ground, wrapping her in a wooden shell as the beast regained itself and scrambled to devour what it could reach. It broke its own nose trying to reach inside the cocoon hiding her body. Hot, foul air gusted from between the cracks in the wood.

It wouldn't stop.

None of them would.

They were a storm crouching from the tangle of Liana's dark deeds. Her endless abuse of Osolda. Zahria was no more than a stray bolt. What could she do against a legion of thunder with a singular desire?

How would she get what she needed from the trees with these beasts in the godsdamned way?

Wait. A singular desire.

If you don't know what they want, then you can't coax them," she'd told Elina. *You can't anticipate what they'll do next.*

But she did know what they want.

The demons were *agonized* by it. Frenzied. They stopped all rational thinking to have it.

"Death," she murmured. Whether it was to wallow in it or to cause it, the beasts were alive because of death. The iron tang of it. The swelling before a life drained away.

She forced her way free from the fibrous shelter the trees had fashioned for her. Waiting was too tame a word for what the beast was doing once she emerged.

From her belt hung her gods. Little silver statues, compact enough to cart poisons and odors from one land to the next, without risk of exposure to the innocent and unsuspecting.

If the beasts' wanted death, she would become something they could not kill.

Sweet End lay beneath the god of death's small silver head.

An enchanting, yet poisonous fume. Its perfume in small doses could knock out her quarry if she was so inclined to apply the substance. Even she had been known to grow faint when using it. But the long-term effects?

She covered her nose with her arm and let the intoxicating scent seep into the air.

Heads jerked up from crouches. Wooly mouths grew slack with drool. Wide, dark pupils began to expand.

"That's it," she whispered, walking a straight path through their tense bodies. She buried her face in the crook of her elbow. "Go," she ordered any living soldier she saw. "Hurry."

So few. So few ran from the clearing.

She turned away from the thought.

One beast tried to leap for her, but its movements were sluggish. Others had lost function of their muscles. They made keening noises.

Zahria unfastened the god of death from her belt and poured out its contents in a winding path around them—one drop at a time.

She left the god sitting in the center of their reluctant formation, fumes still billowing.

There was a series of thuds and whimpers.

But Zahria was already walking deeper into the forest. She let go of her distress. Muttered a prayer for Ardith's soul and thanked the god of death.

She refused to turn back.

A deep voice settled over her then, as strange and surprising as an army of moths alighting on her body. The sensation should've made her skin crawl.

But her muscles lost their tension.

Hunting woman.

The voice was broken into many and yet resounded as one. The forest had never resonated so clearly in her own ears.

Have you come to aid us—

—fulfill us—

—desert us?

What is your—

—answer, hunting woman?

Will you take from us—

—and give to us?

Her breath trickled out in both horror and wonder. She almost wished she had been attacked by the imaginary moths. She had never heard the trees like this.

So loud. Bold. Focused.

We need you.

Will you need us?

"How do I defeat the queen?" she asked aloud, turning in a circle, watchful of anything that moved.

If we show you—

—how it is done—

—hunting woman—

—will you accept our gift?

"I don't have much of a choice, do I?" She sighed. That wasn't true. She had always had a choice. Choosing wrong was what had broken faith in her friends. With Tristan and Ardith gone, what she chose now should matter much less. But it didn't. "I will accept whatever fate awaits me. Consider this my penance to you and to the rest of this kingdom."

I honor you, she thought to the two people she had betrayed and lost before she was fully forgiven.

A buttery light showered over her, enveloping her from head to foot. An unnameable energy coursed through her, pumping off the whispers surrounding her from all sides.

We give you this gift—

—in exchange for our current lives.

We will be no more than husks—

empty of sound—

and without purpose.

Clear this land of us—

—let fire take us—

—and when the soil is free—

—heal us.

We will become whole again.

There was a light rush of wind, like a long-held sigh. The flow of ancient life pouring through her came to an abrupt end.

One last thing—

hunting woman—

a secret.

You must have this secret.

For a moment the voices flitted through the air like the buzzing of insect wings, flocking in droves. Unintelligible. But their secret tipped into her ears. A heavy truth made of brambles that scored her heart.

And then there was a heavy blanket of quiet.

And Zahria was left standing in a veil of inky roots and silver branches, listening to the soundless death of the Unforeseen Forest.

WITH THE FOREST at her back, she called for Heathen.

To her surprise, the horse answered.

He trotted from some grassy bounty she could not see and nosed her cheek, gusts of his breath tickling strands of her hair.

Her dried tears dissatisfied him somehow. She stroked his velvet cheek until he calmed.

"To Greyhold, then," she told him.

WHEN SHE WAS ACCEPTED behind the towering stone arch of Greyhold's gate, she immediately sought out Alistair.

Dell blocked her path.

She settled her hands on her knives and looked up at him. His eyes were red-lined and swollen. He hadn't slept. His forehead was crowded with mussed hair from his restlessness. She itched to comb through the sable locks, as she had relented when once he'd embodied boyhood.

But the young man before her wouldn't have smiled at the memory.

"Does your offer still stand?" he said. Torchlight flickered over the sleepless hollows in his face. Ardith's death had aged him in a way that showed beneath the skin.

She remembered offering her death to him. To him and Ardith both. "Afraid not," she said, her voice rough. "It would seem I'm still needed."

"It's not fair," he choked out. The boy he had been when she'd first come to Greyhold would have said the same. That boy had believed in justice. Now, he had seen too much death to know that there was no such thing.

But she wanted to assure him, however she could. "You fought honorably, Dell," she told him quietly. "So did she. Do not think you are alone in grieving for her."

"No." His smile broke her heart. "I am alone."

She watched his shadow peel away from the stones as he headed away from her, down to men and women he did trust. A sigh trembled out of her. A familiar ache for her wineskin called out to her. Turning away from the path down to the kitchens made her sweat.

And more aware of all the work she had yet to do.

When she found Alistair at last, she'd been directed to a room with canary-colored walls and a silk-sheeted bed, where Elina was tucked. He was crouched over her side of the bed. His hands were clasped together beneath his forehead. Zahria thought she heard traces of weeping.

"Why cry if she's going to live," she said.

His head arose slowly. Tears tracked his cheeks. "I'm relieved," he said. "But these tears aren't shed only for her."

Zahria didn't ask to whom his grief belonged. She turned her face to the window, where the moon's solemn watch awaited. "I'd like to..." She cleared her throat. "I'd like to sit with her for a while."

She felt his long stare. Then, his chair scraped back. He left the room without a word.

Zahria sat confidently in his abandoned seat. But she couldn't bring herself to look at the battered girl lying against the gold-trimmed pillows, her hair unbound and blending in with the tassels. She turned over the rows of inset bookshelves and the old maps of Osolda hanging from the walls, thinking how familiar it all looked. These weren't Alistair's bedchambers.

And then she saw it.

A medal given to General Tristan by the queen. Before their animosity.

A void bloomed inside her. A black rose of regret. And yet the tears she could have shed were not there to soothe the raw edges of it. They had vanished. Her sorrow was dry and cracked. There was no balm left for it.

"I'm sorry for what happened to you," she told Elina, whose breathing was thin, yet unchanged. "I know what I have to do. It's just... look, I don't have to like it." She wound curls around her hand. "And I don't exactly know how..."

A knock intruded softly.

Zahria sighed. "Come in."

A young woman entered. She was missing a hand— and an eye, if the sash covering the orifice was to be believed. Her hair was brown, with streaks of silver running through. And yet Zahria could not guess the woman's age.

She said nothing to Zahria, though the strain in her movements told Zahria she knew she was being measured and weighed.

After a quick, yet thorough survey of Elina's injuries, the woman reached for Elina's mangled arm. Zahria had a knife pressed to the woman's throat before she touched two fingers.

The woman met her eyes. "I'm a healer."

"No," said Zahria quietly. There was a familiar scent hanging in the air now. She didn't know how much magic the woman possessed, but these days, any was enough cause for suspicion. "That's not all you are."

"Maybe so, Huntress, but I am the only thing keeping this woman alive."

"I hope that continues to be the case. For your sake."

The healer smiled, baffling Zahria. "You must care for her very much."

Zahria scowled. And dropped her arm. "It's my fault she's been injured like this. That's all."

The woman's misplaced delight sobered. "And terrible injuries they are. I don't suppose you'll leave the room for a few moments."

"Not a chance."

The healer sighed.

"What's your name?" Zahria demanded.

"Good." She laughed a little when Zahria frowned. "Just Good, Huntress."

"Not very clever."

"No. I suppose not."

"Somewhat presumptuous, then."

"Perhaps."

"How long will she remain sleeping?"

Good's hand was tentative of Elina's arm, but her face remained smooth. Zahria waited for signs of distress, like a wrinkled brow or a widening of the eyes, but nothing happened.

"She's wakened a few times since she was brought to the garrison," said Good. "But periods of deep sleep are normal. Her body needs time to heal, though it does so at a much faster rate than most... people."

So then Good knew. Zahria eyed her warily. "How much is the Lord Alistair paying you to maintain your silence?"

"No more than is warranted, my lady."

"You may continue addressing me as Huntress."

Good raised her brow, but didn't comment on the snideness of Zahria's tone. "I'm going to heal this part here. It's susceptible to infection."

Zahria waved her hand.

When Good took a knife from the small leather bag around her chest, Zahria's hands tensed. But the woman only cut herself.

And cut deep.

"You use bloodcraft," Zahria said, open-mouthed at the realization. "You haven't reported your abilities to the queen."

Good's gaze sharpened. "Which queen?"

Zahria stared down at Elina. "So you're another of hers."

"I am and I am not. I believe in her cause. In the Lord Alistair's. This kingdom is ready to start anew."

"You don't worry that Queen Liana will come for you?"

"Why should she come here? Are you going to tell her?" When Zahria did not answer, Good continued, voice calm. "I have no interest in becoming another of the witch-queen's pets."

Pet. The word only stung because Zahria had heard that same term applied to her at court. And because it had been true. She had pretended not to take offense. But something inside her had cowed. Had refused the responsibility of her choices.

It was also true that she had lied to the slowly mending Elina.

She did know how to do what came next. But she was afraid. Uncertain.

We have no use for cowards.

"Tell me." Her fingers fluttered against the silk of the bedsheets, causing ripples. "Could I make an Exchange?"

This was part of the secret of the Unforeseen Forest. The trees had enveloped her in their magic, restoring her after grief and battle wounds. They had made an Exchange: their withering lives for the chance to start anew with magic fresh from Zahria's keeping. This was the answer to the question of the queen's reign.

Good considered her, without surprise. "You don't practice bloodcraft. We'd have recognized each other as soon as I entered the room if you did. Although..." Good gave scrupulous tugs on Elina's bandages, righting them into place. "You do possess something."

"Magic, as your countrymen like to say."

"Yes."

"Is it possible?"

"Of course it is."

It wasn't Good who spoke.

The voice had been hoarse.

"High One," said Good, bowing her head.

Elina's lashes fluttered.

There were storms brewing in those sea-swept eyes when they finally revealed themselves to Zahria.

She found herself fighting a smile. "Come to join the living again, have you?"

"Going to twist the queen's game on her, are you?" Elina countered. Her voice quieted. "Bold move, Huntress."

Zahria locked eyes with Good once her head lifted. "Will you show me what to do?"

"Will the queen no longer be a problem?"

Zahria's lips quirked. She made sure Elina caught the

mischief in her gaze. "Which queen?"

Good laughed. "You give me hope, Huntress."

Startled, Zahria sat back.

"Really?" said Elina dryly. "Must be nice to feel something other than a head ache. Fortune favors you, Good."

"Hush now, High One," said Good, her smile bright. "I'm about to begin a lesson."

WITH THE HELP OF GOOD, Zahria had a plan ready to present to Alistair. By the time she finished explaining, he was shaking his head.

"No."

"Yes." She looked to Elina.

Alistair glared. "I won't risk your safety, so don't even ask it."

"When have I ever been safe?" Elina reached for his hand. Together they covered an old depiction of the Unforeseen Forest. Its branches were lively, like brown dancers frozen on paper. "Think of our people, cousin."

"I have *always* thought of our people."

"Then trust us," said Zahria.

An odd sound fluttered in his throat. He threw his hands up and walked away.

But, that night, once Alistair's letter slipped from the hands of a Greyhold courier into those of the queen, owls arrived in the garrison city to collect a prize she could not overlook.

An end to dissension from the Sky Clans.

THE WHOLE of Luren was beside itself with excitement. Men, women, and children from even the uppermost Belle District had slipped down the tiers of this city like a silk-made waterfall into the Angel District. Despite wrinkled noses, they invited the commotion.

Where a pearlescent fountain might have stood in the Belle District were the gallows of the Angel District Liana had ordered readied. Those who lived in the dingy filth of this tier of the city called it the Hangman's Elm. Liana had ripped an old linden from the open courtyard behind St. Lura's Church, where people had once come to sing and sacrifice to the saints of strength, justice, wisdom, and mercy, to build it. The poor prayed to the faces of the saints that remained carved into its new wooden shape.

There were no seats for the poor. Only wealth lined the pews circling Elina, whose back was tied to one of the beams up on the platform.

"You're going to have to get your arms around her." Good's voice came from beneath a woolen hood.

"I know," said Zahria. Ending Liana's reign was entirely dependent on this single act.

The queen gave an order to one of her guards. When he threw himself up on the platform and began untying Elina's hands, the crowds cheered.

"What a kingdom," muttered Zahria, her stomach turning over. She knew why the queen had chosen public execution, but why did the people? She didn't understand how anyone could make a spectacle of murder and consider themselves honorable and pious.

"The road to a better world is a long one," said Good, nodding. "But not an impossible one."

Zahria didn't ask the healer if it was bloodcraft which had stolen her hand, her eye. But she said, "How did you come to forgive the world?"

"I don't have to," said Good. "I am guided by my pain. I trust that what hurts will always heal."

Liana rose to stand before Elina, her rain-dark hair spooled into intricate braids looping around her head. Her crown gleamed in the moonlight, showering her crimson gown with silver beams. Zahria wished the ache in her heart away. She couldn't trust what it meant the way Good did.

Elina's face was bruised and defiant. Her chin came up as she faced the crowds crowing for her death. "What has happened to this land?" she shouted. "Do you not remember who you once were? Do you think your descendants will forgive your memory?"

"Dissenter," shouted a man.

"Abomination," shouted another.

"And what of your queen?" demanded Elina, all but snarling in the wake of Liana's smug calm. "What would your saints say of a demon allowed to walk in your midst?"

It was no use. Her words were kindling of a different kind. The crowds roared for her to hang.

Liana smiled. "Citizens of Luren," she spoke over the din. "I give you a traitor of Osolda. She has defiled this city with an attack that many of you have yet to recover from. She plots our kingdom's destruction among the clans within the trees. Why else would I have captured so many of them? It is she who sends beasts to dine on your kin in the country. With her gone, Osolda will finally know peace. Safety. Prosperity." She turned to Elina, a sharp glint to the sound of her voice. "My people. It is in your interest that I sentence Elina of the Nightingales to die."

She took a step forward. In a soft voice that none but Zahria could hear, she said, "I don't envy you."

Elina smirked. "Don't you?"

Before Liana could give the order, someone in the crowd screamed.

This ignited a bonfire of cries.

Ivy had slid over the walls, consuming stone, and trailing the ground like snakes at the feet of Liana's audience. Children were lifted in the air as ankles were tasted. Vines wrapped around the gallows.

Birdsong detonated over the city.

Soaring over the walls were Liana's former captives. Legions of them, from every clan Zahria had seen escape.

Guards reached for their bows, but a sea of hawks swept down, clawing their weapons away.

Liana whirled. Zahria wasn't certain of what she searched for until she found it.

Until she picked Zahria's gaze apart from the crowd's wheeling panic.

"Do you mean to conquer me then?" Liana called out.

Zahria stepped forward. People peeled away from her path like grass blades parting for a snake. "I mean to see this end, Liana."

Elina went free from her bindings. She pulled out one of her knives.

Zahria ran now as Elina stepped in the queen's direction. "For your perversion, detainment, and torture of the clans of the skies. For your greed and mercilessness," she said, a feverish glow to her skin. Her eyes were wide and clear and did not flicker at Zahria's shout. "*I* sentence you to die."

When Liana smiled, a roar exploded past Elina's lips.

She charged.

ZAHRIA DOVE BETWEEN THEM. She held an arm out to block Elina.

"You would let her live?" Elina said, disgust tangling with impatience. "Even after all this?"

"You're wrong." Zahria turned to Liana. "A knife wouldn't make a difference anyway."

"You're foolish to come back here," Liana hissed. "You

belong in a noose alongside her. My traitorous Master of Spies beside you."

"Liana." Zahria stepped closer. "It's over."

"We've been finished for decades."

Zahria shook her head. She reached for Liana's wrists. Pulled back the embroidered sleeves. She remembered how cold Liana's hands had been in hers. When Zahria looked down, she saw what she expected.

Black veins winding through luminous skin.

Liana jerked back.

"You're not wrong," Zahria murmured. "In my heart, I've known that far longer than I knew to accept it. But, this has gone on too far. You've done unforgivable things." The forest's secret washed onto the shore of her tumultuous thoughts. "Those beasts in the forest are your doing, aren't they? If you won't let go..." She took a deep breath. Nodded and steadied. "I'm going to make you."

Bloodguard pooled against Liana's sides, as if to bolster her before she caved in. Her eyes were wide. Zahria wondered if grief was finally slipping through the decades-wide cracks they had both neglected. She wondered if she could wrap her arms around this woman and commit to everything she had promised.

"I've toppled a king and ended holy men," Liana said. Tears spilled down her cheeks. "Do you really think I would ever just step aside?

"No," said Zahria, holding Elina back. Then she curled her arms upward. Vines of ivy towered, then fell like a tide. Bloodguard were caught in their thicket, leaves filling their mouths, rambling ropes tying them down. "That's why I'm not asking you to. I don't need permission to be free of you."

"And you think to let this girl set a precedent for killing monarchs. Go ahead," Liana invited. "Make a martyr of me, Zahria."

"She's not going to end you," said Zahria. Sadness made a mockery of her steadiness. But she stepped forward. Just once more. An Exchange had to be made. "You've already lost, Liana. You can no longer bear the cost your actions demand. Just let go."

"I told you once before." Her mouth was grim, irreversible. She reached for a fallen sword on the ground. "I am above cost."

Zahria started to reach for a weapon of her own, when the queen pulled back the head of one of her guards. She killed him without a flicker of remorse. She made an Exchange with his blood.

With the resurgence of her power, she took the lives of the rest of her bloodguard.

Zahria felt Liana's power roar like the waking of an infallible beast.

Owls barreled from the unseen depths of the palace above. They were a dark flame burning the sky of stars.

"I will never stop," Liana bellowed. Hunger washed over her face. Zahria saw her thoughts climb over this kingdom, poised to leap for the rest of the world. "Twenty lives wouldn't be enough. There are no conditions to power. I am *more* than you, Zahria of Gildesh. I am more than your gods. I make the demons that keep your gods in their heavens." She turned on the city with ebony veins spidering beneath her features. "Osolda is *mine*."

Elina pushed Zahria aside. She hefted a sword from a fallen ally and lunged.

But when Liana faced her, she didn't know Death.

She sent Elina crashing through the wooden beams of the gallows with no more effort than the lift of her hand.

"*You cannot defeat me.*" The owls' fervent cries whirled around her. For a moment, she was made of wings and claws and towering to the sky. "I will finish what I started when I ensnared your people, Elina of the Nightingales. You will be my beasts."

"Zahria," Elina whispered, a whimper trapped in her throat. "Zahria, now. Please."

"My love," Zahria murmured. "What have you become?"

She remembered innocence made flesh. Dove skin, vibrant smile. She remembered a Liana with pillow feathers lost in her hair and a smile that pulled her mouth into a shape she'd often startle at if found in a mirror. A woman who had too quickly shed the girl she had been, taking her kingdom by the reins by ending its last master. That woman had done unspeakable things since, it was true. There was much to answer for.

But, could Zahria execute judgement?

Did this matter not fall to the gods once Liana's time ran out?

"I have become all that this world *deserves*."

Zahria fell backward. Liana had sent her sprawling. Her words echoed in Zahria's mind. What did this kingdom truly deserve? Hadn't she seen the people's fallacies and believed they were well-matched with a queen like Liana? Was Zahria herself not just another wretched flaw that had found its rightful place?

She hadn't run from Osolda for a *reason*. She'd endured a century of a place so radically different from her homeland, staying had made her sick with longing, because this version of herself had belonged here.

But what of the world?

Was there not good worth fighting for?

Zahria thought of Ardith and Dell and Elina. Even Alistair. Even, and perhaps especially, Good. A woman she'd had such a short acquaintance with, and yet, as Zahria's eyes lifted to the crowd, she saw the healer sifting the floor for a weapon. One-handed. Desperation brimming from a single eye.

Zahria didn't know what part of herself Good planned to

part with next, but she couldn't let others continue making sacrifices while she did nothing in the wake of devastation.

Or, worse, while she chose the wrong side.

It was painful to rise to her feet. Her heart still reeled from the thought of what she was to do. "But this has to end."

Everything had to. While the Osoldans chose not to answer to Death, Zahria embraced him. She embraced all her gods as she stepped into the wake of Liana's wrath.

"You will not harm another soul," she told her. "I will not let you." She couldn't. It wasn't who she was. Not before and not anymore.

She wrapped her arms around the queen.

Liana froze. "What are you doing?" she growled. Her eyes changed. Zahria saw her thoughts. She saw the moment when advantage flipped to fear. When dominance was no longer possible as her soul slipped from her body. "What are you doing?" she gasped. She dug her fingers into Zahria's collar. Her body quaked. "Zahria."

Tears filled Zahria's eyes, but they did not fall. "I'm making an Exchange." She kissed Liana's brow, watching as life drained from her. "Your life for Osolda's, and everyone dwelling within."

"You can't," Liana whispered, her fingers weakening against Zahria's tunic. Her lashes became damp. Heavy. "You can't."

They slid to the platform together, Liana cradled against Zahria's chest. "I can," she whispered back. "I can."

"You're... nothing."

"Yes." She tucked her face into hair that had once curtained them both in the dark. "I am nothing like you."

"I wish..."

"You wish for nothing," said Zahria as Liana's eyes shut. "Let go."

The queen's death wasn't peaceful. Nor was it painless. The god of death did not take kindly to whatever battle she waged against him. Zahria saw Liana's campaign even as her tears froze and her skin turned ashen. She felt every minute that Liana's soul lingered in place. The Exchange would not set either of them free until it was complete.

Elina knelt before the silhouette they made, her sword once more in hand.

Zahria's tears finally fell. "She won't die."

Elina only looked at her. "Then let go."

Her eyes squeezed shut. She relinquished her grip on the queen's dying body and backed away. She only opened them again when the sword plunged into the queen's chest. Even then, Liana didn't appear defenseless. She was still fighting to come back from the turn her fate had taken.

But then, she exhaled.

Her chest didn't rise again.

"It's done," said Elina.

But the hooks inside Zahria's heart didn't unlatch and fall away. She looked out as dawn grabbed hold of the sky by its pink-and-orange ribbons and felt like anything but the victor in the match Liana had lost.

SHE'D DEMANDED the keys of the palace guards to enter Liana's chambers. There were only a few left who still had the privilege. When Zahria stepped through, she thought how unimportant all this elegance was.

Gold and marble, bronze serpents and ivory sculptures that told no one who peered inside what Liana had really been like. You couldn't find what mattered to her inside these walls. Zahria no longer knew what those parameters had been like at the end of the queen's life.

She picked up her wineskin and drank deep. Then she

pulled open the windows and poured its contents down the side of the balcony.

She stood there for a long time, at first watching the honey-colored rivulets drip down to the white flagstone paths below, then dwelling in the depth of her thirst—and the control she'd exercised in refusing to fill it. Her gaze sank into the unfolding horizon, where her thoughts could lose themselves inside silver-tinged clouds.

She had ridden through the southern fields of Osolda astride Heathen. She had taken him to the edges of The Unforeseen Forest, where Elina and Alistair's greyguard had awaited them. Fire was set to the deadened husks of the forest. Together they had seen the first inklings of new life pushing from the ground as the ash settled.

Zahria had spent days among the charred remains of the forest, circulating her gift through the roots below like pumping blood.

By the next morning, there were saplings standing, shivering at their own entrance.

"I wonder what it was you had to become in the end," Zahria whispered to the night. "Not to know the beauty of this. To deny it from your own people. I wonder what hatred you courted in your heart." She lifted her empty wineskin. "I hope you found peace from it."

She hoped that eventually she would too.

Alistair had already begun his quest for his own. The Council of Blood and Song was rising to legitimate power in the queen's absence. Unlike before, where Liana had swept the people in the windstorm of her magic and fabricated stories about her royal claims, Alistair had suggested an election. It was the sort of proposition that turned Osolda on its hard head. The nobility weren't keen on losing the foothold they had in this kingdom. But, in time, Zahria had faith that a sly and clever man like Alistair could convince them.

When she heard footsteps, her first assumption was that Good had come to part ways. The healer's home wasn't in the shambles of this city, though she had stayed these last days to heal any who had suffered injuries. She belonged at the garrison city, tending to the wounded who fought behind Dell. Alistair was allowing Dell to lead his own company, for his thirst for vengeance against the beasts who had scattered from the Unforeseen Forest's end needed quenching. Someday the endless bloodshed wouldn't be enough for him. Dell would return to himself.

"Isn't this a bit pathetic?"

Zahria spat at the ground in answer.

"Testy, testy," said Elina. "But better that than seeing you mope for that horrible woman."

"Can I help you with something, Elina?"

The clanswoman kicked at some imaginary rock, for the maids always kept this balcony smooth and shining. "What are your current plans?"

The question rocked her. Zahria didn't know. She wasn't quite ready to leave. And yet it had been her only thought from the moment she had set out to end the beasts of the forest. No, not the forest, she corrected herself. But of the queen. These creatures were not *asarak,* but just another stamp of the queen's experimentation.

Perhaps she could go hunting with Dell for a time. Bridge the gap between them and hope they might be friends again. Or perhaps she could help Alistair enforce the welfare of this city, at least until the council had reasonable control of its citizens.

She wasn't ready to return home. If she were honest with herself from the beginning, she would've turned away from the thought long ago. Even if her homeland still stood, Gildesh would no longer look and feel as it once did. The faces of those she had loved would not be there to greet her upon her return.

She wasn't ready to face that kind of grief. She was still turning over the knowledge of what truly awaited her in her heart.

Would you be proud of me, Jenya?

When the silence didn't fill with her sister's answer, she said, "I have no plans at the moment."

Elina looked aghast. "What a *waste*."

Zahria scowled. "Some of us need time to process what's in our hearts."

Elina frowned.

Moonlight wandered into the room in increments, dancing with the shadows.

"So you still care for the queen?" Elina said, finally sounding tentative. "Even though she's dead?"

"Gods be damned, is everything so black and white with you?" Zahria bit out. "Do you think it's a simple thing to turn out a century's worth of memory? I'd like to see you shut that chest as easily as you seem to demand."

"She was an evil woman."

"The woman you knew was evil," said Zahria. "She was the villain of your little epic. But she had more facets than that. There just wasn't enough time for you to explore them. Believe me, I understand why you would not have wanted to."

Elina's lip curled. "Do you want me to grieve her with you?"

"No. My grief is mine." Zahria sighed. "Gods, you're young. Just listening to you makes me tired."

She did want to see Gildesh, she decided. Not right away. But she wanted to see what it had become in her absence. She wanted to know if the land would wrap her in its heat again. She missed the smell of crushed purple lotus, the lonely prayer of rain on a darkened night, the unrelenting humidity. There was no way to know how much time she had left on this earth—her immortality had seemed some unnatural byproduct of Liana's dark magic and her gods' blessings. Now that Liana was gone, Zahria understood the god of death might even now be lying in wait for her. She wanted to spend her remaining hours doing what mattered and what redeemed.

"Come with me to reclaim my people from the mountains," Elina burst out.

Zahria slowly turned to her.

"We are divided. Some we might never regain. The ones you saw facing the queen with me were only a few of what had been. There might still be clans clinging to their lives in the mountains."

"A very tidy explanation," said Zahria after a moment. "But it doesn't explain why you need me to accompany you."

Elina groaned. "I knew you wouldn't let it remain simple."

"What's simple about a random invitation to join you on a suicide mission?" Zahria threw her arm in the general direction of the mountain chain in question. "The pass is treacherous. The winds brutal. And the climb atrocious. I'll lose my breath just trying. Have you forgotten I'm an old woman?"

"*You* take my breath."

Zahria's heart bounded in her chest. "I can't tell if you mean that as an insult or a declaration."

Elina shoved an impatient hand through her flowing hair. "I don't know what it means, if I'm honest. I only know that I grow impatient around you. I'm always on edge. And it should be uncomfortable, but it's not." She drew in a breath. And took a step forward. "And I want to find out why."

Zahria reached for Elina's face. Her heart beat thickly in her ears. She placed her lips on Elina's, drawing in her sweetness, the earnestness of her youth.

But, for the first time, she understood what it was that Liana had felt when they'd met in the forest a century ago. Zahria had been the one to insist and to pry. She'd tempted Liana closer, but had never stopped to consider how Liana would react being trapped too near. She'd never really asked if the woman she had met that day was still too broken by the past to take on a future with her.

When she pulled away, her smile was soft and sad. "I can't." Elina's gaze clouded with confusion. She instantly tensed. Zahria rubbed her arms, hoping the gesture would soothe her. "You've so much courage in you. You'll only need a little of your store to understand my meaning."

Cupping Elina's face gently, she said, "Sorrow binds. And when you don't wish to be bound that sorrow will torture you. Mine will torture us both." She stepped back. Her every movement was rendered with care. She couldn't stand it if Elina ran from the room with less hope than she had entered with. "I'm no good as I am. My heart broke in this palace. In these very rooms. I need time to hunt down all the pieces I lost. Whatever I don't regain, I need to redeem. I need to justify, if only to remind myself I paid the price of loving and earned my pain. I want to teach the ones I've hurt not to be afraid of theirs. Can you understand that?"

Elina blew out the breath she held. "No," she said. "But I can try. I *am* trying."

"You're young," Zahria repeated, but with more softness. "I might find that uplifting one day." But, for now, exhaustion seeped into her at the mere thought of trying to keep up with another queen—another side of a land she had never loved, her heavy heart dragging behind her. "I'll come find you when I'm ready to start... exploring again."

Elina sniffed. "Maybe I won't want to *explore* with you anymore." But Zahria saw the mischief behind the gesture. More, she did indeed see understanding.

As the silver beams of the new moon drenched the balcony, pooling warmth between them, Elina said, "The trees are gone. The clans of the skies won't be able to settle in this part of Osolda." She reached for Zahria's hand and played with the fastening of Zahria's arm guard. "We will still need to leave. But we will come back. Maybe we can meet again when the saplings have begun to flower."

"I'm no good with promises, but..." Zahria smiled. "You'll have to find me first then. I won't be staying in Osolda for long."

Elina quirked a brow. "Are you doubting my capabilities as a tracker? I might not be so a fine a huntress as yourself, but I know my way around the green of any land."

"Such arrogance," Zahria teased.

Elina opened her mouth to argue, but Zahria pressed a quick kiss to her stubborn jaw. "I look forward to the day," she murmured.

The new moon marked the end of Zahria's long century in Osolda, and perhaps the beginning of true and lasting freedom. The welcome pleasure of the stars lighting up Elina's jeweled eyes felt like a taste.

The first of many.

She intended to savor them all.

STORM MISTRESS

J ade snuck out as soon as Mabel finished looping her red hair into a waterfall of curls down her back.

She'd begged Mabel not to tie her hair into angry knots that pulled on her scalp. "It's no good if I get a headache before Mr. Warrington comes. And what if I'm too sick to read with Mama at night?" Regardless of Jade's plea, Mabel would never deny her. She was too afraid of Jade's father to risk displeasing a girl of nine.

When Mabel finally shut the door behind Jade, muttering and wringing her brown hands about the laundering to be done, Jade heaved a sigh of relief.

When Jade's hair fell to inevitable disarray, Mabel would catch the blame. No one would suspect Jade's climb from the bedroom window, the dirt netted with sand crusted under her heels, nor the sweat staining her stockings at the knobs of her knees. No one would ever think Jade had done anything more than cracked open the spine of one of her mother's beloved books and read throughout the morning.

Mabel liked the quiet, so she never questioned the silence from Jade's bedroom. Until noonmeal, Mabel would wash, dust, sweep, launder, and rinse chamber pots. Jade had offered to help once last year. She'd just turned eight and watching Mabel toil had pricked her heart. Jade's mother, Thaya, had tried to reassure her that Mabel's wages were fairer here than in any other household in the Inlands. *The work is better here than in the quarter,* her mother had said. *Trust me, Jade. There's worse than airing out our urine to be found on Nadara, amongst merchants and pirates and all those in their employ.* And when Jade grew so bored she'd almost whacked herself dusting a windowpane, she had decided to believe her mother and give up her sympathy.

But this year was different. This year was even less about sympathy and more about the secrets Jade had started keeping. Hiding them depended on a few things, like not eating all the way until noonmeal, pretending to be "lady-like" by waiting patiently with a book until her tutor arrived later in the afternoon...

And noting that Mabel didn't muck the pen where they kept a pair of mares until noonmeal was over. Which meant Mabel wouldn't notice Starmine, Jade's pony of the last year, had gone missing. And, if the worst ever happened, and Mabel told Jade's mother something was amiss, she'd take their maid aside and gently remind her that she was Tore Elder's daughter, and a betrayal of Jade's confidence was also a loss of her protection.

Yes, this year was different. Jade wanted things she shouldn't want, like cunning and calculation and command. The things whispered about her father when no one thought she was listening.

Her father was *remembered*, thought of and braced for, which was better than Jade, who so often sat up in her room while her mother flitted about the Inlands and her father fared the seas. Jade was simply forgotten.

Her heart skipped as she coaxed Starmine out of the pen. Beneath her curls, her neck grew sticky with sweat. The sun flushed her skin, until everything felt too warm. She led Starmine past the peach tree her mother sometimes tended when there was time between errands, past the wall of hibiscus Mr. Warrington always plucked from, offering a red bursting bud to Jade at the start of her lessons and making her giggle.

A palm leaf brushed her face like a weighty feather, its many green fingers soft in their passing. Starmine snuffled behind her. The sharp smell of cedar irritated her nose. Jade scratched the pony's cream nostrils and led them both farther into a small forest. "We're almost there."

She waited for the brine of the sea to hit her, but they were still too far. Her heart kicked faster.

She saw Nate waiting for her, just where they'd agreed. His tawny face sported a wide grin.

"Well, what does a *lady* want with my rope?" He revealed what was behind his back. "And my hat?"

She grinned back. And snatched his offerings. With a playful bat of her lashes, she said, "Thanks. Now, turn around." Nate was four years older than her and had started talking about some of the other Inland girls with a certain *tone*. Like when she first realized how close the sea was or how the pirate quarter was filled with beauty that was both dangerous and simple. Rich discovery, piqued curiosity. She didn't trust Nate to avoid those things with her, especially because they had stopped meaning for him what they did to her... Even if she thought his brown eyes pretty. Sort of golden, sort of coppery. "What I'm about to do isn't very lady-like."

"Promises, promises."

Jade carefully rolled up the skirt of her dress, tying the fabric at her waist. "Did you bring the pants? The shirt?"

"Yes, my lady."

She pouted at his back when he tossed them to her. "Cut that out."

"Whatever you say, *lady*."

"I mean it, Nate." She stuffed her hair under the brim of her borrowed hat, until all the red was gone, freeing her from the humidity a little. "I'm the daughter of the pirate Tore Elder. And he'll break your nose and stomp on your privates if you call me a lady one more time."

Nate held his hands up in defense. "You're not anyone's daughter now."

She stepped up to him. Poked his thin chest through his cotton shirt. "What's my name?"

"Jade." She poked him again. He sighed. Then saluted her. "You're Jade Elder, feared pirate's daughter and not a lady." When she stepped back, satisfied, he rubbed his chest. "What's the matter with being a lady, anyway? Your mom's a lady."

"Maybe. But, my mother's mother could change her shape, you know. Maybe my mother can too and she's not really a lady. And they call my father The Ashman." She wished her father was there with them now, smelling of moss and sea-salt and some icily dry scent that Jade imagined came all the way from his frozen homeland in the Far North. If Nate took one real look at Tore Elder, with his kohl-rimmed eyes, long scarlet beard, and the twin axes strapped to his back, Nate would wet himself. "He's not a lady and neither am I. What I want has nothing to do with being good and proper and dumb."

Nate curled his fists. "My mother isn't dumb."

"I never said she was," Jade argued. "She's too nice to be a lady."

"But she is good and proper," he argued back.

"Aye," Jade said, liking the sound of the word. "But who cares about that now? I'm going into the quarter alone again, Nate."

184

His fists relaxed. He seemed to consider something and bit his lip. "Just be careful, Jade," he finally said. "There's some bad talk going around. If you hear the name Mortimer Lowe, go the other way."

"Why?"

"Heard some things." He shuffled his feet, unable to look at her. "Our mothers talking. He's not a nice man."

"Oh. Well, I'll stay away from him if I see him."

When she hugged him, he said, "I think it's great that your father's a pirate. He can protect you and your mom."

Jade shrugged. "Sometimes. But he's not here that much. And Mama doesn't like me to talk about him with other people. I'm not even supposed to say his name."

"At least you know who he is," said Nate, glancing away. "I wish I knew mine."

Starmine didn't like leaving him behind. She nosed around in his pockets and sometimes found things she wasn't supposed to eat, but greatly enjoyed. Jade herself stewed on Nate's sadness, wondering if bringing back a seashell would cheer him. But when the salty breeze caught her astride Starmine's saddle, Jade forgot to feel sorry for her friend. She let the briny wind rake through her worries and snatch up what wasn't fun or exciting as she dismounted.

Ahead of her lay the quarter, the beach, and, her favorite, the sea.

She tugged her hat low and tied Starmine down to a post between dusty-white buildings, outfitted behind timber-cut stalls draped with straw and colorful tarps. Columns of people walked the street to barter with vendors, chewing tobacco, tracing silk patterns, smelling eggs, testing the weight of beads. Chickens squawked in time with swearing merchants. Jade just barely resisted testing one of the swear words she heard, or stopping to run her hand over a shiny gold compass she thought her father would like.

Instead, she did her best to avoid everyone's gazes, keeping her chin ducked and her posture curved. Each time she was jostled, she pressed her lips tight, tight, tight, even when her foot was stepped on or an elbow punched her shoulder.

She was invisible and yet not. *Overlooked,* she thought.

She fell back against a table where black pearl was being assessed. The lapidary started to yell, but then something caught his eye and his mouth slackened.

Forgotten.

Following his line of sight, Jade got an eyeful as well. There was a woman lounging barefoot in the doorway of one of the biggest buildings on the street. Her hair flowed in long, black spirals and her dark breasts nearly spilled out of a peach-colored corset. Jade didn't know what it was, exactly, that made her so eye-catching. The elegant arch of her back? The sultry curve of her smile? Whatever her secret, it made no difference how poorly the broken shutters framed her. No passerby could look away.

"Who is that?" Jade whispered, not really expecting an answer. Her curiosity was so huge she got close enough to make out the white pearls woven into the woman's hair. "Who are you?"

Jade was more startled than the woman, as she was quickly and thoroughly assessed. "You're too young to learn." The woman's smile grew. "Come back to me when you're a little older, *little love,*" she said, her accent sweet and low, like she intended to unveil that tantalizing secret if Jade listened well. "And I'll teach you who I am."

"You're not a lady."

"I am," said the woman. "Just a different kind."

She heard someone say, "I promise we're good for payment next week." A boy. When Jade turned, he was a thin, quaking pillar of desperation and surrounded by meat. Butcher, she realized. Although he was tall, he looked young. Nate-young, in fact. "I promise we're grateful for your investment, Mr. Lowe."

"Hurry," said the woman. "You should come inside."

But Jade was already ducking away from her reaching hands, trying to get a better picture of Mortimer Lowe. *A crow,* was Jade's first thought. *He looks like a crow.* Not in coloring. His eyes were crystal blue, his skin pink in the sun. Not in bearing. He was taller than the boy. But something about him made her think of storms and shadows under the bed. His pointy nose didn't help.

"We had a *deal*, Mr. Feathertooth," Lowe said softly. But Jade could hear him clearly, as everyone on the street had stopped their bustling to listen. His lip curled when the boy barely muffled a sob. "Go on and scurry back to your mother. Send her out. I'll deal with her directly."

Jade shuddered along with the boy. "Please," said Feathertooth. "She's not well."

Lowe sighed. Then his fist sprang out, cracking against the boy's cheekbone. "We have a certain way of doing things, Mr. Feathertooth. You're young yet," said Lowe as the boy cried. "But consider that a downpayment. I expect what I'm owed, plus ten copper bars more, this time next week. Understand?"

The boy nodded and whimpered, and Jade stepped forward, her fists bunched. Her face felt hotter than ever. Her own lips had curled back and she might have been growling. It didn't matter that she hadn't gotten to the beach yet and noon was almost upon her.

She wanted to make Mortimer Lowe hurt.

When she was close enough, she shoved at him.

He was surprised enough to jerk into the boy's stall, causing the pig meat hanging above them to rattle their chains. "What's this?" he hissed.

Then he laughed when he saw Jade.

"And who might you be?" His gaze roved the crowd, as if

searching for someone responsible for her. Jade saw the lady who was not a lady disappear inside the building at her back. "A knight, maybe?"

There was more laughter. This time, it didn't just come from Lowe.

Jade's cheeks burned hotter. "No, I'm not a dumb knight," she spat. "I'm the daughter of Tore Elder."

More laughter.

Then a kind of awkward silence.

"Fuck she say?" said someone in the crowd. *"Ain't that the bastard who wrecked the fort?"*

"The Ashman. Mostly burns down holy things. Monasteries. Churches. Temples. Don't much matter to 'im."

"Captains the Sea's Fire," someone else supplied. *"You don't got a fort big enough, you ain't got a prayer loud enough to keep Tore Elder back."* There was a startled huff, or a deep sigh, Jade couldn't tell which without unlocking her gaze from Lowe's. *"He'd just burn your god down anyway."*

"I remember hearing he'd had a brat. Didn't figure she'd be so small."

Jade's chin lifted higher. People knew he had a daughter. That was all that mattered. Mortimer Lowe had better believe she was who she said, or she'd make sure he paid. "Apologize to that boy." She did her best to mimic the sound of her mother's voice, a kind of elegant and righteous fury Jade had never seen anyone dismiss. "Or I'll tell my father what you've done."

But rather than appearing frightened, Mortimer Lowe smiled. Jade wanted to hunch away from it, hide and run. "It would seem, Miss Elder, that we have a problem," he said, stepping toward her. "Do you know who I am? What it is I do?"

Two very large men suddenly scooped her up. She started screaming and kicking. She bit one in the arm.

Lowe spoke over the man's howl. "Our island only prospers in the name of our Overseer. You know him, yes?" Jade only struggled harder. "And while he's tucked in the Inlands, I am the one they turn to on the street. I am the one who keeps out the unwanted, the dangerous. You see, Miss Elder, your father is not wanted in the quarter, or anywhere on Nadara."

He pulled her chin toward him. "With your help," he murmured. "I'm going to make sure he never comes back."

"Help me," Jade screamed out.

But this wasn't the Inlands.

No one in the quarter reached for her.

"Everyone here has a fine enough memory of your father, Miss Elder," Lowe said. "They don't like what they remember."

Jade kept right on screaming as Mortimer Lowe and his men dragged her deep into the shadows made by the street.

THERE WERE SCREAMS. Her screams.

There were blows to the back, for the lies they believed she'd told when they discovered nothing but a maid and a thin-armed man toting books into her home. Nothing about their findings made her claim sound credible.

There was a spark in the distance, then a fire so consuming Jade didn't think any in her household had escaped. Not Mr. Warrington, who'd been waiting patiently for Jade's return. Not Mabel, whose work supported a family of two boys and one girl. Not even her mother, who would have been anxious to return home after Jade's lessons.

She was made to watch the fire spread from the roof of Lowe's office.

All of this was punishment for her deception. Her false claims. For how could a daughter of Tore Elder live like a lady inside a house so fine as the one cresting the hill, overlooking the quarter? A pirate's child raised in the Inlands, no less, which was the Overseer's territory?

No. Mortimer Lowe was not convinced.

When Lowe and his men were certain she knew next to nothing of real importance about Tore Elder, when they stopped believing she had anything to do with him at all and everything that had come before ceased to matter, they tossed her to the street at nightfall.

The butcher helped, called for a Ms. Anette. The lady who was not quite a lady. What Jade could make of Anette's beauty through eyes nearly welded shut was just comforting enough to make Jade weep into the ground.

"You should have listened to me, little love." Ms. Anette and the butcher were careful when they lifted her. "You should have come inside."

AFTER...

J ade sat on a cushion plaiting feathers into her hair when she met Pala's dark, sloe eyes in the gold-leaf mirror. The black splotches across its surface did not hide the resignation digging frown lines around the other girl's mouth. "Anette wouldn't approve of what you're doing to your face."

"I'm worried."

"Make sure you're not followed and you'll have no reason to be."

"Stop shrugging this off." Pala shut the door behind her. And though the walls were thin, the moans pouring out from the other rooms masked her question from any who might hear what they shouldn't. "Are you sure you know what you're doing?" She walked over to the window and leaned heavily into the opening. "I'm not sure the risks you take are worth it."

"Worth what?"

Pala turned, a grim willow of a girl sparkling in the morning sun. "Worth the loss of you."

"Yes, I'm sure," Jade said, inhaling softly. Weaving the red strands of her hair with feathers dipped in delicate gold kept her hands steady and precise as she spoke. "You arrived after Tore Elder blew a hole through the bay. When his gun captains broke off chunks of the fort. Do you know what becomes of an island without a fort? A beach?" The wind outside her window was a cunning hiss slithering into the room. She cinched the bottom of her hair with a feathered brooch and wondered if Pala was just as chilled by the sudden breeze as she. Then she turned to face Pala fully. "Pandemonium. That's a word my tutor once taught me. It means chaos," she explained when Pala only stared at her. "Nadara has arms and they sprout from that fort. They guard and they invite. They provide security and they sanction commerce for this place. The fort was being rebuilt when you arrived, but you remember what little good it did, don't you, as damaged as it was still?"

Pala had arrived on Nadara's shores hanging onto a strewn plank, near to unconsciousness. She and her brother had sought passage on one of the legal trading ships, aiming for the Overseer, who paid for passage in exchange for servitude. Jade still didn't know what Pala and her brother had been running from, or running toward, but all that had ceased to matter when Captain Wynn aimed from the damaged fort and fired on any ship sliding into the bay. Pala's brother hadn't survived the ship's destruction.

Jade saw the memory strike a blow in Pala, because the poorly drawn coolness she wore to match Jade cracked and revealed a pallor. Death had a way of unmaking even the most careful of defenses. Its footprint remained, even on an island made of sand—or on girls made from the shadows of loss.

"Captain Wynn is a problem, and not the only one Nadara has," Jade said, folding her hands instead of opening them to the gilded brush on her vanity or the seams of her robe. Her nerves were fully awake and pressing for action. The breeze became a tool, chilling the rawness of them. "He took the fort, rebuilt it on his own terms, and caused another mess in the bay because he could. Because pirates like him were given free reign when Tore Elder tore through this place. He made our shores weak, *desperate* to defect to the strongest." She inhaled again, pushing aside memories of falling buildings, sand erupting, fires blazing. The fists and whips of Mortimer Lowe. "Even when that strength is terrible."

Pala nodded after a long moment, heading for the door. But she hesitated. "I'm not asking what bringing him here really means. I'm not going to ask after the trap you're setting for the tomcats. I just want you to remember you're still the mouse. And I want you to remember something else."

Jade rose from her cushioned stool to test the bathwater she had brought up to the room herself. It had been boiling and was now down to searing. A bath was a simple ritual she intended to turn into a cold tactic. "Go on."

"He was disciplined by the sea and lives for the chase of the next prize, same as them all. But he is what he is for one reason, same as them all," said Pala, flicking her honey-almond hair behind her. A nervous habit Jade was sure her friend didn't know about. "Something was stolen from him, some wrong that can never be made right—and he will never forget it. So if you're thinking of wronging him..." The thought of Jade accomplishing such a thing clearly unnerved the girl. "Don't let him catch you, Jade."

The robe Jade wore was hand-painted satin-silk and left a watery trail of seafoam fabric as she met Pala near the door. Patted her cheek. "Pleasure is only a fair exchange when both parties are rewarded. And I assure you, my friend, I have been nothing but fair with the captain."

"Then I won't worry."

Jade smiled, because Pala's lie was innocent. She was just another girl who didn't fully understand her own nature, nor saw the point in trying. "Good." Jade had many friends like Pala, because the alternative was less simple. She had less and less time to account for friends who might one day become enemies. "Now, after you've delivered him here, only knock on the door again if I pass too much time with him or if Anette comes back early from her errand."

When Pala left, so did the coolness of the air.

Everything hung on a precarious balance from this point on, a scathing scratch of a fact against her numerous worries. She found herself at her only window, sucking in the salt-laced air until she no longer tasted ash on the wind, nor smelled burning wood.

Until the hot press of memories faded.

Because she was alone, she gave in to the urge to peel at the paint curling in the corners of her window while her mind raced. She could see the broken patches of ivy swallowing nine-year-old rubble no one had bothered clearing. She could see the merchants, though half-hidden by the drape of red, violet, and tan canvases, haggling with one another. She could see pirates, lured to the island by the promise of the Overseer's gold, hanging limp over tables visible through the open slats of Lowe's Tavern.

Her nails dug into the chipped paint when Mortimer Lowe himself approached. His gaze skittered over the street, winding through half-knit deals and tender negotiations. Every merchant on the street pretended not to feel his interest, laughing harder and longer, clapping each other on the back. But his lips had already turned up. He'd found something he wanted despite the tangle of their limbs and ease of their conference.

That gaze slid up the inn suddenly, locking onto Jade's through her open window. Bits of her hair lifted up in the breeze. Her shoulders were straight under the satin. She offered Mortimer Lowe a smile molded from embers and midnight, revealing practiced mischief and nothing more. Nothing he'd find dangerous. She turned away when a knock cracked against her door.

But the weight of his concentration broke like a thousand pinpricks down her back.

Collect yourself, she thought, quickly taking up a cloth to wash away the fury building behind her cheeks, her eyes, her lips. *Calm is a weapon. Fury is an artifice.*

She forced herself to remember there was nothing to be afraid of. That particular monster of her childhood would lose his foothold in the shadows soon enough.

The knocking stopped. Then the doors were shoved open.

Jade remained in her robe, but only just. She designed a dip toward her cleavage, a slat of flesh going down further until the fabric cinched low at her waist.

Filling up her doorway was a man made of silver streaks and copper skin, a black-cobalt gaze and hard hands. "Captain Wynn," she greeted, dipping her head slightly because it pleased him to be deferred to. "How goes the managing of the *Victory?*"

His smile was always made of his lips instead of his teeth. Many a foe had instantly begged for mercy at the sight of it, or so the stories went. Jade, eying the edges of the scar sunken into the left side of his face, didn't doubt his formability. But when he carved out, "Survived the sea's fire well enough," from a voice as deep as the ocean itself, she began to understand why many found those depths frightening. He looked at her like darkness only just parting.

It was a struggle not to press her hands against her mouth in sheer disbelief. Insult had no place here, between herself and a man built from merciless canonfire and the pillaging of islands much like this one. Inside, however, hope was a soft undulation in the bed of her nerves.

"Was it a difficult task?" she managed. "Did much harm come to your victims?"

"There was some resistance. But when the fire abated, the ash settled. We brought what remained back with us."

"Then this venture has borne fruit, wouldn't you say?"

Wynn's dark gaze remained steady. "If your promises haven't spoiled in my absence."

Now Jade did smile. Cocked her head with it. She disrobed, watching him as she did so. "You require proof?" she said, sinking into the bath. She moaned as the heat of the water sank into her skin, clamoring against the low hum of fear ringing inside her. When Wynn stepped toward her, she didn't cower. Didn't flinch when his knife swept under her throat and pressed against her pulse. She'd have expected nothing less from him, but that his breath was uneven told her she had won the advantage.

"There, on the dresser." She spoke softly, so softly she wasn't even sure he truly heard her as he followed her direction. "A letter signed by the Overseer, delivered from my own mother's hands, promising that should you deliver Tore Elder into his keeping, you will be well-compensated for your efforts."

Wynn opened the letter, read from it. "And if I were to take this document to Mr. Lowe for verification?"

Jade shut her eyes, ordering herself to relax though it was a very delicate game she played. Wynn would find no fear or regret in them anyway. She'd meant what she'd told Pala. Piracy had grown too bold on this island, breathing life into the monsters who'd hung low on the sea, with little refuge on the open water or the port cities of the world. They'd been dying and then Tore Elder had caused a resurgence. His guns had shaped a new battle cry. If the pirates continued to bellow it, and continued to fight with it, then this island had no chance of a foundation.

Jade's home had no chance of a future.

"I would say you are not a man who relies on the word of a common clerk. I would say that you understand that mutual self-interest is a better gamble than simple trust in a pleasure-worker. I would also remind you that I am still in Ms. Anette's employ, and she would no more enjoy my private dealings with you than you would enjoy any betrayal I conjured against you." She smiled again. "But you do what you must, Captain Wynn."

He released a little puff of amusement. Less than a quarter of a laugh and as much quarter as he'd ever give. "Does Anette have any idea how clever you are?"

Jade's lashes fluttered. "Why, you flatter me, captain. Are you trying to seduce me?"

He didn't laugh, but the amusement remained in the quirk of his lips. "No time today," he said, but they both knew it didn't matter if the opposite were true. There was an unspoken understanding between them. They each respected each other enough not to wrench their current dynamic. If they fell into bed now, neither one of them would be able to resist wresting power from the other.

Jade had secrets she couldn't afford to part with. But, there were times when the soft sheets at her back beckoned. When the lock holding back the seductive shadows behind Wynn's unyielding gaze begged to be picked. The man was insatiable by all accounts, but Jade supposed she had fed him something far more satisfying.

The weight of his measure was a palpable thing. "Is there something else I can do for you, captain?"

"One thing." He stepped forward again. "How did you know where he'd be?"

She tilted her head, hoping the careless move hid her alarm. A part of her had anticipated his asking, but the rest of her had hoped he would not have. "How does anyone like me learn anything before anyone else?"

"That's not a real answer."

"You called me clever, if you'll recall," she said, dancing her fingers over the surface of the bathwater. "Would it be truly clever of me to reveal my sources?"

He studied her a long moment. Then, onto the bed, he dropped a pouch full of her promised one hundred silver bars in payment for the information that had enabled him to capture one of the most notorious men in the world.

"A fraction of what the Overseer has promised you," she commented. "Maybe I'm not so clever after all." And yet by encouraging Tore's capture by another pirate, something new was composed from the dreaded battle cry of a sudden, misshapen brotherhood. Wynn was growing stale behind the walls of his fort. And he, being the very worst of the pirates here, had just abandoned anything resembling honor among thieves. Selling out a fellow king of the seas would be the start of their dismantlement.

Wynn added twenty more bars to the pile, just as thin and small as the silvers undoubtedly were, but this time shining copper.

She quirked a brow at him. "Not a very generous tip."

"The income you'll need to report to Anette for my visit today. A courtesy, and all you'll get from me." He leaned down, until Jade's vision was overflowing with his menace. "If anything should fall through from this point on, I'll be coming back to collect more than money, Jade."

Her breath finally expelled when he walked back across the room. As soon as she was certain she could speak without stumbling, she threw out her final demand, one he hadn't accounted for outright. "And the heathen goddess purported to be aiding him in taking his prizes? Was she dealt with?"

Wynn stopped at her door. His hand ticked against the panels. "One of my men claimed to have spotted a girl aboard," he said over his shoulder. "But when we took the ship, there was no one there."

"What are you saying?"

"That stories like Tore Elder's demand ornaments. Something to gawk at so that the last horrible thing that happened won't seem as horrible. One man says there was a girl. The rest of the men, including myself, find nothing. I say the help of a sea goddess is exactly the kind of embellishment the people of this island enjoy."

Jade stepped out of the tub, quickly tugging on her robe. "I don't believe that. And, deep down, I think, neither do you. Maybe that terrifies you. To believe without really knowing if you should. But I can't afford your ignorance, captain. The tales of Tore's latest voyages have been flooding the island with regularity. All of them are embellished. But one detail that crops up again and again is *her*." Jade ignored the knock at her door, and the near-violent need to toss Wynn from the room for failing her. Traditional payment had only been one compartment of this deal. "I don't know who she is nor what she is, but I do know magic has most certainly climbed aboard that ship. It's the only thing that has made his recent hauls possible."

Jade's pulse raced at the thought of a ghost unchecked, some nameless peril wrapped in substantial reputation. Stories like the ones she had heard of her father these last nine years, no matter how tentative the foothold, never warranted a dismissal. "And if it hasn't occurred to you that any form of magic made loyal to a man like Tore could very well set this island ablaze, allow me to assure you that *it is possible*. I have seen the work of magic, Captain Wynn, and the things it can achieve when wielded." Her voice hardened, any deference she had for him lost to it. "Our bargain remains incomplete until you've removed this threat."

Silence passed between them, but Jade couldn't hear the things the captain said to himself. Didn't know the ways in which he might reassure himself, lean closer to the voice in his head that told him magic was something made in the shadows of the world and did not often rise out of them. That things like goddesses or saints or whatever else anyone on Nadara still believed and held dear and true were unmatched by the curse of a world built on sand—and a man who had become someone only emboldened, powerful even, by the curses of this world.

"We hold every proof of what really exists. The Ashman bottled in my fort. This letter promising me payment. The money weighing down your sheets." He opened the door to Pala's stunned face. With a last look over his shoulder, he said, "As we both know you can't really tell me otherwise, our bargain is finished.

"Clever girl or not."

SHE HADN'T SMELLED the unwashed bodies when she was younger.

Her first time through the quarter had been a kaleidoscope of colorful, untouchable things. Actions and insults that couldn't have been repeated in front of her mother, though the woman had lived on the deck of a pirate ship before Jade was born.

Every wide gesture of a merchant was a promise about to be sold. Every smile and ripe swear was a debt being called. And those rare moments of silence were just pockets emptying, leaking copper and silver onto the gaming tables where dirty, sea-worn palms twitched toward the clink of falling money.

The stink meant that business was good.

But there was something else, something *more*, winding through the stench of men and women showing devotion to their wares and tills. An insidious perfume that held a throbbing note of silver snaps in the sky and flame dancing on leaves.

Dread coiled inside her. When Jade tilted her head, the clear afternoon sky was bloated with poisonous tempests. She could hear the sea's harsh rasps even from here.

Jade waited for someone to shudder under the curtain of power slipping over them from the beach, but no one turned with a cry of, "Don't you *feel* that?"

If Pala had been allowed to accompany her, Jade didn't think her friend would have noticed either. There were a rare few who felt that lurch in the belly when magic drifted where it was not invited. A specific palette was necessary to catch the subtlety. Captain Wynn hadn't believed her warning of retribution because he couldn't; his sensibilities were as narrow as his beliefs.

She dodged an overeager pair of hands and slid into the shadows made by the buildings. All of them were slanted, built without longevity in mind. Many had lost the tops of their heads in her father's attack nine years ago, bandaged with canvases instead of stone to keep out the summer torrents and night winds. The people who owned things here either fed expectations of departure or clung to the dream of owning land in the Inlands.

The quarter was a stopgap for most. A temporary reprieve from the edges of civilization, where the unwanted had likely been turned out. A ramshackle construct they convinced themselves they could escape.

So what did it matter if that crow, Mortimer Lowe, took away some of their shine? What did it matter if Captain Wynn roamed restlessly behind the walls of the fort, lording over the bay?

There was no mortar securing the sands beneath their feet.

No one had promised them anything different.

Jade had lived through the cycle of violence and fear of this place. Sometimes when she lay at night, the scars of her beating chafed against the sheets, burning through the softness. She had swum in the shadows of men like her father for nine years, watching their claws rip open bodies and buildings on a whim even as she avoided the keenness of their edges. Some day she would be too slow. She'd be split open by their careless cruelty. She'd end up watching this entire island drown, pinned down to pay the debt of some dangerous man's revenge.

Or, worse, now, the revenge of a goddess.

A large man from the north had once mumbled to her about the gods of the winds and seas and forests of the earth, and their lust for the honeyed inconstancies that made a human. How their curiosity lay them down with mortals, rearing creatures of unmatched power. And while Jade had no way of confirming her father had bred some new menace for her to contend with, she wouldn't see her home drowned out of spite.

At the end of the street, she found a handful of northern monks prostrate on the ground, praying to a figure carved into a wooden barrier. Only northern worshippers of the Mother of Light were welcome here. A faint dawn-rose aura spiraled from them.

Jade stepped forward.

The monks were instantly on their feet, sweeping out silver swords curved from jeweled pommels. "What business?" said the shortest of them, his chin groused with scars.

"I only come to deliver a request," Jade said.

"Step no further."

With a nod, Jade kept still. "My business is with Vane Mercy." She waved at the half-moon they formed. "I have a special proposition for your captain."

"You say," said the monk. "But you bring no guarantees, infidel."

"Tell him I know why the sky changes, the sea rages, and the air smells like smoke." She quirked a brow at him when his scowl deepened. "Tell him he can find me at Anette's inn, and we can discuss what we both know."

When she returned to the pleasurehouse, Pala pulled her aside and nodded toward a turn desperately pretending he wasn't waiting for her. Special requests cost more, and judging by his wide eyes and careworn clothes, he and his crew hadn't had much success with their latest prize.

Jade tried not to curse him the lines he caused her forehead since he seemed innocent enough—for a pirate. "Strange, isn't it?"

"New faces usually are," Pala agreed. "I'm sure he's worth something good." She wiggled her eyebrows. "Says he's heard of you. Says that's why he's just...waiting."

"Strange *and* interesting."

Jade left Pala to warm him up while she went up to change. Years ago, when Anette had agreed to take her on, she thought she'd found a magic house, cobbled out of the island itself. Mismatching chandeliers made of shells and glass swung from the lower level ceiling created by the various rooms above. In the center of the inn, however, a tree wound its way past the second floor toward the roll of clouds, sprouting leaves that strung together a green tourmaline upper ceiling with small shards of the sky peeking through.

Magic of a different kind had been taught to her here: illusions, much like the ones people thrived off of throughout the quarter. *Not staying. Not buying. Not telling.* And yet so many were still here, and they bought as much as they could, and they told her things she shouldn't know, things Anette liked knowing. Illusions built here snared secrets and in turn transformed the coal of broken promises into anything Anette wanted.

Best of all, the Madame also liked sharing. Jade, along with the rest of the girls, had benefited in cosmetics and silks and accessories. Her room smelled of rose-water after each turn because of the Madame's generosity.

As soon as Jade entered, she hid her payment from Wynn under a loose floorboard beneath her bed. She lined her eyes with kohl, added more feathers to her hair, and donned a charm made by her mother. It represented Elda, spirit mother of the sky clans born in Osolda, a country northeast of the island which had suffered more than a century under unjust rule and beast-infested lands.

The way Jade's mother had fashioned the charm, Elda was shaped like a black stork and would ward off unnatural cruelty.

This was all the protection she had, until Vane Mercy could council her to something stronger.

Lightning rippled outside of the room.

The day she entered the quarter had been sunny and bright. The day she had *become* the quarter was altogether different. It was much like today, bursting with tension and dripping with endless rain. She'd been hiding from her rampaging father for weeks. He'd docked uncontested in the bay and found ashes where Jade's childhood home had been. Land which he'd been given as a desperate bribe from the Overseer to cease hostilities in that very bay not long before Jade's birth lay in the thick of ruin and empty of his family.

But he'd refused to fully accept his wife and daughter had been swallowed by a nameless fire.

He'd cut through the quarter searching for the cause, setting things alight in turn, pulling men apart until answers and blood slipped through his hands. No one dared oust Mortimer Lowe, not when he'd had so many contracted to him. Not even when Tore reboarded his ship and cast his guns to the fort, the edges of the street, the tents on the beach.

For weeks, death had tolled.

Jade would smell it on the hands of those who had sheltered her. She'd see it in the crimson streaks slashing the buildings, like an errant and erratic artist had murdered his muse to paint them. She'd hear it when the dust settled after a fired shot and a child's wail broke the silence. The cycle had sustained her. She drank nothing but the blood from her broken lips and ate little more than the dregs of smoke that took days more to dissipate.

When at last Tore Elder had departed the island, and she'd approached Anette for employment, she'd become a creature who breathed only in the shadows, a walking welt of raw nerves.

Under Anette's tutelage, polish was overlaid but did not remake what Jade had become—

A girl so entwined with the anguish and possibilities of the quarter, she rose and fell to the rhythm of debts and deals. She arose rose-scented each day, though not entirely clean of the stench that meant business was good.

That, even when Nadara prospered, death was close.

Who she was now could scarcely afford those quiet spaces in a life, where moments containing her mother's soft hands and books by candlelight, Nate's copper-glinting eyes and gleeful grins, became a precious cache she handled only when her room was black and empty. When turns went back to their captains or to their stalls in the bitter final hours before dawn, and the girls went back to their rooms, wringing the quiet free of echoes of false pleasure. Those night hours when the world seemed to swallow itself...

That was when Jade finally embraced the broken image of her old self, ignoring the misplaced naivety and soothing the muted child she had become in those death-defying weeks, whose sorrow sequestered itself in the back of her mind. A child sundered by the misery of crawling through grit and hiding from monsters whose faces split between her attacker and her father.

Dwelling was a luxury very few in the quarter could afford. One day she might have those spare moments in idle excess. She'd have to face the loss of what had been. But that day was not today.

One of the new girls brought up Jade's strange customer just as she finished changing. Her thoughts went smooth as glass.

Calm is a weapon. Fury is an artifice.

As the girl turned to go, Jade slipped her beloved robe off her shoulder, feigning a shiver as the man tracked the delicate satin ripples against her skin and said, "Ready for me, handsome?"

SHE LEARNED the turn was quartermaster of the *Revenge*—a smaller ship than most, manned by a smaller crew than most, sailing under an enigma to the island called Steel.

"Tell me, sweeting," she purred into the man's ear, sensing his distress in the way his hands clutched her skin. They didn't know whether to hold or let go. He hadn't spoken his name to her. "Does your captain know you've come to see me?"

He moved drowsily beneath her. Reached up to dive his hands into her hair. "No," he confessed, groaning. "Wasn't supposed to come in today."

"Oh?" Jade whispered, grinding down on him. When he moaned, she smiled against his lips. "Why not?"

Secrets accrued interest with enough diligence. They grew thick and tall, built layer by layer, until there stood a spire where there once was an empty plot. Secrets burst with value the better a structure could be seen in the short distance between present and future.

His mouth reached for hers. "Says—" The deliberate slide of her hands caused another groan. "Says he's worried about this place. Says Ms. Anette used to be harmless. Now he's not so sure." She bit his ear and he crushed her mouth down onto his for another taste, even as she wondered what a new captain on the water knew of Anette and her dealings. "Seen captains and crews come in here too many times with less money and less thoughts in their head. Seen Captain Wynn come in too often with less of one and more of the other."

Jade jerked against the man, but he took it as a response to his cold, questing hands. A pirate smart enough to follow another pirate, turn over the other's plans? What kind of creature was Steel? Did he suspect *her*? She rewarded his quartermaster with a smile and let him think her racing pulse had to do with his efforts. "Well, you might tell Captain Steel that Ms. Anette frowns upon theft of any sort," she murmured, heart thudding against his chest. "And, here in her inn, he needn't worry about anything but what's between his legs. Or, rather, let us worry."

Doing her job well meant she had to let go of the outside world, make her customer believe that for this window of time every breaking sigh and every practiced roll of her hips was borne of her lust for him, and only him, and not her design. A skill the likes of which the younger girls would need a decade under Anette's tutelage to master, because, unlike Jade, who had learned years ago the value of splitting herself from the current moment, those new girls were too keen on living inside that moment.

They were brought here or traveled here when the money was good, when the pirates were generous. They had grown up in the prosperity and had no inkling of the wreckage they might find themselves. They had no way of knowing just how rapidly things could change on Nadara.

But Jade knew. She had no choice but to remember always.

Strife was what honed a talent.

Uncertainty forged it's quicksilver edge.

"Tell me I'm everything," Jade panted, her rosy hands coming up to cradle the man's face. "Tell me you'll never deny me. You'll give me everything."

"*Anything*," he muttered hoarsely, panting harder. "Everything."

Detachment with the power to create ruses and ensnare men was easier when the man's hands were cold, when you felt nothing in the first place. But, such as the case with Wynn, and men like Wynn, when their warm, inexplicable draw became a tempting danger, the kind of detachment Anette taught and Jade had had no trouble learning took more than a strong will.

It took ambition.

The need to be more than someone else's overflowing cup. The desire to climb something, make something, be something that served a purpose. When Jade and the other girls led men to their rooms, and they cradled them in their bodies, and they rendered the world with a private softness, they might smile in the dark. For their deceptions were so beguiling not even they could question their own artistry. And when secrets were plucked from the men's bruised, loose lips, no one could question they were divine. All-knowing and powerful with it, holding fates in the palms of their hands.

Women who achieved this kind of divinity were never forgotten, *especially* when their power was least perceived. That was the magic taught to a pleasure-worker.

Jade smiled into her turn's neck. "If Captain Steel warns you away from me, you won't listen. You'll come back to me."

"I—"

"I'm everything," she reminded him, clawing at his backside. Then she stopped her movements. "Yes?"

"Yes," he pleaded. "Gods, there ain't no fury like a woman."

She gave him what he needed then. Held him as he finished, and, thought, oddly, *But what does a woman become when the fury is gone?* And was startled by the sadness lurking behind the sentiment. It snuck up on her like a well-tended secret. She could see it clearly and yet had no conception of when it had started building.

When he collapsed on top of her, Jade was cold again, her thoughts alert and turning. "Did Captain Wynn betray Captain Steel?" she said idly, while stroking his back.

"What?" came the drowsy reply.

She sighed. "I just wondered why Steel cares so much about you coming to see me. Why he cares that Wynn is sometimes here."

The man's breath fanned her ear. "They have history. Used to sail together. All of us did."

History. A polite word to muffle hostility that went fathoms deep.

Jade had trained to catch the tension in a man. She could snap it like bone or smooth it out like muscle. "Why are they angry with each other?" She made her voice wobble, rousing him more from his half-sleep. "Why does your captain want to keep you from a good thing?" She paused, letting her skin rub against his. "This *was* a good thing?"

He lifted his head, showing her softened features. She'd planted the seed of affection, but was fascinated to see it needed no watering from her. Her skills were growing untended. "I *loved* it," he murmured, rubbing her cheek.

Most fascinating of all, she could see he meant it, that his warmth toward her was real, even though he'd lay thirty copper bars at the foot of the bed when their time today was done. "Then why does he care what *we* do? What does it matter if Wynn comes here sometimes?"

Her thoughts were strong and straight in her mind, but his long silence opened the chest of her fears. They spread inside her like fever. They grazed beneath her flesh like the threat of a knife. She didn't *need* to deal with the dark potential of a feud right now. Not while balancing Wynn's coerced injustice of Tore

Elder with the plans she had for Mortimer Lowe. The men of her world already had enough power demanding to be stripped. She couldn't afford to tiptoe around another bloody line drawn in the sand.

She couldn't stand it if her home toppled again.

Steel's man finally sighed. "Wynn stole from my captain, and we've become what we've become so that never need happen again. But Wynn made it happen again, to Steel," he said. "And we don't become what we become because we learned forgiveness."

She wanted to press him. Tease out the hostility between a captain for another captain, a crew for another crew, because if she knew their secrets, she could amend her plans to truly protect the island. Bolster the quarter.

But instead she found herself thinking of the fire Mortimer Lowe had set, the terror he'd brought down upon her. The crippling loss of self and the certainty that she might never be whole without all that had been taken from her.

And could say nothing more.

That was why she heard the creak so clearly, the only sound warning her what was about to happen.

The turn had just begun to roll over—

—when a sword skewered him through the chest.

Jade's scream lodged in her throat.

A girl loomed over them both, her face carved from ochre and speckled with blood. "Almost," she hissed.

Jade rolled from the bed, linen sheets tangling between her legs, while the quartermaster of the *Revenge* choked on his own blood.

Before Jade could turn away, the girl lopped off her strange customer's head.

∼

JADE QUIVERED hard against the cold floor.

The room was spinning. Her hands trembled against the rivets in the wood before digging in for purchase. Her voice would crack if she spoke, so she kept silent, willing herself to calm, though she was petrified between the door and a stranger with a blood-drenched sword.

"What," she managed after a moment of false, agonizing silence, "have you done?" She sucked in a breath when the girl turned toward her, sword still high. "Do you *know* who that is? Who his brothers are? Do you know who you've just *killed*?"

The girl blinked through the blood dripping down her face, lowering her blade for a moment. As though what she had done hadn't truly sunken in.

But it had already started to infiltrate Jade's panicked thoughts. Her fear had already taken on a different shape. The girl had just killed a valued member of Captain Steel's crew in *Anette's place*. There was far worse than the promise of a foul beating for the costliness of what had just happened. Jade didn't know who this girl was, but she'd be damned if she would pay for her severely expensive mistake.

She opened her mouth to scream but the girl rushed her, pinning her to the floor. Pressed her bloodied hand against Jade's mouth, transferring the turn's death onto her skin.

"I will break you," the girl hissed, leaning in and sending a curtain of teal braids swinging forward. Her worn, broad-brimmed hat skewed her cheekbone. "Then I will feed what remains of you to the sea."

Jade screamed as loud as she could behind the girl's hand.

The girl brought her hands down to choke her. Jade's legs kicked against the wood as her breath backed into her chest.

"Who are you?" Jade gasped out. *Hear me, please, someone hear me. Pala. Layla. Anette. Someone.*

"I am Azura," growled the girl through gritted teeth, green

shards for eyes reflecting a deadly passion. Sweat beaded her brow as Jade struggled. "Daughter of Tore fuckin' Elder."

Jade felt something collapse inside her. Not just from her lack of breath, nor the taste of death swelling in her closing throat, but from the hard pulse of shock battering her body. It quaked inside her, toppling light and reason. The world delved dark and bottomless as a nightmare, until all she saw were those icy, green chips for eyes.

Eyes so familiar tears burned.

The doors burst open.

Distantly, Jade heard Pala's voice. "Fucking hells is this?" Jade wanted to warn. Or scream. Or weep. *This is my—* The thought crumbled in her mind before it fully formed. *This is danger. This is worse than anything I could imagine.* "Get off her."

Thunder beat down outside the window, blowing open the glass. Light exploded in a thousand fragments.

The pressure around Jade's throat lifted. Pala ran to her, helping her sit up as she coughed.

When Jade could make out the figures before her, she saw Azura facing Vane Mercy, holding up palms riddled with blue lightning. "You'd dare lay hands on me? Do you know who I am? What I am?"

The captain of the *Infidel's Cry* stood with his long, maroon cloak billowing in the harsh winds pouring from Azura's body.

"What are you are," he said softly, "is my enemy."

Lifting an ivory medallion between them, he spoke in the old language of Feydla, another northern country which shared a border with Osolda, muttering what sounded like prayers, until a dark plum aura smoked out of his skin and permeated the room.

When he stepped forward, Azura stepped *back*. Her fists of lightning were evaporating, the way a candle's flame fluttered before winking out.

"What's happening to me?" she cried. Her gaze flew toward

Jade, and, for a moment, the hatred was gone, leaving nothing but a plummeting fear in its wake. The same fear that had caught Jade unaware from the moment Azura had stormed into the room. "What's he doing to me?"

"I'm purging you," murmured Captain Mercy, once a devout monk from Feydla's coast. A holyman turned pirate was that much more dangerous than the average sort. Jade didn't know she could feel both grateful and wary of a man who stole magic about as often as he stole goods. "In the name of the Mother of Light, you will harm none with your power."

As Azura sunk to the floor, her knees catching her weight, Jade went to her and knelt down. She wanted to grab her arms, but was afraid of more than just the girl's waning power. Somehow, when she had thought of her father breeding a force of magic, the last thing that occurred to her was facing a creature made of limbs and wearing a face sharpened by her father's chin, his *eyes*.

"Did you mean what you said?" she demanded, in contrast to the soft rending in her heart. This was a person who sort of looked like her. Who shared her blood and had flesh over her bones. A person Jade had never met. "Are you really his daughter?"

That hatred returned, and if Vane Mercy had never come, Jade was certain Azura would have seen Jade's death through to the bitter end. "You destroyed my world," Azura said weakly, though that fire in her eyes seared Jade to the bone. Her fingers wrapped tighter around her fallen hat. "This," she said, nodding toward Vane Mercy, "won't stop me." Her smirk was laced with years of poison, as though this hatred she bore Jade was not newly formed. "I will not stop until I destroy yours."

And then Azura whispered the one and only thing Jade had *never*—and would never have—expected to hear while tethering herself to an island constantly on the verge of collapse, away from her father's legacy and in the midst of building her own. "Count on that," Azura breathed as her eyes fluttered closed. "Big sister."

∾

HOW DOES SHE KNOW?

"Jade?"

How does she know who I am? How did she know to come here?

"Jade," Pala insisted, turning Jade to face Vane Mercy, who cast his eyes about the room, ears twitching at the moans coming from the other rooms, and said, "I was told you have a proposition for me."

His contempt for their meeting's whereabouts sat heavily between them. "I confess I nearly didn't come."

It took all of Jade's skill to shutter the kernel of guilt growing in her mind and ignore the unconscious curve of her sleeping half-sister. She notched her chin and said, "Then why did you? It's true we've had no dealings before. And yet you came anyway. Was it the promise of capturing magic?"

The gleam in his grey eyes unsettled her. It was impossible to forget that a man like him rooted his coin from the ensorcelled, taking what he drew from them like poison and turning that power into profit. "It was in the Book," he said, referring to the Feydlan holy text protected by the coastal monks. Jade could only guess his motives for stealing it—honoring his vows or reinventing them to suit—but it was his beliefs which allowed him to corner a market for mystical objects of his own invention. A man so intangibly governed and canny despite it was not to be trusted. His gains hadn't yet become Jade's losses, but she suspected that if he put effort into thwarting her, or any of the other concerns on the street, both Wynn and Lowe would become the least of her worries. "Today, when I opened the Book of Mercy, the Mother of Light made note of our meeting."

"I see," said Jade, speculating on what she could do with this knowledge. A man who showed deference to a book opened possibilities of how he might be governed anew. He'd been a low-rung priority for her while she dealt first with the more immediate problems of Wynn in his fort and Lowe on the street, her father on the sea, but with Azura's appearance Jade had to find a way to fit Mercy into her rapidly magnifying plans.

But her thoughts dragged their feet. "And did your Book tell you of the girl?"

"No." He eyed the headless body of Jade's turn with disdain rather than fear of reprisal. "The Mother's gifts are wrapped in challenges which must be met."

"But wouldn't you say it was your duty to safeguard the island from one such as her?" Jade returned, thinking of the day's severe overcast and Azura's lightning. If she could convince Vane Mercy to keep her half-sister in check, Jade might have more time to consider her options, other alternatives.

At the moment, her mind still reeled like a brawler listing after a blow. Her past limped closer to the forefront of her thoughts, leaving her weak inside her skin, ham-handedly sewing together a plan that might make sense of the death before her and the girl behind her.

The captain almost smiled. "No, I wouldn't claim that responsibility," he said and Jade's hands clenched to keep her steady. "Her powers have been removed and replaced inside this medallion until my death. If she poses another kind of threat, a physical one to you, let's say, that is no longer my concern." A silver lock of his hair slid free from his tie when he tucked the medallion into the depths of his robe. "We'll consider her magic payment for answering your request. Have you anything else to barter?"

Jade turned back to Pala. "Go on and distract Anette," she

told her friend. "The other girls too, if they're watching. I have business to discuss with Captain Mercy." Then she sighed deeply, her clenched fists shaking a little. "And a body to dispose of."

Pala gripped her curled hand, stuffing a sealed envelope into the creases. "Anette left just before I arrived. And this came for you." She eyed the captain over Jade's head. "Shall I come back and knock again if too much time passes?"

Jade squeezed her friend's hand. "If you must," she said with a small smile. "Now go."

When Pala departed, Jade walked to her dresser. "Rum?" she asked the captain. "Or would you be breaking a vow?"

"Some vows are made to be broken," he said, watching her steadily. "But today, I have no wish to drink. What business?"

"I've dawdled too long in this room. Too many men have passed through and now I have a dead body to explain away," she said, anger stirring beneath the words. She had expected a magical blow, some recompense from a mysterious force tied to Tore Elder. Like a curse cast on her by her part in his removal, Jade had suspected whatever goddess belonged to the captain and crew of the *Sea's Fire* would come calling. But she thought she'd had time. And she had believed no one would ever come close to understanding why she'd involved herself in the destruction of Tore's legacy. Did Azura intend to free Tore Elder from Wynn's fort? Was she yet another obstacle in Jade's efforts to remove the source of instability on this island? Didn't that make her another pirate to contend with, too?

Jade briefly shut her eyes. "I have no time to outline my bargain with you, but I will say that should you take the girl off my hands, I have the means to show you my gratitude. I will pay you a visit with the sum of my gratitude as soon as I'm clear of this mess."

A mess that meant more than just a dead body. Somehow, Jade had to make reparations with Captain Steel before he discovered the circumstances of his quartermaster's death, convince the girls and Anette that nothing was amiss, and come up with proof she could pay Vane Mercy for his help in full.

"I have no interest in gold or silver or copper," he said. "What could you possibly have that I would want?"

Jade recalled what she knew of him, how he split his prizes between himself, his crew, and the people of Feydla, particularly those closest to the temples on the coast. Foodstuffs and cotton and timber were regularly transported to help the impoverished there, who were more of Tore Elder's victims. She thought of how Vane Mercy had arrived in the bay summers ago, with the white flag of surrender tacked and his jaw clenched, until he'd been invited to speak with Charles Wynn up in his fort.

The bay controlled commerce and the fort controlled the bay. Take the latter and the riches of the former were all yours.

"I offer you the one thing that has eluded you for far too long." She delivered her sultriest smile at Mercy, for her own benefit more than his. "Control."

He stiffened. "I see."

"You don't. Not fully. But I promise I can offer it to you. For now, begin by asking yourself why should Captain Wynn have come to me today, if his visit had nothing to do with my—" She licked her teeth. "—services under the employ of Ms. Anette? Ask yourself why someone like him would come to me seeking something as though I had the power to give it and wonder until I come to you with an answer you'll want."

For a long moment, Mercy didn't speak. He glanced down at Azura, watching her stir. Then, with his gaze back on Jade, he said, "I'll expect your visit before day's end."

She opened her mouth to agree when a scream punctuated the fact that she no longer had a shut window. *Has anyone heard us?* She peered out and below just to be sure, purposefully ignoring the stretch of the beach at the end of the street.

She knew why the crowd gathered and why there had been a scream. And yet instead of tracing his gaze back to the spectacle unfolding, Mortimer Lowe had his eyes trained on Jade's window.

"You know whose death has been found on the beach," said Mercy at her back.

"I do," Jade said, trembling all over, fighting valiantly to suppress the instinct to jerk back as though stung. It was more than one death the crowds were panicking over. She imagined the crew of the *Sea's Fire* appeared formidable even in death. Captain Wynn had wasted no time laying out his hard-won victory over Tore Elder before Nadara.

And yet Mortimer Lowe left his business untended, leaning heavily against his tavern to watch her silhouette.

And smile.

When he finally turned to go back inside, Jade let out a long breath. "You should take the girl now while the eyes on the street are distracted. I will meet with you as soon as I can."

"Tonight," Vane Mercy repeated.

"Tonight," Jade agreed.

NOT ONLY DID Jade have more unfulfilled debts than when she awoke in the pleasurehouse early that morning, she'd also inherited a sister. One born with the mysterious ability to control storms and an insurmountable hatred for Jade. One who had known or discovered Jade's part in the capture of Tore Elder and the conquest of the *Sea's Fire*—the only place Azura likely considered home.

And, now, thanks to Azura's fierce rage, Jade owed the enigmatic Captain Steel compensation for his lost crew member and a viable explanation for that crew member's death. Ten copper bars, at minimum, to give credence to Vane Mercy's visit to her rooms when Anette came to Jade with inquiries. And, while Jade had made a good show of understanding Vane Mercy's desires, she was far from sure she could deliver them without even greater personal risk than she already faced.

But, if she didn't yield him what she'd promised, she'd not only have yet another dangerous man, who commanded the devout and ripped magic from the body, to contend with, but also the freedom of her equally dangerous sister.

Sister. Jade shivered from the force of her own sorrow. *A sister I've wronged. Skies forgive me. Protect me.* She stroked the black stork against her neck, stunned at her own vehemence. *For I've taken from her what was taken from me.*

Removing the body of Steel's quartermaster required bribes sacrificed from Wynn's payment for her information. Silver bars went to the girls on the floor and the kitchen staff and the sweepers already cleaning the blood. Each of them swore to keep their whispers out of Anette's hearing, but none of them promised to defend Jade should proof of her involvement come to light.

Even when the world seemed quiet and defensible again, her fears were leaves on the wind, blowing sharply past. When she sat at her dressing table of lacquered mahogany and gilded bronze—an indulgence bought with generous tips and Anette's blessing—she yanked at her snarled braid, ripping the feathers out and tearing at the plaits until her temples stopped hissing.

Calm was a poorly won victory, but she wrangled her temper. She opened the letter Pala had passed to her.

A letter, though unsigned, from Jade's mother, Thaya.

You were correct in your suspicions. The man for which the interior bows craves what he has been denied more than ever before. To do so, he must starve the cats drinking from the bay. Once victory is at hand, he will deal with those that remain.

I am afraid. I am afraid my visits will soon no longer be welcomed. What, then, will we do?

Jade burned the letter with shaking hands. *It's begun,* she thought, and carried the charred remains of her letter to the window, watching the ashes float away toward the afternoon sun.

The Overseer, a ducal disgrace still beholden to his mother country, would soon stop authorizing the pirates' ventures on the sea. He would no longer fence their goods and plop gold into their hands. The far-reaching political reasons didn't matter as much to Jade as the fact of what was quickly cresting Nadara's horizon.

Simply enacting a ban on piracy wasn't going to be enough to chase them out. *Does a cat run from a gnat, after all?*

The Overseer's decision would only aggravate the tensions Jade herself had flamed by encouraging her father's capture. Pirates were as likely to band together a second time as to turn on each other, and on the merchants and innocents on the street. Battles for supremacy would crack open the chest of the island and spill blood into the bay. Not one of them would be satisfied until a victor rose up as her father had done nine years ago, loosing his fury on Nadara for his loss and for the Overseer himself, whom Tore had held responsible when no one else came forward.

None of the pirates would stop tearing and clawing, pillaging and burning, until there was one who stood and proclaimed self-governance. A life without fear built upon the fear of others.

Jade's hand tightened on the handlebar of her brush. Running it through the unwoven strands of her hair was a battle of its own. The tangles and snares encouraged her frustration, until finally her arm reared back. Metal struck metal as the brush bounced off the framing of her bed.

Looking into her mirror revealed a swollen-eyed girl whose shoulders collapsed under red tufts. It was not an image so very different from her first night inside the pleasurehouse. Pala would spend days after soaking and parting Jade's mangled hair, but the angles of her face could have cut teeth and did not round for years. Sleep had become a fable. Smiling, a mystery. Food, an obligation. But her first full plate that first night, she had been seated right in full view of Lowe's Tavern. She'd even glimpsed the owner himself in the low light and kept a silent vigil on him throughout the night.

When Anette had told her she needn't be afraid, Jade lied and said she wasn't. When asked if she would stay in Nadara even if passage off-island could be booked for her, Jade had stared at the Madame for a long time. Finally, she had said, "I would."

The realization had come to her some time in those terrible weeks of pressing her body to something thin and all but invisible. It was the reason she had begged her mother to cleave their ties to Tore Elder and patch what was left of either of them until they could stitch something new.

Because it was a miracle that either of them had survived.

The shadows of the quarter, and the small lights within, had kept Jade alive until she and her mother had found each other in the chaos. The darkness had gentle hands and they had nestled Jade as close as they dared while Tore Elder burned and Mortimer Lowe threatened. And when those hands had been severed, or had languished back, the quarter had provided in other ways.

Through scurrying after her meals and dodging the tumble of buildings, Jade had survived. She had become a lady that was not quite a lady. And granting power over the quarter to anyone was granting power over herself. She remembered what it was to be helpless and knew she could never survive it again.

Everything she was depended upon the safety of this place. Nothing else mattered. *Or could,* Jade thought, even as Nate's face filled her thoughts, kindling with a rich emotion she nearly failed to recognize. His hope unfurled a blossom of light in her dimming memory, illuminating all the places where his features were beginning to blur. *If you could see me now, what would you make of me?*

If protecting Nadara meant more sacrifice, more clever plots, Jade would start with the matter of the Overseer's "payment" to the captain of the *Victory*. When Wynn had paid her for the information leading to Tore Elder's capture, the captain had no way of knowing what he was actually purchasing.

For the moment Wynn and his own men arrived in the Inlands to deliver the captain of the *Sea's Fire* to the Overseer, a loyal contingent of trained mercenaries would be lying in wait for him.

"Their orders are simple," she explained to Vane Mercy as the sun set outside the window of Lowe's Tavern. "And there can be no mistake that those orders, once fulfilled, are irreversible. What do you think that would mean for you and your men, captain?"

Vane Mercy folded his hands across the teetering wood table. "You expect me to believe that you have the power to sell the fort to me and my crew?"

Jade's lips quirked. "Sell? To you? Why would I need to sell anything to a pirate, monk or no?" She leaned forward, dipping her voice low. "It's my understanding that a captain of your stature wouldn't wait for anything so legitimate. What I'm doing is trading the knowledge that the fort will be all but empty in two days time as Captain Wynn travels with Tore Elder to the Inlands. What you do with that information..." Jade spread her hands, smiling wider. "That's not for a simple pleasure-worker to say. All I ask in exchange is that you keep the heathen goddess confined in your new stronghold." Azura couldn't matter either. Not while Jade played so many hands at once. Things were already difficult enough to keep track. She didn't have time to fit in an acquaintance and a plea for forgiveness when she didn't know if she needed either. "The girl is a danger to this island, with or without her powers."

Clapping broke out over the other tables as guitar strings were plucked and drums beat to a hip-coaxing rhythm. Anette had leant some of the girls to Mortimer Lowe to aid in the performance unwinding around his patrons, and, in exchange, the girls were permitted to lure some of their more enamored audience members back to Anette's inn.

Pala tried to catch Jade's eye, but Jade pretended to see nothing.

Just as Vane Mercy ignored everything but Jade, studying her with a tangle of suspicion—and something that struck Jade as reluctant admiration. "You're leading a captain as strong as Wynn to slaughter and you expect me to trust you?"

She tilted her head, coy in every bone in her body, and repeated the words she'd said to Wynn that morning, "Why worry about trust when mutual self-interest makes for better partners?"

Mercy considered this for a long moment. "You know of what I do with my prizes, yes?"

Jade nodded. "Yes," she said softly, remembering those who sought the comforts he smuggled to his country's coast.

"My country's king has no respect for the Mother of Light, or her followers," the captain said. "So when The Ashman sacked our small ports, plundered our monasteries, and killed my Brothers, do you know how I thanked my king for his refusal to send aid to the coast?"

Jade's skin chilled. She shook her head.

"If you cross me," Vane Mercy warned gently, the silver bands on his fingers glinting in the candlelight like the edges of drawn swords, "I will show you how I repay those who betray me."

Jade was careful to make no sound as she swallowed. "Understood," she finally said. "Do we have a deal?"

The captain held out his hand. When Jade placed her own in his, he squeezed hard enough to scrape bone. "Indeed, we do."

~

"You did what?"

Zachary Feathertooth, or Mouse, as he was called now, proceeding the day Mortimer Lowe bruised his face and made him whimper in public, was so loud in his exclamation, Jade instinctively slapped her hand over his mouth, checking over her shoulder at the other merchants on the street.

"You know for a mouse, you've got to be the loudest, biggest thing I've ever heard or seen," Jade said in a strangled voice.

Strangely, though, Mouse never seemed to mind his new moniker. "It's honest," he'd told her once, free of the shame Lowe and the others tried to inflict. "I'm not a brave man, and I accept that."

Jade never argued, though she had wanted to point out that Ms. Anette hadn't been the only one to save her nine years ago, and he'd endured the consequences of that when Mortimer Lowe went searching for her again, hearing word that the butcher had something to do with the escape of Tore Elder's daughter from the quarter. Lowe had never considered Mouse was capable of duplicity; much of Jade's hiding had been in the attic of Mouse's home, until one of Tore Elder's canons ripped it from the walls.

Jade never needed much of a reason to confide in Mouse, but everything he had been and done for her since the day she'd been beaten was more than reason enough.

"You did all that last night? Why?" he demanded, chopping down on a featherless chicken. Jade couldn't yet bring herself to tell him about Azura, though her eyes had haunted Jade's sleep. "If something goes wrong... And how do you plan on—" He lowered his voice to a whisper, casting his eyes about too. It was early enough that Lowe wouldn't step out from his room up in his office, but there were still scavengers of information who would sell him what they had come to know. "—paying back Captain Steel for his loss? Word's already gotten out that his quartermaster has gone missing. And with the *Sea's Fire* crew dead, no one wants to piss off Steel *or* Wynn. They'll do *anything* to stay on their good sides, turn on anyone."

"I have a plan, Mouse. I'd always planned to take on Mercy, when the timing was right," she spoke so lowly he had to lean over the dead chicken. "Turns out it's right. And that's why I need you do the next thing for me."

"Ah, gods, I should've known," he muttered. Then, with a sigh, he said, "What do you need?"

She leaned the rest of the way over and kissed his cheek. "Why do you do that?" she wondered aloud. "Give me what I need when I ask?" A big part of her worried he felt indebted to her for how she'd stood up to Mortimer Lowe for him. Years ago, when he'd brought over food and clothes his older sister had outgrown, that was what she'd assumed. But if he admitted that their friendship was less about years of loyalty and more about debts unpaid, then she would have to admit to herself she was still comfortable using that fact to her advantage.

It was that, of everything, that worried her most.

The cunning thing she was becoming could truly call the quarter home because Mouse had helped her survive enough to belong to it. He and Anette were the reasons this place had, however reluctantly, adopted her. She owed him, and loved him, and yet she would use him so long as he let her.

Mouse blushed when she moved away, more from embarrassment than any particular affinity toward her. She knew him that well, at least. "I do what you say," he said, gently enough to suddenly embarrass *her*. "Because you're the best friend I've got, and I don't want to see anything happen to you."

"Oh."

"Yeah. What did you think I was going to say?"

"The wrong thing." She smiled at him. "Which is ridiculous, because you never do."

"You must really want my help," he said, adding dryness to his tone, which helped both of them compose themselves. If they started crying all over each other, no one on the street would believe they were discussing qualities of meat. Jade didn't know if there would ever come a day when their actions in the light wouldn't be so scrutinized, but she hoped she could build the quarter toward it. And yet she knew that she couldn't alter the very fabric of what made the quarter what it was. It was a place built upon the thrift of the unspoken. "Tell me what you need."

"I need you to make some inquiries on the street," she said quietly. "See who would be willing to sell Lowe's interests in their concerns to someone else."

"*You?*" he all but screeched.

"Mouse," she warned. When he settled himself, she continued, "Get quotes from as many of the merchants as you can. And make sure Lowe doesn't get word of what you're up to, or this will all fall apart before it's even really begun."

"You're talking like something's coming," Mouse said, moving to pig meat next. "What am I saying? You've always talked like something's coming. And you always sound so angry when you do."

"Changes *are* coming," Jade said. "In more than one variety. And I'm going to make sure my interests are protected. That you're protected," she assured him. "No matter what it takes I'm not losing my home."

Again, she thought.

But he heard even in silence. "I'll do it," he murmured. "But what are you going to do about Steel? He's going to find out sooner rather than later. This could *all* fall apart sooner rather than later, and then what'll you be left with, Jade? If they don't kill you, let's say."

She tried rolling the tension from her neck, her shoulders. "Believe me, I know what I'm risking," she said fiercely. "And I have the money to pay back Steel. I just have to go see the woman I promised the money to and explain just how much trouble I'm in." Her sigh was laden with burden. "I'll need to borrow Starmine and your wagon."

"That's fine. Just bring them back soon as you can. But how are you going to pay the merchants?"

"I have an inheritance." When Mouse's eyebrows rose, she said, "It's not easily transportable, so I can't use it just yet. But I'll work it out soon enough. Trust me."

"I do." Mouse's gaze held sympathy. "She's not going to understand, is she?"

Jade faced the direction of the beach, remembering the day her whole life had upended itself, all because she'd wanted a little taste of freedom and the sensation of burying her toes in the sand.

"No," she said, turning away from that glimpse of the ocean still so sore in her heart. "I doubt she will. When it comes to the quarter, my mother rarely does."

Starmine let out a low groaning tune as Jade prepared the wagon. Mouse was gentle with the gift she'd given him, even when there was no need. "He could make dozens of trips less than he does," she whispered to the mare, "if he wasn't so worried about overburdening you."

"An interesting day for a ride."

Jade turned slowly, giving herself ample time to school her features. Mortimer Lowe smiled at Mouse, though his attention was on Jade. She continued unwinding Starmine's tether from her post, readying her for the wagon, as Mouse greeted Lowe. "It's a fine day for pickled pork."

There were as many thoughts as migrating birds flitting over Lowe's expression, though Jade had a hard time clipping the wings of one and studying it closely. "That's good news. You can send a pallet over to the tavern first chance."

Mouse's shoulders shrunk, but he didn't disagree.

Jade leapt into the wagon. The bed shook and the wheels croaked. She leaned over to brush Starmine's side, keeping her face turned from Lowe.

"Interesting day for a ride," he repeated, this time at her back.

She repressed a shudder and said, without turning back, "Not really. My mother isn't doing so well of late, so I thought I would surprise her."

He braced his hand on the wood as she settled into the box. She couldn't flick the reins without hurting him. The gesture was clear. "Your mother lives in the Inlands?"

"Yes, as a maid for one of the land-owners." She glanced down at his hand. "Her time on the island is coming to an end. Quickly. I haven't much time myself."

"You seem to have acquired quite a bit of generosity." She kept her expression blank, though inside she heard the crack of a whip. The shouting of his orders to continue. "This wagon, for instance."

Mouse jumped in, his cheer locked taut on his face. "I haven't the heart to deny a dutiful daughter."

"Of course." Lowe stepped back from the wagon. "You must be a favorite of his," he told Jade, winking as Mouse blushed. "I might just come inquiring at Anette's inn, hole up with you myself. Would you like that, love? I promise to be a generous man."

Because Jade couldn't trust herself to respond, she snapped the reins. Her heart eventually slowed to match Starmine's steady trod as the distance between them and Mortimer Lowe lengthened.

They came to a bend and Jade dismounted near a crooked palm with a hunch in its backside. She walked around until she met Starmine's mane and could bury her face in it. She didn't want even the sun to see the tears that fell.

"You remember, don't you?" she whispered to the mare, nuzzling a little. "We curse him, don't we? The both of us. He doesn't scare us. And, soon, I'm going to show him what it's like to be left with nothing."

By the time she returned to the box, her cheeks were dry. She nudged Starmine on.

When the ripe curses and chicken squawks and bawdy laughter disappeared behind her, Jade sank into the smell of cedar and palm and fig, the jolt of rubble beneath the wheels, the earthy smell of sun-warmed rock and soil. White orchids spilled down from trees like light-captured water. Herons snaked with violet and grey feathers flew overhead in search of mild streams.

As a child, Jade remembered longing for more than the vividly ordinary world she and her mother had been buried in. It hadn't served as a fruitful playground in many, many years, and yet Jade found herself missing the exploding, uncomplicated terrain that had enjoyed having her underfoot.

The Inlands had always been gentle with her, valiantly servicing her wild little curiosities. In the tepid wind, Jade silently wished she had appreciated all of its efforts. And then she swallowed the taste of sadness, and reminded herself she could never afford to be a woman who carried regrets.

When Starmine instinctively turned down a certain road, remembering a home that was no longer there, Jade carefully maneuvered her back onto the right path, murmuring tender, silly things the Old Jade would have spoken with far less hardship.

As they crested a much smaller hill, a sharp pang knocked into Jade's breastbone. Nate's house sat on the other side, where a new family now lived and Thaya now served.

Her mother still hadn't uncovered any explanation for the disappearance of Nate or his mother. Jade and Thaya had been anchorless in their own turmoil, racing from one hiding place to the next as both Tore Elder and Mortimer Lowe tore back palms and murdered men, all in search of ghosts who were supposed to be dead. The only clue Thaya had managed to dig out was that the property was sold to her employers by the Overseer, who'd stated that the original owners had sold it to him and fled.

One day, when the quarter was no longer threatened by the brutal whims of those who sailed under the black, she'd seek out the Overseer and coax new answers from him, for a boy and his mother didn't just disappear in a matter of weeks without being seen or heard from again.

The day Jade had learned of Nate's disappearance hadn't been the worst of her life. She had refused the possibility of there being a reason to mourn, telling herself there was an explanation, a harmless one, one that might even have to do with the father he never knew but had fervently wished for every day of his life.

I will learn what happened to you, she swore to herself, hoping the words would ease the burning, frayed edges of despair she hadn't yet released from the depths of her heart. *I will.*

On the days when her fears threatened to burst, she made up a picture of him in her mind:

Limbs as long as branches by now and a permanently upturned mouth. Wide chest to fit the breadth of his heart. Dark hair cut short the way his mother liked. On the nights when she dared to hope, she laced her thoughts with his arms curling around her. Holding. Sometimes for more than holding. Part of her knew it was a fool's wish. That he was likely as different a person as she had turned out to be and would probably have every reason to dislike her now. For her to dislike him. But those nights, when she dreamed of being held by someone she had loved, who might still love her now in a way that was different and possibly pure...

Those nights were always the safest to sleep.

Her tutor's brother now lived in Nate's home. Mr. Warrington had never married, choosing to open his own home to a brother and sister-in-law. After Mr. Warrington was killed, his family hadn't been able to go on there, citing that the books in his study sometimes floated to other rooms and that the library chandelier stayed lit all throughout the night, no matter how many times they extinguished the candles.

Since they couldn't have children of their own, they'd taken Mabel's once they learned of the fire, raising a newly cobbled family on Nate's well-tended land. Thaya often said it would never be a whole one, with the way the youngest still wailed and how all books were locked up in the attic after lessons, but Jade thought that those things weren't signs of emptiness and disrepair.

Instead, she saw them as signs of healing. Slow, painful, and unforgettable healing that might one day become useful in the building of something new.

"Jade," said Mrs. Warrington, a smile pulled wide on her tanned, freckled face. "Are you staying for supper?"

"Wish I could," Jade said, trying to smile back with the same amount of unconcerned joy. "But I have to work tonight."

Mrs. Warrington's face fell. "Oh. Well, I'll just go get your mother for you."

"Which do you think offends her more?" Jade asked her mother when she emerged from the Warringtons' house. "That I'm a pleasure-worker or that I won't eat her food?" Not really expecting an answer, Jade kissed Thaya's cheek. "Hello, Mama."

Jade's mother had once had hair that shone rich auburn in the sunlight, her long curls brushed smooth by their maid's hands. There had never been any question of her favorite pastimes, as she'd adorned her body with the shiniest ones. When Jade was small, they would curl up in Thaya's bed and coo over baubles that spun sparkles into the air. This was usually after an hour of reading, in which Thaya's palms covered Jade's fingers as they turned page after page in the firelight.

"Did you bring the money?" Thaya asked quickly, her eyes shining with hope as they walked toward a small pond at the edge of the property. Her hair was pulled into a style that was anything but fanciful, and her calloused palms slid over the strands to ensure nothing had gone astray. "Did you cart it in that wagon? I hope you didn't tell that boy you were bringing it here."

"Mouse would never steal from me, Mama," Jade murmured, but she didn't bother with defending her friend. Thaya would never understand how Jade could have made *any* friends in the quarter. "And there's been a setback."

"It's my money," Thaya whispered, sounding as fragile as a brokenhearted child. "I risked everything for it. How can there be a setback?"

Because impatience was welling, Jade moved to stroke Starmine's light brown mane. "*Our* money, Mama," Jade said. She'd been going to use her share to whet the merchants' appetites and fully convince them she was a sounder investment than Mortimer Lowe. Instead, she would have to shoulder disappointment along with her mother and regroup. "And I will get you your share as soon as I can. But, for now, I need what's left of the money—"

"What's *left*?"

"—to pay for—"

"How could you use a bar of it without discussing it with me first? I can't live this way anymore, Jade."

"—a problem—"

"Scraping by as a servant to a family who enjoys giving me charity. Sneaking about like a wraith in the night, hoping for a piece of the grand prize. You know that—"

"—made by my *sister*," Jade ended on a shout, her breath exploding.

Silence twined with the wind, rippling the giant, emerald palm leaves standing tall near the pond and loosening the yellow petals stuffed under their sun-kissed heads. Jade barely felt the soft touch of a petal sliding down her cheek.

"What in the Skies are you talking about?" Thaya finally said. She stepped closer, narrowed her eyes. "And what happened to your charm?"

Jade stared down at her necklace, noticing for the first time that the feathers of the charm were charred to a crisp.

She tilted her head back and laughed a long, bitter while. "What happened?" she said, with a hard smile tugging at her mouth. She opened her own hands and finally understood the black stains she'd discovered on her fingers earlier that morning—she'd been touching the charm after Azura attacked her and again before she slept, but stress had kept her from noticing what she was feeling. "The charm was used against my half-sister. Tore Elder had another daughter, Mother."

Thaya blinked several times. "How could he?" she said. "How could he?"

Jade looked away from the tears surging in her mother's gaze. "It's been years," she said, though Azura looked little younger than her. "How could he not?"

Her parents' marriage had never been a welcome area of discussion, but it was even less of a concern to Jade now. Still, her heart twinged when she saw Thaya's unshed tears.

"I'm so tired, Jade," her mother whispered fervently. "I'm

tired of the secrets and the dangers. I'm tired of living in a house that is not my own. Do you know close I am to being found out by the Overseer? How long do you think it will be before his stable master trades the opportunity to flirt with me for a well-placed bribe? How long before the Overseer discovers I've been pumping information from his groomsmen, his maids, his kitchen staff and decides to see me killed for it?" Her voice wobbled. "You don't think of me. You don't think of my sacrifices. How did I raise such a selfish daughter?"

Jade pressed her fingers to her eyes and pleaded for calm. For control. But she might very well carry her mother's words to the grave. It would have been impossible to forget a chorus endured every day in some form since the day she'd lost their lives to Mortimer Lowe—and begged her mother to let him keep what she had helped him steal.

She'd seen what it was to be related to The Ashman. Lowe had opened up her back, her arms, her face looking for the connection she had once been so proud to own. She'd tasted the consequences of that pride, swallowing the iron tang of her own blood as she suffered blow after blow. And she'd watched the madness that had overcome Tore Elder the moment the tether between he and Jade had disintegrated. The gravity of his loss had forced her to understand what would possess a man like Lowe to brutalize a child in search of keys to her father's destruction.

Jade would never forgive, never justify Mortimer Lowe's actions that day on the street, and she'd see that he paid for each of them... but there was a part of her that believed, just as her mother did, that the fault was entirely her own.

"You want your money," said Jade in a ragged voice she couldn't smooth out, no matter how she tried, "I'll get you the means to see yourself far from me and the rest. But know that as long as even the faintest connection remains between you, me, and the father you never really wanted me to claim, you'll never be safe on this island." Jade dropped her hands from her face. "I'm tired too. So, to spare us both further pain, I'll see you removed from Nadara's shores altogether." Jade turned to go. "If it's the last thing I do."

"I know what you intend," Thaya called out. "I've put it together. And if you betray your father this way, what will you have left without either of us?"

Jade couldn't turn back. The tears had overcome her so intensely, so suddenly she had no time to build up a defense. All she could manage was, "A legacy of my own."

And *desperately* hoped that legacy would be enough. Because her father's name couldn't protect her, nor anyone she cared about. That was proven even now. She and her mother had once been mirrors shining brighter in each other's presence. Now, there were cracks in both.

So Jade had to protect herself.

She *had* to protect what was left.

SHE LEFT Starmine at the Warringtons to see her mother's wishes done.

At first, it began with the need to walk.

Then the urge to fly overwhelmed her, as the daybirds overhead flitted and cawed, chasing auburn spears of light as the bright ball of the sun climbed higher in the blue-swept sky. The draw was almost too much to bear, before Jade remembered she couldn't, that once noonmeal was over she was due at the pleasurehouse.

Walking on the rocks to avoid marking her path, Jade slipped into the small dash of a forest where she and Nate once met to share whims and thrills. When she cleared the other side, no longer was there a wall of hibiscus or a pen made for mares. Where her home once stood, Jade could clearly envision the charcoal behemoth of smoke that had stolen the structure into its jaws, chewing until even the surrounding trees collapsed into the cinders.

All that remained of Jade's childhood lay under strewn planks, fallen trees, and a thin coat of ash that even the sea's distant winds couldn't carry away. Why should any have come to clear the property? Why should Mortimer Lowe have scavenged through the dying embers?

This place was nearly forgotten, much like the Old Jade herself. Even her mother had a difficult time finding her way here on her own. There were only two people left in the world who remembered its existence.

Jade had realized this after silently trailing her father through the trees one year, watching as he and a handful of men carted little luxuries, crafted by the foreign mysteries of the world, in heavy chests. She'd held her breath as Tore intoned a deep, breaking song, an *important* song that tracked tears down his cheeks, at once shameless and private, one she had no way of understanding as he'd so rarely spoken in the language of his homeland when he was home with her.

Then he'd had the rest of his men bring out the bodies of those who'd paid the price of his vengeance.

And set them alight.

Her home, in that instant, and in all the years that followed on the anniversary of Tore's loss, became an impregnable sanctity. A ritual filled with sacrifice and mourning and offerings.

It wasn't until Jade overheard him answer one of his younger subordinates that she understood why he offered anything at all to what was becoming his own private cemetery.

"My daughter is angry with me," he whispered harshly. "Until she takes my gifts, her spirit will not rest."

So each year Jade's father offered more and more, burying each gift beneath layers of ash, infiltrating the island from a small, enclosed bay to the west, so no one would suspect how he craved forgiveness, nor see his wan expression when he returned to the *Sea's Fire* without it.

Thanks to Jade's patience there was a veritable, and secret, cache of wealth hidden under years of death and loss. She brushed aside the tears that hadn't quite faded from her mother's visit and stepped forward.

A crack in the underbrush had her spinning around, heart thumping. Some unbearably vulnerable instinct gave voice to a single thought:

"Nate?"

But when there was no reply, and Jade walked closer to the trees she'd entered from, an iguana poked its head from the shadows in search of a perfect drape of the sun.

She stood there with the sound of her heart sinking, and the vaguest sense of memories not her own breathing behind her. She found herself hating what her old home had become.

Too many emotions, and too little practicalities, had prevented her from taking what was rightfully hers. What her father had meant for her.

But, with the leaden weight of her mother's demands on her shoulders and little time to spare, Jade lifted her skirts around a fallen log and began to dig.

BONES HEAVY, muscles sore, skin flushed and caked with old soot, Jade took what she needed and left the rest behind.

She didn't yet have a plan for withdrawing from her childhood burial grounds what would eventually become the deposits to outmatch Lowe's interests on the street. But, now that she knew just how much remained, Jade had less doubts about her plans than when she awoke.

There might never come a day where she wasn't riddled with fear and doubt, fighting to keep hold of a home that bucked her at every turn, but after her house had burned, she'd become the girl who bargained with the likes of Wynn and Mercy and planned revenge against Mortimer Lowe, the man who believed because he owned a thing, he owned it all.

Lives were lost to that fire. Not just Mabel's or Mr. Warrington's. She wouldn't apologize for salvaging the dregs of her own.

Nor would she begrudge her mother for doing the same. The quarter was unruly and restless. There was no peace there for a mother who was not a mother any longer.

So when Jade handed Thaya enough jade and black pearl to not only attain passage off the island, but also to resurrect the dreams torched by a rebellious child, Jade kissed her mother's cheek a final time, and meant it whole-heartedly when she said, "Be well."

As JADE TIED Starmine to her designated post, Mouse informed her that while there was interest in her furtive proposal, the street remained too afraid of Mortimer Lowe to sell.

"Everyone's fear has a price," Jade responded.

Strangely, Mouse's features pinched. It took her several moments to realize he was hurt.

"It's the truth," she said.

And though he was the last one to think himself brave, Mouse said, "But I've never been bought. People aren't transactional, Jade."

"Really?" Her own bitterness surprised her. For some reason, Azura's hateful gaze bored into her mind. If Jade ever did attempt to salvage that relationship, what would Azura's price be? "What town do you think you've been living in, my friend?"

Though she was sorry to have caused him even a moment's

pain, she knew that truth to be the only constant Nadara would ever see on the long, tumultuous road ahead.

The day had become a lingering veil of weariness. She wondered if there was a way to siphon fatigue in the same way Vane Mercy siphoned magic. But, then, she'd probably have to move to a place where convenience and leisure were more commonplace than sorrow and heartbreak.

She abandoned Mouse for her room inside the pleasure-house, washing the morning's sorrow off her skin and wrapping herself in clothes for the evening.

If her hands trembled on the stays of her corset, she wrung them out. If some errant, petulant thought whined about the lackluster stitching or the cracked pattern of blossoms on her skirt, she reminded herself of the cache she'd somehow get her hands upon and utilize for the purpose of protection. Even, quite possibly, indulgence.

Wynn was only a day away from his own destruction. Lowe was about to see his monopoly pulled apart and remade. Mercy would recapture the fort while Wynn was gone, but Jade would find a way to confiscate the control she'd traded him.

Tore Elder would never again pose a risk to her home. The more she built into the quarter, the steadier the foundations would be without his bloodlust muddying the sand.

By the time she made her way to the floor, smiling easily at Anette's patrons and thinking how she could take this place for her own with the amount waiting for her deep in the hills, she assumed she had regained control.

But when the doors of the inn burst open, framing Captain Steel in the wounded red of the late afternoon sun, any conception of control disappeared with the ability to breathe.

Jade's whole body shook when screams broke out amongst the other girls.

Oh, Skies.

Gripped in Captain Steel's wide, bloodied hands was Vane

Mercy's silver hair, the gore-stained strands of which held his sundered head aloft.

Jade's horror ripened as a single, panicked thought broke through her reverie: *Azura.*

An echo of Vane Mercy's voice filled Jade's mind. *Her powers have been removed until my death.*

Molten eyes roved the tables, the stairs, the balconies where hitched breaths were unrestrained, until they landed on Jade, who leaned heavily against a post for balance. Her heart clawed its way to her throat when Steel's amber gaze lingered.

"There you are."

There was nowhere to run. That she might have considered doing so brought her no shame, only regret.

Whimpers unwinding from pleasure sprang up from the shapes around her, but there was no sound, no matter how fraught and penitent, Jade could make that would save her now.

Not even the enforcers stationed throughout stepped to defend her. They knew that when a captain like Steel came for blood, carting death with him, he would simply have theirs as well.

As Vane Mercy's head swung toward her, Steel's footsteps hard and pronounced between them, Jade tried frantically to turn her mind, weave new schemes.

But all that remained were the remnants of old plans dissolving in the brine-soaked breeze, wafting toward her with that gut-clenching tang of iron blood.

Of a flogging and a reckoning scalded in her memory.

Anette entered from behind Steel, setting down elegant purchases from the clothier. "What is the meaning of this, captain?"

The captain of the *Revenge* stilled. Jade's heart pounded as he turned and considered the pleasurehouse's Madame.

Anette's gaze slipped down to the familiar, severed head in his possession, then hiked back up with an intensity that bellied any fear holed up inside her. Her bosom heaved out of a silver-threaded damask corset, which tapered into a pale rose skirt, and yet Jade thought of her father, of fearsome, straight-necked warriors who bowed to none. "You have business with one of my girls?"

Steel's silence stretched thin. Then, with his free hand, he pulled from his pocket a small pouch that clinked against the nearest table. "Thirty coppers," he said, "still the rate?"

Anette let out a long breath.

She caught Jade's eyes, holding them by the hands of fury barely banked. But she did not order Jade to take this turn.

And because Anette had sheltered her, would protect her, even now, Jade shut her eyes and answered Steel. "Follow me."

A stray glance had her breath thinning. Watching the entire spectacle along with the rest of the crowd was Mortimer Lowe. Her fingers dug into the grain of the banister leading up to the second floor. He lifted his tankard high, tipping his chin to her.

Her debts were about to be called, but she'd be damned if she let him rattle her now. She turned her back on him, wishing she knew how to unhook his probing gaze. Or simply understand what had provoked this sudden fascination with her.

Was he catching onto her schemes, or was it something else?

THE CLOSER HER ROOM LOOMED, the quicker Jade tried to plot an attack.

Sweat slid down her spine. Her mind opened to the sounds around her, despite her press for calm. There was the ugly soft-ness of Vane Mercy's oscillating head, the thud of it landing on one of the tables, before Steel said, "Keep him company for me, will you?" to no one in particular. The unrelenting footfalls of the captain climbing after her as they crested the stairs. The creaking swing of her doors.

And still no plot or plan.

She had nothing and no one left to stop him.

She eyed her dresser, which held cosmetic powders and tinctures. If she got close enough, they might be enough to distract him.

She didn't dare edge toward them yet. Her first words to him were quiet. "What do you want from me, captain?"

In the saffron edges of sunlight cutting into her open window, the wizened quality about him seemed to vanish, showing her youth carved of innocence. Most of the scars on his face seemed meager when compared to the one with the most interesting placement: in a fight, another man might try for the eyes or the neck, but Steel had a long scar hooking around the corner of his mouth. As if a knife had gone in and he had spit it back out.

He couldn't be much older than her, and yet he'd seen more trials than she had schemes in her mental armory.

She licked her lips, remembering the remaining silver bars Wynn had paid her. "I think I know why you've come," she said, fighting to smooth the tenor of her voice. "And I'm willing to offer you fifty silver bars and the benefit of seeing me whipped for my small, and unplanned, part in your crew member's death."

His expression unchanged, he walked to her, slowly circled her. When he stopped at her back, it took every ounce of Anette's training to suppress an involuntary shiver. She was at his mercy now, and, like when faced with any wild predator, she refused to give him unnecessary cause to pounce.

He swept her loose red curls onto her bare shoulder.

She shut her eyes, unwilling to believe, yet desperately hoping nonetheless, he only expected a tumble from her. She'd swallow her disgust if he lifted those blood-dried hands to take what he wanted.

She'd give him anything she had if it meant he'd let her live.

"Just tell me what you want," she whispered. "Please."

He leaned into her ear. "That's not as simple as you might imagine." He held his breath a beat. "My lady."

Her gasp echoed like a wave. He spun her in his arms, holding her close enough for her to see eyes that weren't quite dark, not quite light.

"Sort of coppery." Tears flooded her throat. "Sort of golden." Her breath hitched.

"Nate."

His arms unraveled around her and he stepped back, composure untarnished.

Of all the many changes sprawled across his bronze face, his bare arms, the long length of his deep sable hair, this was the one that dug a fissure in her heart. *Where's your smile?* she thought wildly. *Where's your warmth?*

You have facial hair, she nearly blurted, but there was nothing inviting silliness on his face so she kept her foolishness to herself.

Her voice broke. "Where did you go?" She didn't dare take a step in his direction, though the effort to keep her arms from reaching him cost something dear. Her patience crumbled as quickly and as completely as her childhood had. "*Why* did you go? How could you leave?" Another thought jarred her so violently, she reeled back. "How long have you been near enough to tell me the truth?"

His nostrils flared slightly as he inhaled. The only sign her outrage had touched him.

But the possibilities answered for him.

As long as she'd known a Captain Steel had existed. Perhaps longer, as he hadn't always had the *Revenge,* or it's crew.

He'd had the *Victory.*

And Wynn was a much older resident of the quarter.

A familiar hollowness layered over her shock. The offense he seemed inclined to ignore. What else was Nathaniel *Steel* asking for if not her precious calm by reflecting nothing of his own feelings?

How could you not tell me? How can you not smile at me?

Then she remembered the visit to the quarter he'd helped her achieve. She remembered how, later that night, every inch of her bruised, lacerated body had howled, how her very soul had curdled with shame and failure. She remembered that in the mire of her loss and pain, she had barely had the where-withal to sustain herself, let alone think of Nate, and how he must have fared tracing the smoke back to her home with no hope left in the dark.

There had been no room for him in those early weeks, full of terror and agony. And she'd avoided seeking him out because of that shame and failure.

Her next breath shuddered out, damp with tears unshed. "Your father is Charles Wynn."

This time his inhale was deeper. He still refused to speak, and, for the first time, Jade wondered if this was his new way of hiding his emotions from her. When they were little, he'd hidden his face or his hands. Now, it seemed he preferred to shroud himself in silence.

She didn't want to let him collect himself so well the Nate she knew shrunk deeper inside.

Jade took a challenging step forward. "Every day of your life, every day we ever had together, you spoke only of what it would be like to have him in your life," she murmured. "I gather it didn't go the way you imagined. Neither did my fantasy, if it helps." She shaped her voice into something far more fragile than a whisper. "Where's your mother, Nate?"

A spasm wracked his body, and she went to him instantly, wrapping herself around him in ways more intimate than any other man she'd held in her service. Ways that had nothing to do with the clothes on their bodies or their skin igniting with warmth. She pressed herself as close as she could, clutched as tightly as he could bear.

And, still, he hadn't spoken a word.

He didn't touch her with his bloodied hands.

"Where is your mother?" she repeated, unable to let the words sit. She *needed* him to confide this much in her. Her fingers grasped at his waist. *It's unbearable to me, too. I can't stand the thought of it.* "Did he kill her?"

Nate untangled himself from her. His hands were hard against her skin... yet he gently shoved her back. "It doesn't matter."

She didn't believe him for a second. And she deserved better. "She was your mother, Nate," she told him. "But I loved her too."

Somehow the silence that descended then was not truly quiet.

"She's gone," he finally said, with enough tension to tell her all she needed to know about why a boy so enamored by the idea of having a father would break faith with the man he'd been hoping for all his life. "And I'm not here to relive the past."

Aren't you? Jade was shaken. *How can we do anything but after what we've lived?*

"I'm here to collect your reparations to my crew." His gaze met hers, boring into her with his impatience. The need not to need her, or speak with her of the things that hurt, which both of them had lost the chance to mend for the other. "I don't want your money. I don't want your blood."

Jade made herself think of the head of Vane Mercy, drenched in blood Nate did want. Her thoughts around his death clicked into place. "How did you know about my deal with him?"

"Lowe and Anette aren't the only ones who know the value

of information." He glanced around her room, taking in the hand-painted panels of her folding screen, the drape of her satin robe across her polished table. "And you aren't the only one capable of pickpocketing secrets. I make it my business to know what lay in the shadows of the quarter."

Secrets were *her* trade; she breathed the business of shadows. Thoughts crowded her mind. *He's a pirate now. He kills for self-interest. The violence here will continue.*

But she had to be clear. "You killed Vane Mercy because you want Wynn's fort?"

"I killed him because he was in my way," Nate corrected. "He didn't know me. Didn't like the look of me. Now his pious little crew knows not to confront what they don't like. His deal with you about the fort was a bonus."

And a loss for Jade. The half-sister she betrayed might have already gotten free of any bindings, of the crew Nate had warned away, and was even now plotting her retribution.

"You knew about the fort before you killed him. You sought him out and taunted him."

Nate's lips quirked in a black-tinged reminder of what a full grin from him once was. "My men would swear otherwise."

"I don't trust your men. I don't trust you."

"I never expected that you would," he said, fisting hands covered in death. "I want to know why you traded the security of that fort in the first place. Why you were so sure Mercy wouldn't have a fight on his hands when Wynn returned from the Inlands. Why you let Wynn have any part of your father. Tell me the truth," he told her, with eyes that would never look quietly into hers again for all the rage shored behind them, "and you and I will be squared. I'll square it with my men."

"You come here with demands for *my* truth?" Her shout stained the cool, calm veneer she'd decided to wear. Her voice broke. "If you had walked through my door at any point in the last nine years, I'd have gladly told you. I asked you where the hell you went and you refused me an answer. You think I care so much about being even with you that I won't deny you?" Her short laugh laid bare all the bitterness churning inside her. He had gone and ruined every sweet lull she'd fashioned around his memory to pacify her fears. He was breaking apart her faith in him before the instinct to trust him had the chance to truly take shape. "Your first mistake was telling me who you were. We both know you won't kill me now. You can go hang your head out that window and shout to everyone who's daughter I am, remind them of why I'd been beaten and torn from my home. You can make them hate me and have Mortimer fucking Lowe drive me out, but I will not hand you my secrets. I will not justify my reasons to you."

The silence he relied upon hummed.

The sound of his quiet fury knocked her heart faster.

Calm is a weapon. Fury is an artifice. She curled her own fists tight, relishing the flare of pain. *I have resources at my fingertips, skills in my arsenal, and an endless well of iron will.* She ordered her mind to cool.

"Is that where the scars came from?"

Her concentration snapped. "What?"

He finally reached for her again, turning her chin so she could peer over her shoulder. She frowned at her reflection. Then she noticed the scars slithering up from the opening in the back of her corset, laid out starkly in the dying light without the thick mass of her hair to cover them.

Her voice was quiet. "What does it matter anymore, Nate?"

"I'll kill him." His hands fell to his sides. "I'll kill Mortimer Lowe for you."

"What does it matter?" she repeated, because having him kill Lowe wasn't her answer. She did not want to perpetuate the same things as her father. Maybe if Nate knew and understood, even a little... "Everything I've done has been for the island, because Nadara and I are the same. We both tire of tyrants and their bloodsport. The quarter is the reason I'm alive, and I will not see it destroyed by squabbles for power." She stepped forward, letting her breath fan his mouth. "So you can have the fort. You won it square. But you and I? We won't ever be if you continue to use it the way your father has. The way my father would have if he'd had any interest in staying here. If Vane Mercy had even attempted to do the same, he would have had a very short stay inside that fort. Do you understand?"

He plucked up a curl, rubbing it between his thumb and forefinger. She held herself still. "I didn't choose this life," he said suddenly. "And damned if I was grateful for it. But I made something from it anyway. I broke from his shadow, biding my time because it ripped me in two. It all ripped me. But I was never afraid. Not once." He breathed in deeply, fixed in place by her curls. "Except when I looked out my window one night, before the world shifted under my feet, and saw your house burning."

Their noses touched. Their breaths were curling into one soft, invisible shape.

"I've never known fear like that before or since." The shaking she'd been trying to prevent poured out. She couldn't be still with him anymore and yet she didn't know what to reach for or how or if any of this even meant he would want her to. "When I showed up back here, I decided I was done waiting. I was going to move on Wynn whether it killed us or not. Told my crew he was guarding some prize meriting a fortune. I didn't know the prize was your father. I didn't know you were in the quarter until I saw you with the butcher early this morning."

He bent, pressing his cheek against hers, and stunned her heart. He breathed her in and sighed, like a man rising from bed in peace after enduring restlessness for far too long. When he leaned back, tears had at last gathered for him to see.

"I've never been so grateful to see someone in my life." His thumb reached up to stroke her temple, catching a single drop. "Yes, I understand you. And if you're saying there's a different kind of future in store than what I had in mind when I woke up this morning, I'm saying I won't stop you from building it."

She drew back, more wary of him than ever. "Thank you."

"I won't stop you," he said, his features hardening, filling in all those cracks in his calm, until he resembled Steel more closely than Nate, "unless you try to stop me. I'm going to take the fort. It's not just what I have to do, but what I want. Stay clear, Jade, and the bloodbath won't spread. But if you try to send anyone after me, I promise you won't like the results."

She couldn't answer him when he squeezed her hand. The pressure was gentle, and yet the warning stung.

It was all too much. The punch of his words. His closed expression. Her thoughts teetered inside her head. She sat hard on her bed and let the silence stretch.

When he finally left her there, she could only rub a hand over her heart.

Because, whether she gave verbal assent or not, it seemed they had a deal.

THE MISFORTUNE of living in the bedlam of past mistakes came with the opportunity to relive them. To wheel all of the wrong turns and end up finding the right ones far too late. Jade had found the craggy rocks behind the quarter, winding down the back door of the pleasurehouse, at a time when the last thing she wanted was to be reminded of her past. Both continued to be terrible, treacherous spirals, traps for unseasoned wayfarers.

But there came a time when Jade could no longer resist either, testing herself against the sea's fortitude both in reality and in memory.

Had she known this secret path existed, might she never

have crashed against Mortimer Lowe in defense of Mouse to feel sand and sea between her toes? Might her pride have continued to fill the sail that was her father's name?

Would the name Elder have carried her farther, quicker than just Jade alone when she'd grown enough to manipulate its weight?

But the answers no longer mattered. She had changed. Thaya and Nate had changed. Her father had as well. And yet what was this grief writhing beneath her skin?

Jade had tried to be right and whole despite what she had lost. She'd sidled closer to the quarter, when perhaps she should've run from it. And then her hollow healing had filled to the brim with her quiet rage, turning her into a creature who couldn't live without the sea-spray in the air, the flowering vines that climbed into the buildings, who would fight the turmoils of unsteady merchant alliances and wars for dominance among the pirates if it meant she need never fall out of place again.

Like the bird lost to it's nest, forever chirping in defense of the shadow it casts on the ground.

No matter the ebb and flow of her feelings toward the sea, when the burning brightness of its blue rush touched her eyes, and its white foam licked the stones black beneath her feet, Jade wanted to forgive the child she'd been who had craved its soothing curls and mysterious troves. But she only found that confusing tangle of anger in her still, burrowing hooks into her fight to belong with the quarter.

If she set them free, what remained, other than the layered whispers that sometimes woke her from nightmares?

Don't go, you idiot. Turn back. Take up your mother's books and let Mabel put pretty knots in your hair. Don't say it. Don't ever say his name.

You can love him and never speak of him.

For a brief moment, she shut her eyes.

The sea-winds were anything but gentle, the deep-water cuffs against the reefs entirely defiant, and yet Jade could relax here, amongst the raw honesty of the sky unturned.

Daylight melted into the horizon, and Jade invited the change to come.

She opened herself to the rearranging of her limbs, the sprouting of feathers, the jet smoke eyes that meant she could see through the darkness made by the moon.

She shrugged away her human skin and donned the nut-rind cloak of an ashy-faced owl. Her cindered charm glowed warmly against the plume of her breast.

Elda was pleased, her mother would have said as Jade took flight for Vane Mercy's former stronghold tucked away near the wrecks—ship-spattered shores that had taken more lives than the pirate had himself.

Years ago, Jade had believed her mother dead in the fire that had consumed their home. But Thaya had simply walked through another door, one buried in long-lost memories, imprinted in the far corners of her knowledge, waiting for the chance to be of use.

Jade had never met her grandmother. Thaya had been swaddled and combed and fed by her father for most of her life. And when Tore Elder had happened upon her, showing her his distaste for abusing women, Thaya had went with him to ride the seas until the world ended. She'd never sought out her mother's people, the men and women who formed clans of the skies and took flight in all manner of shapes.

There was nothing to go back to anyway, Thaya had told Jade. *The bitter-blooded queen of Osolda had taken them, remolded their contours, their thoughts. The owl clan had been destroyed, my mother along with it. What would have been the point in seeking out the rest?*

Desperation had forced Thaya to search deep for new opportunities. She taught Jade to make use of them too. And together they worshipped what little they knew of Elda in secret, toting her charms and pretending they knew something of what it was to belong to a broken world away.

Jade's mother used her abilities when there was absolutely no other option. Jade monopolized them. She'd followed her father whenever he'd docked in his private bay. It was how she knew of his many plans, the shape of his ship, the scent of magic like hers and yet not which hadn't come ashore with him. *Azura.*

It was the reason she could sneak into the cove where Vane Mercy's men lingered, their bodies lined with grief and nerves. Azura was not with them. Jade could see the cost of their surprise when her half-goddess sister must've burst through her bindings, fresh lightning and storm clouds brewing inside her again.

Their sunken faces never turned in Jade's direction. Never saw her sneak into the tent where their captain had slept.

Where he'd once guarded a certain holy text, which gave him knowledge of the impending future.

And they paid her no mind when she reemerged from the animal-hide flaps in her owl skin once more, setting a return course in the night sky.

JADE MADE herself walk the beach when she returned to the quarter.

She had to see for herself the depth of her debt to her sister, whose life she had thoughtlessly torn apart to win an important advantage in a game tacked with too many of her sacrifices, her gambles.

The heads of the *Sea's Fire* crew were piked and staked to the sand. A note was displayed on a longer spike than the rest, which read *They tasted victory not their own.*

Jade memorized each of the newer faces, wondering how many of them were friend or foe to Azura, which ones had taught her to tack lines and hoist sails, to differentiate between Tore Elder's tempers. *This is what it's like when he's angry. This is what he is when he has a yen for something he cannot reach,* she imagined these men, their horror-stricken expressions now sealed into their decay, telling Azura with lively grins over dragging beards, nurturing her, protecting her.

She could imagine it so clearly because this was the life Jade had turned from. The life she might have had, had she come to her father, her mother in tow, and asked him to take them far away from Nadara so that she never need know pain like that day again. Some of these faces had filled her dreams, moving her small hands over ropes and clucking the brim of a hat much like Azura's in jest.

Jade had loved the sea so much. As much as that born sailor, Tore Elder, giant and cocksure, breathing fire across its jagged, gemstone surface atop a ship with a dragon for its figurehead. At first, she hadn't felt deserving of either of them. Not strong or brave enough. And then she thought of deserving better, of staying stationary despite the temptation to veer off and set the course of her life on a too-distant gleam. She wanted a home that couldn't be taken from her. She wanted to keep her heart somewhere more fortified than the wooden belly of a ship. And, most of all, she didn't want to spend her life chasing a thing because she could not have it.

She'd rather chase something she could change.

People aren't transactional, Mouse had said.

Yet, walking away from Tore Elder's dead crew, Jade understood there was no fate in which Azura wouldn't come to collect Jade's debt, for she had proven just how vulnerable such a home was and destroyed it. Her actions couldn't be forgiven away on the simple fact of shared blood.

Jade didn't know when Azura would come, but the wait

wouldn't be long. The same rage that lurked quietly within Jade would spit and claw within Azura until every last drop of it was spent. That was the impulse that had slain Nate's quartermaster and had all but consumed Jade's breath. That was the sum of Azura. Jade had witnessed it all firsthand.

But, in the surrounding death, Jade had turned over one more advantage to keep her afloat another day. She couldn't fill the dead with life again for Azura's sake. But she could offer her the living.

Maybe giving Tore Elder back would be enough to reconcile their accounts.

As she set foot on the street again, Mortimer Lowe peeled out of the shadows made by his tavern, smoking a red-burning cigar.

For an instant, Jade froze. And because he would enjoy her hesitation should it continue, she forced herself to move to the safety of the pleasurehouse.

"You're feeling pretty confident these days, aren't you?" he called to her.

She turned back slowly, standing on the threshold.

"Leaving the promise of turns to go on so many errands these last days," he went on, blowing out smoke. She still couldn't shake the feeling of his being a crow, especially not when he stood bolstered by the darkness, looking at her through the grey mist of his cigar. "Might say to some you're feeling confident about the monthly tally. That you have enough tucked away to afford leaving so many customers untended. Now how could that be?"

She made herself smile. "Turns can be generous tippers."

"Would that were so, seeing as the tavern could use that kind of generosity." His eyes were narrowed on her face, and he wore that smirk that sometimes woke her in cold sweat. "Isn't it funny that Captain Wynn should come into Anette's place so many days, then Tore Elder's crew turns up dead?" His shoulders lifted off the building. "It's Jade, isn't it?"

She stepped back through the doors, ensuring everyone on the floor would see her. See him. "I'm flattered you've been keeping an eye on me, Mr. Lowe, but I need to report to Anette."

She had never, not once these nine years, let him get this close, this often. Every day she had hidden from him in secret, then in plain sight, seemed like a miracle. But the day he'd taken her, her hair had been covered by Nate's hat, which had shadowed the green of her eyes. Not to mention the possibility Lowe *couldn't* remember what that young girl had looked like. He'd been so preoccupied with his own retaliation, he hadn't thought to catalog her appearance the way she would have, not knowing he'd need the information when her father came tearing through the quarter.

"Now there's no need to look so afraid, Jade. I have questions, that's all."

"And if I don't want to part with the answers?"

Though if he asked the wrong questions, she'd be happy to oblige him. She'd let him tell her what he thought he knew. Maybe then she might finally understand that oil-slick shine he'd been taking to her.

"Well." His smirk grew into a smile. The kind he wore when there was bloodshed to be had. "You'll have to pay. You seem to have the money these days. Almost like magic."

Jade should have known. His precious claims for protecting the quarter only ran as deep as his pockets. Being the Overseer's man didn't rise him out of simple greed. He used the things beaten to his advantage, then cashed them in for little luxuries. Like the first cut of meat from the butcher, the freshly died cotton he wore, tailored to perfection by the very clothier he'd taken them from. Everything he did was to make himself important.

A smoother, more cunning rat than the rest.

"Or I can go to Anette and tell her I think you're holding back some of the take? Anette's got a special rule about that, doesn't she?" he said conversationally, taking another step toward her. "Maybe she'd take an offer from me. Sell you to me to keep you out out of her hair. See that no more dead captains stain her tables."

When Pala called out to her, an enforcer not far behind, Lowe's lips thinned. "Think on my terms, Jade," he said lowly. "I'd hate for us to become enemies." He ducked out of the candlelight flowing out from the doorway. "After all, here in Nadara, all magic comes with a price."

"Are you all right?" Pala said when Lowe vanished back into his hole in the wall. "What did he say to you?"

"Nothing worth repeating." Jade's eyes caught on the large bruise shading Pala's light brown skin. "What happened to you?" she demanded, shoving down the shivers Lowe had caused her. "Who did this?"

There were shadows in Pala's gaze. "One of the turns." She winced as Jade tested the injured area.

"Did you tell Anette?"

"She said a few nicks to the hull is better than wrecking the whole ship. Don't," Pala said, gripping Jade's arm. "She's afraid. Things are changing, Jade. They're changing fast."

Jade looked back out into the night, where she imagined Mortimer Lowe still watched. "Yes," she said, her tone vicious. "Things *will* change."

◆

TALK FILLED the long tongue of the street.

After a gluttonous two days spent behind the walls of his fort, filled with enough rum and coin and girls from Anette's inn to stir bouts of envy on the beach, Captain Wynn and his crew left the quarter astride dark, muscular horses in the direction of the Inlands.

Trailing a man behind, a woolen sack covering his head.

Ain't that the bastard who wrecked the fort?

The Ashman, supplied another voice beneath Jade's window. *Burns down churches, the fucker.*

And whatever else he feels like. Wynn showed 'im. Cackles exploded. *Guess our fort was finally too big for the bastard.*

Jade serviced her turns through the morning with mutterings like these breaking through her concentration. She tried to sweat the words out, placing genuine effort into the construction of mutual pleasure. But, each time, each turn, Jade's thoughts would turn back to the crew massacred on the beach, and eventually her skin would stay cold.

None of her customers complained. But, inside, shame was doing its damndest to unspool her.

As soon as she'd collected enough payment to keep some of the suspicions about her in check, she left for that place near the wrecks, from where Vane Mercy's crew had yet to unchain themselves. Icy shame was replaced by a franticness that burned to be unleashed.

Jade held her calm. She forced her nerves into hiding.

"What do you want?" hissed one of the women, priestess markings from the east glowing against her deep skin. She nicked Jade with her knife. "I should gut you right now for what was done to my captain."

Jade held her palms up. "He came when I called," she said, her steady tenor drawing in the crew of the *Infidel's Cry*, "because the Book of Mercy told him to."

The dead captain's fellow Feydlan monks stood straighter at this.

"He told me," she continued, reaching into her bag, "there was more to come. That his dealings with me weren't done." She gingerly placed down the sack of silver bars Nate had rejected into the hands of the cook steaming beside their spit. He'd taken his eyes off his roasting pork to listen intently and she liked the look of him. "I'd like you to check the Book and then listen to what I have to say."

"We heard about that dead quartermaster," said the priestess, still hissing. She dug the knife deep enough to pierce cloth. Jade heard the echo of a head splintering from a body, a life dividing from the living. "Why should we trust a crew-killer like you?"

"Because I didn't kill him," Jade said easily, ignoring the priestess' snort. She'd paid for that quartermaster's death, she reminded herself, by keeping out of Nate's way. Her fault was small compared with Azura, who'd done the deed. But the sting of guilt remained. "The one who did may be after me still. You know her. You held her in your captive."

More of Mercy's men and women turned at this, their ears pricking.

"I see you lost some of your number," Jade went on, keeping her eyes trained on their faces, rather than the hands clenching their pommels. "And you haven't seen a new captain elected. One might wonder why that is, but I know."

One of the men broke from Vane Mercy's tent, speaking for the first time. "Let her go. It is written," he murmured, almost in wonder. "This meeting is written. She has a proposition for us we cannot ignore."

"We don't share the same god," snapped the priestess, shoving Jade aside. "Gods, in my case. Why the hell should I listen to that book?"

One of the Feydlan monks stepped forward. "Because our captain believed in it. He'd want us to see this done." He turned to Jade. "What business?"

"Things are changing in Nadara," she told him while glancing at the rest and taking a seat by the fire without being asked. She smiled right into the eyes of the cook who'd been tending the pork. "Your captain wasn't killed on my errand. That would imply that a simple pleasure-worker like me had that kind of power. But what I do have is connections. I make it my business to know things." She leaned in as if telling a secret. "You are a dying breed. The Overseer will see the pirates of this quarter, of his own making, extinguished before he refuses the warmth of a certain fire."

"Homesick fool," the priestess hissed again. Not a fan of much, that one. "Begging for scraps from his mother country, is he? Now that he's done playing the rebellious son? Bastard."

Jade nodded. "And I think the reason you haven't yet chosen a new captain, gone outside to search for one when you couldn't agree on one from within, is because, deep down, you know those of Vane Mercy's ilk, his caliber, are facing extinction," she said. "Think about who's left on this island. There was Mercy. There was Elder. There is Wynn. And now there's Steel. But where have their betters gone? Killed by any one of them or lost to the seas. And their lessers, *your* lessers? You won't find a captain among them."

"What do you suggest?" The priestess cocked her head, a sneer working over her plump lips. "You captaining us?"

A bit of laughter huffed out at this, but Jade didn't mind. She'd developed a thick skin against it long ago.

If she didn't convince them of what she had in mind, she would have no way of restraining Azura should the worst happen. She'd lose her life to a girl who would make her pay with every breath.

And Jade was drowning in enough debts. Every time she fulfilled one, another emerged. By staying in Nadara, the gambles of possibility and enterprise would be her lifetime.

She didn't want Azura to make her regret choosing such a life.

"How could I captain a crew with your seasoning?" she admitted, spreading her hands. "That wouldn't just be impossible, it would be a waste. No, for now, I offer you the fifty silver bars in that bag to become my temporary guards. I have many threats coming against me now, for the things I know. One of them the heathen goddess you so badly want to pay back for your losses. I ask only that you allow me the chance to reason with her should she come down on Anette's inn, then, failing reason, to do what I'm paying you to do."

"Which is?" said another monk.

"Protect me," returned Jade, eying each one of them, "from the demons who would destroy me. From the remains of Nadara's monsters who would spite me."

"Like common sellswords," sneered another priestess.

"Sellswords are worth their weight in gold," Jade said, an inner satisfaction pooling at the gleam coming into their eyes at the mention of bigger profits. The possibility of hauls all onto their own, not to be shared with those weaker than them on the coast of Feydla. There was a pang in Jade's heart at that, but she didn't have time for the kind of mercy the captain of the *Infidel's Cry* had preferred. "And wouldn't you like to have secured a prospering occupation when the Overseer starts putting anyone still clinging to notions of piracy to the noose?"

Jade rose. "I could come back with letters and ledgers and all manner of documentation to support my claims, but you already know I'm telling the truth. You're starting to see it. Feel it in the shifts of the tide. Change *is* coming," Jade said again, her voice strong as the arcing sea-winds. "What do you want to be left with when it arrives on our side of the island?"

She waved a hand toward the bag of silver. "I'm going to leave you this, as a show of good faith," she said, though the potential loss of the money frayed her confidence. She still hadn't come up with a way of transporting the cache her father had buried with her old home. Leaving Wynn's bag of silver behind was the last of Jade's outlandish maneuvers and she had to play it with flourish. "I'll let you think on my offer. But you should know there's more where that came from. Enough to protect you from the things you can't control."

"And you can?" This from the priestess harboring hostility toward her. But she had calmed enough to study Jade with clear eyes. "Protect us?"

Jade said, "I can."

∼

ANETTE HAD WRENCHED Jade aside for those overdue explanations, but Jade only confessed enough to prepare the Madame for what was coming.

There had been a flogging, swifter than Jade's first and only, and less taxing, for her counts of insubordination.

Not the theft of secrets, never that. But Jade *had* broken both ends of Anette's one rule—*always share the pot and never bring back trouble when you do.*

Still, Anette's heart hadn't been in it, though she committed wholly to the display of discipline before the rest of the girls. Anette's unflagging resolve was actually what Jade had always liked about her best.

Pala was tending Jade's wounds when Azura's lightning spat into the open ceiling above the bottom floor, striking the trees growing into the building like incorrigible limbs. Fire sparked quickly, then died. Azura's ship-killer torrent of rain submerged the fire before it could consume.

No wonder Tore had voyaged the world ablaze with unthinkable victories. This was the might of a divine mistress of storms.

When Azura emerged from a vicious swath of mist clouding turn from pleasure-worker, she drew her sword. "Where is Jade?" she bellowed into the heart of all the screams.

Jade did not bother with hiding. "Go," she told Pala, who did not listen, and called through her open doors, "I'm here."

A gust of Azura's storms sent Jade crashing back against her empty tub, wheezing from the pain radiating through her spine.

When Azura swarmed in, pieces of her mist stitching her back into a person with a raised sword, Jade didn't scream. Instead, she stated the truth, "I didn't know we were sisters. I didn't know you were a person I could hurt."

Azura kept on coming, unfazed.

But her hurt was plain beneath the anger, despite the depth of both.

How quickly had Azura found the beach and the deaths littered over it? How long must she have stood amongst the pikes bearing the heads of the *Sea's Fire*'s men?

Jade saw she had destroyed any chance of a bond before they'd ever met. Nothing she gave back would change that.

Pala leapt up to defend Jade, but before Jade could warn against such foolishness, Pala was thrown aside.

Jade made no move to defend her, or plead for her life, for if she showed even a moment of weakness, of caring for someone other than herself, Azura would redirect her rage, if only to see Jade suffer more.

Jade said, "I'm going to help you get Tore Elder back."

The sword shivered in the air.

Jade felt its shadow over her body and tried not to tremble. "I was an ungrateful child. Impossible, spiteful, petty, and impulsive," she told Azura quietly. "You sit so often in the same chair you forget your own weight. When the legs of that chair snap, it might sting when you land on the floor," she said steadily, laying everything bare before the sister she'd betrayed. "But the last thing on your mind is thanking the wood for holding your weight all that time. Then you learn what it is to fall through a hole in the ground. How long it takes to dig your way out. Later, you still don't thank the wood or the nails. You don't pray to them. But you remember. You remember what it is to be brought so low there was nowhere for you to sit... and nothing left to depend upon." Her breath did tremble then. Azura's eyes blistered with rage, but her hands hesitated.

They hesitated.

"I *know* what I took from you," Jade said. "I won't say I'm sorry for what I did, even knowing what it cost you. I've already lost what you have lost and can't ever afford to lose it again."

Jade didn't dare move other than to straighten her spine, to pretend the hurt in her back away. "But I know how to get you Tore Elder. I've come up with a plan to do it."

A plan that might mean the end of everything Jade had been working for. Mercy was dead and Steel was Nate. Tore Elder had been captured, broken from his men. She'd always known that if Wynn succeeded in capturing her father, he would be the last true threat of unchecked piracy.

Taking Tore back from him now could spark the violence she'd hoped to avoid. It could turn into a loss so vicious, Jade might not survive it.

But she owed her sister. And freeing Tore was a better chance of survival than not.

Azura's voice was a quaking, furious thing ready to spew when she spoke. "*You killed my family.*"

Contrary to Azura's storm, Jade's voice was calm as a still lake. "Not all your family, no."

Azura lifted Jade by the throat. "You've taken *everything* from me."

Jade kept her fists to her sides. She didn't struggle. "And I will get you back what's left."

Azura threw her to the floor. "Fight back," she raged. She flung lightning at Jade's robes, her tables, her mirror, her dressing panels, the soft sheets of her bed, until everything was smoking, melting husks. "*Fight back.*"

They were just things Jade told herself. Things she could buy back. "If I thought you would kill me now," she said, "I would fight you. But you can't do it now that the seed of your father's return is in your head."

Something in Jade's statement brought Azura's boiling to a sparking simmer. "*My* father?"

Jade's smile was empty, even bitter at the edges. Toward herself or toward the first pirate she had ever dared to love, she couldn't know. "I gave up my right to him a long time ago," she said. "Can I tell you what I have in mind to save him for you?"

Finally, the storm inside the inn evaporated. The crackling mist cleared. Azura's thunder-striking hands dissolved into true limbs.

The screams below died down.

"Everything I tell you now, every way I help you from this point on, clears me of your death warrant," Jade said softly. "While I'm sure you can think of plenty other methods of retribution, I want your word that once I deliver Tore Elder back to you, you will not ever, by your own hands or another's, kill me."

"Cold-blooded, calculating," murmured Azura, a vibrating husk of the writhing fury she had been. "I never expected any of it from you. I didn't know you, but I knew of you. Those *eyes.*" Her face unraveled into desolate lines of incredulity. "Those eyes are mine. They're his. The grief he carried for you was always stronger than his love for me. And all I could ever do was curse the day you were born to him as I was. And this is how you repay him for his devotion. A cold, slick bargain while he rots up in that fort."

Ignoring the shame that tried again to make itself known, Jade honed in on mention of the fort. "You've been misinformed," Jade said slowly. "Your father is not up in that fort."

Azura threw her head back and laughed. "You offer a plan but you don't know the truth?"

"What are you talking about?"

Pala whimpered as she stirred, drawing Jade's eye. Azura

laughed again, this time the sound fettered with delight. "Do you know how I found you in the first place?" said Azura, her words clipped and harsh beneath the echoes of her laughter. "Because I saw this one deliver the *Victory*'s captain to your door. All the way from up in his precious fort. I heard every word of your deal with him because of her."

Jade's heart thudded. *You aren't the only one capable of pick-pocketing secrets.* "I asked her to—"

Azura cut her off. "And, later, I followed her back to that fort. Again and again, she went back. Came back with a bruise this time, didn't she?" She reached down to grab up Pala by the hair, causing Pala to shriek. "This one deals in secrets, just like you, big sister. *Your* secrets. Didn't I see her just the other day talking closely with Steel after that monk's death? Didn't I see her go to Wynn again after that?" She shook Pala, who refused to look at Jade, as though the secrets were going to come pouring out. "I'm supposed to trust you to get my father back when you can't even trust yourself?"

Jade trembled all over. She felt her eyes going wide with disbelief, couldn't stop the tears from brimming in them.

Azura smiled at their wet trail.

They turned the board on me. Wynn. Possibly even Nate. Perhaps he and his father had reconciled while Jade's back was turned to more urgent matters. Her plans might have been unraveling from the beginning. *Pala helped them do it.*

"Why?" Jade croaked, thinking of all the years she and Pala had pressed together in a single bed, sharing whispers and giggles, telling tales sometimes real and sometimes not, cocooning one another from the painful blows of the past in a way only sisters knew.

But before an answer could quiver past Pala's lips, a gunshot went off below.

The steep rasp of Captain Wynn's voice floated up the stairs. "I have a message for Jade," he called out.

Jade's eyes shut. She inhaled deeply. Rubbed away her drying tears.

"Where are you?" he mocked, clinking money as though he were coaxing a mutt. "Come out, sweetheart."

"You can no more help me," Azura muttered, "than you can help yourself."

Jade opened her eyes, stared directly into Pala's. "How many men did he bring with him?"

"I don't— Jade let me—"

"*I* don't have time for your useless apologies," Jade snapped, selfishly pleased when Pala paled. "You've left me with a mess. Now you'll help me clean it up."

"Please, you don't understand—"

"Jade," Wynn shouted. There was a shriek down below. Something crashed. "I've grown tired of your games."

She heard Anette attempting to soothe him, telling him Jade would be right down. He wouldn't hurt her, but Jade didn't want to let him have the chance.

"Tell me how many men," Jade spat, "or I'll let the goddess show you what you deserve."

Azura surprised her in keeping quiet at this. Perhaps she could sense the danger unfolding below, or perhaps she just wanted to see what Jade would do. Was that the nature of creatures born from strange conjurings and couplings between the elements and men? Did they enjoy human tempests the way a cat relishes the delicious resistance of a mouse?

"He didn't want to bring his men into this," Pala whispered. "I didn't tell him about Azura, but I told him you'd been gone for long stretches. That you'd been awhile with Captain Steel. He didn't like that. He didn't like the idea of you winning him to your side."

"I expect not," Jade muttered as relief wound through her. *Nate's not against me. Thank the Skies he's not against me.* "Well, if he came alone, then he's in for a surprise. I have Vane Mercy's former shipmates surrounding this building."

Pala blinked, her mouth falling open.

Azura's menace swelled at the knowledge Jade had surrounded her.

"I trust a rare few." Jade spoke to her half-sister but kept her gaze on Pala, whose head lowered. "And I don't make the same mistake twice. If it's a fight Wynn wants, that's fine. I'm ready for him. Then, when he's finished making his threats, we'll take Tore Elder back from the fort." She finally turned to Azura. When her half-sister hesitated still, she said, "If you could take him back alone, you would have. But you don't know where they're keeping him, and you can't find out without hurting him in the process. So, little goddess." She didn't bother with holding out her hand. Not when those green eyes sputtered with ripening rage. "Will you take my deal or not?"

The tension downstairs was rising to a pinprick, ready to explode any moment.

Finally, Azura said, "I will."

WHEN JADE WALKED DOWNSTAIRS, no one would ever suspect she'd bartered her life back from a goddess.

No matter the scattered beliefs of Anette's patrons, such outcomes would seem impossible. But Jade had survived that, so she would survive Wynn, a mortal man thinking himself the better player.

What did you hold over my friend? She wondered as she approached his towering height. *How did you get her to betray me?* Jade thought vaguely of the bruise on Pala's face and speculated.

"Captain Wynn," she drawled, glancing about at all the gawking tables and seeing that he'd shoved an enforcer through one of them, explaining the noise following the gunshot. "Back so soon? How were the Inlands?"

For a moment her obvious unconcern seemed to throw him off. But he adapted quickly. That was part of what made him formidable, Jade realized at last. He recuperated from the surprises thrown at him and flung out his own power. She hadn't believed he could outsmart her, not with greed so core to the life he'd chosen, helpfully blinding him to her wit.

You called me clever. She hoped he hadn't forgotten. This time she wasn't only armed with letters and smokescreen answers.

"Should I claim surprise?" she said. "Okay, I'll play. What can I do for you, captain?"

All trace of amusement on his face had fled. His stare was cold obsidian. "It's more about what I can do for you."

"Oh?"

"Recently one of the merchant vessels came to me with a discrepancy on their manifest," he said, sitting down in a chair he dwarfed, all the while holding her gaze with his own. "You see, I had warned all the little fish not to forget who I was, and how there was nowhere in this world I wouldn't go to settle with them for a mistake. In this case, I wanted them to keep eyes out for a girl who might try to book passage off the island."

Jade did her best to appear interested, and she hoped the struggle not to show her boredom knocked him down another peg. "Seems like a shameful waste of resources to me," she said, even smiling a little. "Anyone who knows me knows I would never leave the island."

"I admit," said Wynn, holding up his hands as if this were no more than a friendly wager gone wrong. Jade knew better. "I didn't know you well enough for that. But the discrepancy remained. This merchant's manifest stated that a young woman *had* in fact tried to buy passage onto his ship. You know

Mortimer Lowe owns majority in a great many of these ship-ping vessels, yes?"

Now Jade's heart was starting to pound. "Your point, Captain?"

Now Wynn smiled, his teeth shrugging from his lips at last. "The name on the manifest was Thaya." Jade's heart dropped. "Last name Smith. But we both know that's a lie, don't we, Jade?"

When Jade said nothing, could say nothing, he said, "I met you once when you were born, you know. In the days when Tore and the other captains and I rarely had quarrel with each other because there were no shortage of prizes in the world. He called you his Precious Jade."

Hearing this was a tug on the fuse inside her. The coil seared so brutally it took everything in her not to open her mouth and scream. *You can love him and never say his name. You never have to tell the truth.* Those had been her mother's words before they were hers. Now Wynn hurled a bit of that truth, goading her to deny. Or to beg. Either was a victory.

"And when he and I drank too much in his quarters, laughing between swallows," Wynn continued, "he'd told me how his wife, Thaya, still hadn't found her sea legs, how she'd been yakking up worse even after you were born. It's strange, isn't it," he murmured, rising to cage her against a post, "the threads that tie one life to another?"

Jade didn't know how she managed to speak. Or even breathe when he was so near and all she wanted was to tear him apart. But she couldn't make a move against him. She understood now the reason why he'd come alone: her mother was trapped with the rest of his men inside the fort. If he didn't return, they likely had orders.

She didn't show him the fear shaving her nerves. She only said, "What do you want?"

He leaned closer. "I warned you, didn't I?" he said, almost

pitying. He pitied her for letting it come to this. "I warned you I'd come back to collect more than money if you crossed me. Now your poor mother will have to pay your dues."

Jade held her breath. She saw it in his eyes, the interest, the cost of him asking her for anything when he had all the advantage. "Unless?"

He stepped back, gave her breathing room. "Whatever trap the Overseer has laid for me, I want you to undo. And because both you and he have pissed me off, I want him to pay me double what I'm owed for the capture of Tore Elder. I don't care if you have to fuck and beg the man blind and deaf to do it. But you will. In the end you will get me what I'm owed."

As soon as he shoved his way clear of the doors, her knees trembled. The bold hues of the inn were blurring together in her vision.

Mama. Papa.

The words were winter flowers drowned by summer rains. They weighed. The memories inside them had washed away, leaving only a faint scent of the sweetness that had been.

Jade had gambled as a child and lost to Mortimer Lowe. She'd gambled again, playing a longer hand, and had once again lost everything. All she had left was a half-goddess sister who loathed her and a bruised liar of a friend waiting for her upstairs.

Skies, what have I done?

Jade slid to the ground and wept.

∼

BUSINESS TOOK off without her as she cried, though there were whispers. No one reached down a hand to help her up, because there was no one left with the urge inside them.

Only those whom she'd paid and those whom she owed debts. She'd seen to that.

You're being ridiculous, you look ridiculous. Get up. The closest she could manage was curling her knees up to her chest, muffling her sobs.

She'd lost everything. One selfish, childish act in the underbelly of an island she should never have loved and she'd lost every prominent point on the map of her life. She'd disappointed them. She'd used them with little shame, little mercy.

People aren't transactional, Jade.

What will you be left with when all the rest is gone? When the fury dries out who will remain?

She'd hoped for a legacy. A home without conditions to house the story of Jade Elder, unspoken queen of the quarter who needed no crown, only loyalty. *Only love me,* she thought pathetically, her sobs easing. The ache in her chest was harder still to bear. *And I will protect you. I will protect us all.* But struck bargains ignited even the most enduring roots of love, until everything turned to ash.

Did she know the names of the merchants whom she sought ownership of, other than Mouse?

Did she have devotion that wasn't purchased through desires?

What will you have left without either of us?

If they don't kill you that is?

A thousand times she could have turned back. A thousand times she could have played her hand a different way.

And she'd failed.

When she unfolded herself from her seashell shape, anger had rejoined her. She screamed. But the music of the pleasure-house didn't stop to keep time with her. The world kept turning new leaves even when it burned. She screamed and screamed. Tossed a chair, then a table. She gripped her head and gave herself pain.

The smack knocking her face askew tipped her balance. Her cheek blazed.

When Jade righted herself, Anette was there, hands on hips, bosom heaving, corkscrew curls blowing lightly in the breeze. She had none of the poised, sensual calm of Jade's first memory of her. Her cheeks were rosy and the lines of her mouth so tight, she looked on the verge of a scream herself.

"Do you know," Anette said slowly, "why I have no lines on my face?"

The question could not be answered as Jade was. Her mind was still spinning, her anxiety still scraping.

"The reason," Anette said, "is because I don't worry. I don't fear. I don't crack when the world tries to shatter me. What is my one rule?"

The Madame's words were slowly sinking in. Talk of a rule reminded Jade of the stinging in her back. "Always share the pot and never bring back trouble when you do."

"Sit." Anette had turned table and chair back upright and forced Jade down. "You've been lording, Jade. Spinning turns, taking chances, and holding your gains over everyone. Look at me," Anette snapped. "Watch me. *Always share the pot.*" She snatched a plate from one of the kitchen staff and delivered the order to a man drunk outside, holding himself glum against the open window. When he looked up at her, taking the food, there were tears there. A grateful smile. When she went back to Jade, she said, "Do you see now? I choose who to share with, but I always do. That man will never come in here and cause a ruckus in my place. In fact, he might leap to defend me should I ever need it. I didn't hold the bowl over his face and say, 'look what I have that you don't.' I didn't say, 'I have what you need, what are you going to give me for it?'" She leaned over the table, catching Jade's chin in her hand. "Is that what I did with you, little love? Give you something for something else?"

Jade's voice was a broken whisper. "No," she realized. The truth of that only enflamed the cracks. She'd chosen to work for Anette because she'd seen her power and hadn't been able to teach it to herself.

But she hadn't really learned. She hadn't listened well.

"No," Anette echoed her. "Because that's the quickest way to bring trouble to your door. The kind Mortimer Lowe taught you." She squeezed Jade's jaw gently. "You didn't lose everything because you gave Mouse something for nothing. Nor was it because you snuck away from your mother's skirts when you shouldn't have. You lost what you had that day because you lorded your name over a crowd that would never have thanked you for it.

"You learned tricks and enchantments from me, but you weren't much different than you were today, standing before the captain like you didn't know what it was to lose to Mortimer Lowe. Like you could crack him apart by the force of your will, same as you wanted to then."

Anette sat back, tucked a loosening curl back into place. "You haven't been playing your game smart. People like me, like Wynn, like Lowe, we don't crack easily. It's not how we made ourselves and we respect each other for it, no matter our feelings on one another. What will you make yourself into, Jade?"

The silence that fell between them couldn't be termed comforting, but it warmed something that had gone cold in Jade since her schemes began. The possibilities of what she could do with this feeling rattled inside her.

The Madame scraped back her chair, but Jade grabbed her wrist. "I want to buy up most of this place, if not all," she said quietly. "Not because I want to take it from you, or because I think it belongs to me more than you, but because I'm making myself here. I'm going to be more than anyone expects here."

For a long moment, Anette didn't so much as sigh. She didn't, thankfully, pat Jade's head and tell her those kinds of dreams were wasted on her like. "If you live to pay the kind of sum I have in mind," Anette said at last, "you'll get the reins without a peep from me. You'll probably have earned them by then."

Jade let her go, feeling light-headed and fragile.

And as deeply grateful as she'd been when Anette came to help Mouse pick her from the street, laying her down before an unconditional hearth for no other reason than to tend to her battered soul.

Azura had found Jade, carrying the same duress Jade had experienced then. Nate had found her too, holding in just as much pain as she had known then.

Jade hadn't tended either of them. Instead, she'd tossed them both into that hearth to maintain the sanctity of her plans.

No more. She needed a new tactic.

It was time to start paying back the cost of all her myriad lies and gambles.

BLUSHING new-dawn light tenderly kissed Jade's feathered brow as she flew over villas bigger than the bluffs which had kept her old home from falling into the quarter.

The Overseer's estate shadowed the wakening hills, the towering palms, and touched the sky like a pronged white-and-terracotta crown. As Jade winged closer, she swept past the main villa, the blooming courtyards, and the plantations where indentured servants from around the world, save for the Far North, plowed through the heat. Jade had heard a rumor about the estate having its own prison facilities. She imagined that would be where he kept the ones worthy of some kind of trial. A dark stamp of civilization dressed in finery and pomp.

She began to grasp why her parents had chosen the life that they had. Leaving behind their homelands was perhaps a brave acknowledgement that they didn't belong in the civilized world and never would, because the rules were small boxes with metal bars.

Rules without justice was a cage. Destruction, even with purpose, a noose of the soul. Cold-blooded greatness was possible here, from the shadows of the quarter to the polished depths of the Inlands. So were grave mistakes and bitter rivalries.

Was Jade truly so absorbed with protecting the wealth of Nadara spread before her, she'd become as bold and callous as the very men she had begrudged for near a decade?

"I don't mind the Nadara you want to build," she explained, with none of her wind-rough fear, only her calm, after being led by a very stout and stern majordomo with crisp cuffs. He'd left Jade in the heart of the Overseer's largess—wide purple couches beneath blue-glass windows framed in marble, jade vases holding reddish lilies in the air, walls scrolled with gold-threaded petals and jewel-toned ivy vines. "Doesn't change much for me and mine," she said to the disgraced duke behind a desk of polished mahogany, fingers curled over his plush chair like talons. "I will have the backing of the street regardless."

"So what is it you do want?" he said sharply, pointed up like an arrow in his chair.

Everything hinged upon her answer. She knew this. She knew that if she wanted to take down Wynn, and fulfill her promises to both Azura and Nate, divest Pala of her secrets, save her mother, and protect Mouse and the rest of the merchants from that vulture—no longer crow—Mortimer Lowe, Jade had to not only entice the Overseer into solidifying terms, she also had to make him believe she could be— "Your partner," she said, because she could accept nothing less. "I want to be your partner."

If she was the quarter, she was also the beach, the bay, and the fort. If she could keep herself tethered to all those places dependent upon commerce and security, then she was already one half of the island. The half that served as an outer layer of protection for the Inlands should a new threat ever embolden itself. Jade had to prove she could maintain control of all of it.

She had to prove she had the power to guard against pirates like Wynn, who let their arrogance overcome them, and to evade the greedy grasping of wealthy land-owners and merchants not unlike Mortimer Lowe. If Jade had power over the island, then she had power over herself.

She would have a stake in her own future.

"My partner?" The Overseer's fingers ticked against his desk. "You want to replace Mortimer Lowe."

"Is Mr. Lowe your partner?" said Jade, sitting back in her own chair, languidly crossing her legs. "Or a greedy, heavy-handed thug long past his prime?" She wanted to implore that the man would never be anything more than a greedy wretch. A poison clogging the wells of profit and prosperity. But a man like the Overseer would only mistrust that kind of passion. "No, Your Grace, I have no interest in being what he is." She had a different candidate in mind for the replacement of Mortimer Lowe, a direct conduit between herself and the Overseer who was far more honorable. She didn't know if the job would lighten the darkness of her shared past with Mouse, but she hoped it showed him some measure of her trust in him. "I'm talking about something much bigger."

He rose to pour himself whiskey that made Jade think briefly of Nate's eyes. "What do you have to offer me that he doesn't?"

Always share the pot, Anette had said. Jade still wasn't entirely sure how to replicate the meaning here, but she thought it might mean honesty. Full disclosure.

"You should know," she said, "that I had my mother spy on your workings here. I tasked her to pluck valuable whispers from the crevices of your halls and the furrows of your fields. I also lied to many people about what you would do on my behalf. Those lies were supposed to send Captain Wynn to your door, and I had hoped when he arrived with threats about payment..." She trailed off to eye the sleek, silent, and cloaked men stationed at the only two sets of doors in the room. "You wouldn't disappoint in dispatching him. I profited from those lies, because I knew your mind on such matters thanks to those whispers. Just as I know what you intend now."

"Do you?"

"I know you need pirates like Captain Wynn removed from that fort. You need them removed all together if you're to prove your prowess to those countries across the sea." She saw interest kindle in the way his fingers flinched against his glass. "I need that too. I'm as much tired of being taken from as you are, I imagine."

The Overseer smoothed his hands over his desk. "And what is the price for fulfilling all my desires?" he said, almost mockingly. "I *imagine* its quite exorbitant."

Jade leaned in, placed her hand across from his, fusing the space between them with all her wanting. His throat jumped in response. "Only that I might be the pulse in the shadows. The one you come to when you need loyalty you can rely upon," she said softly, though her urgency nearly overwhelmed her. The breadth of this arrangement could turn the board from Wynn to her. It could mean so much more than simply securing her parents from Wynn's fort. Her advantage would remain as imperceptible as prying secrets from the unsuspecting. But, if outed, she'd never have to truly hide.

Jade and the quarter were bound irrevocably by blood and loss. If the Overseer agreed on that point, that to attempt to separate one from the other would collapse them both, she'd never be made to run. She could finally cling to what really mattered without being afraid of losing everything.

"This is not a demand," she said. "This is not even about a

balanced exchange. I just want my home safe, prospering under my hand, and I'm willing to prove to you how far I will go to see it done. Seeing Wynn removed from the fort is a benefit you can't ignore."

"You intend to break into that fort? Alone?" His skepticism iced his voice, cooled the sweat on his brow. "Just how will a simple pleasure-worker like you manage such a thing?"

She'd been hoping he'd be inclined enough to ask. Rising to open the stained glass window, she said, "You've been to Feydla, haven't you? Ask yourself who rules Feydla's neighbor now that a certain blood-thirsty queen has perished?" The answer came to him and stunned him. He stared at her as if she grew heads rather than wings. "Did you see me arrive with an escort or a steed?" *There,* she thought, *I've trusted you with an advantage.* Never mind that in the same breath she had also insured her escape should their dealings sour.

"I can get inside easily enough." She smiled. "And, forgive me, Your Grace, who ever said I was going to do it all alone?"

"Before I even entertain the idea of continuing this conversation," he said, haughty in every tense, primped muscle, "I want to know why. Why do you want to partner with me if you claim to have so much? Why tether yourself to an island with an uncertain future?"

"A few well-placed whispers and a hearty hand can take you far," she murmured, an idle finger teasing the mounds rising from her cleavage. "Shadows are dark, sensual things. But what about the light? What about shouts of allegiance outside your window made under the sun? These are not so exciting but they bestow promises. Recriminations. It's the reason wars are fought and must be won." She shifted beneath her dignified shawl, hiding the curves of her breasts from sight. He'd only glanced down once, but that was enough to prove her point, for he was regarding her with that hawk-sharp look again, quickly rebuilding his defenses. Underhanded tricks only diverted for so long, and truly utilizing all that Anette had taught her, all that she had nurtured on her own, meant becoming something more than just an idle distraction.

"How long," she said slowly, "can the midnight games we play hold value while guarantees are traded in the light? How long before men like Wynn and Lowe send this island to the bottom of the sea? Overseer, this island is my home. And I can no longer afford to gamble with its safety."

Her heart pounded the longer he stared directly into her. Half-fledged promises were at the tip of her tongue. But she bit them back. For the first time, Jade found herself unable to risk a promise without knowing the consequences.

"He stole from me once, you know," she said instead. "Lowe. At one point in my life, he made me believe nothing that mattered was left and that I mattered even less than that. You can avoid finding yourself in the same position."

The Overseer's reply was curt. "What are you suggesting?"

"Suggestions won't make you believe me. I'll get you proof that it's not just Wynn or his ilk that should worry you. When you enable a man like Lowe, you'll end up with far worse than bruised pride." She lifted a fruit off the tray his manservant had brought into the room. "So. Will you trade with me in the light?"

They spoke until that light faded.

JADE SHUT Pala's door behind her. "You thought to toy with me," she said. "You wanted to prove yourself the better player."

Pala rose from her stool quickly, hands fluttering. "*Never.*"

"Then why?" Jade's fists curled. "Because, trust me, I've gone over every reason in mind, and I can't think of anything except your pride."

"What about love?" whispered Pala brokenly. "I was trying to protect you, Jade."

"I had everything under control," Jade all but shouted. "You forced my hand a different way. *You.*"

"I know," Pala said, covering her face. "But by the time I thought to stop, it was too late. He had me." When she lifted her face, her cheeks were drenched, apology spilling from every pore. "He had me and I couldn't stop."

Jade sucked in a cleansing breath. "I know you love me," she said quietly. "You're one of the few who do. But I can't trust you."

Pala stepped forward, catching the shine in Jade's eyes. "Unless?" She held out her hand, same as she had years ago when Jade found herself alone amongst all the other girls.

Jade reached back, held tight in spite of everything. "Unless you commit to helping me."

Once she let go, and Pala left to prepare, those hands shook. Negotiations with the Overseer had strung out her nerves like broken shards held up to the sun. She knew he might have seen more than she wanted to show. But, with each pulse of her wings taking her from his estate, a tunnel of flame built inside her. An inferno promising failure caught in a whirlwind of hope. Her bird-body had shivered from the force of her apprehension.

But there was no other choice. Not when Wynn had seized all her bargaining chips and taken still more. And not when the loss of it all had invigorated her instead of hollowed her out, as it had when she'd been a child. There was a stronger chance she would succeed because she had grown stronger.

Her fears left a glassy trail that would lead her to burrow under her bedsheets and lament her choices. She left them behind.

She needed one more person to help her solidify her plans for the fort.

"When this is done," Jade said into the warm sliver of distance between hers and Nate's faces, "you'll have to convert. Reform your articles. You'll be nothing more than large merchant vessels, importing and shipping legitimate hauls should you choose to leave the island. But you *will* have uncontested control of the fort." She brought their faces closer, until their noses touched and she could see every trace of a thought run over his expression. "Can you live with that?"

They were seated openly in the pleasurehouse, with Jade snug in Nate's lap. Her legs were sprawled over his hips, touching the cold wood of their chair. When Pala delivered a report to Wynn, she would say they had only been enjoying each other. That Nate was using, not plotting, and Wynn had nothing to fear.

A dozen other eyes would say the same.

"Please say you can," she whispered against him, barely resisting the urge to just crawl into him. Wrap him in her thrall until he had no chance of disappearing again.

"Most of the men are hunters," Nate said, ever cool while she shivered in the heat they made with no effort at all. It maddened her, in the same way his sun-fired aloe-in-smoke scent maddened her. She wondered if he'd puffed on tobacco before coming here. She wondered why he smelled so much like home to her. "How do you expect me to convince them to drown their instincts and do what's unnatural to them?"

Jade cupped his face, willing him to understand what was at stake. "By explaining that they might live to do anything at all. Besides," she murmured. "I don't intend to let the Overseer have final say over *everything*."

He regarded her thoughtfully. Then, slowly, so slowly, he hooked a curl from her cheek and wrapped it behind her ear. His other hand squeezed her waist and suddenly she was flush against him. Their bodies were fitted together line by line, angle to curve.

"And what do you intend for me?" he said.

She nuzzled his neck, and not only because she wanted Wynn to hear about it. The world had narrowed to a needle-point and she and Nate were wound tight at its edge. "My intentions are to help you achieve your revenge, just like I promised." She lifted her head from beneath his clenched jaw. "That's what this is all about, isn't it? You know the way in, I know the way out. We're in this together, Nate. Your father won't know what hit him."

This time, he didn't say the thing that would bruise her heart. He didn't warn her this alliance was temporary, that at some point he'd grow unsatisfied and try to buck her from the shadows she sought to rule without a title. He only looked at her, softening a little, holding up more of her red curls.

"You feel good," she murmured into his ear, a little startled by the truth of it.

"I followed you," he said. She jerked against him, disbelief tainting their closeness. He clutched her tighter. "I don't know why I had to be the one to go. I guess I told myself I couldn't trust my men or anyone else to do it. But I followed you the day you went to visit your mother."

Her palms were icy on his neck. "Did you tell your father about my mother?"

He didn't flinch from her. His gaze remained steady and hot with that indomitable rage never far behind. "No," he said. "I followed you back to the place where your old life ended. Where mine did, since Wynn came for me not long after." His heart kicked hard against her breasts. Strangely, the fast beat called to her own. "And you called out for me. Why?"

She could have responded with, *tell me you'll help me and I'll give you the answer. Tell me you'll help me get my mother and father back and I'll give you whatever you want. Anything you want.*

And yet Nate hadn't stolen from her. He saw what was

buried beneath years of neglect and death, and he hadn't laid claim on her prize.

With Mouse's words still ringing in her ears, she relented without an asking price. "Because I needed you," she said, the words stirring his hair gently. "Because you weren't there, hadn't been there for years, and I still needed you. I don't know why it was so hard to forget you, but somehow you made it impossible."

His head fell forward and his struggle for breath warmed her neck.

"Don't hide from me anymore, Nate. Don't leave me alone again."

He hesitated. Her pulse was a strong beat in her ears. The sound of its course thickened when he pressed a soft, quick kiss where his breath had landed.

Her arms quavered around him. *I know what you've made yourself.* Instead of urging her back, the thought had her tightening her hold until he gently separated them.

His voice throttled toward her when he finally spoke—a low, merciless tempest giving birth to a promise as withstanding and jagged as a bluff: "Never again."

SPOKES OF RUINED ships jutted between the rocks as Jade spoke out to all those she and Nate had gathered. "They're not going to think we'll try the tunnels," she said, "because it would be stupid with them so well-guarded. But that's the kind of arrogance we can count on."

Nate's first-mate piped up through a straggly chestnut beard, "He'll have double the men down there, while the rest of the fort isn't so carefully guarded."

Jade beamed at him. The man was three times Nate's age and bald as a scrubbed pearl, and had, after a single introduction, become Jade's favorite person on the island. He was an Osoldan like her, and her affection fell on his wide, drunken gestures, his scathing victories in a game of dice, and the ruthless medley of weapons strapped all across his body. He'd passed the time easily with her as the others arrived, regaling her with blood-curdling ghost stories belonging to the fields to which he'd been born as he trounced her roll after roll.

Nate unfolded a yellowed map of the fort across a moon-drenched rock, which Jade had stolen from Mortimer Lowe's office, along with a cache of other documents that would interest the Overseer. He pointed to the southern tip of the fort. "That's their weak point. They just don't know it." The night's breeze bit his cheeks russet, but his voice didn't clatter behind his teeth. "There will be a sprinkling of men inside the watch-tower, but that's nothing half a goddess couldn't handle."

Azura's piercing gaze pushed up from the shadows made by her hat's brim. "Depends on the results you're looking for."

Jade indulged in a biting laugh. "Are you saying you can't do it?"

Just as she expected, Azura's rage rose to the surface, stirring heat in the air. "Would you like another demonstration of what I can do?"

"No need, no need. I have a good memory. So do most here," Jade said, opening her arms out to Vane Mercy's former crew, whose expressions varied from stunned horror to biding wrath. "If you're worried about killing the men, don't be. I doubt anyone here will miss them."

She looked to Nate for confirmation, and he nodded. "Anyone I cared to take from Wynn is already with me."

"I might not be able to control how far I go," Azura muttered, the air around her rippling with her impatience.

"Don't worry, you'll have an eye on your back."

"*Whose?*"

Jade went back to the map. "My sellswords—" she ignored

the chaffing hisses at this "—will lie in wait in the water, while the majority of Captain Steel's men flank the western wall, waiting for the doors."

Mouse, who'd remained quiet throughout, said, "What about me? Why am I here?"

It hadn't taken as much effort as it should have to get him to come. Even when he was hurt or irritated, he'd still come to her when she summoned him. "Because you're the best friend I've got," she told him, echoing his earlier admission to her, causing him to shuffle his huge feet a bit. "And you're the only one who knows how to lure out Mortimer Lowe without making him think you're up to something."

Mouse cracked a smile, despite the wary, stoic glances Nate had locked on him from the moment he'd arrived. "But what are *you* up to, Jade?"

She grinned back, finally feeling like things were defensible and possible again. "Haven't you been listening?"

"There's no way Wynn isn't going to notice," interrupted Nate's first-mate, staring bleakly at the map. *They must have been friends once,* Jade worried. *Can he do this?* "How could he not?"

"Leave that to me," answered Pala, wearing Jade's borrowed shawl like a blanket over a laughably thin corset and skirt. "I can buy you all a distraction."

Azura had returned so resolutely to her silence, Jade had almost forgotten she was there. "And where will *you* be in all this?"

Jade looked over her shoulder at the last person she had ever expected to turn up at her door, the girl who blasted a hole through her plans from that first day, and said, "Where you least want me to be, little goddess."

She reached up to finger the blackened charm in the hollow of her collarbone. "At your side."

THE CHILL PRESENCE of the mist shivered along Jade's wings, threading damp and white through her feathers as they fluttered. Gray rains were the only sound pinning down the silence. The men guarding the top levels of the fort were watching with red-rimmed eyes and skin bristling from the cold.

Thick air made it harder for them to see shapes in the water below, obscuring even the wide set of muddied shoulders ducking low, curving around erratic heartbeats.

Men Nate had recruited were waiting for their moment to strike.

When Jade landed on the craggy tip of the watchtower, her ear valves screeched with the opening of the fort's doors.

Pala walked through, her shawl gone, her skin pebbled from the cold night. "I have a gift from Anette," she told the guards eying her, leaning over as if to tell a secret. "He'll find it between my thighs."

One of them chortled.

The other waved her forward and escorted her to the captain's rooms.

It wasn't long before she re-emerged, impishly calling back to the captain she was going to find rum to prime their next bout.

All the men had eyes on her.

Jade flew down to the doors and shifted into her other self, as though the human skin was simply waiting between one puff of the mist to the next. It didn't take much for her to lift the bar. The doors were the real problem.

Azura appeared from the milk-skinned air as Jade grappled the doors open for Nate, bringing lightning down on the watchtower to cloak the harsh, dragging noises of the wood.

"Did you see that?" Jade heard someone from the watchtower bellow down. "Gods be, that was closer than—the doors!"

The wick inside the watchtower flared and the men along the walls unsheathed their swords as Nate and his men barreled their way into the fort.

Mens footsteps' banged down the fort's outcropping like drums, pistols and muskets bursting. Those at the entrances of the tunnels called down to the rest, pouring from the hole in a steady stream.

Some of Nate's men drew swords, some lit the barrels of their own weapons. An iron grenade snicked to life, then went flying for the men remaining on the walls.

The explosion rung louder than the clap of thunder overhead, shooting out shrapnel.

Shots rained down. Captain Wynn emerged from his rooms, barely clothed, and with two pistols in hand. The moment he caught sight of Jade in the chaos, he aimed one weapon.

Nate shot first, catching Wynn in the side. "Go," he shouted back at Jade. His father wasn't going down from a flesh wound. Wynn climbed down to meet Nate head on.

This is his fight, she reminded herself. "Don't die," she shouted to his backside. Without waiting for his response, she transformed again as Azura brought down a ferocious barrage of lightning on the gun captains racing for the fort's canons.

They'd heard what the others, well into the thick of their own fights, had missed.

A violent whistling sound was charging toward them from some unseen depth in the mist hanging over the water.

The blast shook the watchtower, poised at the edge of the southern tip.

The entire fort quaked.

"Open fire," one of the living screamed.

But Nate's first-mate and the rest of the crew had already launched the next shot from the cannons aboard the *Revenge*.

Jade arced high overhead, loosing an ear-splitting cry.

In answer, the former crew of the *Infidel's Cry* howled from the belly of the darkness below. Each of them awaited the destruction of the watchtower from skiffs stopped a safe distance from the cliffs.

When the southern wall of the fort fell, those men and women would climb up the cliff-face and into the tunnels, dispatching any of Wynn's lingering men.

Another cannon shot did the deed.

The southern wall crumbled in an explosion of stone and debris, crippling the men fighting in its shadow.

Nate.

Jade winged low, avoiding one of Azura's lightning strikes. She saw Nate's bloodied fist crack against his father's red-smeared jaw.

A broken caw pulled her attention away from the battle. Her gaze locked on Pala, who jangled a set of keys.

At the signal, Jade landed at Azura's back, a human again, and said, "Let's go."

With a bitter quirk of her lips, Azura brought down another hair-raising belt of lightning on the men whose blades had separated the *Sea's Fire* crewmen from their heads.

She turned to Jade, not wholly human, crackling sparks surrounding her in a halo, and said, "Now we can go."

Jade didn't think her half-sister would appreciate her unfurling smile, so she turned to follow Pala's lead.

Dank darkness soared over them like the wet mouth of a beast.

Jade grabbed one of the torches off the wall sconce and led them deeper into the darkness. Though she kept her owl body away, her night vision was still sharp and had no trouble avoiding tossed wood, forgotten skulls, and rubble.

"How do you know he's down here?" Azura demanded, not bothering with keeping her voice low, though Jade was doing her damndest to muffle even an errant heartbeat.

"There were brigs on the map I stole from Mr. Lowe," said Jade, dodging a dribble of musty water from some unseen crevice. "Wynn wouldn't have kept either of them in one of the cells above. He wouldn't have wanted either of them out in the open."

"Why is that?" Pala asked.

"Because my mother would have bat her dirty lashes and promised them all manner of things to get her out with no more than a doe-eyed look," Jade said. "And as soon as the little fish forgot the dangers beneath the surface and got close enough, *her* father would have snapped their necks even if it had meant breaking his own hands to do it."

"He's not just *my* father," Azura snapped, deliberately kicking a skull.

"Oh, I'm sorry, I didn't realize you were interested in sharing him, but there's simply no need."

"You don't need him?" The soft currents of lightning emanating from her half-sister began to glow from soft yellow to blazing blue-white. "You say that just because you think I do?"

"You two are—" Pala hesitated. "You know what, I don't want to know."

Jade sighed, stopping. She swung her torch around, but she needn't have bothered as Azura's power had sharpened her own vision. "You're going to need *someone* after what you've lost. Might as well be our father. This way you're less likely to hold my sins against me."

"Not likely," came Azura's answering mutter, resounding up to the ceiling.

A retort—like, *remember our bargain, little goddess*—might have left Jade's lips if they hadn't come to a set of metal bars painted with red-rust. There were stirrings in the darkness behind it.

"Mama?" Jade called out.

A weak flutter that might have been her name echoed lowly from inside.

Her heart stuttered in her chest. "Give me the keys," she said, tossing down the torch.

"Allow me," said Pala, whose hands were far steadier. Each wrong key pumped Jade's heart faster. Azura's impatience was a tangible gale at her back, ruffling her curls.

It seemed like an eternity before Jade and Pala could manage wrenching the metal gate open, the bitter scent of blood and rust circulating with each hard tug thanks to Azura's snapping winds.

Jade shoved herself through the small opening. "Mama." She drew a quivering, bruised Thaya to her side, holding her until the shock and weariness gave out, then helping her stumble into a standing position.

Jade made herself look over at the man who coughed out, "Little Gust," as Azura wept over his broken body, the rage that had broken down doors and windows, that might one day tear apart ships and leave a trail of blazing scraps behind, had sapped from the well within her.

No, Wynn had never believed Jade's deal had been so simple. He'd never taken Tore Elder with him that day he'd left on horseback.

All of it had been a ploy. He'd likely suspected Jade all along, because... those wounds...

Tore Elder could never have mounted a horse. It would be a miracle if they could even get him to his feet.

They'd torn her father apart.

Papa, something small and half-forgotten inside her whimpered.

She'd done this.

She'd given her father to a man who'd given him no quarter, maybe even in part because of boredom.

There was some resistance, Wynn had said, the way a butcher talks about pickling meat. *But when the fire abated, the ash settled.*

This was what the monsters of Nadara did when tested like her father or when caged like Wynn up in his fort, prowling for opportunities because the vast sea with all its promise had been shrinking beneath his feet. When the world started changing, men like Wynn sought alternative methods of filling their appetites and restoring their pride.

And Jade had helped sate Wynn's.

She thought she heard Tore say, "Leave me." He curled into Azura's arms and murmured, "Leave me, Little Gust," into her quaking shoulder. She'd taken off her hat to hold him, as though he were already dead.

"We have to go," said Pala gently. "We don't know how the tides are churning up there."

Azura set down Tore. Mopped her face with the back of her hand.

Then she cocked a pistol Jade had never seen before in her mother's direction.

HORROR WAS a broken note in Thaya's melodic voice. "Jade?"

Pala stared at the weapon in Azura's steady hand. "You... What are you doing?"

Jade didn't dare move a muscle. "We had a deal," she said, though she knew the reminder was futile. She'd bargained for her own life, not her mother's. *Always share the pot.*

But once again Jade had been so consumed by her own arrogance, her own life, she'd never stopped to consider what suggestions of retribution might have been tumbling through Azura's mind. Thaya's weeping wouldn't deter her, just as the thought of men's screams on the *Sea's Fire* when Captain Wynn finally boarded hadn't stopped Jade.

A shared gift from their father, who could switch from generosity to cruelty just by the flick of his hand.

"You killed my family," Azura said. "*His* family. I promised to let you live. But now I'm done making promises."

As Azura's finger twitched on the trigger, Jade decided. She told herself there would be no more transactions made in the name of survival. If a deal required bloodshed, Jade would have no part of it, no matter how enticing, no matter how certain the prosperity.

She was finished with putting herself before the ones she loved. Chasing a thing no matter whom her pursuits hurt.

Like father, like daughter after all.

When Azura's gunshot finally rang out, smoke trailing after the clamor, Jade closed her eyes and shoved her mother behind her, sealing her final bargain made in the shadows.

TOO MANY THINGS happened at once for Jade to be sure of the path fate had taken in those endless seconds before her death.

But one thing she knew for certain was that she still breathed.

When Jade opened her eyes again, Pala had been shoved into the bars. And her knife—a constant companion living the way they did—was buried in Azura's shoulder blade.

With a quick glance over her own shoulder, Jade saw the smoking tail of Azura's bullet flowing out from a narrow hole in the wall.

Thaya wept harder as Azura wrenched the knife from her body, stepping toward her with vicious intent. "Jade," she screamed.

Before Jade could stop her sister, that weak cough broke the air. "Jade," came the faintest whisper, charged with an even fainter sense of hope. "My Precious Jade?"

Those were the words that pulled Azura back.

"Little Gust," rasped Tore, his hands roving the dirt, grasping through rubble. "Don't hurt my jewel. Don't."

Tears crowded Jade's vision, but she couldn't go to him. The devastated cracks in Azura's face made the move unthinkable.

All I could ever do was curse the day you were born.... The grief he carried for you was always stronger...

"Dead," Tore wept through swollen lids, his arms flexing desperately against the ground. His muscles failed under his weight. "Thought you were dead, my jewel. Where are you?"

Jade looked helplessly at her mother, whose gaze held no answers. Their drenched faces could've been mirrors.

"Thaya, you never said," Tore whispered. "You told me you agreed... her spirit was angry..."

Jade's mother had given her that—the right to decide how she would proceed from this point on, the freedom from giving Tore the truth because Thaya already had.

Jade's rage was the foundation of everything. A fury born from a childhood twisted with misery, for which she had blamed the man grasping for her from the floor.

A chain of inward grief rattled inside her. An array of broken memories littered her mind. If Jade brushed against the long, ugly trail, she would bleed out.

She'd destroyed their father in order to protect her home from destruction. She'd caused a man to mourn to spare herself pain. She'd watched the quarter come undone from the throes of his rage, because she'd been terrified of what he would do if he found her.

For how much worse would he have become had he discovered the horrified, hungry thing so far-flung from the little girl he remembered?

She longed to soothe the raggedness of her memory, the blazing in her soul.

But, she'd already taken enough from her half-sister.

Azura, whether it was to her knowledge or not, had started dissipating into a punch of white mist leaking into the brig. As though she could hear that same unnerving jangle that meant a heart was coming apart and was trying to escape it.

Jade started to open her mouth, to tell him there was no one here by that name, that Jade Elder was a ghost, one who would finally stop haunting him. She would no longer make him pay for being only what he was.

But then a fully human Azura dragged Jade forward. Shoved her down beside their father. "Tell him."

Sorrow knotted her voice, spilling fresh down her cheeks. "Papa," she said aloud for the first time in more than nine years. She clasped his shaking hand in hers. It was no more than a sad, worn limb now. "I'm sorry." She burrowed into his chest. His heart was so frail, so weak. Tears, his and hers, leaked into the lines of his throat. "Oh, Skies, Papa, I'm sorry."

His hand reached up to touch her hair, the strands indistinguishable from his own.

The ceiling quaked in time with her heaving breaths. Before Pala could draw her back, warn them all again, Jade wrapped herself in calm once more, reeling her sorrow back inside with a patient hand. "I'm going to get you out of here," she whispered into her father's ear, fighting not to break when he could barely nod in response.

"Can you manage lifting him?" she asked Azura, who nodded without a word.

Between Jade and Pala, Thaya kept her balance as the four women made their way through the fort, with the leviathan Tore held in Azura's unearthly arms, each of them gritting their teeth against the jolts of canonfire exploding overhead.

"There's an exit coming up," Jade said. "If that map is to be believed."

"I'm curious," Pala said, taking her role as distraction seriously the longer the terse silence stretched, "what else did you take from Lowe's office? There was a stack in your room," she went on when she caught Jade's look. "They looked like manifests, but I don't know why you would need a bunch of musty, smelly papers."

The comment gilded Jade's smile. Pala eyed her with twitching lips. She, too, knew the twists Jade's guarded thoughts could take, even if she couldn't always guess their final shape. She would have been surprised to learn how many of them were limned with hope.

Those musty, smelly papers were yet another maneuver yet to be played. Jade had delivered the entire stack to the Overseer just before their siege on the fort.

Her skin shivered at the first touch of fresh, salt-hammered air. She and the rest rose out of the bowels of the fort with the cardinal dawn, their breaths bloated with all their efforts, their eyes skimming over the beach.

Pala gasped as Mortimer Lowe approached from a path netted by swaying palms.

The girth of the trees shadowed even vultures circling for their meat.

"I thought I might find you here," said Lowe, backed by half a dozen men, all as wide as the deck of a ship, and enjoying the benefits of his retainer. "Then again your friend, the butcher, didn't take much coaxing." His smile was the curve of a scorpion's tail. "Since you seem disinclined to empty your pockets to me direct, how much, in your learned opinion, do you think Charles Wynn will pay to take the woman who broke open his fort off my hands?"

Pala glanced back at the holes above them, where the fighting had begun quieting.

"Oh, you didn't believe Captain Wynn would ever lose his beloved stronghold? He'd push anyone who dared to take it from him right into the fucking sea." Lowe pulled a knife from his belt. "Don't make this harder than it has to be, love."

When he started toward her, Jade broke from Thaya's side to meet him halfway. "You asked me how much Charles Wynn was willing to pay…"

A frown turned over Lowe's smile.

"But the better question would have been how much your employer is willing to pay," Jade said, glancing at the men he'd brought with him and nodding, "for you."

Lowe spun around just as two of the men came forward and shoved him to his knees. Their orders from their true employer were clear. Shock kept Lowe from struggling under their steel hands. They locked his wrists in the manacles he'd meant for Jade.

I could kill you. She stared down into his glazed eyes, tendrils of satisfaction buried under years of vendetta pulsing beneath her skin. *I could finally have your blood on my hands, because I'm finally bigger than you.*

Stronger.

"I've waited a long time for this," she admitted, her eyes dry whereas the Old Jade might have wept with conflated pride. That little girl had been nine years old, after all, and she'd been dragged into the shadows by a man three times her size who had delivered a list of torments down her body, wringing it out again and again as his impatience thickened. Of course that little girl wouldn't have known what to do with the rising flood crashing into Jade's thoughts, her emotions. She wouldn't have known what to do about her father stretching his lungs for one more breath or about a sister entrenched in heart-sickening turmoil or about the men up in that fort tearing each other apart.

But Jade did. She'd listened well and learned.

"But I'm not going to kill you," she told Mortimer Lowe. "I'm not even going to bother with reminding you who I am or why it was necessary to stamp my vengeance on you, though you deserve to be haunted the way I have been. All that matters is your days of carving your advantage from the toil of others is done."

Still, she thought she deserved *one thing* after all this time.

Though her fists ached to deliver a fraction of the pain she'd endured, all she did was pull his chin toward her face. "The Overseer knows what you are. I've given him a list of all your illegal shipments and takings made under your service. You made it simple enough, leaving your paper trail tucked in your desk," she murmured.

"You're nothing but a lazy cheat, Mr. Lowe, and now you're finished."

He screamed as she had screamed from the quarter once, his heels digging deep trails in the sand as the Overseer's men dragged him back to the shadows his greed had birthed.

ALTHOUGH NATHANIEL STEEL conquered at the fort, Jade hadn't celebrated at Anette's inn, for The Ashman died three days after the battle was won.

His daughters' pleas hadn't grounded him. He'd gone to join the Skies, if Jade's mother was to be believed.

It was not... the outcome Jade had wanted. What she had done to pour him into his deathbed perpetuated that she only ever saw him as a monster to be quelled.

No matter how deep the grief of that burned, she couldn't claim it out in the open, joining her sister in intermittent bouts of waspish silence and storm-conjuring wails. She wouldn't demean what she had done to satisfy her regret. *You can love him and never say his name. You never have to tell the truth.*

But she was, "Jade Elder." Saying her full name aloud after nine years clogged her chest. Made her wish for her father's hand.

Tore Elder had ruled the seas with a handful of other men and now all of them were gone.

In the end, she hadn't wanted to be a pirate king's daughter anymore than Nate had wanted to be a pirate king's son, and yet, in the end, he'd also had the strength to look his father in the eyes and show Captain Wynn what was to be done for the failures that had cost Nate his old life. He had been honest.

Jade would never be able to convince herself she'd done the same—the lie would only stretch thin with time instead of grow calloused against its abuses. Some part of her would always remain guilt-ridden.

But she wouldn't fail those who had saved her by once again ignoring their lessons, remembering that neglecting them had cost two daughters their father, one a ghost and the other a goddess.

Another dawn was rising over a scarred Nadara, brutal in its unflagging beauty, but Jade ignored the itch to shift forms and ascend into the day's light. *Calm is a weapon*, she'd recited again and again over the years. *Fury is an artifice.* But she realized now both emotions were reality, both could do harm if unchecked, and wondered if there was a method of living sequestered between the two.

She wondered if someday she would pause long enough, in the rapids of her life, to achieve a state of true peace.

She spared a glance for the fort, already in the process of being repaired, thinking that once fortified again, it might make a good, safe home for her childhood cache. Nate and his men were transferring Jade's wealth to the coves near the wrecks, where Nate and his men would guard it until a new plan was solidified.

Pieces of the cache would be fortifying the street soon

enough. Witnessing a cuffed Mortimer Lowe scream en route to the Overseer's estate, where he would await a civilized trial and judgement, had strengthened the merchants' resolve to sell Jade his interests.

She was officially, and yet unofficially, queen of the shadows, capable of both building and demolishing, expanding and setting parameters, all with the backing of those whose trust and loyalty she intended to earn.

One soul at a time.

She rubbed her arms as the sudden chill leached the little warmth she had. "I've been waiting for you," she told the encroaching mist.

Azura didn't yet make herself known, but Jade felt her there, hovering with all manner of roars and bolts, her anger an unending froth.

"Family may not always be a gift, but it is what you make it," Jade said to the churning air, "I'll always be responsible for destroying your family. You may always hate me for it, even should you come to love me someday. Maybe when you're utterly tired of human skin, you'll swallow my home whole. And when pieces of the land, of my heart, spew into the sea, I'll have no one to blame but myself. Worse, I would understand why you did it, why you couldn't do anything else."

What was only an angry wisp of teal hooked on the wind became a girl made manifest. Storm clouds sniped at each other in the distance as Azura's ankles delved into waves that seemed to beckon her closer.

"I never asked," Jade said, tilting her head at the seafoam, "Your mother?"

Azura's nod was a swift, jagged motion.

Jade had more questions, but she was sure Azura would neither entertain them nor answer them without veils attached. Why bother, when there was no trust or affection between them?

"I want you to know," Jade said after a long moment, "that what I give you now is not some means to earn your forgiveness, nor is it a plea for your understanding disguised in earnestness. It's not meant to be anything other than what it is." Gradually, she crossed the sea's threshold and handed Azura a set of papers. "Hold tight. You don't want them to fly away."

"What are they?"

"A second chance. *Your* best chance."

Jade tried folding her hands, but couldn't settle so she let them hang loose and trembling at her sides. Azura watched her struggle with that same cat-like intensity, as if the vulnerability intrigued her.

Jade cleared her throat. "Those papers were drawn and designed to give you a new home. One that is yours to defend or break apart and feed to the sea." She worried her bottom lip and fell back on folding her hands. "A ship. One that belonged to Vane Mercy."

Azura's gaze sparked on the name. "You'd have me sail the ship of the man who tried to strip me of what I am?"

Jade stood her ground. "I'd have you remake the ship of the man who tried and failed to unmake you." She shoved back the hair falling in her face thanks to Azura's winds. When her gaze was free, she saw her sister valiantly resisting the shedding of tears that had nothing to do with fury or grief. "You are what you are, as are we all. His former shipmates have agreed to sail under your banner, if you'd allow them."

"Why?" Azura croaked.

"Because as much as I enjoy their protection," Jade said, stifling a snort. "They're hunters, ones who acknowledge you're the last of Tore Elder's voyaging prowess. And while the Overseer is putting an end to endorsing piracy, I've worked very few exceptions into our understanding of one another. After all, merchant vessels around the world can't be completely free of fear, or the global tax system might collapse."

When her miserable attempt at humor was unmet with even so much as a smirk, she said, "It won't hurt me to see you sail under the black. I thought it would, because I wanted all of them gone. The pirates I've known all go feral at some point, devouring even the ones they love. But I trust you. I trust you not to be as cruel as he may have taught you. Take the chance, Azura."

She rifled through the papers herself. "Look, I've named her for you."

"You did what?" Azura snapped. "It's *my* ship."

Jade ducked her head to hide her smile. "If you don't like it, you can always change it." When no wayward bolts of lightning came down on her, she lifted her head. "But I think you'll appreciate the symmetry.

"I dubbed her the *Storm Mistress*."

KEEP READING FOR AN EXCLUSIVE
BONUS TALE—

AND PREPARE FOR BOOK ONE OF THE
GODS' FATE SERIES COMING AUGUST
2019.

GOOD

For someone who had witnessed so much death, Good had rarely visited Greyhold's crypt. A dank structure holding up the garrison city by its stone claws, its narrow, arching hallways teemed with the lost echoes of long-tethered spirits. Their whispers snaked through the shadows and wound through the cold gusts seeping into the darkness.

So it was said, anyway.

Still, Good averted her eye. The rest of her features remained carefully smooth. Golden wisps of power belonging to Sumora, Osolda's saint of sun, embroidered the firmly knotted sash darkening half of Good's gaze. The soft, decorative blessing bought on a whim in one of the village markets obscured her left eye. On the days in which the loss of that eye ached, the sash's firm grip staunched the worst of the memories ready to pour from the old wound.

She'd grown so used to tightening the fabric alone each day, the greyguard were always startled when she managed, in part, with the stump of her right hand.

Then again, these days, the greyguard were ill at ease when her shadow so much as sidled up to theirs.

The tiniest of smiles moved her lips. Healers and soldiers shared the same secrets, the same nightmares. They both warred with mortality and hoped to win. And yet, looking up at the statue erected for Ardith Bryer, a true grey soldier at rest with her still cloak and sheathed sword, Good wondered how it could be that she, with the narrowest of perspectives, saw more hope than those whom she had ushered back from their deathbeds.

It was the same with Cana, who once saved Good from a blood-strewn path years ago. She hadn't pretended a lonely, broken girl away. She hadn't ignored the bright burden of a worthy risk. The completely sightless Cana had taught Good the beauty of a world wrapped in darkness. She'd shown Good how even brusque kindness and patience—those sharp pulses of light—became more radiant when cast in the shadows.

Others did not see as they did.

Cana always said it was the strangest thing, living in a sighted world with no vision.

She pulled a small idol from her cloak and laid it at Ardith's stone-clad boots. The wooden god of death held a blank expression, its gaze almost pointedly enigmatic. Good's father had once told her there was a mythical temple in the south-lands of Gijaran where the gods wore knowing smiles and held out their hands for the offerings of humans. Their desires were written into the golden halls if you looked closely enough. Their jealousies were inlaid with emerald, their fury beaming from slats of amber. But Good couldn't see past the severity of the miniature oak god she had commissioned from the local woodsmith. She'd wanted it for Ardith, in the hopes that if her spirit were trapped, the god of death would guide her—perhaps to the River of Souls said to lie in those southern lands of her father's country.

The longer Good stared, however, the more her skin chilled. An ache beat beneath Saint Sumora's sash. The knowing softness of the crypt whispered against her like the slow crawl of ice on glass.

Forcing an even breath, Good recalled her mother, and the sensation of holding her hand in the fields of the lost near their old home:

Lost spirits want you to think you're bloodless. You must show them you're not.

The knife her mother had once given her slid into her palm. She made a careful cut on her opposite wrist—deep enough to draw excess blood. Shallow enough to avoid a serious injury.

In the hungry quiet surrounding Ardith's statue, Good let her blood fall over stone and wood, and made an Exchange.

A harsh gust of warm wind blew through the underground hall, whipping up the short strands of her silver-streaked hair. The press of what she did not see lifted as the god of death spilled crimson tears.

"What do you think you're doing?"

The raised voice startled the flow of her magic. The edges of her skirt now suffered stains of both blood *and* muck. With her privacy lost, Good leaned her wounded wrist against her stomach and used her free hand to sift for a bandage and wrap from her crossbody kit.

She lifted her head as Dell Aldain's boots spat up murky water from the grime of the earthen floor. He stopped too near and stared hard at her bandaged wrist.

When he finally met her gaze, Good knew her expression showed nothing. But, inside, her heart stuttered at the cutting things spoken by his soft grey gaze.

They'd never truly been friends. She, Ardith, and Dell had always been three spokes on a wheel that needed to keep turning if Osolda was going to be something more than a place of terror and hardship. And yet with Ardith lost, another spoke replaced the last until Greyhold's pace balanced again. This,

Dell hadn't reconciled. Nor had he forgiven Good for something she had no name for. She didn't know if it was a thing intrinsic to her he hated, like her magic or her need to heal, or if he loathed her simply because she reminded him he had lost his friend.

One whose ghost he did not want to share.

But Good remembered the way Dell and Ardith both had forgotten their prejudices long enough to smile at her—or offer her water instead of a wineskin on a particularly brutal day of failing the dying. Because, somehow, they'd noticed she only used alcohol to clean rather than clot what needed mending. Good remembered feeling her heart stir toward the shadow Dell and Ardith made as they walked side by side, silently awed at a friendship stitched together so tightly they formed a single entity when their backs were turned. Working alongside them as command of Greyhold shifted from a dead general to a secretive noble in a few, short years, she remembered wondering if she was considered part of their shared history, if they would forget her should their missions stretch for long enough.

Had she sighed more loudly, Dell might have flinched at the weight carried by the sound.

Instead, as ever, her sorrow was quiet. It was a thin shape in the heavy silence between them.

She'd joined the garrison city's ranks as its healer because doing so had meant she belonged. Without question. She couldn't lose that. She couldn't bear being adrift again, desperately hoping someone out there might share their anchor. It would be too much like losing her hope. And because she knew too well what she was without trust in the world around her, Good finally said, "I'm sorry."

Not because she was ashamed, nor because she thought it would change things between them. She was only sorry that he had lost someone and didn't know how to shift his grief in a way that would make it easier for him to carry. For others to help him carry.

She was sorry because they had once been the same. Had he met her before Cana had found her, he might have recognized himself in her. Whether he would have hated her all the more for that, or not, made her glad he didn't know—though she hoped someday she could tell him about how she had quelled the monster within her.

She wanted to assure him that he would heal.

His jaw clenched. "I didn't ask for an apology." His eyes could have carved glass. "I asked what it was you were doing, leech. Were you performing blood rites over my friend's grave?"

She didn't say the right thing. She knew it when she whispered, "She doesn't belong here," and watched his hands tighten into fists. His anger made him fiercer in his greyguard armor, whereas when Ardith had coaxed his humor, he'd become clunky and off-balance. His confidence bolstered him too well.

How do I cool his hate? How do I make him smile, Ardith?

For if he was smiling, he wasn't hurting her. He would return to the shy, awkward recruit too green to know how Ardith's death might mold him anew.

Good tried for comfort and said, "I want her spirit to be at peace."

"What does your kind know about peace?" he suddenly shouted. He made a grab for her arms and lifted her off the ground. She shook in his hold. "What good has bloodcraft ever brought to this saints-damned kingdom?"

She flinched when his spittle landed on her cheek. Her reaction struck him somehow, opening a wound that shocked him stiff. He stripped her of her chance to respond by dropping her.

The fall was so abrupt she fell. She was forced to look up at him and pretend the fear skittering over her bones had nothing to do with him and everything to do with this place.

The crypt was made of invisible eyes and frozen touches. They lingered at the edges of Dell's aggression as though poised to emerge.

Gods, she would run if she could. She would run from them both if she was sure she wouldn't be caught. All she had was her hope. She clung to it as she watched some battle playing out over Dell's features.

Could he want to help her up? Or was he only repulsed by the thought of touching her?

Did he hate her because she was the enemy he knew or because he didn't want her to be?

She slowly picked herself up from the cold, wet ground. There was hesitation, for a moment, but then she said, "It's all right, Dell." She thought of the one thing she had wished for following the terrible things she had done. "I forgive you."

Rather than lash out as she half-expected, he turned away from her. Lurking in the quiet were the words he wanted to wield against her. He was already thinking of how to hurt her again.

But when he finally spoke, he surprised her still. "You can't give what others won't take." His head lifted, but she couldn't see what new resentments boiled beneath his skin. "Keep your forgiveness unless I ask for it, leech."

His heavy footsteps pushed him deeper into the darkness of the crypt.

Good closed her eye, shutting out Dell's retreating backside until the rapid thud of her heart quieted, and she was alone among the fallen soldiers of Greyhold.

※

WHEN EVERYTHING within her had stopped quivering, she

joined the bustle of the main street again, shaking off the cold, dim deed of visiting Osolda's brave, unsung dead.

The first time she'd entered through the iron grate sitting like teeth in the open mouth of the city, she'd been overwhelmed by her country's sudden obsession with building towards the sky. From the road, she'd confused the solitary turrets in the distance with dawn-hazed mountain peaks prodding copper holes into the sky. Standing in the shadow of its towering height had instantly turned her stomach, as it would have done for any of her village in the eastern hills beyond the Unforeseen Forest.

There was nothing grey or soft about this fixture of Osolda's strength. And while Good's childhood had vanished in a tempest of blood and death long before arriving in Greyhold, the deep blue breadth of the city had threatened to crush her underfoot. Her entrance had dredged her in smoke and screams and stone-dust. One of the region's chronic storms had upended the torch of the soldier leading her further inside, coughing up gusts that would blur the path ahead with leaves and straw.

The garrison city, bloated with chaos and curses, mud and weaponry, was a beast which dared you to carve your place in its hide.

Good, for all her promises, all her lessons, hadn't been able to resist, not for a moment.

She'd found her way without help. And she'd been carrying on that way ever since.

Dell couldn't turn her into a burden or a blight. She'd been both those things and had fought every day since to live differently. She was no longer a creature of her past.

A shout snipped her fears before they could unwind into her nerves. They might have taken possession of her thoughts for the rest of the day had a boy and what looked to be his mother not scrambled through the iron grate that had once daunted her.

She could see his instant awe and terror before he shrugged them away and helped his mother forward. Her left arm shook around his shoulders as she hacked a cough so deep it wracked the entirety of her frail frame. The next wave sent both mother and son to their knees as a few of the greyguard approached.

"*Blood,*" one man hissed, sighting the stains trailing down the front of the woman's cotton shirt.

Good shivered. Could the woman have some kind of plague? It seemed Osolda was forever turning out the sick, but none had ever ventured here, where there was little sympathy and none to help. This was the reason Good visited the surrounding villages as often as possible. These soldiers crossed swords with death enough to know how canny a god he could be, even if they didn't believe he existed.

Pure-blooded Osoldans knew no death saint, and the lack stole their compassion for the dying.

"Healer," croaked the boy. "We came to see the healer."

Good was already hastening her stride, but one of the greyguard blocked her path. "I can help them," she said slowly, recognizing the woman before her as one of Dell's subordinates and a regular member of his hunting parties. She'd been missing for some time, tasked with some secret mission from Greyhold's lord and master. "Please let me pass."

"If she carries plague, healer," said the guard, "we can't let you treat her within these walls."

"Then let me take her out of them," Good snapped, sweat dotting her brow as the boy struggled against the hold of another soldier. Patches of blood were blooming beneath his mother's hanging head. He cried out when another soldier wrenched his mother upright. Old memories loped toward Good. The looming threat of an onslaught shredded her patience. "Let me pass, damn you."

The boy's panic made him foolish.

He wrenched a sword free from his oppressor's belt and turned on him. He didn't aim to kill. Good could see that. But then he and his opponent grappled, and somehow where there had been a hapless, desperate boy now stood a murderer wearing blood not his own.

His mother screamed. His face drained of all his hard-won color. His breaths grew rapid and thin as blood pooled beneath the fallen guard.

Good tried to break free of her shock, but she heard her own screams, smaller, thinner, more wretched. When the boy reached for a power not unlike her own, using first the small pools of his mother's blood, then his victim's, to defend himself, Good didn't see him. She saw herself standing in a vast green field, wearing the blood of far too many, her mother's body swaying in the wind. Fog had come to blanket her, but the blood was so bright. She had craved it and it had consumed her. She was a girl made of crimson whose heart and mind had just been shattered.

No.

The memories were sifting for a place to root no matter how violent her attempts to dislodge them. Panic unfurled in her chest, constricting her heart.

No. She was good now. She was *good*.

Just as she'd sworn.

"Good." Dell's voice was a scathing swipe through fleshy echoes. His voice scraped and she already hurt everywhere. "*Good.*" He continued shaking her until she returned to the present.

Until she noticed there was one more motherless child in this world, and he had been killed before he could grieve that fact. *She must have tried to protect him,* Good thought distantly, noting the way the boy's mother lay over his body, their blood feeding the mud.

"You will report this," she said quietly, and Dell's gaze

snapped to hers. "You will tell Lord Alistair what happened here, or I will."

Though his face had hardened, his voice was unsteady when he spoke. "He was using bloodcraft against us."

Good arose slowly, her bones protesting the sudden pressure of her stance. "He was also a boy. And we failed him, Dell. We failed them both." She glanced at the greyguard gathered around the bodies frozen in their distress. "We all did." She was a healer and she had been paralyzed by her own wounds. She'd done nothing to save them. "Report this," she repeated. "Because if you truly believe in what Osolda could be, this kind of injustice cannot go unanswered."

When he said nothing at this, she went in search of something to heft the mother, the boy, and the soldier off the ground. For if she was to lay their spirits to rest, the act required she tend their bodies first.

Her own mother would have expected nothing less.

"I'm sorry," she whispered aloud, hoping for some small relief, because those two words were a cacophony running through her entire being. It was a punishing litany she forced herself to withstand, even knowing there might come a day when she no longer could.

THE FEMALE SOLDIER who'd barred her from helping the two dead strangers buried just outside Greyhold's walls came to collect Good barely an hour later.

"I'm sorry," said the soldier, causing Good to wonder if her apology was for the needless death she hadn't allowed Good to stop, or for whatever punishment she thought Good was about to endure. "But your presence is requested in the former general's offices."

Good's nod was sharp enough to draw out a wound. "If you would help me with my things."

"Healer?"

Good motioned behind her, where two packs were strung tight on the edge of her former bed. "They're quite heavy," she said, "and I'm very tired today."

When she started by the soldier, her arm was clasped in a mud-spattered gauntlet. "This is a thankless city, healer, and far from perfect, but I ask your forgiveness." A light squeeze came then. "For all of us. We need you here."

Good didn't know this woman, but she found herself smiling a little, though there was a sadness building beneath her skin. "I can't stay," she told the woman. "Not when I can't treat my own kind within these walls." When the soldier blanched at this, Good's voice was gentle. "And not when they are so easily slaughtered in a place which I thought my home."

In her single field of vision, the boy with her gift welled from the shadows, his features crisp and clear. A bolt of shock struck her.

But when her gasp hit the air, the soldier looked puzzled. Her stare joined Good's, but she could not see the same things.

Good held her voice inside until she was sure it wouldn't crack. "What is your name?"

Dell's subordinate returned her steady gaze, though questions thick with confusion filled the brief silence. "Esma."

"Esma, please call me by my name." Her smile drifted away. "I am Good. And my leaving is not a question of forgiveness. I do forgive you."

"But do you forgive yourself, Good?"

That hint of a smile returned. Another fissure cracked open her heart, but her pain was soundless. It didn't matter when two people were dead thanks, in part, to the agony that lived within her. She turned for the door, pulling her crossbody kit over her head as she went. "That is something I still don't know." She ignored the spirit standing beside Esma. His eyes were rounded with woe. Misery straddled the shoulders he'd used to bear his mother's weight. "And I'm not sure I ever shall."

When they entered the Lord Alistair's offices, Good hadn't expected the heir of the sky clans to join this meeting.

Elina of the Nightingales stood proud in leather travel clothes dyed a rich burgundy, adorned with polished shoulder armor and silver chains finely smithed to resemble feathers. Her hair dwindled down to her waist like a freshly hammered sheet of gold. Her eyes reminded Good of the elegant peacocks she had once glimpsed in her father's drawing books. In them swirled a fury so bright not even the most opaque of lies could shadow the truth of it.

Lord Alistair of the Wrens, and of the Council of Blood and Song, concealed his emotions with practiced skill, but the subtle tightening of his features bespoke the depths of his own anger.

Good prepared herself to face it. She said only, "I make no excuses, High One. My lord. I was not diligent in my duties."

Elina scoffed.

Good's cheeks reddened. "Whatever punishment you deem fitting, I will accept. But once my penance is served, I am leaving Greyhold."

Elina opened her mouth, but Alistair stemmed whatever tide of thoughts threatened to emerge. "Do you intend to return?" he asked softly, for everything about him was soft. Expression, hands, clothes. He was a delicate man enrobed in an armor invisible to all but Good. She shielded her emotions the way he did, though she doubted their reasons were the same. He held secrets inside him that could never leave his keeping, for this kingdom depended on his safeguarding them well.

"I do not," she announced very quietly.

Dell entered the room just as she did.

His mask of indifference was faulty. Good could make out the hairline cracks in which his despair seeped through. Grief and guilt were two forces he had no true defense against, no matter how he might try to convince himself otherwise.

"I accept full blame for the incident," she said so forcefully, Dell spun to her, eyes wide. "Commander Aldain left his post to investigate and then was focused on my care. My panic had made things worse for the three dead. The greyguard lost control because of me."

What are you doing? his gaze asked. As commander of the greyguard, any misdirection or ill action taken up by his underlings was his responsibility.

She didn't know what she hoped this would change. She only thought it might be the friendly thing to do.

"While we do think it's best you leave," Alistair said, "we do not agree with where you place blame, Good."

"My lord?" Her heart throbbed. She hadn't expected his easy agreement. She thought they might agree that Greyhold was her home, and that to abandon it would be painful to them all.

Except that wasn't the life she lived here.

She wasn't a friend to any of them.

When she'd come to the garrison city, she'd kept herself at an appropriate distance, never bothering to bridge the obvious divide between them. She had lost much because of what she was, and hadn't believed she deserved to hold anyone's hand or heart. The responsibility of friendship was both a foreign terror and a desperate wish, yet she had relegated herself to something secretive and deadly, a creature that belonged only to the spaces which couldn't be seen.

No wonder they feared her.

No wonder Dell misunderstood her.

She was fulfilling the prophecy they had written for her the moment she had entered the keep.

The spirit of the boy killed with his mother stood before Dell, who stiffened at the near contact. Good moved closer to him, reaching for his wrist.

The spirit vanished. Dell shook her off, his brow furrowing. She smiled gently at him. His confusion caused another line in his brow.

Before he could gather himself and his anger, the door behind them creaked open again.

In walked Esma.

And she wasn't alone.

Zahria of Gildesh made Esma's secret mission clear when she strode in, boldness in every line of her, behind the lone greyguard.

Good's smile widened. Perhaps she could claim a friend, after all. "Huntress."

Zahria returned her grin. "Been gone a year, Good, and I'd swear you have another streak of silver. I'd hate to think the stress was getting to a young thing like you."

"Isn't there a custom about avoiding commentary on a woman's age?" asked Elina with a dry tone. "Or general appearance?"

"Little bird," Zahria crooned. "Have I made you jealous?"

Though her cheeks heated, Elina simply rolled her eyes. "You're here for a purpose, Huntress."

"And what purpose is that?" spat Dell. "She helps kill an evil, false, bloodcraft-wielding queen and suddenly she's not our enemy. Have you all forgotten whose side she started on?"

"None of us have forgotten," Good said, unable to stop herself. "I know she's on ours now. Why can't you—"

"What, forgive? Betrayal might be common among your kind, *Good*," he snarled. "But here in Greyhold betrayal has weight. She killed Tristan."

But you don't blame her for just Tristan's death. Good thought of his possessiveness of Ardith's ghost. The way he clung to her memory, wouldn't allow himself or another kindness of any kind. "I grieve Tristan too," she murmured. *And Ardith, though you wouldn't like me to.* "But Zahria has done her best by Osolda." *And is trying to do her best by you.*

The huntress in question hadn't even spared him a glance. But one of her hands made a whitening shackle over the opposite wrist, which she had curved behind her back.

She, too, defaulted to hiding her pain.

Good took a step toward her. "My friend," she said, struggling to hide swift surprise. At closer inspection, the witch-queen's former lover no longer appeared weighed down by the horrors of the past. And yet there was a deep weariness that worried Good. For the first time, Zahria looked nearly, wholly human. "Why are you here?"

Zahria's answering glint of a smile brimmed with gratitude. "I think the birds should explain."

Alistar nodded. "Osolda has been infected for a long time. And, although the queen and her poison are gone, that infection festers. There are more dying and sickening every day," he said. "Not all of the fields have returned to prospering. And the clans of the skies have not all united." He rose from his chair, hand sliding over a map of Osolda as he abandoned his desk. "Unity is paramount now more than ever."

"Why?" demanded Dell.

"Feydla continues to feign a desire for peace, with lofty promises and backhanded blockades, but it's been clear for some time that they are little more than our enemy," answered Elina. She wrestled back strands of her hair, pulled forward by her passion. "There's something sinister brewing beyond our borders and I need all of you with me if we are to succeed in excavating Osolda's true essence. Its true might and glory."

"Dark fates are coming for us from near and far," said Alistair. "Will you help us? Will you help Elina mend the broken pieces of this country until there is balance again?"

Good felt the faint stirrings of hope. She thought it gone after all that had transpired this day. But a chance to heal the world had opened up rather luminous possibilities.

She didn't hesitate. "I will."

～

LATER, Dell stopped her from reentering the crypt. "Why did you assume responsibility for this afternoon?"

His hand all but burned through her cloak. A chill had picked up, blowing the brown strands of her hair into her eye. "Because I worry about you," she confessed, and her reward was his unfathomable suspicions. "About what you're becoming, Dell Aldain. I worry that you don't see all the ways in which you're losing yourself."

His smirk held nothing of the boy Ardith had pummeled and prided in. "You're a strange creature, Good. You belong to the darkness of this world and refuse to see it." He leaned closer, barring his teeth. "You can convince yourself otherwise, but I see you."

"And I worry," she continued, "that you never will. See me, that is. Did you know I had hoped, once, that we could be friends?"

That useless mask of his returned. "I don't befriend leeches."

She shook her head, and left him with his hate, alone, in the cold. She hoped to see the day when he would thaw at last.

Her return to the crypt had little to do with him, or even Ardith. Her presence had been requested.

Sconces lit the way to Ardith's statue, where Zahria awaited.

"What is it?" said Good, instantly concerned. She'd known something hadn't been right about the huntress, but hadn't been sure of the right course of action. She hadn't wanted to breach Zahria's privacy by openly inquiring after her health.

"What ails you? I brought my tonics with me. Poultices if you were injured on the road. I—"

Zahria laid a comforting hand on Good's shoulder. The stark difference in height between them reminded Good of her smallness again. And when she was small, she was helpless. She wasn't going to like what Zahria would say.

"There's no need," said the huntress. "None of it will work."

Good set her chin. "Then I have my magic."

"That's what I'm counting on, but it won't be enough to save me."

"What are you talking about?"

Zahria blew out a breath. It sounded strained now that Good was listening for its quality. "I'm dying, Good. And we both know you can't cheat the god of death. You'd know that better than most, even without knowing him."

But I do know him. I know him too well.

The certainty of Zahria's statement could not be refuted. To try anyway would only grieve them both more.

But, oh, it hurt.

They hadn't known each other long, but that was not the source of Good's pain. She hurt for this woman who had fought for a century to make her life mean something, only then to find new meaning right at the end of her life. "Did you find your family? Do they know?"

Zahria's smile gleamed true. "The family that remains are of those who had been," she said. "Yes, they know. I couldn't be anything but honest with their like. They're... pure. Much like you. You'd like them."

Good averted her eye. "You think too highly of me, huntress."

"I hope not. I'm going to need you to sustain me on this journey. If I'm to help Elina revive Osolda, I have to be at top form in the time I have left." Zahria stared up at Ardith's stone-carved face. "Let's hope I last longer than I think."

"I'll see to it," Good said, with a firmness that bellied her fear. She hoped she could guarantee for her only friend what she had never been able to before. The god of death was a force to be reckoned with, and battling him back would not be an easy task.

"Now what shall I give you in return?"

Good blinked. "I don't expect payment, Huntress."

"I insist."

Good thought hard. "Gijaran," she blurted. "Take me to Gijaran."

Incredulity widened Zahria's gaze. "I hardly think I'll have enough wherewithal to survive two journeys inside the last moments of my life."

"Not physically," Good said quickly. "In spirit. I'd like you to tell me stories. My father used to, before..." It became difficult to speak, so she swallowed the words down past her sorrow.

"You'll tell me more about him," Zahria decided. "Where he's from. What his name was. When you're ready." She laughed. "After all, we could be cousins. In the meantime, I'll tell you whatever you want to know, though I have one more favor to ask of you."

"Name it," said Good.

Zahria grew quiet. Her lips tightened, as though she were holding something back.

Finally, she said, "I'd ask that you keep this to yourself, will you?"

And then smiled.

Leaving Good helpless to deny her. "That's hardly a favor. I won't tell unless you ask me to."

When Zahria turned back to her former friend's statue, tears marked silent streaks down her cheeks. If ever there was a time Zahria might have been ashamed of them, she wasn't now. Gilded by the firelight of the crypt, she was a testament to hope, and the worthiness of keeping it close. The dead were no more than faint flickers beside her.

Good ignored the pulsing ache beneath her sash, and the vague silhouettes of the dead crowding around them—including the boy whom she wished hadn't lost his life so soon.

She reached for Zahria's hand, lacing it with her own as the world's most famed huntress silently wept in the darkness.

THANK YOU FOR READING!

PLEASE TAKE THE TIME TO REVIEW
HEIRS OF FATE ON YOUR FAVORITE
RETAILER SITE.

ACKNOWLEDGMENTS

Heirs of Fate was never supposed to exist.

Let me backtrack a little: these novellas were never supposed to link up the way they did. A series was never supposed to come together from what originally began as a bunch of loose threads. You see, I thought I was writing short stories that might have influence from fairy tales that I loved.

I didn't end up writing those stories. Or at least not the way I'd imagined.

Instead I ended up with three really long novellas that, when woven together, make up the backbone of a brand new fantasy series.

These characters will find you again. Hopefully, in ways you won't expect.

But because Heirs of Fate does now exist, there are several people I want to thank for not only getting this book out into the world, but for helping us develop Wonder Heart Books into a bold storytelling platform with a loyal community attached.

None of this would have gotten very far without my sister, Gabi, and her incredible talent as an artist. Every single cover, art print, and even some of the graphics are thanks to her skill and patience. We wouldn't have garnered nearly the same level of interest in these stories without her beautiful art, and I certainly wouldn't have ended last year as sane as I did without her.

Francina Simone, you have helped shape me into a stronger, more seasoned writer. The stories inside this book would not have been what they are without your brilliant critiques. Thank you for all your patience and expertise.

Bethany Pullen, I'm so grateful to have you in our corner. You've helped us shape this marketing campaign. You've kept us organized. You're a fountain of wisdom and creativity, and we can't wait to implement so many of your new ideas. Thanks for all your incredible work behind the scenes and on our instagram page @wonderheartsociety.

Huge thanks to Claire at Eight Little Pages for taking such exquisite care with our hopes and dreams for this paperback. We could not have asked for a better design!

To the WHB street team, we really need t-shirts.

I specifically want to thank Alex @littlebookqueen, Ashley @pages_of_horror, Hira @bookvenger, Jess @jessreadsalatte, Jess @as.you.like.it, Kate @thebitchbookshelf, Kelsey @kculver88, Laura @laurabookish, Julianne @cinamoonbooks, and, our newest member, Scarllet @iamlitandwit, as well as all our previous street team members.

Penny, Jenni, Maegan, Alecs, and Alicia, my earliest readers, thank you for taking a chance on a little known writer like me.

Those of you who helped with the cover reveal tour for Heirs of Fate: THANK YOU. Next time I will have the book done early enough to incorporate each and every one of your names. Your participation truly meant the absolute world to me. Thank you for saying yes to Wonder Heart Books.

I'm also extremely grateful to my friends and family. All those "of course you can" conversations and cheering emojis got me through. I love each and every one of you immensely, and I'm so happy to celebrate all the milestones for Heirs of Fate and beyond together.

But, don't forget, dear reader, that this book was dedicated first and foremost to you. Thank you for picking up Heirs of Fate and letting everyone know how much you love these stories. We are able to keep doing this because you are with us.

Thank you, thank you, thank you.

ABOUT THE AUTHOR

Amara Luciano is a smiley YA fiction author who is obsessed with tortuous endings, so much so her books are almost always about dark, magical misfits making really questionable decisions. She's the co-founder of an independent publishing company called Wonder Heart Books. She also shares muse magic and true tales for staying peacefully creative on her podcast called Love Your Fails, Win Your Magic. She loves heart-ready smiles, chocolate anything, and people who win love by daylight. Her spirit animal: a Kara Danvers-Arthur Curry cross-mix. Her motivational mantra: "If I can see it in my heart, I can hold it in my hands," a la Cara Alwill Leyba.

You can knock on her social media doors @amaraauthoress pretty much everywhere, but she likes Instagram best. Head on over, there's always room by the bookshelves...

VISIT AMARALUCIANO.COM
TO LEARN MORE.

instagram.com/amaraauthoress

CPSIA information can be obtained
at www.ICGtesting.com
Printed in the USA
FFHW022052110319
50944601-56375FF